THE
CHARM

by TRACY HEFFERON

PRELUDE

LORNA STEPPED FROM THE WARM, scented bath onto stripped wooden floorboards, wrapped herself in an over-sized cream towel and looked down at the puddle of water pooling around her feet. She really must remember to buy a bath mat. And a wok, come to think of it. Necessary household objects she desperately needed but always forgot to buy. So for now, the floor – and a frying pan – would have to do.

She smoothed white musk lotion onto her body and massaged it in gently, inhaling the familiar scent that had cocooned her since she was a teenager. Her skin was the colour of alabaster, as white and translucent as a porcelain doll. She unfastened the tortoiseshell clip that held the twisted rope of hair on top of her head, allowing her deep red curls to tumble over her shoulders and down her back.

The white cotton nightdress slipped over her head and fell to her ankles. It was an old-fashioned kind of nightdress, high at the neck and edged in broderie anglaise, but she loved it all the same. She looked at her reflection in the mirror that stood by her wardrobe. Her green eyes surveyed the coffee-coloured freckles that lay scattered across her nose and cheekbones, freckles she despised as a child but had grown to love as a woman. She reached for the little pot of lip balm and dipped her middle finger into it, slicking sweet, chocolatey cocoa butter over her pale pink rosebud lips. She looked far younger than her twenty-eight years and for that, she was extremely grateful. She needed to attract a mate and a youthful appearance was nothing but a bonus.

She padded barefoot across the hall into her fashionably sparse sitting room. There she gathered together a pink candle, a tiny bottle of lavender oil and, from the huge floral display standing majestically on the mantelpiece, she plucked two pristine white rose petals.

Next, she went into the kitchen to retrieve the box of matches she kept under the kitchen sink, along with a small china plate, and took all of the objects back to her bedroom.

She looked out of the window and up at the sky. The moon above her, suspended in an inky infinity of stars, was getting larger by the day, moving from new moon to full moon. Tonight the moon was a waxing moon. Tonight was the perfect night for casting spells.

She moved into the centre of the room and walked slowly round in a full circle, sank to the floor and, with trembling hands, carefully lit the candle. She placed the rose petals on the china plate and unscrewed the lid from the bottle of lavender oil, tipping it forward slightly so that three precise drops spilled out and landed silently onto the petals.

'Love's truth burns bright, I welcome my soul-mate on this night'.

She tilted the burning candle so that hot, molten wax dripped onto the petals. Her delicate fingers moulded the warm wax, petals and oil together into a coin-shaped disc and when it was cold and hard, she pushed it underneath her pillow. And there it stayed for six more moons, until one cold,

6

dark, frosty night in mid-November, when she retrieved it from the safety of her bed, tiptoed barefoot into the sparkling garden and buried it beneath a rose bush still in full bloom.

ONE

LORNA FLIPPED OPEN the large, leather-bound diary and turned to today's date. She scanned the list of orders and jobs to do for that day and then leafed through the following pages detailing the week ahead. The weekend had been busy, as it was every year, being the first of the wedding season. She worked every weekend although Sundays were usually delivery-only days, which meant she was back in her flat by noon, drinking tea, munching marmite on toast and reading the papers. Monday was catch-up day and comprised of housework, grocery shopping and placing flower orders for the following week. It could never be classed as a day off. Those were few and far between. To all intents and purposes, Lorna worked seven days a week. Running a business single-handed was hard bloody work but running your dream business single-handed was most definitely worth it.

Lorna trained as a florist after leaving school at the age of eighteen. She passed three A Levels with flying colours but decided, despite months of vehement protest from her parents, not to go to university. She wanted to own a florists shop, a string of shops perhaps. She wanted to earn money, to own a house, buy a car and make something of herself. University life didn't appeal at all. She was a home-bird who thrived on familiarity and routine. The thought of living and studying in a dusty city miles away from everything and everyone she knew, living in squalor and surviving on tins of spaghetti hoops, filled her with horror.

So she set the wheels in motion by enrolling on a college course in floristry and as she studied, she gained priceless work experience during the evenings and at weekends alongside an eccentric but highly-regarded florist by the name of Tobias Montéfiore. Or Tony Montogomery as stated on his birth certificate.

Under his expert guidance, she not only passed the course with distinction, but became a much-sought after name within the industry in her own right – producing stunning designs for stately homes, magazine photoshoots, society weddings and the occasional B-list celebrity. Tobias snapped her up immediately and she worked as his partner for four wonderfully hedonistic years until, at the tender age of twenty-four, she made the bold move of renting a dilapidated and long obsolete butchers shop in the small village of Casworth. The village was close enough to her friends and family to avoid feeling isolated, but far enough away from Tobias to evade the aggravation that being in direct competition with one's mentor can bring. And it was the best decision she'd ever made.

She used her life savings to put down six months rent on the old butchers shop and totally revamped the premises from top to bottom. With more than a little help from her father and two brothers, she ripped out the ancient butchery counter and shelving racks, invested heavily in an exorbitantly-priced polished wooden floor, chiseled off the cold, white tiles from the walls and painted the newly-plastered surfaces the colour of lilies. She cleaned, scrubbed and bleached every nook and cranny to within an inch of its life until it looked like new. A smart wooden counter was installed, a beautiful crystal chandelier hung where the ancient fluorescent strip light once flickered, and the shop was filled with cast iron buckets crammed with flowers of every colour, variety and scent.

She sold single red roses in February, sumptuous bouquets and exotic potted plants for mums in March, holly wreaths, poinsettia and Christmas trees in winter, and a profusion of floral tributes for birthdays, gestures of gratitude and slightly more lugubrious occasions in between. But the biggest money-spinner of all came during the summer months, when she was inundated with orders from a seemingly never-ending procession of blushing brides, all demanding dreamy bouquets, colossal floral displays for the church and reception venue and dainty button-holes for the wedding party. Lorna often wondered if Westminster was slightly over-exaggerating the extent of economic decline in which the country was currently floundering. The wedding market was certainly showing no signs of slowing down or tightening its corset. Far from it. Business was positively booming.

Lorna lived just a few doors up from the shop, in a newly-converted building called The Maltings. The building had been bought by a local property developer and skillfully converted into four separate dwellings. It boasted an impressive entrance hall, a laundry room, a spacious communal garden and garaging and parking for eight cars at the back. Lorna occupied apartment number three on the first floor. In number one lived a retired police officer and his battleaxe of a wife. A professional couple of newlyweds lived in number two, the flat directly beneath Lorna's, and number four was empty – its thirty-something owners having purchased it as a security blanket before migrating to the other side of the world to make their fortune.

Lorna was proud of her achievements so far. She'd come a long way in just a few short years and the sky was her limit. She closed her diary and made a mental note of the commissions she had to complete that week and, despite a heavy wedding workload on Friday and a bouquet to deliver to the village primary school for the retiring headmistress, the next few days were straightforward and pretty laid back – just the way she liked them.

Stock was delivered twice a week and she kept it all in a special cold room at the rear of the shop – a room which had originally housed great, waxy, pig carcasses and strangulated chickens hanging upside down from hooks in the ceiling, all waiting to be jointed and dismembered by a skilful butchers knife. It was one of the reasons the old butcher's shop was so perfect for a floristry business – the Victorian building lent itself beautifully to the purpose of selling flowers.

The delivery man drew up alongside the shop at 9am on the dot. Lorna was always the first delivery of the day on Tuesday's. He was a peculiar chap. Cheerful enough, just not very talkative. Considering Lorna had seen him every week for the last four years but hardly knew a single thing about him, struck her as a little odd. This morning was no different.

'Hi Pete!' she said, her voice light and sunny.

He pushed the shop door open with a jangle and strolled over to the counter, his clipboard layered like mille-feuille with the day's orders.

'Morning,' he replied dourly, handing her the clipboard,

avoiding all eye contact. 'Nice day. Make sure it's all on there, love,' he added, nodding at the clipboard.

Lorna scanned the order form and cross-checked it against the original order printed out from her laptop.

'It's all there, thanks Pete.'

She picked up a pen and scribbled her signature at the bottom of the sheet.

'Right you are, I'll go and unload.'

Their conversation was exactly the same every single delivery day. Lorna smiled.

'I'll help you'.

'Right you are,' came the monotone reply.

Soon the cold store was crammed to bursting point with flowers and buds and plants once more and Lorna began re-stocking the shop. The whole place smelt glorious. She never tired of smelling flowers and greenery all day.

The brass bell over the door jangled again, announcing the arrival of a customer and Lorna looked up, mildly surprised at someone being up and about so early.

'Only me, duck. Just to let you know I'm about to cut the grass. I might do them borders an' all. Need doing. Not been done since last year. Got any washing out or owt?'

George was The Maltings' gardener. The residents held a meeting after they'd moved in and decided to employ the local odd job man to maintain the garden every fortnight. It was a fairly big space, with a small pond and established trees lining its boundary. The apartment owners were busy people with busy careers or busy social lives, or both, and gardening was the last thing they wanted to do after work or at weekends. They paid George ten pounds an hour to keep everything looking park-like and he did a sterling job.

Lorna stood up straight and arched her back, stretching her spine like a cat after a lovely, long snooze. The accompanied pained expression indicated all was not well.

'Blimey, that's getting harder, George!' she said. George laughed at her.

'Wait till you're as bloody old as me, gell! Then you'll know about it!'

Lorna smiled. She'd heard that particular conviction more than once before.

'I'm sure I will. I've been on my knees too long unloading these flowers. I've seized up! And no, no – there's no washing out. I got it in last night. I had a feeling you'd be here first thing this morning.'

'Okey doke. I'll crack on then. Good weekend?'

'It was ok,' she sighed, recalling her gloomy Saturday night in front of the TV – a bottle of wine and a bowl of curry-flavoured super noodles her only company. 'I had a very busy day on Saturday in here, what with all the weddings. And on Sunday I went to see mum and dad. Mum's been a bit off lately so it was nice to catch up and make sure she's ok.'

'Nothing serious I hope?' George asked, a look of concern creeping over his weather-beaten face.

'No. Nothing serious. Ladies things… you know. She's at *that age!*' replied Lorna, gesturing with her fingers to indicate her mother was going through the dreaded menopause.

'Oh dear. Enough said. Glad I'm a fella!' he chuckled. 'Right, I'm off then duck. I'll pop in later in the week to collect me money.'

'Ok, George, thanks… and yes, see you soon.'

And off he shuffled, whistling a merry tune as he went.

GEORGE UNLOADED the mower from the trailer that he towed from the rear of his battered old Land Rover and wheeled it down the side passageway, through the gate and into the garden. The grass was lush and long and green, but within ten minutes it resembled a miniature football pitch, resplendent in alternating pale and dark green stripes. He fetched his trowel and started turning over the earth in the borders, fishing out weeds and stray stones as he worked.

'What the devil is that?' he muttered as he forked over a clod of earth, revealing a pink, waxy, coin-shaped object from the soil.

He picked it up, wiped it on his trousers and studied it closely.

'God only knows what *that* is,' he said to himself, tossing the charm into the garden refuse sack, along with a pile of rotten leaves, grass cuttings and wilted flowers from a spring now past.

For a fleeting moment, a lonesome cloud drifted in front of the sun and the garden fell into shade. A gentle breeze whispered through the newly-emerged leaves of the ancient rowan trees that stood guard, like soldiers, around the edge of the garden. And precisely one mile away – across the fields of flourishing wheat, peas and barley – a certain Joseph Edward Hardy breathed in a long, deep lungful of sweet, fresh air. It felt good to be alive.

TWO

LORNA LOOKED AT the ancient French clock that hung above the shop door for what felt like the hundredth time that day. The clock was a gift from her parents to mark the florists opening and it kept perfect time, despite being so old. It was 4.57pm and she'd been clock-watching all afternoon.

A steady trickle of customers had wandered in and out of the shop throughout the day but most of them had come in purely to browse. As well as the customary abundance of flowers, Lorna also sold a small range of trinkets in the shop – pretty little pots and vases, hand-painted mugs and china bowls, handmade candles fragranced with peony, freesia and tuberose, and a variety of organic soaps and bath bombs. She never intended to sell anything but flowers when she first opened the florists but the diversity in merchandise, the opportunity to be able to offer her customers more than just botanical goods, enhanced her business and customers would often nip in to buy something as a last minute gift or a stocking filler.

The village was a profitable tourist magnet. It was a typically English chocolate-box village, set in a valley sliced in two by a silvery, serpentine river and surrounded by fields, woodland and gently rolling hills. The village was frequented by walkers, cyclists, artists and photographers, and the history buffs – who could be spotted a mile off due to their avant garde appearance – were never very far away.

The big draw of the village was the church. St. Kunegunda's – a magnificent, Grade One listed building dating from the fourth century – stood majestically on top of a hill, the highest point in the village, standing silently, dignified, keeping watch over the network of narrow roads and lanes below her, with their thatched cottages, terraces and grand stone houses. The church itself graced what was once the site of a significant Roman palace and the whole place exuded an atmosphere of importance and wealth and opulence. Casworth was always busy, even in the winter, but especially so in summer, when the three pubs were filled to the rafters and the numerous B&B's and self-catering holiday cottages were booked solid from May through to September.

The tourists were good for business but not today it seemed. Today they were just looking. Lorna had sold a couple of pot plants, several small bunches of pre-arranged flowers wrapped in cellophane and a lavender-scented candle but that was about it. She waited patiently until the big hand finally shifted to the number twelve and decided to call it a day. Five o'clock. Home time.

She'd already packed away the outdoor area and arranged Mrs. Godbeer's lilac and white retirement bouquet, placing it in a vessel of icy water for the morning, so all that was left to do was move the remaining buckets of flowers into the cold store, give the floor a quick sweep, cash up the depressingly spartan till and set the alarm. She glanced at her mobile to check for texts and saw Rose's grinning face beaming back at her. She tapped the screen and her message appeared.

'Meet you in the pub at 7. Are we eating?'

Lorna tutted. Rose always asked if they were eating. Every

16

single Thursday night. And the answer was always yes.

She sent a one-word reply and immediately felt mean. She quickly tapped out a second text saying she was looking forward to seeing her. She cleverly added a smiley face on the end to make it appear even more friendly and pressed send.

She walked to the shop door and flipped the sign in the window from OPEN to CLOSED, programmed the alarm code into the keypad and stepped out onto a baking hot pavement, locking the door behind her.

Inside her own four walls, she kicked off her shoes and wandered into the cool kitchen. She was ravenous. She couldn't wait until gone eight o'clock to eat so she grabbed a banana from the fruit bowl and stood at the sitting room window eating it, gazing out onto the pristine garden below. She looked at the rose bush where she'd buried the charm six months ago and wondered why the spell hadn't worked. She was adamant it would. It had worked for others so why not her?

Warm, golden sunshine flooded the garden and she was tempted to sit outside for half an hour in a bid to give the merest hint of colour to her skin but she had to wash her hair and to get it dry by 7pm, was a task in itself. She tossed the banana skin into the kitchen bin and made her way along the hallway to the bathroom.

THE PUB WAS PACKED, which was a surprise. Friday and Saturday nights in the village were always popular with locals and visitors alike, but Thursday's, as a rule, were usually pretty quiet. Perhaps it had something to do with the upcoming bank holiday weekend – maybe everyone had had the same idea and taken Friday off work to make a long weekend of it. Tonight was the start of their mini holiday, the lucky buggers.

Lorna walked to the bar and waited patiently to be served. She glanced around the hop-strewn, heavily-beamed saloon, picking out plenty of familiar faces, all of who were laughing and joking, swigging beer and sipping wine. She nodded and smiled at those who caught her gaze.

'What can I get you, Lorna?'

Kevin, the permanently pissed landlord – or PPL as the girls liked to call him – stood in front of her, rubbing his hands together. How he made a profit from The Vine was anybody's guess. He started drinking at 11am and didn't stop until closing time. Seven days a week, fifty-two weeks a year. He must be preserved from the inside out, like a jar of pickled onions, Rose would say.

'A large glass of Cabernet, please. And can I also have a large white wine and soda and a Bacardi and coke please?'

'Coming up, love,' he replied, giving her a creepy wink and gazing at her chest for a fraction longer than was totally necessary. Lorna shuddered.

'*Hiya!*' came the all too familiar greeting from behind her.

She turned to see Rose, a vision in fuschia, and Evelyn, more somberly dressed in head to toe black. What a curious trio they made.

Rose, forty-eight years old and statuesque in height, was quite a large but well-proportioned woman. Her snow-white hair hung to her waist and she possessed the most beautiful, flawless skin but a truly awful set of teeth. Her eyes were the colour of a glacial lake and were arresting in their beauty. She'd thickened around the girth with the onset of middle-age and despite years of hearty encouragement from both of her friends, she'd never owned a properly fitting bra. She either had four breasts – two normal-sized ones with two smaller ones spilling out over the bra cups – or two breasts swinging pendulously somewhere around her navel. And she always wore the brightest colours she could possibly find – never co-ordinated with anything or toned-down with more muted hues. If Rose decided to wear jade green, then jade green it was from head to toe, including matching accessories, nail polish and eye-shadow. If nothing else, Rose was striking. And she always smelled absolutely wonderful.

Evelyn was the polar opposite of Rose. She only ever wore grey or black or a washed out in-between shade of charcoal, as she liked to call it. She was thirty-two years old and as skinny as a rake. Her hair colour changed by the week. Today it was deep purple but the last time Lorna saw her it was peroxide white. And the time before that, it was a gorgeous, pale, baby pink. Lorna often wondered if an impending crowning glory disaster was on the horizon and Evelyn would wake up one morning completely bald. She had deep green ivy tattooed around her arm, trailing up to her shoulder and down her back and piercings in places that would make your eyes water. And she had a beautiful face – full lips and deep chestnut eyes that were permanently accentuated with black kohl and layer upon layer of glossy, jet black mascara. Lorna thought she looked like Clara Bow minus the obligatory 1920s bob. And her dry, wicked sense of humour won her an army of admirers. She had the mind of a man and the mouth of a sailor and by god, could she make you laugh.

Then there was Lorna – beguiling and enchanting, with an allure that captivated many. She was prepossessing to look at, small but perfectly formed. She won admiring glances from both men and women and her beautiful hair – the colour of a blood red sky – together with her fine bone structure were features envied by every female that set eyes upon her. She wore pretty, girly clothes – dainty prints and polka dots, cotton dresses nipped in at the waist and pastel cardigans, ballerina pumps and elegant kitten heels. She hardly ever wore trousers. The closest she got was when she wore her one and only pair of jeans on very rare occasions, usually when she was spring-cleaning the shop. She was feminine in every way – elegant and demure – like the delicate patterns she wore and the fragile blossoms she sold.

'I've ordered your drinks,' Lorna told her friends, nodding towards the bar.

Rose leaned forward and kissed Lorna on the cheek.

'You look lovely,' she said, reaching for her wine.

Evelyn kissed Lorna too, eyeing her up and down.

'She always looks lovely,' she groaned, looking over at Rose.

Lorna smiled and handed Evelyn her Bacardi, scooping up the glass of red with her other hand.

'Thank you! You both look gorgeous too. I love your hair that colour, Evelyn. And Rose, bright pink really suits you.'

'I hope it does. I'm about to paint my bedroom this exact shade over the bank holiday! Hot Pink it says on the tin!' she cackled.

Lorna and Evelyn shook their heads and laughed.

Rose's house was like a Dulux paint chart. Every colour of the rainbow adorned the internal walls. You needed your sunglasses on just to walk through the front door.

The ladies found a spare table – shoehorned between a table full of old men playing cards and another smaller table, seating four middle-aged women sharing bowls of chips and swigging back vodka and tonic.

'Busy tonight isn't it?' Rose said, stating the obvious.

'It's the bank holiday I think. Everyone's starting early because the weather is so good,' replied Lorna.

'It's gorgeous isn't it! I got so fed up last week with the cold and the rain, I did a little spell to bring on the sunshine. I've been gloating to myself ever since I woke up on Monday morning, opened my curtains and saw the sun!' said Evelyn.

Lorna and Rose laughed.

'Well done, Evelyn!' they chorused, applauding her wholeheartedly.

Rose took a large gulp of white wine and soda. Quite why she bothered with the soda was a constant source of amusement. She said it was the healthier option. But as she downed at least four glasses of the stuff each time they went out, health didn't really come into it.

'Any news anyone?' she asked.

Evelyn shrugged her shoulders.

'Not really. Work is as boring as usual. I'm just glad I get to have the whole summer off for the first time since I left school!'

Having spent most of her career sweating it out in a hospital kitchen, last summer she spotted a vacancy in the local paper for a cook to run the kitchen in her local village primary school. She applied and to her surprise and utter delight, she was offered the job. She could cycle to work, the pace was so much more relaxed in a school than in a manic hospital kitchen, her working day was shorter, and best of all – the real perk of the job – she had fourteen weeks holiday a year! This was to be her first summer holiday, all six glorious weeks of it, and she planned to use her time very wisely. Firstly, she wanted to visit family in Ireland, then take in a festival or two and lastly, decorate her hall, stairs and landing. She'd been single for eighteen months but, unlike Rose and Lorna, didn't mind being on her own one little bit. She had her cats and her garden and her friends and her hobbies. If somebody special came along, she'd snap them up in a heartbeat. But if they didn't, then it was no big deal.

'You are so lucky,' groaned Lorna. Rose nodded in agreement.

'I'd give anything to have a week off work, let alone all bloody summer! I can't remember the last time I had a break, can you Lorna?'

Lorna's eyebrows dipped and her forehead wrinkled as she tried to recall her last holiday.

'It was when you went to Greece with Tosspot,' said Rose.

'I think you're right, Rose. But I did have that mini-break in the Cotswolds for Hattie's hen weekend. Does that count?'

'No. It doesn't. You need to get out more,' sniffed Evelyn.

'Says you!', retaliated Lorna. 'You hardly ever leave Fordbridge nowadays, Little Miss Humdrum!'

'You cheeky sod!' gasped Evelyn incredulously. 'Neither do you!'

There was silence for a couple of seconds as the ladies

looked at each other blankly before roaring with laughter.

'You're right, I don't!' cried Lorna. 'The furthest I go is to Sainsbury's every Monday. Oh, and to my parents. And your two houses!' She picked up her wine glass and took a generous slug. 'God, I'm so boring.'

For a second she looked wistful, distant almost, remembering her former life. The one she shared with Dan. Her two friends noticed her look of despondency and quickly tried to change the subject.

'Well, let's make a pact to get out more then! We ought to have a girly holiday!' said Rose excitedly.

'Sounds good to me! Let's get our diaries out next time and make a plan. Where do you fancy?'

'Anywhere hot and cheap.'

'Spain it is, then.'

'Talking of hot and cheap, how's it going with you, Rose? Are you still shagging that bloke from the old time music hall?'

Rose pretended to slap Evelyn.

'You bugger! He's not from the old time music hall! We met at the singles dance club in Stamford! And yes – we are still… dating!'

Rose flushed the same colour as her dress, necklace, lipstick and shoes.

'At least I am actually using my bits and pieces!' she quipped.

Evelyn raised her eyebrows.

'If I could find a man half decent to use my bits and pieces with, Rose, I would use my bits and pieces quite happily! I'm not even looking, to tell you the truth. I'm quite happy on my own. As I've told you a million times. What about you, Lorna? Any news?'

Lorna swivelled her glass round and round, watching the deep red wine inside slosh from side to side. She looked straight into Evelyn's eyes.

'I did a spell,' she said tellingly. 'I made a charm. But it didn't work.'

'You made a *charm?*' Rose felt a tingle of excitement creep up her spine. 'When? You didn't tell us!'

Lorna took a deep breath.

'Last November,' she said, her voice tinged with sadness.

'Last November?' cried Rose.

'Well... I made it before then, but I buried it last November.'

Evelyn drained her glass and sighed, shaking her head.

'I know I should have waited until June but... I'd been thinking about it for a while. I felt lonely. That's all. And it was a waxing moon, perfect conditions. So I made a love charm.'

'Where did you bury it?' asked Evelyn, suddenly serious, the smile gone from her face.

'In the garden. Under a rose bush, like I was supposed to'.

Lorna's friends looked at each other.

'And was it a safe place? I mean, there's no chance at all that it can be or could have been dug up?' asked Rose pensively.

Lorna thought about the question and shrugged.

'No. I don't think so,' she said shaking her head slowly and swallowing her last mouthful of wine.

'Are you absolutely sure though, Lorna?'

The perturbed tone to Evelyn's voice unsettled Lorna and

a nervous tingle started to form in the pit of her stomach.

'Well, safe enough.' She took a deep breath. 'I mean, I don't do the gardening, if that's what you mean. I don't weed or...'

Rose interrupted her, stopping her in her tracks.

'So who does?' she asked urgently, her voice, like Evelyn's, becoming increasingly anxious.

'Stop it! You're scaring me.'

'Lorna. WHO does the garden?' urged Rose.

Lorna froze. Her heart began to thud in her chest and she suddenly felt very, very hot.

'George. George does,' she whispered.

'Who the fuck is *George?*' hissed Evelyn, leaning forwards, her eyes flashing.

'The gardener. He's always done the garden. Ever since we moved in to The Maltings. I saw him just a few days ago. He came into the shop for a chat and then went off and cut the grass and tidied up.'

'How deep did you bury it?' asked Rose.

'Er... oh, not deep. The ground was frozen solid, what with the long winter...'

'For god's sake Lorna! Is there any chance he could have dug it up?' Evelyn looked at Lorna in the disconcerting way she always did when she was pissed off.

'I... I'm not sure. I...' she stuttered.

Lorna's eyes began to slowly fill with tears.

Rose reached out and took her left hand. Evelyn grasped her right.

'It's ok, Lorna. Please don't cry. It's ok. Everything will be alright. We will go now, to your garden, and we will find the charm and we will bury it again. This time deeper. And there it will stay. Until the spell works and…' she took a deep breath. 'And he comes to you.'

Rose smiled at her reassuringly and Lorna's heart began to beat at a slightly less frenetic pace. The three friends stood, picked up their bags and left the pub. It was a balmy summers evening and the air was hot and heavy and perfumed with the heady scent of lilac – the perfect night for a spot of moonlit gardening.

ANGELA – A PLUMP, highlighted housewife who thrived on village gossip – leaned over the table towards her three friends, her blouse straining at the buttonholes, hardly able to contain her ample breasts and bulging belly.

'Did you hear that?' she hissed, taking a shifty glance over her shoulder to make sure the recipients of her impending lambasting were out of earshot.

'Bits and pieces. What were they on about?' asked Jan, jabbing her forefinger at minute crumbs of chips at the bottom of the bowl.

Jackie looked puzzled and started fiddling with her new phone.

'Spells. Magic. Making charms. Burying them in the bloody garden!'

She took a hefty gulp of vodka and almost choked on an ice cube.

The other three women abruptly stopped what they were doing and stared at her agog, mouths gaping, eyes on stalks.

'I always knew there was something funny about her from the florists! Nobody would listen to me though! And the other two she hangs around with… freaks, the bloody lot of

26

them! Especially that one with the long white hair and funny teeth!' Angela spluttered, her hands twitching nervously as she fiddled with the hemline of her navy cardigan.

'Can you believe it, Liz? Can you actually bloody believe it? Here! In Casworth! I dread to think what the vicar's going to say...'

She looked at the women, the fear of god instilled within her. They gawped back in disbelief, shaking their heads in unison. Her voice was low, rasping and barely audible as she whispered shakily.

'Those three... those three, sat there just now, as bold as brass... are bloody *witches!*'

LORNA, EVELYN AND ROSE gathered at the bottom of the garden and knelt on the grass in front of the rose bush where Lorna buried the charm the previous winter. It was immediately obvious that the soil had been recently turned over. Lorna remembered George telling her he was going to dig the borders and dug them he had. And bloody thoroughly, by the looks of it. The edges of the lawn were straight and neat and the earth around the plants was as fine as breadcrumbs and free of stones and clods. George always did a good job. The garden looked immaculate.

'Are you sure this is the one?' asked Rose, pointing at the rose bush.

'Yes. Definitely. It's the bush directly opposite my sitting room window. The others are either too far to the right or too far to the left. This is definitely the one.'

Evelyn handed Lorna the trowel. 'Dig'.

'And when you dig it up, don't touch it with your right

hand. Press it back into the soil with your left. And cover it up with dirt. That way the spell won't be broken,' added Rose quickly.

Lorna dutifully began to dig.

She started directly in front of the bush, and dug to a depth of about five inches, her heart beating faster and faster with every trowel full of earth she extracted from the ground. And then she moved further each side until she'd dug a huge trench in front of the rose bush. She glanced nervously from friend to friend.

'It's gone.'

'Are you sure?' asked Evelyn.

'Yes. It's not here. I didn't bury it as deeply as this. I know I didn't. The ground was frozen, I could hardly get the trowel into the earth.'

Rose breathed in dramatically and let out a long, frustrated sigh. She looked sadly into Lorna's eyes.

'Then the spell is broken, my love. And the consequences don't even bear thinking about.' She got up from her knees and smoothed her crumpled pink skirt.

'You must do the reversal love spell under the next full moon. And this time dig deep. As deep as you can. And use geranium oil, not lavender. It is very, very important you do not use lavender again.'

Lorna nodded slowly, absorbing and heeding to Rose's valuable advice.

The three women stood and walked back across the sun-dappled garden, through the back entrance of The Maltings and up to Lorna's flat. It was still early in the evening but none of them much fancied going back to the pub. Lorna opened the fridge and took out a chilled bottle of Sauvignon Blanc.

'Anyone hungry?'

'Famished.'

'Bloody starving!'

'I only have pizza in, I'm afraid…'

'That'll do. I'll get some glasses. Evelyn, put the oven on.'

THREE

THE SUN SHONE BRIGHTLY through the wooden slats of the venetian blind, casting stripes of intense white light onto Lorna's duvet. She turned over in bed and reached for her phone, sliding the snooze button to off, halting the irritating buzz of the alarm. Her head was slightly fuzzy from the wine she'd drunk the night before but she was thankful she didn't have a full-blown hangover. She had a busy day ahead of her and the last thing she needed right now was to feel ill as she went about her work. Drinking on a week night was never a good idea at the best of times but she'd enjoyed herself nonetheless – after the initial shock of discovering the charm had been dug up, that is. She toyed with the idea of asking George if he'd discovered a strange, pink, waxy object with petals stuck in it whilst he was gardening on Tuesday morning but decided it was probably best not to mention it at all. He was a nosey old sod and would undoubtedly start asking questions – questions that would be rather difficult to answer, least of all truthfully.

The trio sat in Lorna's candlelit sitting room, drinking wine, eating pizza and dodging salad until well after midnight. They talked about all sorts of things from old boyfriends and suffering the humiliation of back acne at the age of forty-eight, to the forthcoming Casworth May Day celebrations and the first time they'd met each other, nearly ten years ago. And at the end of the evening, they did as they always did – their farewell ceremony.

Kneeling down, facing one other in a circle on the floor, each woman reached out her left hand to grasp the right wrist of the witch beside her. They lowered their heads and closed their eyes.

'Live each day as if it were your last, for one day you will be right.' said Rose softly.

'Love yourself first and foremost. For when you truly love yourself, loving those around you will come as easy as breathing. And we all must breathe.' whispered Lorna.

'Learn your life's lessons – each as it comes – for that is the reason we are here.' Evelyn said, giving Lorna's wrist a gentle squeeze.

'Enjoy your life, because if you do not, someone else will enjoy it for you and your time on Earth will have been wasted,' chanted all three women in unison.

They broke the circle of hands and looked up, smiling.

'Goodnight, my loves. And Lorna? Don't you worry about a thing. Everything will work out just fine. And in it's own good time. Just you wait and see.'

Lorna nodded. She loved Rose and her weird, Welsh, Wicca ways.

'Thanks for dinner sweetheart,' Evelyn said, as she hugged Lorna tightly.

And with that they were gone. Back to their homes, their lives, their animals. Until the next time.

SHOWERED, DRESSED and breakfasting on granola, yoghurt and honey, Lorna felt decidedly more human than when she first dragged herself out of bed an hour before. She had to deliver the headmistress's bouquet to the school office first thing and by 8.30am she was in the shop, setting up for the day and running a feather duster and a damp cloth over the already sparkling clean surfaces. She spritzed the air with expensive vanilla room fragrance – a quirky little ritual she'd inherited from Tobias – and locked the front door. She fished the bouquet from the bucket of icy water in the cold store, dried the dripping stalks with a tea towel and wrapped the flowers in a layer of chiffon, followed by a layer of pretty paper and finally, a layer of cellophane. She tied it securely with a thick, purple, satin ribbon and let herself out of the back door and into the alleyway that ran up the side of the shop. She retrieved her pride and joy – an old-fashioned white bicycle, with big, shiny wheels, a brown leather saddle and a beautiful, hand-woven wicker basket strapped to the front – and placed the bouquet gently inside the basket, along with her purse and bunch of keys, and wheeled the bike through the gate and out onto the street in front of the shop.

She turned right, crossing the road, and pedaled through the newest part of the village. Large, stone houses now stood where sheep once grazed, each boasting five or six bedrooms, several bathrooms, landscaped gardens and long, herringbone-paved driveways leading to triple garages. She cycled along Main Street and back into the past, with it's streets lined with cottages from a bygone era – quaint and tiny, thatched and tiled, sometimes crooked, sometimes grand, some with roses and honeysuckle around the front door, but all quintessentially English and admired by many.

The road snaked round to the left, past the newsagents and

post office, and then up to the first of the village pubs – the more upmarket of the three – the one that sold moules-frites, Wagyu steaks with triple-cooked chips and only the finest Chablis. Past the village Manor House, shielded from prying eyes thanks to its preposterously high stone wall – only the slate tiles on the rooftop and the canopies of ancient trees visible from the road. The village was quiet. Its breadwinners safely ensconced in their workplaces, its children at school and its housewives at home watching the final few moments of BBC Breakfast before the call of the gym beckoned. After just a few minutes pedalling, Lorna rounded another corner and began her ascent up the ever-narrowing street, towards the school and the oldest part of the village, with its imposing church dwarfing and outshining everything in its shadow.

She leaned her bike up against the wall of the Victorian red brick school and carefully lifted her wares from the basket. She pressed the buzzer on the wall and waited patiently.

'Can I help?' said the detached voice through the intercom speaker.

Lorna noticed the tiny camera positioned just above the buzzer and smiled into it.

'Hello! It's Lorna Mills from Fleur. I'm delivering the bouquet you ordered.'

'Oh yes, Lorna. Do come in'.

There was a loud beep and Lorna pushed the door open with her side, careful not to crush any flowers. Inside the reception area was a set of double glass doors leading into the main part of the school and a hatchway with a sliding glass panel that acted as a barrier between the outside world and the school office. It was like Fort Knox.

A friendly face suddenly appeared at the hatch and the glass door slid to the side.

'Oh, my! Aren't they wonderful?' gasped the school secretary.

Another lady appeared at her side.

'Oh yes! Beautiful! Oh you are clever! Miss Godbeer will love them. The colours are so… so… her!' she gushed.

Laura handed over the bouquet and the secretary swiftly handed it to the other lady.

'Quick. Go and hide them, Caroline! Miss Godbeer could pop in at any second and we don't want her seeing them before she has to,' she whispered.

Lorna smiled.

'Have you got an invoice or anything for us, or have we already paid?' asked the secretary.

Lorna shook her head.

'No. Whoever placed the order on the telephone paid with a credit card. Here's your receipt.'

Lorna dug her hand into her pocket and pulled out the receipt stapled to her business card. She handed it to the secretary.

'Thank-you for your custom,' she said cheerfully. 'I hope your headmistress has a very happy retirement.'

'No… thank-you for such a wonderful display! It's just perfect. And that's very kind of you. I am sure she will enjoy every minute of being a lady of leisure. She's already booked a round-the-world cruise, the lucky so-and-so!'

'Wow! That sounds amazing!' said Laura, feeling a pang of regret for not having travelled the globe before launching her own business.

Lorna got back on her bike and made her way around the side of the school, past the graveyard, along the pathway by the church, where the road bent sharply to the left and curved steeply all the way down to the bottom of the hill, where the bakery was. She fancied some fresh bread for lunch and maybe a cake for the weekend. Her parents were popping over for lunch and Lorna knew how much they loved a liberal slice of Victoria sponge with their cup of tea.

She took her feet off the pedals and started to freewheel down the hill. She stuck her legs out at either side and pretended she was eight-years-old again.

She breathed in deeply – the intoxicating scent of an early summers morning filling her lungs. She looked above her, and through the verdant, virgin leaves of the horse chestnut tree, the sky was the most dazzling shade of deep cornflower blue she'd ever seen. Sunlight dappled the road in front of her and the warm breeze caressed her bare arms and legs and made her hair dance behind her. A sense of happiness washed over her like a wave breaking on the shore and she felt glad to be alive.

But there was somebody in the road in front of her. With momentum building rapidly, she careered downhill, almost out of control, with alarming speed. Her feet found their spinning pedals and her right hand pulled on the brake lever sharply, causing the brakes to squeal, the wheels to wobble and the bicycle to judder violently. She was going to crash.

The figure in the road staggered sideways and lost his footing, falling backwards and landing heavily on the grass verge next to the wall that enclosed the church grounds. His sharp reflexes prevented him smashing his head on the stone

– but only just.

Lorna slowed down considerably but still managed to mount the verge, narrowly missing the unfortunate person sitting forlornly on their backside in the cowslip. She jumped off her bike, allowing it to fall with a clatter to the ground. She turned and saw a man looking back at her.

'Oh my god. I am so, so sorry,' she cried. 'I could have killed you.'

She felt an overwhelming desire to rush to him and help him up but the man hauled himself to his feet and set down the rucksack he was carrying on the verge beside him. He dusted his trousers down and straightened his back. He looked at her and cocked his head to one side, squinting into the sun, a ghost of a smile playing on his lips.

'Phew… that was close,' he stammered. His voice was soft and low and she detected a very faint local accent.

Lorna stood opposite him – biting her bottom lip and shaking her head – her heart beating louder than a drum. He stared at her for what seemed like several hours and then smiled shyly. He was quite possibly the most beautiful creature she had ever seen.

She felt a prickly, almost painful, heat creep up her chest, neck and up to her cheeks. And then her spine tingled from her tailbone to her ears and all the way back down again. Her stomach not only did a somersault but an Olympic Gold Medal winning triple twisting yurchenko.

She needed to get a hold of her self. She was acutely aware that she was making a complete idiot of herself, standing gawping at a man she'd almost maimed for life. She breathed in deeply through her nostrils and exhaled slowly through her mouth, drawing even more attention to her neurotic state.

'Are you ok? I mean, did you hurt yourself when you landed on the ground?'

The man shook his head and smiled again.

'No. I'm fine. Honestly. I should have been looking where I was going. I didn't see you... I didn't realise you could...' he said apologetically before trailing off to silence.

Lorna's heart melted. He was gallantly trying to take responsibility for the accident when it was quite clear that it was entirely Lorna's fault.

'Er,.. I think it should been me apologising to you actually! I'm really too old to be pretending I'm on a rollercoaster ride whilst riding my bike. My stupidity could have caused a very serious accident.'

The man smiled again, his right cheek dimpling. He was becoming more adorable with every heartbeat.

'Well, there wasn't a very serious accident. I'm still in one piece, and so are you. Thankfully.'

Lorna nodded.

'I'm sorry again. Really, really sorry.'

The man chuckled and stooped to pick up his rucksack. He threw it over his left shoulder and looked up the hill towards the church and then back at Lorna.

'It's ok. I promise.'

And with that, he raised his right hand to his brow and did a funny little salute before dipping his head, his eyes not leaving hers for a single second. He then turned and without a word, strolled up the lane alongside the churchyard.

Lorna picked her bicycle up off the verge, surveying it for

damage although there was none, and wheeled it down to the bottom of the hill. She stopped only very briefly to turn and take one last look at the beautiful man with the green eyes but he'd already gone.

She propped her bike up against the bakery and wandered into the shop. Its door was thrown wide open, allowing the tantalising aroma of freshly baked bread to drift into the lane outside, tempting all and sundry to step inside and sample its wares.

'Hello Lorna, how are you? Gorgeous day, isn't it!'

'I'm... er, a little shaken actually. I almost had an accident on my bike.'

'Goodness!' exclaimed Sue. 'What, just now you mean?'

'Yes. I was being a bit stupid and freewheeling down the hill and almost knocked somebody over. I still can't believe I didn't kill him. Or myself, come to think of it.'

'It wasn't that silly old Tom Sharpe, was it? Not right in the head, that one. Always roaming around the village, making a nuisance of himself. We were only saying the other day, he'll end up getting run...'

Lorna interrupted her.

'No. No, it wasn't Tom. It was a complete stranger. I've never seen him before in my life.'

'Oh? At this time of the morning? Bit early for walkers, isn't it? You sure he's not one of those from the new estate?'

Lorna shook her head.

'I don't think so. Although he might be... I don't know everyone in the village just yet! He looked too young to own one of those places though? He had a rucksack with him too. He could have been going to sketch the church or something

I suppose?'

Sue shrugged.

'Could have been. It's a beautiful morning for drawing and the likes. Did he hurt himself?'

'He jumped out the way and fell on to the verge by the wall. I felt terrible. But he was so nice about it. A real gentleman.'

She felt her cheeks flush.

'Ah... was he now?' laughed Sue, knowingly. 'Bit of a looker was he?'

Lorna laughed with her and nodded.

'You could say that!'

'Well, he'd stick out like a sore thumb if he did live in the village. I'm pretty sure we'd all know about it if we had a new local heart throb! Your Dan was the last...'

Sue stopped talking mid-flow. It suddenly occurred to her that discussing the much appreciated good looks of Lorna's ex-fiancé – who, precisely one year ago, ran off with one of the barmaids from The Vine – was pretty bad taste, so she shut her trap before she caused any further offense.

Lorna smiled weakly.

'Sue – the man today was a million times more handsome than Dan ever was.'

Sue grinned. She knew only too well how much heartache Dan had caused Lorna and how she'd been left devastated by his betrayal.

'That's my girl,' she winked. 'Now... what can I get you, my love?'

FOUR

SATURDAY IN THE SHOP was manic. Lorna managed to deliver three bridal bouquets to their respective brides on time, along with five bridesmaids posies and numerous buttonholes, and she trundled back into the village well before opening time. Her extremely old but highly efficient Morris Minor Traveller, which, apart from her bike, was the only method of transport she'd ever owned. It had covered approximately 238,880 miles in its lifetime – the distance between Casworth and the Moon – and it was her car and a delivery van in one. Forty-three years old and still boasting its original maroon paintwork and ash wood trim. It cost her a fortune to run and maintain but she loved it. It even had a name, Cherry, coined from the colour of its glossy red bodywork.

By the end of the day, she was exhausted. All she wanted to do was go home, run a hot bath, put her nightdress on and eat dinner in front of the television. It was the beginning of her weekend and she relished Saturday evenings, knowing she could go to bed at any time, in any state, without fear of the alarm clock waking her up at some ungodly hour the following morning. But tonight, rather reluctantly, she'd agreed to go to Rose's house for dinner after causing ripples of excitement by telling her about the poor, unfortunate man she'd almost killed the day before.

She'd tossed and turned in bed for hours during the night.

The heat was stifling. The weatherman warned it would be a sticky one, and a sticky one it was. The windows were wide open and the cotton sheet that covered her had been kicked to the foot of the bed but still she was uncomfortably hot. There wasn't even the whisper of a breeze through the slats of the blind and the airless room made her glad she lived in a country that enjoyed four distinct seasons. She loved summer but this was ridiculous! It was bordering on tropical. And they'd only just welcomed in the month of May!

She lay motionless in her quiet, dark room, conscious of her steady heartbeat and her slow, deep breathing. Her mind wandered to the man in the lane that morning. She visualised his face, his hair, the shape of his body, his clothing. She remembered every single detail about him. She wondered if she would ever see him again. It was highly unlikely, especially if he was, as she and Sue suspected, a tourist. Or maybe he was a student, studying art or photography. Perhaps his visit was a complete one-off and he was destined never to return to Casworth again. Her heart sank several fathoms. She'd never experienced an encounter quite like that before – an all-encompassing, almost alarming, feeling of attraction to a total stranger. She likened it to being hit in the chest with a sledgehammer. Stopping her dead in her tracks, winding her, making her heart bang like a bass drum. She'd heard the phrase banded about several times before but she'd never really known its true meaning, until now. And it was utterly ridiculous! Even more ridiculous than the weather! She didn't even know the man's name. And she doubted she ever would.

Irritated, she reached for the phone charging beside her

bed and texted Rose.

< Nearly killed somebody today on my bike. No idea who he was but I think he might have been the love of my life. >
She pressed send.

She looked at the time and immediately regretted sending it. She hoped Rose was fast asleep or at the very least, bonking her waltzing partner, because if she didn't have her phone on silent, and the text woke her up, all hell would break loose. Rose was a light sleeper and the slightest noise stirred her.

The phone buzzed back. Lorna grabbed it. It had to be Rose.

< What do you mean the love of your life??? >

< Oops... did I wake you? >

< No. I'm still up. Can't sleep. Too flaming hot. Splashed cold water on my pulse points and everything. WELL??? >

< It was just a feeling... like he was the one. >

< Don't be so daft! Did you arrange to see him again? >

< Course not! >

< WHY NOT??? >

< Because I almost ran him over! And what's with the three question marks all the time??? >

< I'm EXCITED!!! >

< LOL. Go to sleep. I'll tell you everything tomorrow. >

< Tell me now! >

< No. I need to go to sleep. >

< Come round to mine after work. I'll do us some tea. Shall I ask Evelyn? >

Lorna groaned. She knew she'd be tired and hankering for her sofa come 6pm. Why, oh why, did she open her big mouth?

< If you like. See you tomorrow then. >
< Good. Nighty night. >
< Night. >

AS ANTICIPATED, by 6pm Lorna was exhausted and yearning for a lie down with a bottle of wine and a microwave lasagna for one. But after a shower and a change of clothes, she felt refreshed and ready to take on the world. Rose lived less than two miles away in one of the neighbouring villages. The journey took just a few minutes by car and was nearly always a pleasant one, with the exception of winter time, when journeying to Barnston was more akin to driving on a toboggan run. The winding country lane cut through ancient woodland and gently sloping hills, with pheasants and rabbits dotting the landscape and the skies home to the illusive red kite once more.

Rose lived in a delightful two-hundred-year-old stone two-up, two-down on the main road through the village. It had a primrose yellow front door with climbing yellow roses neatly arched around it. The house sat directly on the pavement and entry was via the front door straight into the sitting room, with its cast iron woodburner and polished wood floor. The kitchen was at the back of the house and had a stable door that opened out onto the compact but very pretty back garden. Upstairs there were two bedrooms and a shower room. One room for Rose, the other for her business – The Beauty Room – a white painted room, with a therapy couch and a small trolley filled with lotions, potions and creams. Rose worked from home massaging and plucking, exfoliating and peeling an army of loyal clientele. She was a highly-skilled beauty therapist with ladies travelling to her from miles around to endure her signature Brazillian wax. She was held in such high regard and her name revered by many, that she'd been escalated to near mythical proportions for her talent in removing pubic hair.

The house was perfect for Rose, who'd lived there alone for eighteen years. Her eight-year marriage to Edwyn hadn't produced children and after finding herself unexpectedly and quite suddenly divorced at the youthful age of thirty, she never remarried and subsequently never became a mother. It was her only one big regret in life – and the reason why she doted on Lorna so much. She was the daughter she never had.

Lorna knocked on the door and walked straight in. The smell of roast chicken filled the air and Lorna followed her nose through to the kitchen, where Rose stood, basting the bird and turning the roast potatoes.

'Rose! Are you cooking a roast dinner?'

Rose shrieked, splashing hot oil over her worktop.

'Oh you bugger! You made me jump! I didn't even hear the door. I must have been away with the fairies.'

The two friends embraced.

'What time is Evelyn arriving?'

'She's not. She's going on a date!'

'On a date? Who with?'

'Some lad she met at the school yesterday. He turned up to teach PE apparently, some sports company that goes round to different schools. Anyway, they got chatting while he was unloading his balls and hoops and the like, and after the lesson, he popped his head round the door and asked her out. As brazen as you like! And she was in her hat and pinny and everything! She made me die telling the story!'

Lorna laughed.

'I can't believe it! And there she was on Thursday night saying she loved being on her own and how she never met anyone decent. It's so weird!'

'I know. And then there's you and your mystery man. And me and my dancer. There's hope for us all yet!'

Rose opened a bottle of wine and poured them both a large glass. She handed one to Lorna.

'You can have the one, love. And if you want more, you can crash out on my futon.'

Lorna took the glass from Rose and sipped the chilled Chardonnay.

'I can't stay Rose. Mum and Dad are coming over tomorrow. I've got to tidy the flat and do a few jobs. It's May Day on Monday remember, so I won't get a lot done then. Are you and Evelyn coming over for the maypole dancing?'

'Yes as far as I know. Unless Evelyn is half way to Gretna Green come Monday morning!'

Rose put the chicken and potatoes back into the oven and ignited the gas ring to cook the broccoli and carrots. She washed her hands in the sink and dried them on a tea towel, before carefully applying hand cream and sliding the silver pentacle ring that lay on the windowsill back onto the middle finger of her right hand.

'Let's go and sit in the garden. It's such a lovely evening.'

THE GARDEN WAS a very precise square of lawn with fruit trees at the bottom and a wide strip running up the right hand side, filled with every vegetable you could possibly imagine.

The left border was crammed with shrubs and flowers of every variety. The fence around the garden was adorned with trellising and wires from which clematis, honeysuckle, grapevines and climbing roses cascaded, creating a magical waterfall of colour and scent. The little patio outside the back door basked in its perpetual sun-trap and on it stood a faded wooden table and four chairs, bought in the days when the fourth chair had an owner. Occasionally it was a resting place for one of Rose's cats, but more often than not it now stood empty of an occupant. And the other three ladies would nod to it and smile and remember.

Rose adored her garden and visibly sank into a deep depression at the end of autumn as all around her withered and died.

'Oh, Rose. You are so clever.' said Lorna as she gazed at Rose's horticultural handiwork. 'Your garden gets better every year! It's like something from Gardener's World'.

'It's my only real passion in life, as you well know. I've always had a soft spot for Alan Titchmarsh. Writes porn when he's not gardening, you know.'

'Oh, Rose! He doesn't!'

Rose raised her eyebrows and nodded fervently.

The two women sat down and raised their glasses to the two empty chairs in front of them.

'So... tell me all about yesterday!'

Lorna suddenly felt awkward and a little embarrassed. There was nothing much to tell but she took a deep breath and started at the beginning, telling Rose all about the entire days events – from delivering the retiring headmistress's bouquet to the school, to choosing which cake to buy from the bakery. And every minute detail in between.

Rose looked puzzled.

'So, did Sue not know who he was? I mean... if he was going up the hill to the church, he must have walked right by her shop? She's so nosey that one, doesn't miss a trick. She must have seen him?'

'No she didn't. I described him – well, I said he was good looking – and she started going on about the lack of handsome men in the village and how the last person in the village to turn heads was Dan. And then she shut up.'

'Oh'. Rose looked disappointed.

'Mmmm,' murmured Lorna, nodding her head and pulling a face.

'Silly cow,' spluttered Rose.

Laura's grimace broke into a smile.

'Well!' Rose continued. 'Why did she have to bring that waste of space up again for?'

'I don't know. Wasn't really thinking I suppose'.

'Trap as big as the black hole of Calcutta, that one.'

She gazed wistfully at the garden with its whispering trees and cradled her wine glass.

'Your mystery man sounds lush, Lorna. It's a shame you don't actually know who he is. You'll have to start making enquiries around the village. See if anybody new has moved in.'

Lorna knew most of what was going on in the village already. She had her business, which attracted genuine customers and those who liked to wander in purely for a spot of idle chit-chat. She very much doubted she would be able to discover any information about the village newcomer. If indeed, he was a newcomer. She knew almost everyone in Casworth, and they knew her. If he did live in the village she was pretty sure she'd have seen him before, and she was certain Sue would have done. After all, she was the nosiest woman within a ten-mile radius, along with Peggy from the Maltings, and every single resident bought her baked fayre at least twice a week.

Lorna resigned herself to the fact that maybe her spell casting skills weren't as refined as she thought they were. And anyway, the spell was broken. For the time being at least. The next waxing moon was several weeks away and she couldn't do the reverse love spell until then. To do so would be far too precarious. She had to be patient. She looked at the empty chair to her left and remembered Oriel's oft-repeated words of wisdom. Good things come to those who wait. And wait she would.

FIVE

Ten years earlier...

ORIEL – A TALL, DEMURE and somewhat ageless lady of uncertain years – unlocked the doors to the community centre and strode into the hall, setting down a portable CD player on the table and plugging it in. She selected a CD entitled Tranquility from her enormous, leather holdall and inserted it into the player, pressing play swiftly followed the pause button.

She unlaced her trainers and took them off, along with her white sports socks, displaying perfectly pedicured feet and pillar-box-red toe-nails. Next, she unzipped her tracksuit jacket and removed it and then peeled off her sweat pants – revealing an emerald green unitard – folded both items of clothing neatly and placed them in her bag. Her body was lean and toned, her limbs long, her neck swan-like, her spine elegantly curved. Her thick, raven black hair was tied low, at the nape of her neck, and hung down her back like a well-groomed horse's tail.

She stood barefoot on the cold, tiled floor and reached her hands high above her head, stretching her fingertips towards the ceiling, titling her hips from side to side, before bending forwards from her waist and rolling down vertebrae by vertebrae, until the palms of her perfectly manicured hands touched the floor. Slowly she uncurled until she was upright once more.

She glanced at the clock on the wall. 6.55pm. Her fingers idly toyed with the silver pentacle that swung from a delicate chain around her neck. As if bang on cue, the community doors swung open and two ladies walked in, both middle-aged, dressed in leggings and t-shirts and carrying mats rolled into tight coils under their arms.

'Hello ladies! Lovely to see you!' greeted Oriel, her cut-glass accent so clipped and refined, she almost sounded like royalty.

The ladies gave her their names and Oriel wrote them down in a large spiral-bound notebook. She took three pounds from each of them and placed the money in a battered old tin.

The doors opened again and another woman walked in. Her long, white hair was woven into a plait and she was clad from head to toe in violet. She looked a little self-conscious as she made her way across the hall to join the other three ladies, but Oriel made her feel welcome straight away.

'Such a pretty colour!' she called out, eyeing the woman's lycra ensemble.

The woman smiled back.

'And what is your name?' asked Oriel, pen poised.

'It's Rose.'

'And such a pretty name too!'

Oriel wrote down Rose's name and Rose handed her the class fee.

'Thank you.' acknowledged Oriel. 'I will try and remember all your names tonight, I promise. By next week, I will have memorised them all!'

Three more ladies walked into the hall, followed by a confident young lady in cropped, black, lace-edged leggings and an oversized black top.

Oriel greeted them all like long-lost friends and wrote their names down one by one.

Claire, Joanne, Debbie and Evelyn.

Oriel eyed the clock once more. It was 7 o'clock on the dot. She clapped her hands and the assembled women fell silent.

'Ok ladies! Wonderful to see you all! And on such a miserable night too! Thank you all so much for coming. My name is…'

There was a creaking sound from the back of the hall and a very young and unusually pretty girl peered her face around the door, her complexion as white as snow, her deep red hair loosely piled on top of her head.

'Hello… I'm so sorry. Am I late?' she whispered.

Oriel beckoned her inside.

'Of course not! If anything, I am early!' replied Oriel with a dazzling smile.

The girl practically tip-toed across the floor to join the others.

'And you are…?' asked Oriel.

'Lorna. Lorna Mills.' she replied, nervously.

'It's alright, Lorna. We won't bite! Will we ladies?' Oriel laughed.

The ladies shook their heads and smiled.

Oriel added her name to the bottom of the list in her notebook and closed it.

'Just a baby…' she said, winking at Lorna. 'We – or rather,

you – are all in the same boat. This is a brand new class and you are my very first ladies!'

Lorna took off her jacket and put her mat on the floor. She felt out of place in this room full of older women.

Oriel glanced around jauntily at her new clients and placed her hands on her hips in an authoritative manner.

'Right! I'll tell you a little about myself before we start. My name is Oriel Trewhellor-Fitzpatrick. I have been a yoga teacher for nearly forty years since discovering the practice whilst travelling through India. But I am also an holistic therapies practitioner and tonight, you are all here to learn the art of meditation.'

The assembled women looked at each other and nodded, as if showing their mutual admiration for this tantric goddess standing before them. And simultaneously, every single woman thought the exact same concurrent thought – if Oriel had been a yoga teacher since the 1970s, then she must be sixty-years-old at the very least. If not older. How could this be when she didn't look a day over forty?

Oriel smiled, her brain detecting and registering their innermost thoughts. She continued her speech.

'I moved to Stamford recently, from the island of Jersey, where I spent many happy years. I met my second husband there and I ended up following him back to his hometown when he yearned to return to his roots.' She paused dramatically. 'The things we do for love...!'

She flashed her film star smile once more and everyone smiled along with her.

'Which is precisely why I am here and starting this class tonight.'

Her eyes wandered lazily from woman to woman, uncomfortably slowly, scrutinizing each one until she had looked deep into the eyes of everybody standing before her.

'Do you all know what meditation is?' she asked, the tone of her voice changing from lighthearted to really quite sinister in roughly a millisecond.

Some nodded, some shook their heads, some just stared at her blankly, almost too scared to speak.

Oriel's eyes flashed the same emerald green as her unitard and her lips pressed into a thin, crimson line.

'Meditation is the ability to focus one's mind for a set period of time, to enable one to think deeply, to contemplate, to reflect, to relax. Meditation can be silent, it can be accompanied by chanting or assisted by gentle music. It can be practiced for religious purposes but it can also be practiced very successfully by non-believers...'

She paused, her finely-plucked eyebrows arched to perfection.

'... those of us who are on a spiritual quest in their lives. Those who believe in something significantly greater than the presence of a God... a presence which, after all, cannot be proven.'

She reached up and touched the silver pentacle resting upon her breastbone once more.

'And that is why I am here. For all of you. To teach you the art of meditation. And once learned, it will become a gift to treasure, a gift which will stay with you for a lifetime.'

The hall fell into deathly silence. Not even the sound of breathing or the feint detection of a beating heart could be heard.

Oriel raised one eyebrow and looked at the women.
'Shall we begin?'

THE FRIENDS' FIRST meeting was a bizarre occasion. One they often discussed – sometimes with laughter, sometimes with sadness – throughout the ten years that had passed from that cold, wet, windy night in November until now. As the weeks rolled by, original members left the class and new members joined, but Rose, Evelyn and Lorna remained faithful devotees. They always arrived a few minutes early and soon everyday, mundane pleasantries evolved into more personal conversations. Within a few months, real friendships had started to form.

Oriel flitted between all three friends like a butterfly. She was always keen to join in with conversations the women had as they got changed, and occasionally, she joined the trio for a drink at the pub after classes, especially if it was a pleasant evening. The marked difference between her and the other three was that she kept her personal life very much to herself. She was guarded and Lorna, Evelyn and Rose knew very little about her. They knew she lived with a man called Roger. They knew she lived a privileged life – her home was on the smartest street in Stamford, where houses fetched upwards of a million pounds apiece. She was childless. She was educated. She was well-travelled. But that really was all they knew – mere snippets of information that had been drip-fed into the conversation from time to time. More often than not, Oriel usually liked to sit back, glass in hand, and let the other women gabble ten to the dozen, revealing their deepest, darkest secrets as though they had known each other their entire lives. Oriel was a great conversationalist. She would start debates about all sorts of diverse subjects, and then sit back and let the others do the talking – interjecting here and there when she felt it was appropriate to do so. She asked many questions, but rarely did she give answers.

The three friends built up a close bond over a short period of time. Oriel was regarded as a friend to all three women – a kind, generous and funny friend – but she wasn't part of their inner circle, their clique, their gang. Until one afternoon in May, six months to the day after their first meeting. A day that would change their lives forever.

SIX

IT WAS A GLORIOUS Sunday morning. Birds sang in the hedgerows outside and in the distance, church bells rang, coaxing villagers from their beds, reminding them there was a ten o'clock service to attend.

Lorna rolled over and peered, bleary-eyed, at the alarm clock. After a long evening at Rose's, and only one glass of wine, she decided to drive back home to the comfort of her own bed. Rose's futon was like sleeping on a mat of bricks and Lorna wasn't too fond of waking up with a stiff back. Or a cat on her face, come to that. So she made her excuses and went home.

She lay on her side, watching the minutes pass by, thinking about nothing in particular. She had a busy day ahead of her. The flat was a tip and needed a damn good clean. She was constantly amazed at how much mess one person could make in a week. Her parents would be round at 2 o'clock. This wouldn't do. She heaved herself out of bed and flipped open the blind. There wasn't a cloud in the sky. If it stayed like this until tomorrow, it would be the first May Day she could remember that wasn't a complete wash-out. Last year, it was so cold, everyone had coats and jumpers and boots on and the turnout was very poor. The year before they'd suffered the misery of sleet. Everyone had legged it to the marquee and that's where they stayed. It was warm and it sold beer and burgers. People stayed there all day and got falling-down drunk. The traders pitched outside on the school field, with their cake stalls and merry-go-rounds and tressle tables full of bric-a-brac, packed up and went home.

The May Day organisers would be rubbing their hands together with glee if this good weather kept up. All proceeds from the fete were going to the Village Hall Preservation Fund, and by god, did the poor old village hall need preserving. The roof leaked, it was cold and draughty and the decrepit guttering needed replacing. It was the church's poor cousin. Standing side by side, one was literally funded to the eyeballs, the other scratching around in the dirt for loose change. At least this year, things looked a little more promising. The coffers would be overflowing and everybody would be happy.

Lorna made herself a cup of tea and a slice of toast and switched on the television. The BBC was full of news stories about forthcoming pension strikes and the lighting of the Olympic flame. All rather dull.

She aimed the remote control at the tv and fired. The screen went black. She sat on the sofa debating which mundane chore to start first – hoovering or cleaning the bathroom – when her phone began to ring.

'Hello?'

'Oh hello darling.'

'Hi mum. Are you ok?'

'Yes, thank you. I'm fine. But your dad's not. He's got a dreadful cold. Well, flu really. I didn't believe him yesterday when he was shuffling around, sneezing, groaning, drinking too much brandy and generally annoying me. But today he can't get out of bed. He's aching all over, shivering one minute, boiling hot the next...'

'Poor dad. So lunch is off today?' asked Lorna, secretly hoping her mother would say yes.

'Yes, dear. I'm so sorry. I hope you haven't gone to too much trouble?'

'No. Not at all. I bought a cake for tea and I thought we could go for lunch in the village, seeing as the weather is so good'.

'Oh, how disappointing. It would have been lovely. I'd say pop over here instead but I don't want you catching your father's germs. I'm sure I'll be next.'

'Are you sure mum? I could bring the cake over?'

'No. You stay there. Take it easy. We'll see you next weekend or something.'

'Well, if you're sure. Give my love to dad won't you?'

'Yes, dear. Of course I will. I'll keep you posted as to how he is. Man flu can be fatal you know.'

Lorna smiled. She couldn't tell if her mother was making a joke or not.

'So I hear'.

'Bye bye.'

'Bye. Give my love to dad.'

'Will do. Are you eating enough?'

'Yes mum. Bye.'

Lorna put the phone down. She loved seeing her parents but her mother was one of those irritating women who still thought her children were toddlers. She overly fussed about every aspect of their lives and although Lorna's brothers quite enjoyed being pandered to, Lorna hated it. She reminded her mum every time she saw her that she was actually twenty-eight years old, managing to live alone quite happily and running her own business quite successfully. There was really no reason to worry. But Jilly Mills disregarded everything Lorna said. Was she getting her five-a-day? Was her car Mot'd and taxed? Did she switch off all her electrics at night? At the mains? Did she have fully functioning batteries in her smoke alarm? Was she getting enough sleep? And vitamins? It drove Lorna mad.

She would drive over to see them in the week after work. Dad would be over the worst of his flu by then and she could wangle dinner out of them at the same time. Mum may be a hopeless nag, but she was learning how to cook and at times, she turned out some pretty edible food.

Lorna showered and dressed and succeeded in hoovering, dusting, cleaning the bathroom, changing the bed linen, watering the plants and scrubbing the kitchen in just over an hour. Then she loaded the washing machine and switched it on before finishing her mammoth chore-a-thon with a trip to Sainsbury's.

When she got back home, she took the linen basket full of damp clothing out into the garden to hang out on the washing line to dry. One of Lorna's neighbours, Peggy, the wife of a retired police officer and the source of all village gossip, sat in a deckchair soaking up the sun, reading The Sunday Times. The newspaper was far too large to hold and read properly in a deck chair.

'That newspaper is nearly as big as you, Peggy!' laughed Lorna.

Peggy lay the paper down on her lap and smiled.

'Yes, it is rather! Good article on colonic irrigation though.

Apparently it's coming back into fashion.'

Lorna had no idea colonic irrigation had been fashionable in the first place.

'Oh! How nice.'

'How are you dear? I don't see you very often, always working aren't you?'

'I suppose so. I do love it though. '

Lorna put the basket down on the grass and began pegging out her clothes.

'And I'm fine thank you. How are you? And David?'

'Oh, muddling through, you know. As you do when you get to our age.'

They were hardly at deaths door! Both Peggy and David were only in their early sixties! Lorna often overheard Peggy chatting at WI meetings and to say she was overly dramatic was something of an understatement. She always had some dreadful, incurable ailment that was baffling medical experts worldwide, provoking coos of sympathy from her clutch of jam-making friends. Of course, in reality, she was as fit as a fiddle.

'You look very well to me. You've got a lovely colour!' remarked Lorna.

'Oh, that's all that's left from our holiday in Madeira. Wonderful place. We go every year, you know. We've got a holiday home there.'

'Yes, I remember you saying. I've never been.' replied Lorna lightheartedly and continued to hang out the washing.

'You ought to. Mind you, probably a bit old fashioned for you. Tenerife would be more up your street. Lots of old folk like me and David go to Madeira. Hotels are smashing. Lovely gardens, very quiet. They have full afternoon tea every day, you know, whether you're hungry or not, and bingo in the evenings. It's marvelous.'

'Sounds perfect,' replied Lorna, making a mental note to never succumb to quiet holidays involving full afternoon tea and bingo when she reached her sixties.

'Are you going to the fete tomorrow?' asked Peggy.

'Yes. I'm really looking forward to it. I'm going with a couple of friends.'

'The WI need more cakes for their stall, if you've got time. I know I reminded you last week but I know you're a busy girl, being one of those new-fangled career women and all...' she said, with more than a hint of sarcasm.

Lorna pegged out the last item of clothing and picked up her basket.

'I've made one already. A coffee and walnut sponge. Where shall I take it?' she answered breezily, cleverly finding a welcome home for the shop-bought cake she'd spent ages choosing from the bakery on Friday morning.

One-nil to me, you old bag, she thought.

Peggy almost choked on her tea.

'Oh! Right! Super! Er... have you got time to pop it up to the hall today? The ladies are there this afternoon, getting the stall ready. I can't go up, of course. I've got terrible bowel problems. The doctors have no idea what's wrong with me. They are sending me for...'

'Lovely. I'll cycle up with it after lunch.'

And with that, she turned on her heel and strode off through the garden, grinning from ear to ear.

'Bye, Peggy!' she called.

She was through the garden gate and up the path before Peggy even had time to answer.

Lunch was a can of tuna, some limp lettuce, cucumber, cherry tomatoes and a blob of salad cream. Hardly cordon bleu cuisine but it filled a gap. And it contained real vegetables, which would please her mother. She took the coffee and walnut cake out of the shop wrapping – revealingly emblazoned with its Sue's Village Bakery logo – and wrapped it carefully in cling film. Nobody would know the difference. She walked round to the florists, unlocked the alley gate and wheeled out her bike, placing the cake in the basket. The village was very busy, as she thought it might be. The three pub gardens were overflowing with people, enjoying their lazy Sunday afternoon in the sunshine. As she pedaled towards the village hall, she said hello or nodded to at least a dozen cyclists and even more ramblers.

Inside the hall, several men were setting up long and very well-used tressle tables and members of the Village Hall Committee were expertly directing where they should be placed. They even had a table plan. It was all very impressive. Brightly-coloured bunting had been strung from beam to beam and bunches of daffodils and tulips stuffed into vases of all shapes and sizes added vibrant splashes of yellow and red. The WI area had already been set up and occupied the entire space in front of the stage. The tables were draped in lacy, white tablecloths and laden with jars of jam and chutneys and pickles of every description. A huge variety of cakes, from Victoria sandwiches and mounds of flapjacks, to delicate, pastel-iced cupcakes and deep, luxuriantly rich fruit cakes took up an entire table. Three elderly ladies from the institute fussed behind the stall, counting the float money over and over again and writing price labels for all the produce on sale.

'Hello Maggie. I've bought a cake for you,' interrupted Lorna.

Maggie looked up and smiled broadly.

'Oh, you are an angel. What is it my love?'

'Coffee and Walnut. I made it this morning,' she lied.

'You are a good girl. Thank you so much. It looks delicious.'

Lorna felt slightly guilty for pretending she'd made the cake herself but she didn't dwell on her shortcomings for too long. She'd paid five pounds for that cake and was pretty sure Sue had made it for a quarter of the cost!

Lorna handed over the cake, spent a few minutes chatting about how wonderful the stall looked and how delightful the weather was, and then made her excuses and went outside to retrieve her bike. She decided to wheel it through the churchyard and cycle home via the back of the village, which was by far the oldest and prettiest part.

She pushed her bike through the gate from the lane next to the village hall and over some old flagstones into the churchyard. She loved looking at gravestones, particularly the ones in this churchyard. The grounds surrounding the church were exceptionally well looked after and boasted so many beautiful rose bushes and shrubs and trees, it was almost like wandering through the garden of a stately home albeit with centuries of dead people in it.

As she made her way up the steep, gravel pathway to the church, she saw a man in front of her, standing with his back towards her, filling up what looked like a watering can

63

from the tap on the wall. She stopped still in her tracks. She recognised him in an instant. It was the man she'd almost knocked over.

Her mouth went dry and her heartbeat began to bang loudly in her ears. She started to push her bike gingerly towards him, not knowing whether to stop and say hello or just walk straight by. She didn't have to make the decision. He made it for her.

Joe glanced over his shoulder to see who was crunching up the gravel behind him and, when he saw her, he slowly stood up, placed the watering can down beside him and turned to face her.

Lorna felt her face begin to burn again. Her eyes drank him in. He wasn't overly tall, around five foot ten at a guess. He had dark brown hair that was cut short at the sides, a little longer on top, and was slicked back off his face. His eyes were hazel and his lips full. He had broad shoulders, strong-looking arms, narrower hips and he wore a white shirt with the sleeves rolled up, sandy-coloured cotton trousers and brown work boots. He was even more gorgeous than she'd remembered him being. If Rose could see him right now, she would describe him as lush. Lush was her favourite word.

'Ah, it's you,' he said softly.

Lorna was momentarily dumb struck.

'Yes… I was just walking through the churchyard… on my way back home,' she replied, trying desperately hard not to muddle her words or start stammering.

'Such a lovely day,' she tailed off in almost a whisper.

Joe smiled and nodded, tilting his face to look at the cloudless sky.

'It is.'

Lorna took a deep breath. She couldn't think straight and was struggling to concoct a coherent sentence.

'So… do you work here? At, at… the church, I mean?' she stuttered.

For god's sake Lorna. You sound like a moron, she told herself angrily.

Joe nodded again.

'Yes, sort of. I look after the grounds. I water the plants, keep the graves tidy, sweep the leaves out of the porch, make sure the church doors are always at their best. They are so old, you know. They need looking after…'

'I've never seen you before, that's all. In the village, or here, I mean,' she gabbled. 'Mind you, I don't go to church very often. It's not really my thing.' she added, absent-mindedly playing with the tiny silver pentacle around her neck.

'Mine neither. It's just a job. But I do love the outdoors.'

They stood looking at each other for what seemed like an eternity. Lorna studied his face. He looked like a film star.

'Would you like to sit down?' he asked, gesturing over towards a bench positioned just outside the church porch.

Lorna nodded and pushed her bike over to the bench and leaned it up against the stone wall of the ancient building.

The bench was dedicated to a rather grandly named Cressida Houghton-Washingley who died in 1968 and who, apparently, 'loved this place'. It overlooked the churchyard, the primary school and its playing field and the picturesque high street below. It was a very good place for a bench, Lorna mused. Ms Houghton-Washingley had good taste.

Lorna and Joe sat down side by side. Lorna's adrenalin

levels were still as high as a kite and she felt nervous, ecstatic, sick and giddy all at the same time. She couldn't quite believe her luck. She could have quite easily cycled back the way she came. And she never would have seen him.

'Do you live in the village?' she asked, knowing full well that he couldn't possibly. There were no film stars in Casworth.

'No.' Joe shook his head. 'I live in Lutton, the next village along. What about you?'

'I live here, yes. I live alone and I run the florists at the far end of the village.' she replied, highly impressed she had managed to inform him that she lived by herself so early on in their conversation.

'Ah,' he said, nodding slowly. 'I know where that is. I walk by the flower shop on my way home each day.'

Do you, she thought? Each day? Lorna was amazed she'd never seen him before.

'Do you live in Lutton with your girlfriend?' she asked, feeling a sudden surge of bravery taking hold of her tongue. She braced herself for his reply.

He looked at her with an element of surprise. He seemed quite taken aback by this intrusion into his personal life.

'No! I don't! I don't have a girlfriend,' he replied, sounding offended. 'I live with my sister,' he added, his voice softening.

His words made her heart soar and her inner-self do a funny little jig.

'Oh! I'm so sorry. I just assumed…' she said, trying hard to rectify her insolence.

'I'm single. I've never married.'

Lorna thought it was an odd thing to say but she didn't

want to interrogate him further. She thought she might scare him off altogether if she asked any more stupid questions.

'Me neither. I mean… I'm not married. I was engaged once but… we broke it off.'

Joe smiled. He turned his body to face her, reaching out his right hand. He looked deeply into her evergreen eyes. His eyes weren't hazel at all. They were the colour of newly unfurled fronds of fern.

'My name is Joe.'

Lorna took his hand in hers. His fingers were long and his skin was tanned and smooth. She didn't want to let him go.

'Hello, Joe. My name is…'

'Lorna,' he whispered, before she had time to finish her sentence.

Lorna gasped.

'How do you know my name?'

The corners of his perfect lips turned upwards into a shy smile and he lowered his eyelids.

'I just do.'

SEVEN

JOE WALKED THE MILE to Lutton slowly, his rucksack slung over one shoulder, his battered, dirty work boots treading a path they'd walked a thousand times. The road was a winding lane – little more than a track, certainly not wide enough for two cars to safely pass side-by-side – connecting one village to another. Except Lutton wasn't a village. It was a hamlet. A cluster of stone houses with traditional, cottage gardens, nestled in woodland with a subsidiary of the River Nene babbling through it. The lane from Casworth snaked through the village, over an old stone bridge, past a tiny Norman church with an extremely rare wooden steeple, further still, ending abruptly in front of the monumental, cast iron gates of Lutton Hall.

Joe approached the village as the sun began to set in the sky, creating a celestial watercolour across the heavens. He looked at each house and cottage in turn as he passed by. Nothing much changed in Lutton. The hamlet looked just as it had a hundred years ago, with the exception of the occasional conservatory or summer house dotted here and there and an abundance of large, shiny cars parked on driveways. He crossed over the bridge, pausing briefly to glance down into the cool, clear water below, and then made his way past the church, turning left at the red post box set into the wall of a now redundant post office – the post office his parent's once ran, his childhood home. The air was heavy with the scent of moss and lichen and as he walked along the densely-wooded Lover's Lane, he could hear his sister's birds singing their last song of the evening.

The garden was in full shadow at this time of day. Thick woodland shielded it from the outside world, blocking out any light from the setting sun. The grass was long and overgrown and full of weeds and the once-immaculately pruned rambling rose and honeysuckle were now tangled together in an inharmonious mass of delicate, perfumed flowers and barbarous, lacerating thorns. Next to the back door – with paintwork faded and peeling – stood Alice's green, rubber wellies and the washing line that was strung between the two garden walls was empty, apart from a solitary, sun-bleached yellow duster that had seen better days.

Joe pushed open the kitchen door and placed his rucksack on the formica worktop. He could smell dinner and was glad that Alice had eaten already, seeing as it was getting late. He crept quietly into the darkened front room so as not to startle her. The television was on with the volume turned down low and a small lamp in the corner of the room cast a warm glow onto the cream walls, illuminating the collection of photo frames huddled around it. He tiptoed up to the sofa in the middle of the room and peered over the back. His sister lay on her side, her head propped up on the large, square tapestry cushion she had made as a young girl. Her body, petite and elfin-like, was covered with a soft, olive green, chenille throw and her long hair tumbled over the arm of the sofa like newly-spun flax.

Joe edged around the side of the sofa, sinking to his knees, and looked at his sleeping sister. She looked so peaceful, so beautiful, so child-like. He lifted his hand and stroked her hair and then, with the side of his index finger, her soft downy cheek. Her lashes fluttered briefly and she opened her eyes. A faint smile flickered across her face and she reached out a slender hand to touch his jaw.

'Joe...' she murmured, closing her weary eyes again.

Joe leaned forward and kissed her forehead tenderly.

'My Alice,' he whispered. 'I'm home'.

MAY DAY DAWNED. Another pristine, summer's day. At last, a fete day without wellies and umbrellas. Lorna woke to two texts, one from Rose, one from Evelyn, both asking the same thing.

Those two have brains like sieves, she said to herself.

She text them back.

< Meeting at the school gate entrance at 12 noon. For the fourth time. You pair of numpties. >

She pressed send and waited for a sarcastic reply to bounce back. But there were none.

She was still floating somewhere above cloud nine after yesterday's completely coincidental meeting in the churchyard. She kept going over the scenario in her head until it seriously started to make her brain ache. And when she became momentarily distracted by something else, such as reading emails or making breakfast, her stomach did a little lurch every time she re-remembered what had happened. She hadn't told Rose or Evelyn about meeting Joe yet. She wanted to tell them at the fete. Not that there was very much to tell. Their encounter came to an abrupt end when Lorna received a phonecall from the customer who'd ordered the birthday bouquet for Bank Holiday Monday delivery. She was in a terrible flap. She'd made a mistake with the date and her mother-in-law's birthday was actually that day. Was there any chance she could collect the bouquet in person at around teatime? Lorna was mildly irritated to say the least. She hadn't even assembled the damn bouquet yet. She agreed to do it but she was still annoyed. Their incompetence had spoiled her afternoon, which, as it happened, had turned out to be rather an eventful one.

She explained to Joe that she needed to go to work unexpectedly for an hour or so and he nodded and smiled and said he had to get on with his work too. And that was that. He hadn't asked to see her again and she felt uncomfortable doing the chasing. But as Joe shook her hand for the second time that day, and tiny electrical impulses ran through her fingers and up her arm and into her chest, she knew she would see him again. She just didn't know when.

Lorna walked to the school and waited for her friends to arrive. The school field was already buzzing with people and she could hear music and laughter and smell the mouthwatering aroma of sizzling onions.

She felt a hand slap her backside and turned to see Evelyn grinning at her.

'Look at you! All dolled up like a forties sweetheart!'

Lorna smiled. She looked down at the red and white polka dot sundress and red patent wedges and then back at Evelyn in her black vest top, faded black jeans and black gladiator sandals.

'Look at you! All dolled up like a Marilyn Manson groupie!'

'Touché! If only,' replied Evelyn dryly, kissing her cheek.

'Where's Rose?' Lorna asked.

'Just parking the bloody car. That's the trouble with these sorts of events. Nowhere to park. I left her round the back near the bakery. She said for us to go in and get her a glass of something nice and she'll meet us on the grass.'

'I'm amazed she's driving. She normally lets her hair down at do's like these.'

'Said something about meeting old Twinkle Toes later for a bit of how's your father.'

'Oh really! Getting serious, is it?'

'Sounds like it! I wonder what he looks like? She's described him as looking like a cross between Richard Madeley and Noel Edmonds.'

'Bloody hell… does that mean he has longer than average hair and a perma tan?'

'I suppose the tan is compulsory if you're into ballroom dancing, or whatever it is they do.'

'Isn't it salsa?'

'Same thing. All dancing is completely naff.'

The two women laughed and walked into the beer tent to join the never-ending queue for alcohol.

Rose came into view, a feast for the eyes in top to toe tangerine. Lorna wondered where she found tangerine slingbacks in the twenty-first century but Rose obviously had a knack for tracking down things like these. They were probably genuine 80s footwear bought off ebay for pennies. Or maybe she'd hoarded them since her mid-twenties. Lorna imagined boxes and boxes of gaudy-coloured stilettos stashed under Rose's bed. Rose was giddy and in a very silly mood, waving and giggling as she teetered across the field towards

72

them, her heels sinking three inches into the grass with every step, causing her walk like she had one leg shorter than the other.

She plonked herself down on the grass in a less than lady-like fashion.

'Are you alright, Rose? You seem a little bit merrier than usual?' asked Lorna, handing her an enormous glass of rosé.

'Yes! I am fine! Just happy! And hot!'

She took a generous gulp of wine, swallowed it, and then took another.

'Ooh, that's better! That'll cool me down!' she sighed.

Lorna and Evelyn looked at each and shrugged their shoulders.

'I'll have some of what you've had Rose. I could do with livening up.'

'Oh Evelyn! I'm so sorry! I forgot to ask! How was your date? Rose told me all about it.'

Evelyn looked at Rose with raised eyebrows and huffed.

'Disastrous. I've not had chance to tell Rose yet either. So I'll tell you both now you're sat here.'

She took a deep breath.

'It started out ok. He's lovely looking. Not really my type but it's not every day you get asked out by a good looking fittie, so I agreed to go out with him.'

'He's a PE teacher, isn't he?' asked Lorna.

'Sort of. He runs a company that goes round different schools, getting kids to try out new sports. He coaches and stuff.'

'Fit in both senses of the word then!' giggled Rose.

Evelyn looked at her and raised her eyebrows again.

'Anyway. We went out for a drink, to The Bull and Swan, and had something to eat. It was all very civilised to begin with. He asked me about myself and he chatted about himself and then he just got more and more boring as the night wore on. He told me about the boiler system in his house and how many sodding radiators he has running off it, for gods sake. By the time the waitress came round with the pudding menu, I was starting to nod off. I said I was stuffed and maybe we should just get the bill. He agreed, thank god, and we split it.'

Rose and Lorna were in stitches.

'Then what? Did he want to nip back to yours for a quick coffee?' asked Rose.

'I didn't give him chance. I gave him a quick peck on the cheek and said it'd been a lovely evening. And then I legged it!'

'Oh Evelyn. You do make me laugh!' said Lorna.

'You'll never meet someone being so picky! If he was as lush as you say he was, I'd have put up with him being boring!' said Rose, her broad Welsh accent making everything she said sound twice as funny.

'I'll never meet anyone. And anyway, I don't care. I don't want to. I'm quite happy as I am,' she mumbled grumpily.

Lorna winked at Rose.

'So you say.'

There was a brief lull in conversation as the women drank their drinks and absorbed their surroundings. The school field was the busiest it had ever been. Locals and people from neighbouring villages alike milled around the stalls, standing in groups drinking ale and chatting or sat on big picnic blankets, eating burgers and hotdogs and other barbecued delights. The food was always fantastic and tonight, along with the Rockabilly band and the comedy duo that were booked as entertainment, there was a mammoth hog roast planned with two suckling pigs and all the trimmings.

Lorna broke the silence.

'What's all this I hear about you and Twinkle Toes getting serious, Rose?'

Rose tossed her head back and laughed.

'Twinkle Toes! His name is Graham! And yes, things are looking pretty hot between us. I'm staying at his tonight!'

'Not if you keep knocking back the rosé you won't be...' chipped in Evelyn.

'Blimey. You move fast. Is he divorced?' asked Lorna.

'Of course he is! You don't think I'd be staying in the house of a married man do you! Goodness me!'

'No! I didn't mean it like that. I meant is he a divorcee? Like you?'

'Oh. I see. Yes. He is. He's been divorced for four years. He's a bit older than me.'

'How old?'

'Nearly sixty.'

'Nearly SIXTY?' Evelyn almost choked on her beer. 'You should be aiming younger than, not older than!'

'He's a very young sixty, I'll have you know! He'd put a lot of men half his age to shame. He even trims...' Rose gestured with her eyes and mouthed the words 'down there.'

Lorna and Evelyn grimaced.

'Good god, Rose! You'll be saying he's got a nipple ring next.'

'No, he's not got one of those but he's very good with his

tongue.'

Evelyn pulled a face of sheer horror.

'Stop right there, Rose. I really, really don't want to hear about Twinkle Toes' pubic hair beauty regime or his oral skills, thank you very much!'

Lorna had tears of laughter in her eyes.

'Me neither!'

Rose smiled and finished her wine.

'You're only jealous!' she declared, waving her empty wine glass at them.

Lorna looked at her old friend.

'I might have a story to tell as well…

The two ladies looked up startled.

'The man you nearly killed?' whispered Evelyn.

Lorna nodded slowly, the corners of her mouth struggling to keep the smug grin at bay.

'You make me sound like a murderer.'

'Have you seen him again?' Rose asked excitedly.

'Not only seen. Spoken to!'

Rose and Evelyn gasped.

'And… he already knew my name…'

Lorna spent the next twenty minutes relaying every minute detail of the day before. Every now and then one of the women would interject with a question or a comment but they sat and let their friend tell her story without too much interruption.

'I wonder how he knew your name?' pondered Evelyn, her forehead wrinkled with deep contemplation.

'I've no idea. It's been bugging me ever since he said it. He must know me from somewhere? Or know somebody who knows me?'

'It's not as if your name is above the shop. That'd be a dead giveaway if it was. But it's not,' added Rose.

'I don't know, Rose. It's a mystery.'

'He sounds like a mystery, never mind anything else,' quipped Evelyn.

'And you don't even know when you're going to see him again?'

'Nope. I had to dash off, didn't I? We didn't make any plans to meet up. But I've got a funny feeling we will. I can feel it in my bones.'

Rose sighed and heaved herself to her feet.

'Talking of bones, I'm going to get myself something from the barbecue. Anyone want anything?'

The three women made their way over to the food marquee after a swift detour to the drinks tent. The grill was set up just outside the entrance to the main tent and inside was row upon row of food stalls, selling everything from fresh farm produce to handmade and highly calorific pies, pasties and sausage rolls.

'Let's just pop in here for a nose first,' said Rose, always keen to sample as much free food as possible.

They wandered from stall to stall, consuming cubes of mature cheddar cheese on cocktail sticks, hunks of smoky, spicy sausage and wafer thin crackers delicately flavoured with rosemary and parmesan.

'Ooh, look!' called Evelyn. 'A stall selling choccies!'

The other two followed, neither of them adverse to the pleasures of chocolate and both with their hands already in their bags to retrieve their purses.

The two women behind the stall were familiar to Lorna but she didn't know them by name. She recognised them from the village. Both wore the Casworth Housewives Uniform which comprised of highlighted, flicked-back hair, padded gilets worn over pastel, striped shirts with the collars stood up, three-quarter length chinos in navy or beige and, of course, obligatory leather pumps. They looked at Lorna, and then Rose and Evelyn in turn, and scowled.

The fatter and shorter of the two women spoke first, her voice shaky and high-pitched and verging on hysterical.

'Sorry. I'm not serving you lot,' she spluttered.

The three friends looked at each other and then back at the plump woman.

Rose was the first to speak.

'I beg your pardon?'

The stallholder looked uncomfortable and shifted nervously from pump to pump.

'I said I am sorry, but I'm not serving you.'

Rose smiled sweetly.

'And why, may I ask, is that?'

The woman looked at the slightly less-rounded friend by her side in a manner that suggested she needed a bit of moral support. The friend stayed deathly silent and looked straight ahead. All the onus shifted onto the plump woman. And she looked furious.

'I know what you are!' she suddenly blurted out, her face the colour of aubergines and her eyes bulging.

Rose glanced sideways at Evelyn and then at Lorna.

'Excuse me?'

The woman repeated what she'd said but this time even

78

louder. Small globules of spit flew out of her mouth like a snake shooting it's venom.

'I know what you are!'

There was a second of hesitation before Rose spoke again.

'You know what we are?' she asked calmly, knowing exactly what was coming. 'And what, my dear, are we exactly?'

The woman shot right back at her, now in full flow, oblivious to the sideshow she was now creating and the audience that had started to gather around her.

'I heard you!' Her head jerked to the left to look at her feeble partner in crime. 'We heard you!'

Her voice lowered slightly but it was still very much audible to every single person in the marquee.

'Last week in the pub. Talking about making charms and casting spells.'

Evelyn slammed her pint down on the table top of the stall, spilling most of its contents and soaking dainty little boxes of handmade violet creams in Roman Gold ale.

'Now, just look here, you stupid bitch...' she spat.

She placed both palms flat on the table and leaned across the stall until her nose was almost touching the plump woman's face. Her eyes flashed with rage and her voice descended to just a whisper.

'If I were you I'd shut my mouth. As in right now. Because if you don't, I might just start causing a scene.'

The plump woman made a face and sneered.

'Is that a threat? Hey? Are you threatening me? You're WITCHES! All three of you! I heard you! Disgusting, it is! And you...'

She turned to Lorna, thrusting out a trembling arm and

pointing at her accusingly.

'...you live and work in this village! You should be ashamed of yourself.'

Lorna's eyes grew wide and her heart started to bang in her chest with anxiety. She hated confrontation. She wasn't like Evelyn. Evelyn lost her temper at the drop of a hat and would argue with anyone about anything if provoked.

Evelyn felt a duty to protect Lorna, who wasn't anywhere near as mentally strong as she was. She seized the woman's arm, momentarily revealing the small pentagram tattoo on her wrist that was usually covered by a multitude of bangles.

'You leave her alone. She's done nothing wrong! She is an honest, good, hardworking woman. We all are!' she screamed.

'Evelyn...' Rose tried to intervene.

'You know nothing, you fat old cow! Absolutely nothing!' shouted Evelyn, her grasp tightening on the woman's arm.

'Get off me! Get off me!' shrieked the woman.

She turned to the assembled crowd, who were standing, staring, mouths open, rooted to the spot.

'These women are WITCHES!'

The crowd gasped.

Evelyn let go of the woman's arm. She placed her right index finger on the star-shaped tattoo on her wrist, stared straight into the eyes of the plump woman and began chanting.

'By spirit, by water, by air...'

'No, Evelyn!' cried Rose, swiftly reaching for her wrist, breaking contact between skin and symbol.

'They are not worth it. Please Evelyn. Leave it,' whispered

Lorna, taking Evelyn's hand.

Evelyn looked at the two women behind the stall. They look petrified. She took a deep breath and shook her head.

'No. They're not. You should do your homework before you go around making accusations,' she retorted, her eyes filling with hot, angry tears. 'We are just normal people.'

'Come on, love. Let's go and get something to eat. And perhaps another drink to calm you down.'

Rose led them out into the sunshine and insisted they go and find a nice spot to sit in while she bought lunch.

The crowd dispersed, shrugging their shoulders, quickly becoming distracted by the temptation of bramble liqueur samples and miniscule wedges of still-warm cheese and onion quiche.

'She was going to put a bloody spell on me!' the plump woman blabbered to anyone who would listen. 'And she's ruined at least twenty pounds worth of my stock!'

'Serves you right for sticking your oar in. I'd have given good money to see you turned in a toad,' laughed the egg-selling farmer on the opposite stall.

'You may mock me. But you mark my words. There will be divine intervention. Exodus 22:18. Thou shalt not suffer a witch to live. It's there in the Bible for all to see.'

The farmer looked at the plump woman and slowly shook his head.

'You live in cloud cuckoo land, Angela'.

Armed with more drinks and three huge Angus beef burgers sandwiched between great, white floury baps and dripping with tomato ketchup, mustard and fried onions, Rose made her way precariously across the school field, tangerine heels sinking and tray tilting dangerously to one side.

'Trust you to sit as far away as you possibly could. I'm going to regret wearing these bloody shoes today.'

She set the tray down on the ground and sat on the grass. She looked across as Evelyn.

'How are you feeling, love?'

'Fucking angry.'

Evelyn picked at the black polish on her fingernails. Rose glanced over at Lorna and caught her eye.

'I know, love.'

She looked up at the deep blue sky above and watched as a Red Kite circled majestically.

'But we've all experienced it before. Ignorance. People hear the word witch and think you must wear a pointy hat, ride on a broomstick and turn people into toads.'

Evelyn smiled. She looked so pretty when she smiled. Like a little Emo elf. Lorna stroked her arm.

'It's why we don't ever talk about what we are, Evelyn. We know who we are. And why we are what we are. Nobody else needs to know.'

Rose nodded in agreement.

'Maybe we were a bit loose with our tongues last week. Perhaps we have learned a lesson from today. The only folk who understand us are our own folk. And they are getting few and far between these days.'

Evelyn looked at Rose, her deep brown eyes swimming with tears.

'I'm sorry I lost it. And I'm sorry I started to cast a curse… I… I haven't used black magic for such a long time. I've had no need to. I frightened myself you know... how easily it came back to me. If you hadn't stopped me Rose, I would have cursed that woman...' her voice trailed off and she looked down at her hand, angling her wrist so she could see her tattoo.

Rose put an arm around her friend.

'But you didn't. Don't be too hard on yourself, my love. You were angry and you were defending us all. You've got a temper on you, we all know that. But it's part of who you are and we love you for it.'

The three women linked hands briefly and smiled at each other.

'Let's eat!' cried Lorna, handing round the burgers.

'Wow, these look fantastic!' said Evelyn licking her lips. 'I could never be a bloody vegetarian!'

'Me neither!' laughed Rose. 'Although, saying that, Graham is one...'

'You're kidding! Oh Rose!'

The sun was still blazing as the arena in the middle of the school field played host to a variety of entertainment acts – from a troupe of Highland dancers and a pack of dogs leaping through hoops of fire to a local boy band, all with identical Justin Bieber haircuts and a ventriloquist who'd made it through to the live finals of Britain's Got Talent three years ago.

By the end of the afternoon, Lorna, Rose and Evelyn were well-lubricated and had all but forgotten the scathing attack on them earlier in the day. Lorna was known by many in the village and she spent most of the afternoon chatting to people she knew – some well, some hardly at all – about all sorts of things. But witchcraft wasn't a topic of conversation, for which she was very grateful. She knew villagers must be gossiping about her. It was a small village and she was pretty sure the plump woman would have started circulating the conversation she'd heard in the pub as soon as she possibly could. But nobody had mentioned the rumours to her, even though some desperately wanted to.

The last act of the afternoon walked out into the arena to huge applause. Dressed from head to toe in white, with straw hats, red sashes and little silver bells strapped to their legs and shoes, the Car Dyke Morris Men looked resplendent.

'Always amazes me that a village with such religious foundations permits pagan revelry to take place in the shadow of the Great Almighty,' mused Lorna.

The three friends watched as the eight men waved white handkerchiefs, whooped and yelled, clashed wooden sticks together and danced their merry way through a series of ancient, English folk rituals to the delight of everybody at the fete. For their final dance, the men performed the intricate sword dance. As they jumped and turned and twisted and hopped, six swords magically entwined into the shape of a pentacle and emerged from a cloud of white to a tremendous cheer and held aloft for all to admire.

Lorna, Rose and Evelyn looked at each other and grinned.

'If only they knew…' sighed Rose.

Lorna looked at Rose and smiled.

'Love is all around us…'

Evelyn bowed her head and ran her fingers through the lush grass.

'Spirit, water, air, earth and fire…'

They linked wrists and held the circle until the pentacle was lowered and the swords extricated once more.

'To us,' declared Rose, raising her glass.

'To us,' Lorna smiled.

Evelyn's eyes, for the third time that day, brimmed with tears.

'To us,' she whispered.

EIGHT

Nine and a half years earlier…

THE CREAM, OBLONG envelope landed on the doormat with a thud, along with a handful of bills and marketing flyers that were destined straight for the bin. The paper was thick and expensive and the script on the front, in pale lilac ink, was something of a work of art. Lorna recognised the handwriting immediately. She only knew one person who was an expert in calligraphy and who also happened to own an antique, ivory fountain pen from which flowed lavender-scented ink – and that was Oriel.

What on earth is she writing to me for, thought Lorna, picking up the envelope and sniffing it. Yep. It was definitely from Oriel. She opened the envelope carefully and slid the card out from inside. Dark green ivy trailed along the top and down the side of the card and inside, in the same lilac ink, Oriel had written…

Darling Lorna,
Please join me for supper on Saturday 12th May at 7pm.
16, Rutland Terrace, Stamford.
Much love,
Oriel

How strange. She read it again. It didn't even sound like

an invitation. It was more of an order. There was no RSVP date, which implied there was no acceptance or decline to be made. She had to go, whether she liked it or not.

'Anything of any interest?' asked Jilly, breezing past her in a cloud of Coco Mademoiselle.

'Loads of bills and an invitation.'

'For me?'

'No. For me, amazingly! A supper party.'

Jilly pulled the face that her own mother called 'the sucking lemons face'.

'One of Tobias's extravagant do's again, I suppose?'

'No it's not actually. Tobias said he's never going to throw another party again after last time.'

'The wine incident?'

'Hmmm... it never did come out of his carpet. Two thousand pounds down the drain, he said.'

'So... who is it from?'

'Oriel. The lady who teaches the meditation class I go to.'

Jilly took the stack of brown envelopes and takeaway flyers from Lorna and walked down the hallway towards the kitchen.

'Very nice indeed. Darling... On your way back from college tonight, could you pop into the paper shop and pick up my magazine. I'm not going to have time to get it. I've got back-to-back meetings and deadlines and god knows what else all day and I'm not going to be able to get out of the office until at least seven o'clock. And I want to read it tonight with a glass of something nice.'

'Ok, will do,' sighed Lorna. Her mother was so annoying at times. It wouldn't do her any harm to show a bit of interest every now and then in her life. Thank god her father showed a little more enthusiasm.

'And make sure you get you and the boys something decent to eat tonight. Not just a couple of slices of toast.'

'Yes, mum.'

Since when had she ever dished up toast for tea? Her mother wasn't just annoying. She was really annoying.

LORNA REMEMBERED to collect her mother's precious magazine on the way home from college that night and she put it on the kitchen table for her to find when she finally got home from work. As usual during the week, she had to get herself and her two brothers tea. Being the eldest child had its drawbacks. She tried to have as little to do with them as possible. They were typical teenage boys. Into rugby, football, computer games and looking at pictures of naked women. She didn't doubt for one second that either of them had experienced a naked woman first hand. They both possessed pustular acne and bum fluff on their chins for starters. They were also exceptionally lazy. Lorna resented having to do anything for them. Even bunging a pizza in the oven caused her to feel aggrieved. But it was one of her many household chores given to her to make her mother's life easier, so she always made sure catering for the three of them was quick and easy and devoid of much thought. Tonight, she prepared pasta with a tub of fresh, ready-made Carbonara sauce she found in the fridge. She ate her bowlful in front of the tv and then went to her room and changed out of her college clothes into leggings and a sloppy t-shirt. She yelled goodbye to her brothers, who were both safely ensconced in their airless, testosterone-drenched caves upstairs, and cycled half a mile to the community centre.

She'd been attending the meditation class for six months, and over that time, through an horrendous winter and an only marginally better spring, had become good friends with both Rose and Evelyn. Lorna was the youngest in the entire group at just nineteen years old, but had connected instantly to her two friends, despite the age gap between them. Evelyn was like the big sister she never had and Rose was the warm, comforting mother she didn't have. Evelyn was loud and outspoken and had a brilliant, sarcastic sense of humour. She possessed a dark streak of rebellion that ran through her like a seam of coal through rock – a couldn't-care-less attitude that Lorna found fascinating. She wished she had a dark streak. She wished she had fire in her belly and a sharper tongue, but so far, those personality traits hadn't surfaced. She was determined, focused and ambitious for sure, but defiance wasn't her middle name. She was always a nice girl. And then she became a nice young lady. And now, she had a feeling she was on the verge of becoming a nice woman.

Rose was Rose – kind, caring, compassionate and a true friend. She was unlucky in love and totally broke after a messy divorce, but she was – as Lorna's grandmother liked to quote – the salt of the earth. Lorna was very glad she'd met them both.

She locked her bike to the railings in front of the building, walked into the main foyer and through to the ladies cloakroom. Evelyn and Rose were already there along with a handful of other people.

'Hiya! How are you?' asked Evelyn, shoving her sports bag

into a locker and slamming the door shut.

'I'm fine thanks. You?'

'Yeah… I'm alright.'

She gave Lorna a funny look, which Lorna couldn't quite decipher. She frowned back at her.

'What?' she mouthed.

Evelyn sidled up to her.

'Have you had anything through the post today?'

'What like?'

'An invitation? From you-know-who?' nodding her head towards the main hall.

The penny dropped.

'Oh… that. Yes. I have. I'm guessing you have too?'

'Hmm. So did Rose. Nobody else here did though. Well, as far as I know. Nobody is talking about it anyway, and you know what this lot are like for idle gossip. Especially regarding The Green Goddess.'

Rose glanced over, her eyebrows raised.

'Sounded more like a demand to me, not an invite…' she remarked.

'That's what I thought. Are you going to go?'

'It's this Saturday, isn't it? Bit short notice to be honest. I've got a lot of gardening to do. And I'm not going if you two aren't,' said Rose in her sing-song accent.

'Me neither. Sounds a bit weird to me. I mean, it's not as though we know her that well, do we?' added Evelyn.

Lorna could tell her friends were itching to go.

'Does that mean we're all going?' asked Lorna, with a wry smile.

'Yes!' came the simultaneous reply.

Oriel didn't mention the supper party at all that evening. She merely gave the three ladies a knowing smile as they gathered in the hall in front of her. After the class, she walked over to them as they got changed and told them she'd see them all on Saturday.

RUTLAND TERRACE was a row of magnificent, Georgian townhouses, four stories high, with black railings and a little gate, steps down to the basement and steps up to the front door. Oriel's house had a glossy, black door with an intricate stained-glass panel sitting above it. Either side of the door, on wrought iron brackets, hung glorious hanging baskets, creating a waterfall of colour and fragrance against the mellow, cream stonework of the wall.

Rose, Evelyn and Lorna shared a taxi to the party, none of them wanting to arrive alone.

'Bloody hell. That's what I call a house!' Evelyn gasped, as the taxi drew up alongside number sixteen.

'Must be worth a bob or two, hey?' agreed Rose, craning her neck out of the cab window to get a better view.

They paid the driver the surprisingly extortionate fare for such a short journey, and climbed the five steps up to the big, black door with a degree of trepidation. Rose pressed the brass doorbell and from somewhere deep inside the house, a series of bells began to chime.

Oriel answered the door almost immediately. She was dressed in white linen palazzo pants, a white voile tunic with a dainty white vest top underneath, and white beaded sandals. She looked immaculate and could easily have wandered off the set of a Martini ad.

'Darlings! So lovely to see you. And all arriving together too! Please do come in.'

She held the door open wide and the three women stepped into what can only be described as the pages of a glossy interior design magazine.

The hall boasted a highly-polished parquet floor that shone like glass, a lofty ceiling from which a dangled an elegant, crystal chandelier and at the far end of the room, a mahogany staircase with deep cream carpeted insets, swept majestically up to the first floor. An ornate Italian mirror hung on one wall, various watercolours of rural landscapes on another, and an antique rosewood grandfather clock stood guard like a soldier up against the third wall – ticking softly and in perfect time – as it had done for maybe two centuries or more.

'Your house is so beautiful, Oriel!' gasped Lorna.

'I'm so envious! I can't even afford a two up, two down!' said Rose with a sigh.

Oriel glanced around her, surveying the wealth and opulence that surrounded them.

'Yes,' she agreed. 'It is. I'm very lucky. Very lucky indeed.'

She sounded wistful, as though her good fortune wasn't solely of her own making. She had already told the women that she was very fortunate to have met her second husband, Roger, and that it was she who had upped sticks and moved from Jersey to Stamford to live with him.

She led the women through the hall and into the kitchen, which was vast and expensively fitted out in cream, handmade units with thick granite worktops and cool slate flooring.

'We're out in the garden' she told them, gesturing with her

hand in the manner of royalty.

From the kitchen they walked into a stunning, octagonal conservatory. It was humid and bright despite the wooden, slatted blinds at the windows screening the glare from the setting sun. It was furnished with several expensive java sofas, a colossal glass-topped table with miniature Grecian pillars for legs and huge potted palms in terracotta pots. From here they stepped through French doors into the equally stunning garden.

'Oh my god! You have a pool!' shrieked Rose.

Oriel threw back her head and laughed.

'Yes, we do! But for what it's worth, it's a complete nightmare to keep clean, costs an absolute fortune to run and we only get to use it approximately four weeks a year due to our lousy weather!' she gushed. 'The climate in Jersey was so much milder than here. We swam outdoors every day from May to October, sometimes beyond that.'

'I bet you wish you still lived there, don't you?' said Evelyn.

Oriel put her hands on her hips and cocked her head to one side – deep in thought – her raven hair falling over her shoulder like a curtain of black silk.

'Not really... I miss the weather... and the seafood... and the lifestyle, of course. But nothing else. The people I never cared for. There is a dreadful air of snobbery that hangs over Jersey like a bad smell. You can't escape that. And anyway, I left behind painful memories...'

There was a long pause. Nobody asked the question but all three women desperately wanted to know the cause of her pain.

'Life for me here is so much more... rewarding.'

Evelyn furrowed her eyebrows and looked at Oriel. What a very strange turn of phrase. What on earth was rewarding about living here? She concluded Oriel was a gold-digger. That was the only explanation for the lifestyle Oriel lived. None of it was hers. It was all Roger's. It had to be.

Oriel clapped her hands together.

'Enough of the past – let's look ahead to the future! Our future!'

She walked slowly over to the ice bucket, which nestled in a purpose-built wrought iron holder, and pulled out a bottle of champagne. She dried it with a linen cloth and holding the bottle at a 45 degree angle, expertly removed the foil, followed by the cork. There was no loud pop, just a discreet hiss as the bubbles were unleashed. She poured the pale, creamy liquid into four crystal flutes and handed a glass to each woman.

The three friends looked at each other with an element of reservation. None of them felt relaxed and all of them felt more than a touch of anticipation.

Oriel raised her glass.

'To our lives – as we know them – past, present and future.'

The three friends held their glasses aloft, chinking them together softly. The wine was chilled to perfection and Lorna was suddenly very glad they were getting a taxi home.

'So, Oriel. Is anyone else joining us?' asked Rose, glancing around the empty garden. It certainly didn't look like it. The table was laid for four people and there were only four sun loungers placed around the pool.

'No, darling. Just us! I thought it would be nice for us to have a little get-together. A chance to relax, to chat, to eat nice food, drink nice wine…'

'Where's Roger?' Lorna asked.

'Oh… he's away. He works away a lot.'

She seemed momentarily tongue-tied and started to stammer.

'A… a… and I'm left in this rambling pile all by myself!' she pulled a sulky face and stuck her bottom lip out like a child.

Stupid woman, thought Rose.

'Sounds like an ideal living arrangement to me!' enthused Evelyn.

Oriel smiled weakly.

'It has its perks, I suppose.'

She took a sip of champagne and proceeded to top up everyone's glasses.

'Drink up! There's plenty more where that came from! We have a cellar and it is packed to the rafters with wine from all over the world. Roger doesn't know half of what he's got down there. I'm sure he lost track many years ago.'

As the champagne flowed as fluidly as the conversation, and the sun began to sink in the sky, Oriel disappeared into the kitchen to prepare supper.

'Isn't this all a bit odd?' said Rose.

Evelyn and Lorna nodded in agreement.

'Just what I was thinking. It's almost as if she's building up to something.'

'But what?' asked Lorna, looking puzzled.

'Fuck knows. But I'm enjoying this champagne. If I have any more I might just start skinny dipping.'

The three women laughed loudly, the bubbles from the

wine aerating their blood stream, infusing them with an infectious sense of frivolity.

'What are you devils laughing at!' called Oriel, as she crossed the terrace with a large, oval tray laden with food.

Rose stood to help her but almost toppled over, so quickly sat back down again.

'Ooh… I think the bubbles have gone to my head everyone! I've not drunk this much since twat face left me!'

'We were laughing at Evelyn,' replied Lorna with a grin. 'She said if she has another glass of champagne she might be tempted to skinny dip.'

'Skinny dip all you like, darling. We're completely private here you know. All girls together! Go for it!'

'I would do if I'd bought my inhaler… I forgot it. Me and exercise don't mix very well, Oriel. I end up coughing and wheezing like a sailor on forty fags a day! I've had asthma all my life.'

Oriel set the tray down on the table and started unloading it. There was a large, white, china bowl piled high with Spaghetti Puttanesca, a wooden bowl filled with fresh, green salad, a platter of artisan breads, a wedge of Parmesan and lots of little bowls filled with olives, pimentos, smoked pine nuts and olive oil with a dash of balsamic vinegar. It looked gorgeous and before long, the four women had polished off the lot and washed it down with more champagne and a couple of bottles of vintage Rioja.

'The Italian's do the best food in the world, in my humble opinion. But they can't do wine. That crown belongs to the Spanish,' declared Oriel, as she opened a third bottle of red.

The sky gradually faded from indigo blue to the inky

darkness of space, illuminated only by a full moon and several billion stars.

Oriel looked up at the moon and idly fingered the pentacle around her neck. She looked at the three women, chatting together, laughing, happy. She took a deep breath and waited for a lull in the conversation.

'Ladies… I've brought you here for a reason.'

Evelyn kicked Rose under the table and Rose's eyes darted nervously from Lorna to Evelyn and back again.

'I want you to hear me out. Let me talk and then you can ask me as many questions as you like afterwards.'

The three women suddenly felt quite sober. They'd waited all night for something to happen. It was inevitable. Oriel hadn't invited them here for a knees up. It wasn't a social invitation. There was an underlying motive and all three women knew it. Lorna, being the youngest and most naïve of the trio, thought maybe Oriel was about to announce her retirement. Rose thought she was going to tell them she was getting divorced. And Evelyn was absolutely convinced Oriel was a transsexual and was going to tell them that she was born a boy called Trevor and had had the chop.

After what seemed like an eternity of waiting, Rose broke the ice.

'Go on then, love. Spit it out.'

Oriel took a deep breath and placed the palms of her immaculately manicured hands on the table in front of her. She looked at the women in turn – a piercing, fixed stare which, if the women hadn't been so bloody plastered, would have put the fear of god into them.

Oriel spoke very slowly. It was almost as if her vocal chords had been slowed down from 45rpm to 33.

'You three women are very special. I picked up on this quality just moments after meeting you last winter.'

She picked up her wine glass and took a large mouthful.

She's pissed, thought Evelyn.

'You – all three of you – possess something only a person like me can detect. An aura, a superiority, something quite… quite magical.'

Lorna had to suppress a fit of the giggles by digging her fingernails into her palm. Oriel continued.

'I know I told you I practice yoga and holistic healing and this is true. I do. But my practices stem from something much, much greater.'

She took another sip of Rioja and lowered her eyes for a split second before looking directly at them again.

'I practice the art – the religion – whatever you want to call it… of Wicca.'

The women looked at each other, perplexed, not knowing what the hell Wicca even was.

'You may not recognise the name immediately, many people have never heard of it before. Wicca is a relatively new religion based upon an ancient pagan way of life, by which one lives happily, harmoniously and healthily with nature and the world around us. Mother Nature and the Gods and Goddesses protect each and every one of us. Wicca is the ultimate force behind my life… to me it is everything.'

She paused and again reached for her pentacle pendant.

'To me, Wicca is my life. To you, Wicca is…'

She paused dramatically.

'Witchcraft.'

Lorna felt her spine tingle and the hairs on her arms stand on end. She felt hot and cold and then hot again.

'You are a witch?' whispered Rose incredulously. 'But you look nothing like a witch!'

Oriel smiled, the same, soft, knowing smile.

'And neither do you.'

'That's because she's not!' protested Evelyn.

Oriel shook her head slowly. She reached out and grasped the wrists of Lorna and Rose and looked straight ahead into Evelyn's black eyes.

'Ah… but you are. I can feel your energy, your spirit. All of you possess the exceptional and unusual attributes of each and every white witch I have ever met. Together, we can use that energy to create something powerful. Something magical. Something so strong, not one of you will ever want to turn your back on it. And you will have everything you have ever wanted in life. Health, wealth, happiness, love… I can promise you a life worth living. If you follow me.'

She surveyed their faces and knew instinctively that she had captured their imaginations. Each of them had a reason to sit up and listen but she knew she shouldn't push them too hard. She didn't want to scare them off or make them think she was a lunatic. She was neither scary nor mad. But she needed to form a coven and these three women sitting before her were the women she wanted. The women she needed. There was just one more thing she had to tell them and she knew – right there and then – that it would captivate them enough to say yes.

'I appreciate this may all be a bit too much for you to take in, so please take your time thinking things over. I will say just one more thing, however. Everything that has happened to me throughout my life, all the success, the good fortune, my relationships, money, health, everything... I can, hand on heart, attribute to Wicca.'

Again, her fingers touched her pentacle, as if seeking reassurance from it.

'I have used the Tarot, cosmic ordering, spirit guides, spells, charms and potions – everything Wicca places before me – in my quest for a good life. And Wicca has never, ever denied me.'

Her face, now bathed in soft, warm candlelight, softened and her voice lowered to a whisper.

'But the most incredible thing of all... and the reason we have been called to work together... is this. Our initials combined spell out the most magical word of all – the word that is at the very heart of Wicca. A word that is the essence of Wicca. And that word is lore.'

The four women looked at each other, mouths open, eyes wide. They were still reeling from the revelation that Oriel – this beautiful, clever, successful woman who'd just cooked Italian food for them – was a witch. Now she was telling them their meeting was destined to be.

Oriel looked at Lorna. She reached out and touched her hand.

'L.' she said softly.

She placed her own hand on her breast as she said the letter O and then turned to Rose.

'R.'

And finally she placed her hand on Evelyn's forearm.

'E.'

'Together they spell lore. A word which means a body of traditions held sacred by certain people – passed from person to person using the spoken word – ancient traditions that continue, never ending, throughout the passage of time.'

Nobody spoke. There was a stillness in the air and high above, the moon cast it's luminescent glow upon them, bathing everything in silvery moonlight.

Each woman suddenly felt an unexpected rush of intense exhilaration – a heady concoction of mystery, intrigue and a sense that they were about to become involved in something that was not only controversial, but in most societies, completely taboo. Their bravado may have had something to do with the amount of alcohol that was coursing through their veins but none of the women felt afraid. Oriel had promised them a life of happiness, health, wealth and love. What more could they ask for out of life? And it was only a bit of white witchcraft. Totally harmless hocus-pocus! Mumbo jumbo even. What could possibly go wrong?

Oriel sensed victory.

'We were destined to meet, all four of us. It was written in the stars. And together we can achieve great things.'

THAT NIGHT, WHEN EVERYONE had gone home, the excesses of the evening had been cleared away and the house and garden were spotless once more, Oriel removed her clothing, her watch, her earrings and her pentacle necklace and tiptoed – naked – down into the cool, musty wine cellar. She carefully rolled back the large, square jute rug that covered most of the room and put it to one side. She felt blindly underneath the wooden chest that stood against the wall and pulled out a collection of items and placed them on the floor. She walked back to the wall and turned off the electric light and crawled on her hands and knees until she was kneeling in the middle of the inverted pentagram that was painted in white on the basement floor.

She lit the black candle and placed it just outside the top of the circle and then bowed her head. She dipped her index finger in the bowl of thick, congealing pig's blood to her right and used it to draw three lines across her left wrist. The pungent smell of putrid bodily fluids stung her nostrils and her stomach heaved. She closed her eyes and imagined a blade cutting deep into her flesh with each smear. As she opened her eyes, she looked at the bloody streaks on her wrist and then directly into the flame that flickered before her. And then she started to speak.

'Lucifer, my father, my brother, fallen angel my sister... At the end of this day I thank you for each gift that you have bestowed upon me. For teaching me ancient ways, for experiences both good and bad – for they have made me stronger. For the people you have taught me through. For the pleasures in which I have partaken. As I sleep, I ask that I may enter your dark realm and be in your unholy presence until morning light. Guide me unto yourself and may I be forever grasped in your mighty wings.'

She leaned forward and blew out the candle with one breath.

'*Ave Satanas,*' she whispered to the evil spirits that enveloped her like a veil of iniquity. And the whole world turned black.

NINE

'HI PETE!' said Lorna, glancing up from her diary, and then at the clock. 'You're early?'

Pete pushed the shop door open with an elbow, his arms full of clipboards and papers and a huge roll of cellophane.

'Morning,' he replied, handing her an order sheet. 'Yes, I am love. I've got to get done early today. Knocking off about mid-day. Wife's due… make sure it's all on there, love,' he added with a nod.

Lorna pressed her mental rewind button and replayed that last sentence again. She tried desperately hard to compose herself and not sound as shocked as she felt.

'Wife's due?' she spluttered, failing miserably.

'Yep. Going in for a sweep.'

Lorna was confused.

'I'm sorry Pete. You've totally lost me. A sweep?'

Pete smiled. This was, in itself, a very rare occasion.

'A sweep!' he laughed. 'You know, to bring the baby on.'

Lorna raised her eyebrows and opened and closed her mouth like a goldfish. The baby? But he must be at least fifty-five years old!

'Oh!' she gasped. 'I had absolutely no idea you were married, Pete! Let alone about to become a father!'

Pete grinned from ear to ear.

'Ah… it's been quick, I grant you that. I met her online and flew her over. And she never went home! Married within six weeks, we were.'

He looked like the cat that had got the cream.

'And... where is 'home', Pete?' she asked nonchalantly. She had a sneaking suspicion where this was heading.

'Thailand. Oh, she's a beauty, Lorna. An absolute beauty! Young, pretty as a picture, a wonderful cook. I must be the luckiest man in the world.'

Yep, she thought. That's exactly where I thought this might be heading. She felt slightly sick at the thought of Pete, with his greasy hair and ankle-flapping trousers, and his poor, young, beautiful bride.

Lorna was more than a little dubious that his purchase from Thailand had married him for his good looks, personality or charm, but if he was happy – and he really did look glowingly happy – then that's all that mattered. And if nothing else, from what she'd read about these types of marriages in countless magazine and newspaper articles over the years, they were usually rock solid and lasted longer than conventional marriages.

'I am really, really happy for you, Pete.'

She leaned over the counter and kissed him on his cheek.

'Next time you come in, please bring a photo of your baby! How exciting!'

Pete blushed and looked coy.

'I will do.'

She ran through the order quickly, making sure it was correct, and signed the top copy.

'Yep, it's all there thanks, Pete.' she said, handing him the clipboard.

'Right you are, I'll go and unload.'

Four years of the same old delivery day chit-chat but today a very different conversation altogether. Lorna smiled.

'I'll help you'.

'Right you are.'

THE DOORBELL JANGLED just as Lorna was closing the door to the cold store. She walked through the archway into the shop to see her most valued customer standing at the counter. Verity French.

Verity lived on The Ridge – a nickname coined by villagers for the most exclusive, prestigious part of Casworth. A raised area of land located at the top of Bluebell Hill, on the road leading out of the village towards town, The Ridge boasted around eight or nine houses in isolated splendor, overlooking the valley below, each one architecturally different to the next, eminating each owner's personal sense of style and taste perfectly. Or lack of it.

Verity resided in a rambling, red-bricked monstrosity with towering, polished white pillars guarding the grand doorway, with various Range Rovers strewn across the sweeping, block-paved driveway. She hadn't done a days work since marrying a South African orthodontist back in 1990 and spent her days – like so many of the village's kept women – shopping, lunching on lettuce and Perrier, partaking in numerous Zumba classes and having sex with the various workmen hired to maintain their extensive properties and grounds.

Verity's floral bill almost rivaled that of Elton John's and Lorna was very glad to have her as a customer. She ordered huge displays each week to grace all her main living areas and Lorna delivered them to her every Friday in her trusty Morris Minor. Just in time for the weekend, when Verity and Johann entertained a whole host of different people, from business associates and friends and family to all manner of societies and social groups and – so rumour had it – the Lincolnshire branch of the swinging fraternity.

Lorna knew such acts of debauchery went on in the village but she turned a blind eye to them. Each to their own, her grandmother always said.

'Good morning, dear! Ooh, now what are these?'

Verity pointed theatrically to a display of striking, lilac-blue flowers.

'Blue Ginger. From Hawaii. Aren't they lovely? I thought I'd give them a go. They last for ages and look so pretty with stargazer lilies and lots of greenery.'

'I'll have them all! I need the usual displays this week, maybe one blue and white, one blue and cream and how about for the hall... all neutral... cream lilies, cream large head roses and...'

She paused to think.

'Peach germinis, white lisianthus, maybe some grasses or palms?' added Lorna.

'Yes!' she clapped her hands together gleefully 'You know me so well, Lorna! Now... the only thing is, can I have them on Thursday instead of Friday? It's just that I'm hosting a posh jewellery party on Thursday night and I'd like the flowers to be there then because I have some people coming who I want to impress!'

Lorna smiled and took out her pad and pen to write down the order.

'Of course, that's not a problem.'

She had all of the flowers in stock so there would be no need to place a special order this week. She worked out the cost of each display and totted the amounts together.

'That will be £275 in total, but with your 10% discount... £247.50 please, Mrs French.

Verity took out her credit card and handed it to Lorna.

'Money well spent. I'm holding a very large dinner party on Friday evening. We're getting the caterers in. And I'm wearing blue – the very same shade as these!' she enthused, jabbing a neon pink-tipped finger at the Blue Ginger. 'I will be colour co-ordinated with my flowers!'

'You are always so busy, Verity! Do you ever get a weekend off?'

'Hardly ever, my love. On Saturday evening we've got a bit of a free-for-all on. Barbecue, swimming, roulette for the boys...'

Lorna took the card and inserted it into the chip and pin machine.

'Oh... I nearly forgot. What's all this I hear about a bit of a spat at the fete yesterday? Between you and your friends and that dreadful, fat Angela?'

Bad news travels fast. The village had only been up and functioning for just over an hour. Lorna looked up from the card reader.

'Oh, nothing really. Just a misunderstanding.'

'Angela said something about witchcraft? I told her not to be so bloody stupid. That woman lives in a fantasy world,' she said crossly, punching her pin number into the machine with some ferocity.

Lorna felt her cheeks burn and she forced mock laughter.

'I know! How ridiculous! She said she'd overheard us chatting in the pub and basically put two and two together and got five. That's all.'

'Well, I put her straight. I know what she's like. The trouble is, some of the more, er... shall we say obtuse ladies in the village don't. She's a terrible gossip, you know.'

Lorna smiled at the irony of Verity's words. She processed the payment, removed the card from the reader and tore off the receipt. She handed both to Verity.

'Thank you Verity. For sticking up for me.'

Lorna suddenly gasped, causing Verity to jump out of her skin. Directly over her shoulder, Lorna could see a man peering through the shop window. He was shielding his eyes against the sun with his hand and his forehead was pressed right up against the glass. It was Joe.

Gauging Lorna's alarming reaction, Verity glanced behind her and looked at the stranger peering in through the window.

'Are you alright?' she asked Lorna.

Lorna was flustered. She couldn't do two things at once – gesture to Joe and speak to Verity at the same time. Her eyes were firmly fixed on Joe as he smiled at her and she waved back at him, albeit limp-wristed and a little feebly.

'Er... yes. Yes I'm fine. I've just seen someone I know, that's all.'

Verity looked back at Joe again and then at Lorna, shrugged and shoved her purse into her handbag.

'I'll let you get on then. See you Friday, darling.'

Lorna watched as Verity left the shop and walked across the road to her white Range Rover. It's blacked-out windows made it look like something a pimp would drive. Not a charity-fundraising, swinging, Zumbamaniac.

Lorna beckoned Joe to come inside and all at once, he was there, in front of her, with only the counter between them. She wasn't expecting this today at all.

'Hello!' she said, shyly.

'Hello.'

And there was that smile again. Lorna felt her stomach churn over. Here we go again.

'How are you?'

'I'm well, thank-you. And you?'

Bloody fantastic, now you're here thanks very much, she screamed inside and her inner-self did a little cartwheel.

'I'm good thank you,' She gestured to the gas guzzler pulling off over the road. 'The lady who just left placed a large order so I'm very pleased. '

'That's good,' he replied.

His eyes looked around the shop, taking everything in.

'This place is wonderful. It's how I imagine a jungle would be! And it smells so nice.'

Lorna laughed. The shop did a have a jungle-like feel about it, she supposed, with its palms and tree ferns and exotic flowers. And the early summer heat made it feel almost tropical.

'It's my itty-bitty corner of heaven.' She paused. 'Or my office, to you.'

A flicker of a smile played on Joe's lips.

'Do you run it all by yourself? Do you own it?'

'Yes. It's all mine,' she replied, looking around the shop. 'I opened it four years ago. Before that it was a butchers.'

'Yes,' he said, nodding. 'I remember.'

Lorna looked at him. He was so beautiful. Her eyes wandered down to his shoulders and up his neck, to his lips and further to his eyes. Great pools of sea green flecked with amber. She wished she could dive right in and swim in them forever.

'What about you? How is work? Did you have a good bank holiday weekend?'

He walked over to the shelf where the soaps were stacked one on top of the other and picked up a pale pink rectangular bar. He closed his eyes and sniffed it.

'Sweet pea. My most favourite smell in the world.'

He put it back and turned to face Lorna again.

'Sorry... work is fine. I was just on my way back to the church. I have to clear some old graves that have become neglected. I thought I would stop by and say hello.'

He knitted his fingers together in front of him and the smile fell from his face.

'And no, I didn't have a good weekend. Alice is unwell. I've spent the last few days taking care of her.'

Lorna remembered he'd mentioned he lived with his sister when they'd met in the graveyard a few days ago.

'Oh, I'm sorry to hear that.'

Lorna saw real sadness in his eyes. It sounded pretty serious.

'What's wrong with her... if you don't mind me asking?'

Joe shook his head slowly.

'No, of course not. She has something wrong with her heart. It makes her very weak. Sometimes she can't even make it upstairs to bed, so she sleeps on the sofa and that's where she stays until morning.'

'That's awful. Why isn't she in hospital?'

'She has been but was discharged. A nurse checks on her every day, when I'm at work. And then I look after her in the evening.'

Lorna thought they seemed so young to be going through such an ordeal. It sounded as though Joe was Alice's main carer, which must be a huge burden on him. She wondered where their parents were? Obviously they weren't around, but where were they? Joe didn't look much older than twenty-five-years-old, which probably meant Alice was either slightly younger or slightly older than him. She thought she'd better not ask any more questions. They could wait for another day. The atmosphere in the shop had gone from being electrically-charged to pancake flat in just a few short moments. But it was Joe who changed the subject.

'If I had any money I'd buy you one of these,' he said softly.

He walked over to a container crammed full of red roses and chuckled.

'But you probably wouldn't be too happy with me, considering you work with flowers all day!'

Lorna felt a wave of heat creep up her chest to her neck. It was the first indication he'd given that he liked her.

'Oh I don't know… I may work with flowers all day but I'm not given them very often. The gesture would be quite lovely, actually.'

He turned and walked to the counter.

'Would you go out with me one evening? I don't know… for a walk or something?'

A walk? What was wrong with going to the pub or out for

111

dinner? Lorna was so taken aback by this sudden invitation of a date, albeit a weird one, that she nodded very quickly and perhaps a little too eagerly.

'Yes! That would be great! A walk! How… lovely.'

Joe seemed pleased with himself and leaned over the counter towards her. For one heart-stopping moment she thought he was going to kiss her.

'Thank-you. How about tomorrow night?'

'Tomorrow?' She didn't have anything planned. 'Yes, that's fine. I'm free tomorrow.'

'Good. I'll meet you at seven o'clock then. Under the village sign.'

And with that he turned on his heel and was out of the shop, stopping only very briefly to raise his hand at her through the window, the same funny salute he did the first time they met.

Lorna stood for a while looking out onto the road. Her heart was thumping and her legs felt wobbly. Did that just happen? The whole encounter seemed so surreal. She'd spent the whole weekend thinking about him and then, out of the blue, he'd just strolled into her shop and asked her out.

There was something different about him. He wasn't like other men she'd met. He was astoundingly attractive, visually perfect in every way. If she had to conjure up her dream man, this is what he would look like. But he was oblivious to his good looks. He was softly spoken, with an endearing local country accent. He was polite and courteous and there was an air of old-fashioned charm about him that she had never encountered before in a twenty-five-year-old man. She thought about Dan and how dissimilar he was to Joe. They were about the same age and both highly attractive but so far, that was the only comparison she could make.

She reached into the drawer under the counter and pulled out her phone. She scrolled through the phonebook, adding Evelyn and then Rose to the list of recipients and started tapping away.

< Joe has just been in the shop. We're going on a DATE tomorrow night! X >

She pressed send.

Within seconds the phone buzzed back at her, making her jump.

It was from Rose.

< Bloody hell! Well done, you! Let me know how it goes the second you get home! >

Evelyn's text took slightly longer to arrive.

< It's been some time Lorna. Make sure your landing gear is in order. You need to be prepared for all eventualities. >

Trust Evelyn. Lorna had never had sex on the first date. It was a rule of personal respect. If the occasion arose tomorrow night, however, she might have to reconsider her morals. After all, rules were made to be broken.

< I'm not that kind of girl, Ev. And he's not that kind of boy. >

Quick as a shot her phone buzzed again.

< There's always a first time. And ALL boys are that kind of boy. >

Lorna smiled and threw her phone back in the drawer just as the shop bell jangled again and a normal working day resumed once more.

TEN

WEDNESDAY MORNING dawned and throughout the day Lorna's stomach was securely tied up in knots. She kept busy by assembling two of the three huge displays Verity French had ordered for tomorrow. A steady trickle of customers wandered in and out, most of them wanting to snap up the beautiful hanging baskets and bargain bedding plants that Lorna had on display on the small patio area outside the front of the shop.

By the end of the day, Verity's most elaborate display, the one destined for her grand entrance hall, together with several bouquets, were safely stashed away in the cold store ready for delivery first thing in the morning. The hanging baskets had completely sold out, which was great news for her bank balance. She made them up herself at a minimal cost and sold them for twenty pounds each. Half the village had her baskets gracing the façade of their plush homes.

After a quick tidy up and a check of the cold store just to make sure she had everything she needed for the following days commissions – the other display for Verity and two almost identical bridal bouquets – she set the alarm, locked up and headed home.

The blistering heat wave showed no signs of abating and even at 5.45pm, it was hot enough to don your bikini and sunbathe. Children hung around the grocers next to the florist in shorts and t-shirts, licking lollies and ice creams with extreme velocity before they melted and dribbled down hands and arms in sticky rivers of sugary gloop.

Outside The Maltings, Peggy was unloading bags of groceries at the front door before David drove their car round to the garage block at the rear of the building and parked up for the evening.

Lorna groaned inwardly. She really didn't have time to stop and chat about haemorrhoids or infected psoriasis or whatever it was they were suffering with this week.

'Hello dear,' said Peggy ominously. 'Just finished work?'

Lorna smiled sweetly at Peggy.

'Yes, another day over. It's been a busy one. And a hot one.'

'Hmm. Well, you can put your feet up now, have a glass of wine.'

'I might just do that.'

She rummaged around in her handbag, desperately trying to locate her front door keys before Peggy could strike up a conversation.

'Good May Day fete?' she asked, her question loaded with sarcasm.

Lorna stopped dead in her tracks. She knew what was coming.

'Yes, lovely thank you. And you? I did see you there, didn't I?'

'Oh yes,' she trilled sharply. 'Me and David always go, come rain or shine. Have done for many, many years.'

Lorna heaved a sigh of relief. For one second she thought Peggy was about to mention the incident in the marquee. She put her head down and without responding, headed towards the doorway to the communal hallway, keys in hand. She had to manoeuvre around Peggy and her numerous carrier bags bulging with toilet rolls and cornflakes but Peggy swiftly took a step forward, blocking her escape route.

'What's all this about a fight in the food tent?' she sneered.

Lorna really didn't have time to stand and explain anything to anyone at the moment. Least of all to bloody Peggy.

'I'm sorry, Peggy. I'm really pressed for time. I'm going out at seven and need to get ready.'

Peggy leaned forward menacingly and glared at her.

'People are talking.'

She licked her thin, puckered, coral-smeared lips. 'About you and your... how shall I put it... odd choice of pastime.'

She raised an eyebrow and smirked.

'It doesn't take much to ruin a reputation around here, you know. Don't you forget that,' she hissed.

She was so close to Lorna's face, Lorna could smell the rancid stench of stale coffee and tobacco on her breath. Together with the odour of cheap, market-stall perfume and stale cigarette smoke that permeated every inch of the woman, being up close and personal with Peggy was a pretty unpleasant experience. Lorna jerked her head back in revulsion and the hairs on the back of her neck bristled.

'What is that supposed to mean?' she snapped, her eyes flashing with anger.

Peggy smirked. Her deeply-tanned and leathery face looked much older than its' sixty-five years. She wanted a reaction and she was getting one.

'You heard.'

The flood-gates in Lorna's kidneys opened and adrenaline surged through every vein in her body, causing her pupils to dilate and her heartbeat to quicken. She didn't need this. Not today of all days. Today was supposed to be a good day.

She spun round, pushed past Peggy into the hallway and up the staircase to her front door. Her hand was shaking so much she could barely insert the key into the lock. Once inside, she slammed the door behind her with such force, the picture on the wall swung from side to side. She leaned up against the door – the wood felt cool against her hot, damp skin. She closed her eyes, tilted her head back and allowed salty tears of frustration to spill down her cheeks.

'The stupid bitch!' she shouted, throwing her bag down onto the hall floor.

She walked through to the kitchen and ran herself a glass of ice-cold water from the tap. She stood at the French windows in the living room that overlooked the garden and drained the glass dry. She watched as David carefully parked the car in front of his garage and made his way through the gate, across the garden path and out of sight. She felt sorry for him, being married to such a cantankerous old cow. He was quite likable really. He was good at moaning but he seemed pleasant enough. Peggy never had anything pleasant to say about anyone. How she'd managed to become so well liked in the village was anyone's guess. And for her to imply that she could shatter Lorna's reputation, her business… What was she going to do? Launch a witch hunt? Track her, Rose and Evelyn down and burn them at the stake? She felt an overwhelming desire to put a curse on her right there and then. She could quite easily write her name in charcoal on parchment, tear it, severing her name in two and hexing her in a heartbeat but she knew from experience that a curse

117

wasn't the right way to go about dealing with a problem such as Peggy.

She ran a bath and spent a good twenty minutes immersed in tepid water infused with lavender, practicing the art of deep breathing to calm herself down. She wrapped a bath sheet around her wet body and made beans on toast for tea. Then she brushed her teeth, combed through her damp hair and cleansed and moisturised her skin. She opened her wardrobe doors and deliberated far too long about what to wear. Nothing too flashy or glamorous, she told herself. It was only a walk after all.

She eventually settled on a sleeveless, lemon brocade dress. It had a nipped-in waist and a full skirt with a lace edged petticoat, and a deep V front and back. She slipped it over her head, fastened the zip and slid her feet into soft cream leather ballerinas. She took a step back and admired her reflection in the mirror. She looked passable.

Butterflies began to flutter around inside her tummy and she noticed her hand tremor slightly as she applied mascara to her lashes and a slick of apricot gloss to her lips. She picked up a yellow hair slide with a huge lemon flower attached to it and clipped it into her long, red curls. Next she spritzed a fine mist of perfume onto her damp skin and adorned her ears with dainty, creamy pearls. Now she felt ready.

She glanced nervously at the alarm clock by her bed. It was almost seven o' clock. A deep feeling of anticipation rose from the pit of her stomach and tingled into every nerve ending in her body. She had no expectations about this evening. She hoped desperately that she and Joe would get on well but it wasn't a certainty, and that scared her a little.

It was a while since she'd had first date nerves, she wasn't used to them at all. She hadn't really experienced that many first dates, most of her short-lived relationships had grown through friendships. She wondered if Joe was as nervous as she was. He seemed pretty laid back, if a little shy. Maybe he was a bag of nerves as well? Or worse, had changed his mind about meeting her and wasn't even going to show up.

She briefly contemplated downing a glass of wine, purely for relaxation purposes, but just as her hand was reaching into the fridge for the bottle she'd opened the night before, she changed her mind and closed the door. Joe would think she was a raving alcoholic if she turned up reeking of booze!

It was now just a few minutes to seven o'clock. She grabbed her handbag, a cardigan and house keys and, with another cautionary glance at her reflection in the hall mirror, she walked out of the front door, locking it behind her and skipped effortlessly down the stairs into the hallway – briefly eyeing Peggy's front door, half expecting her to burst out and ask her where her broomstick was.

Outside it was a perfect summers evening. The air was warm and the heat from the sun still packed a punch. She inhaled the intoxicating smell of summer – an uplifting concoction of cut grass, pollen, blossom and fresh air – and wished she could bottle it and take it out on cold, crisp, winters days and allow the heavenly scent to seep out and infiltrate every square inch of her dark, gloomy apartment.

She pushed the incident with Peggy to the back of her mind and walked slowly, and with a degree of trepidation, to the corner of Station Road.

The road to Lutton snaked sharply to the left so as she

stood underneath the village sign, she couldn't see anything but tall, overgrown hedgerows. Neat, village allotments bordered the left hand side of the lane and a field of wheat grew taller by the day on the right. She checked her watch. It was seven o'clock exactly.

As if by magic, and bang on cue, Joe appeared around the bend and strolled purposefully over the junction of the two roads to where she stood, her knees buckling, amongst the four-leafed clover.

He was dressed in his usual sandy-coloured trousers, white cotton shirt and brown boots. His sleeves were rolled up to his elbows and the top three buttons were undone, revealing smooth, lightly tanned skin. His hair looked freshly-washed and had been slicked back neatly. Over his shoulder he carried a ruck-sack and in his right hand, a rose. He looked less like a film star today, more like an American GI. There was something about him that made Lorna feel physically weak. She'd never felt like this before. Ever. And she was about to spend the entire evening with him.

He walked up to her slowly, a shy smile playing on his lips, his eyes crinkling at the corners, and nervously handed her the rose. It was newly-bloomed, freshly-picked and probably from his garden.

She smiled and took the flower, noticing that he had carefully, and very thoughtfully, removed all the thorns from the stem. Her breathing quickened and her mouth felt as though it was filled with sand.

'Thank you, Joe,' she said, taking the rose from him.

The flower had custard yellow petals edged with deep crimson and was absolutely beautiful. It didn't even look real.

'It's called Joseph's Coat… it's from our garden.'

He looked at her face and saw instantly how happy the gesture had made her.

'It's been growing there for years. My mother planted the bush when I was a boy.'

'Your very own rose…' she whispered, raising the flower to her nose and breathing in its heady perfume.

'We'll have to find you your very own rose now,' he replied.

Lorna looked into his eyes. The sea green of yesterday had intensified into an iridescent, jewel-like jade that sparkled and shimmered like the Indian ocean. He held out his hand and Lorna took it. If her heart beat any faster, she thought she might die.

They walked down the lane at a leisurely pace, talking about one another's day, the glorious weather and the pretty countryside they were walking through – their hands entwined the entire time.

They walked past the remnants of what used to be the village train station. All that remained now was a pile of red bricks overgrown with ivy, nettles and bindweed – a reminder of yesteryear and what was once a thriving and essential part of everyday, rural life.

'They are talking about clearing all of this and building new houses on the land,' Lorna remarked.

'Really?' he asked, sounding surprised. 'That's such a shame. It doesn't seem so long ago when you could board a train here and travel to Peterborough or Stamford or… well, anywhere really.'

Lorna nodded.

'I love train journeys. It's such a romantic way to travel.'

He squeezed her hand and looked at her with excitement.

'Let's go on a train one day, you and I! To London. Or Scotland! Or the coast!'

Lorna laughed.

'I'd like that.'

They crossed the disused railway line, wild with grasses and weeds, and into the water meadows that stretched out verdantly towards the river. A pathway cutting a swathe through knee-high grass led them to a small footbridge that spanned the river and together they crossed it, stopping half way to admire the sticklebacks below and the enormous flat, green lily pads. Over the other side of the river, the path forked – veering to the left towards the village of Waterford and to the right, alongside a towpath right by the waters edge.

Joe stopped and slipped the rucksack from his shoulder. He crouched down, unzipped it and took out a neatly folded plaid blanket, which he proceeded to unfold, shake out and lay on the grass. He gestured to Lorna to sit down and, only when she'd slipped off her pumps and sat with her feet curled beneath her, did he join her. He reached into the bag again, this time pulling out a green bottle with a stopper in it.

'What on earth is that?' she giggled.

'Homebrew,' he laughed. 'Elderberry wine. Would you like some?'

Lorna nodded eagerly.

'I've never tried Elderberry wine before! Only Shiraz and Cabernet! Oh and some god awful stuff my grandad made out of potatoes!'

'Potatoes? Was it Poitin? That stuff'll blow your head off!'

Lorna grimaced.

'I don't know what it was called! He called it potato wine. It tasted revolting! And like no wine I've ever tasted before!'

They laughed and Joe delved into the bag again. He pulled out two old, chipped china mugs and set them down on the rug next to the wine.

Lorna looked at him with a combination of curiosity and total confusion. Joe noticed her bemusement and his cheeks flushed pink. He shot her a reticent glance.

'I... we... don't have any glasses at home. I'm sorry,' he stuttered apologetically. 'Will these do?'

Lorna felt her heart melt into a puddle of sticky, red mess and it was right there and then – underneath a perfect Monet sunset – she fell in love. She nodded her head and watched as Joe removed the stopper from the top of the bottle and poured the rich, red wine into the two mugs. He handed her one and took the other.

'To us.'

He clinked his mug against Laura's and raised it to his lips.

He must be absolutely skint, she thought, feeling a strong surge of endearment towards him.

'To us,' she echoed and took a sip. It tasted so much better than it smelt!

The conversation flowed easily as they gradually began to discover more about each other. Lorna talked about how she'd become a florist and told Joe about Rose and Evelyn. And he told her about his work at the church and how he had always lived in Lutton and had rarely ventured out of the village. He was a good listener, definitely preferring to take a back seat and let Lorna do the talking.

'Now tell me about yourself. You've only really talked about your shop and the village and your friends.' Joe propped himself up on one elbow and rested his head on his hand. 'What about you?'

Lorna set her mug down on the blanket and Joe topped it up. She took a deep breath and exhaled slowly.

'There's not much to tell, really... I'm twenty-eight-years-old. I grew up and went to school in Stamford. My parents still live there. I've got two brothers, both younger than me, both still living at home. Nick, the youngest, has just finished medical school and is working in Leicester General. Ryan, who's two years younger than me, helps my parents run their magazine.'

'Their magazine? What's it about?' asked Joe, looking genuinely interested.

'It's a kind of lifestyle magazine. It's really taken off over the last few years. They've converted their garage into an office and they work from home. It's all about the local area – things to do, places to visit, what's on, where to eat. That kind of thing. And it has features too, which is where my brother comes in – he's an excellent writer – and of course they also sell lots of advertising space, which is my mother's domain.'

'It sounds really interesting! Weren't you tempted to get involved as well?'

'God, no! I mean, I love my family, don't get me wrong, but I couldn't work with them all day, every day! My brothers have always been major pains in the backside, real mummy's boys, and my mum... well... she can be hard work!'

Laura laughed nervously and swiftly told herself to shut up about how annoying her mother was. They always say look at the mother to see the daughter… and she definitely didn't want Joe thinking she was a potential basket case. She wasn't anything like her mother. Her father, yes – her mother, no. Never.

'My father is great though. He has always been supportive of me, encouraged me in whatever I wanted to do. He has his faults, but don't we all?'

Joe took a mouthful of wine and licked his lips. Lorna watched him and suppressed a stomach-wrenching desire to lean over and lick them herself.

'We do. I certainly have mine.' His eyes lowered and he swallowed hard. 'You're lucky to have parents. I lost mine a long time ago. There's just Alice left now.'

Lorna felt terrible. There she was prattling away about her family, without a single ounce of regard for the fact that Joe might not have a family himself. He hadn't exactly said as much but she'd already guessed his parents were absent from his life. But she was shocked to hear they weren't even alive anymore.

'Shit, I'm sorry Joe. I just assumed your parents lived somewhere else. I never thought for a moment that they were…'

'Dead? It's ok. You weren't to know,' he interrupted, plucking a daisy from the grass and studying it intensely.

There was a gentle stillness in the air. Neither one of them spoke, both lost in thought. The river flowed, the evening breeze stirred the long, trailing branches of the willow tree and the sun sank lower in the violet sky.

'How did they die?' Lorna asked eventually.

Joe poured the remainder of the wine into the two mugs

and pushed the stopper back into the neck of the bottle. Lorna was starting to feel slightly woozy. This elderberry wine was strong stuff. She must learn how to make it. She'd always fancied the idea of foraging the countryside and turning her gatherings into alcohol.

'My mother went first, just days after Alice was born. My father brought us up alone but died very suddenly when I was twenty.'

Lorna tried to comprehend what it must have been like losing a mother so young – and that meant Alice was younger than him. She would never have even known her mother. And then to reach early adulthood and lose your remaining parent... it was so sad. Joe's father's death was very recent, so it was not surprising that the wounds were still so raw. Lorna felt an overwhelming sense of appreciation to have her all of her family here, alive and well – with the exception of a very severe dose of man flu.

'Can you remember your mother?'

Joe shook his head.

'Barely. I was only three when she died. I can remember her standing in the garden pegging the washing out while I played in the dirt. I can remember Alice being born. She was born upstairs in my parents bedroom – I heard my mother screaming in pain and then suddenly, my grandmother came downstairs holding this tiny little baby, all wrapped up in a towel.' His face softened as he recalled precious memories. 'And I remember my mothers smell. Lily-of-the-valley.'

He shrugged his shoulders sadly. 'And that's about it.'

Lorna, her bravado heightened by the effects of the Elderberry wine, reached over and touched his hand.

'I'm sorry. You must miss them both very much. Especially your father... it... him... you know, it being so recent and everything...'

Joe looked up, his eyes misty with tears. He folded his fingers around hers.

'I do. But I still have Alice.' His thumb caressed the top of her hand. 'And you.'

When they finally pulled away from each other, after what seemed like an eternity of kissing, it was getting dark. Lorna's heartbeat had regained a steady seventy-five beats a minute and her oxygen levels were now near normal. She hadn't felt this happy for a very long time. If ever. Dan had floated her boat but his touch, his caress, his smell, his kiss... never turned her into a quivering, blob of jelly like Joe's did.

Joe glanced upwards through the willow branches at the sky above.

'How did it get so dark so quickly?' he breathed, reaching over to Lorna and hooking a tendril of fiery hair behind an ear.

'I don't know... I think we must have been preoccupied with something far more important than watching night close in,' she joked, her stomach lurching at the mere brushing of his fingers against her cheek.

They looked at each other in the twilight. The sky was now indigo blue and studded with stars. The full moon shone like a mirror, its halo of light radiating outwards, creating nature's very own night lantern.

'We'd better go,' sighed Joe, standing slowly and reaching out a hand to Lorna.

Lorna groaned. Did they have to? She could quite happily

stay here all night, even if it did mean getting hypothermia and being eaten alive by midges.

She grasped Joe's hand and he pulled her to her feet. She put her arms through the sleeves of her cardigan and fastened the top button. She hadn't noticed how chilly it had become until now and there was a real nip in the air. Joe picked up his rucksack and slung it over his shoulder and firmly clasped Lorna's hand.

They walked the mile or so down the lane, back into the village, in virtual silence, both appreciating the tranquility of the evening and the inner sense of wellbeing that the closeness from another human being can instill.

As the orange glimmer of the streetlamps in the village grew closer, Lorna felt an impending sense of dread descend on her like a heavy, dark cloak. She didn't want him to go but she knew he must. He had to attend to Alice. That was something he had to do, day in day out, regardless of personal circumstances or a social life. Or whether she liked it or not.

Joe walked her to the front door of The Maltings and slipped his arm around her waist, drawing her to him. She breathed in his scent again – an alluring blend of clean linen, warm skin, sandalwood and the sharp, fresh aroma of ozone. She wished more than anything that she could fall asleep enveloped in that smell and wake the next morning with it permeating every square inch of her body. But he had to go.

Joe pulled his lips away from hers and in the warm glow of the Victorian-style lamp positioned over the doorway, his eyes wander lazily over her face and body, as though he was memorising every single bit of her and storing it mentally, until the next time they would meet.

'When can I see you again?' she asked, biting her bottom lip, doing her utmost to stop herself dragging him into the building, up the stairs and into her great, big, empty bed.

'Soon,' he whispered. 'You tell me when and I will be there.'

Lorna's mind raced through her mental diary. Tomorrow she was seeing her parents and Friday, she was having dinner with the girls. Saturday would be a good day.

'How about Saturday? I'm at work during the day but we could do something afterwards?'

'Saturday…' he pondered, his forehead wrinkling into a deep frown. 'How many… days away is Saturday?'

Lorna laughed at his bizarre question but then, as she watched him turn over his hand, revealing his palm, and splaying his fingers, realised he was being deadly serious.

'Oh… er…' she stuttered, almost disbelievingly. 'Three days away? Three nights from tonight?'

Joe counted three fingers, folding each one down as he did so. When it was clear in his mind, he smiled shyly and looked into her eyes.

'That's good. Three days time. Shall I come to your house? After work?'

Lorna nodded.

'That would be lovely.'

He leaned over again and kissed her gently on the cheek.

'Thank-you for tonight. It has been wonderful.'

CLUTCHING THE ROSE he'd given her several hours earlier, she watched as Joe disappeared into the night.

'What are you doing lurking about in doorways at such

129

hours?'

The gravelly male voice startled her.

An old man emerged from the darkness, his battered old tweed cap pulled over his eyes, the stubble on his chin as white as snow. He pulled sharply at the dog lead he was holding, causing the poor Jack Russel attached to the other end of it to yelp in pain.

'Sit, you stupid dog.'

'Goodness, Arthur. You made me jump!'

'I should think I did. Girl like you, hanging about on street corners in the dark. It's nigh on ten o'clock!'

'Oh! Is it?' Lorna gasped. 'I had no idea it was that late! I've just got back home… I was just waving a friend off.'

'Down the Lutton lane?'

'Yes. He's walking home. To Lutton.'

Arthur peered towards the shadowy figure disappearing down the lane. There was not much to see, apart from the silhouette of bushes and trees against a starlit sky.

'Is he now… No footpath or 'owt along that road, you know. He'd do well not to get run over. Or savaged by a fox.'

Lorna tutted to herself. Silly old fool.

'Oh Arthur! I'm sure nothing like that will happen. I'll ring him later, when I get in, just to make sure he got back alright.'

It occurred to her pretty quickly that she'd do nothing of the sort. She didn't have Joe's telephone number. Come to think of it, he didn't have hers. She'd never even seen him with a mobile phone.

Arthur shrugged and made a huffing noise and continued on his evening walk with his skittish dog – the last one before bed.

Safely back in the comfort of her own home, Lorna kicked off her shoes and padded barefoot into the kitchen where she placed the Joseph's Coat rose in a glass of water. She knew she had to text Rose and let her know how the date went but she was too exhausted. She glanced at her mobile and saw that Rose had text her four times already. She turned her phone off and plugged it in to charge. Rose would have to wait. She undressed and hung up her dress and cardigan and washed her face before climbing into her cool, clean bed. Alone.

She went over the evening in her mind at least five times, and every time she thought about their first kiss, her stomach rolled like a wave crashing onto a beach. His lips were so soft, his skin smelled so divine. They had got along so well. And Joe told her he had both Alice and her in his life! It was almost too good to be true.

He was obviously struggling financially, seeing as he didn't even own a couple of wine glasses. And he was quite possibly illiterate, considering he had no idea when Saturday was and had to use his fingers to count the days of the week. He didn't own a mobile phone. Or even a bicycle, let alone a bloody car. But he was charming. Enchanting. Kind. Polite and sweet. And breathtakingly, toe-curlingly, gorgeous. And that was more than enough for any woman. Any more would be plain greedy.

ELEVEN

JOE STOOD FACING the tall pair of grey, marble gravestones. They were almost identical apart from the inscriptions engraved upon them. The stone on the left bore the name Elizabeth Mary Hardy, and the stone on the right, Edward John Hardy.

Joe's parents final resting place lay in a sheltered corner of the churchyard, underneath a four-hundred-year-old Cedar tree, which cast dappled sunlight onto the graves all day long until twilight descended. It was a quiet, tranquil place and Joe often tended the graves as part of his job for the church, always spending a little more time on his parents plot than the others.

He bent to pick up a handful of dead leaves and a discarded cigarette butt and tossed them into a nearby waste bin. He returned to the graves and knelt at his parents feet, pulling up stray weeds and fishing out odds and ends that had blown onto the green glass chippings that covered them like a blanket of glittering, precious stones.

'Wallo, boy!' a familiar voice called out behind him, alarming him somewhat.

Joe pushed himself up off his knees and dusted his trousers down. Behind him, standing beside the bin, shovel in hand, was Victor Freshwater – the church's longest-serving gravedigger.

At eighty-two years old, Victor had dug graves, six foot

deep, seven foot long and three foot wide, by the hundred, for sixty-six years. It was the only job he'd ever known. His father was a gravedigger, and his grandfather too, so it was only natural that Victor followed in his men folks footsteps and took to the spade to put bread on the table. He worked at three other nearby churches, walking from one to the other, wherever and whenever he was needed, in all weathers, wearing little more than a shirt and trousers. Even in the depths of winter. He was a strong man, fitter than most men half his age. He put it down to a life free of worry, stress and strain, which was certainly true, but the fresh air and exercise he reaped every day, along with the tot of whisky before bed and a good woman by his side, all added to his enviable state of wellbeing.

Joe strolled over to him, wiping his right palm on his trousers and reached out to shake Victor by the hand.

'Hello, Victor. Are you digging today?'

'Yes, son. Not the deep stuff, just the filling-in today.'

Joe looked around him.

'Who's died?'

'One of the ol' workers from Milton. Been retired a week and dropped down dead. Just like that.' Victor puffed out his cheeks and shook his head. 'That's what 'appens. You need to keep workin'.

'You should know all about that, Vic,' Joe said with a wry smile.

'Aye. Keep workin', do summat every day to occupy you and your noggin. Or you may as well be bloody dust, eh?'

Joe nodded.

'What'ya been up to today? Clearin'? Weedin'?'

133

'The usual. Watered the rose bushes, cleaned the step and the door. Tidied graves. Shocking what you find scattered around. Bottles, dog ends…'

Victor tutted and sighed heavily.

'Disgustin'. I blame the youngsters. No respect these days. Come in 'ere at night, they do. Drinkin', smokin', gettin' up to no good.'

He nodded over to where Elizabeth and Edward lay.

'They'd turn in their graves at how things are now. Good people your mam and dad. Your mother was a fine woman. Taken too soon. You keep their patch lookin' orderly, Joe. They'd be proud of you, son.'

Joe smiled weakly and lowered his head, looking at the mossy ground beneath his feet.

'Thanks, Vic. That means a lot.'

'And how is Alice, son? I hear she's not been too good?'

Joe shook his head slowly and looked forlornly at Victor, the amber in his eyes glinting like gold in the brilliant sunlight. He ran his fingers through his hair and breathed in deeply.

'Not good… not good at all. I'm just counting the days now. I know the end is close.' He reached into his pocket and swallowing the sob that threatened to choke him, pulled out a white, cotton handkerchief and wiped away a silent river of tears.

'I fear the next time I see you Vic, you'll be digging for my Alice.'

THE TOASTER POPPED up two slices of perfectly browned white bread and Lorna idly spread them with butter followed by a smear of marmite. She placed them on a side plate along with a giant mug of tea and carried them to her bedroom on a tray. She set it down on her bed, opened the slats of the blind a fraction and flicked the radio on, instantly filling the room with the breakfast show and a constant stream of jovial banter.

She sat cross-legged on her bed and reached simultaneously for a slice of toast and her mobile phone. She knew there would be a barrage of texts and missed calls from Rose and quite possibly Evelyn, and as she never switched her phone off or went to bed without answering them, she guessed they would probably be worrying themselves sick by now and imagining her lifeless body, hacked into pieces and residing at the bottom of a ditch.

She switched the phone on and sure enough there were five texts and eleven missed calls. All of them, apart from one, were from Rose.

She dialed her immediately – it was 8am so she knew Rose would be awake. She answered on the first ring and, from the tone of her unusually high-pitched voice, sounded extremely stressed.

'Hello... is that you?'

'Who did you think it was going to be?'

'Oh thank god! I almost got in my car last night to drive over and check that you hadn't been murdered.'

Lorna spluttered and had to swallow her toast very quickly for fear of choking on it.

'Bloody hell Rose! Are you mad? What on earth did you think was going to happen to me?'

'Just that! That you'd gone off on your walk with a

complete stranger and he'd strangled you or something! I called Evelyn and she calmed me down, saying you were most probably bonking, but I had a funny feeling, a deep, sinister feeling…'

Lorna howled with laughter.

'Oh Rose! You are a loony. But I do love you,' she said, taking a gulp of hot, sweet tea. 'And thank you for worrying about me. But I'm absolutely fine and still alive. I was just so tired when I got back. I saw your texts…'

'You saw my texts! Why on earth didn't you just send one back then? I've not slept a bloody wink! And I've got two facials and a back, sack and crack to do today…'

'Maybe have a lie down before you do that one. Anyway – I thought you didn't do men?'

'I don't. It's for bloody Graham. I talked him into it. I told him body hair was a turn off. And that it was much more sexy and above all, hygienic, to be smooth and hair-free.'

'You are waxing your boyfriend? The poor man. And poor you! What an ordeal. I can't think of anything more horrific than ripping the pubic hair off you boyfriends boll…'

'Stop changing the subject! I'm very cross with you still. But I am relieved to hear you are still alive,' Rose took a deep breath. 'So… how did it go?'

Lorna had so much to tell her but it would have to wait until tomorrow night. She had to get showered and dressed and into work. She had one more display to make for Verity and needed to get them to her before three o'clock that afternoon. She also had the bridal bouquets to put together, both of which had to be delivered early the next morning. It was going to be one of those days.

'That, my dear, will have to wait. I will tell you one thing though…'

'What? WHAT? Tell me…!'

'We did get along well. Really well.' She heard Rose make cooing noises on the other end of the phone but divulged no more.

'I'll see you tomorrow night at Evelyn's. I'm taking a lemon tart and a bottle of white. It's your turn to do the starter.'

'You bugger, you!'

'Bye, Rose!'

'Piss off!'

THE DAY DRAGGED. Lorna found herself wandering in and out of the cold store just to keep cool. The main display for Verity took until mid-day to assemble and after a quick call to her number one customer to check if a lunch-time delivery was convenient, she loaded her van with the colossal displays and trundled off along Main Street, towards The Ridge at the far end of the village.

As she approached the church she slowed down to a snails pace and craned her neck, scanning the churchyard for Joe. She could just make out two figures standing underneath the cedar tree by the side entrance to the church, where the rose garden was. But she wasn't sure Joe was one of them. They could have been anyone – mourners, tourists, grave enthusiasts or anyone else who liked hanging around dead people for that matter.

She was past the church and through the oldest part of the village in seconds, climbing the winding hill up to The Ridge. As she drove, she passed several walkers, all from the WI, who would normally have stopped and waved – her instantly recognisable Morris Minor familiar to everyone in the village. Today, however, they lowered their heads and avoided any kind of eye contact.

That old cow Peggy! What on earth must she be saying to them all? The next WI meeting was on Monday, Lorna's day off, and she was determined to go along as usual for a coffee and a biscuit and a natter, just to gauge what kind of reaction she got. She knew Peggy would have already tried to blacken her name, together with Angela and Co, so her welcome on Monday would probably be somewhat frosty. But there was no way on this earth she was going to allow anyone to tarnish her reputation as an excellent business woman and a real ambassador for the community in which she lived and worked. She knew everyone, was well respected and well liked and she did a lot for the village, from promoting fundraising functions in her shop to donating raffle prizes and supporting anything and everything that helped the village thrive. She wasn't going to stand by and allow a bunch of gossiping old fishwives to bring her down. Not without a fight.

She indicated right and pulled into Verity's sweeping driveway and immediately spotted her outside the front door hastily waving off a shifty-looking, paint-splattered individual who looked at least ten years younger than her. She looked disheveled and slightly rosy-cheeked and, surprisingly, a little bit embarrassed. Lorna didn't imagine for one minute that they'd been discussing the latest Dulux colour chart. She was just very relieved she hadn't turned up half an hour before or who knows what might have greeted her at the front door.

The painter and decorator winked at Lorna as she parked her van and opened the rear doors.

'Afternoon!'

Lorna smiled back and continued unloading the displays. Verity rushed down the steps to help her.

'Oh, Lorna!' she exclaimed. 'They are stunning. Just… just… super!'

She turned to the painter and waved him away in a manner more accustomed to shooing stray cats off your lawn before they started shitting on it. Lorna, ever the professional, remained silent.

Together they carried the flowers into the house and positioned them where Verity's flowers always stood – in the hall on a Louis XVI sideboard, in the dining room as a table centerpiece, and on the mantelpiece over the vast fireplace in the drawing room. The lavishness and the grand scale of the house reminded her of Oriel's home. They had similar tastes – rich, opulent and filled with interesting objets d'art and priceless antiques. And beautiful floral arrangements, of course. Despite the ostentatious exterior of the property, the interior was very tasteful indeed, albeit a little more footballer's wives than Oriel's home.

'Are you all set for your busy weekend?' Lorna asked.

'Yes, darling. Tonight is a cinch. Canapes and nibbles already delivered by Waitrose and the wine is chilling. Tomorrow the caterers are expected at around two o'clock and the waiting staff should be here early evening. Everything is sorted. Well… apart from me. I still have to have my hair done and a spray tan – although heaven knows why. I'm almost the colour of leather as it is. I think I might be addicted!'

She cackled like an old hen, her face barely moving as she did so. That's not the only thing you're addicted to by the looks of it, thought Lorna. She mentally totted up Verity's presumed collection of addictions – spray tans, Botox, sex with workmen, sex with other people's husbands, flowers, exercise, low carb diets, most probably champagne and the odd smattering of cocaine to round it off nicely. Verity's life was a melting pot of excesses and seemed a world away from her own humdrum existence. The most daring thing Lorna had ever done was have sex in the back of a car. And that was with Dan. After they'd got engaged. All pretty lame. She wished she could be more audacious. Like Evelyn. She had experienced life to the maximum and had probably tried just about everything over the years. So had Rose, to a degree. But Lorna was very safe. Very sensible. Very predictable.

'Now, before you go… what are these blue flowers again, sweetie?'

'Blue Ginger. It's a funny name. You don't associate the word ginger with blue, which is why it's easy to forget. It's from Hawaii.'

'That's it! I knew the name had a colour in it and I kept thinking about Jamaican Ginger Cake… funny what snippets of useless information your brain clings on to! I will tell all my friends who comment on them – Blue Ginger!'

The two women laughed.

'Oh and Lorna, darling. Saturday evening – you're very welcome to pop along! Just bring your cossie and we'll promise you a wonderful evening.'

I bet you will, thought Lorna.

She imagined the scene on Saturday night around Verity's pool. Like a Roman orgy but with hot dogs. She wouldn't mind spying on the shenanigans but there was no way on this earth she would be participating.

'Oh what a shame. I'm going on a date on Saturday night. Or I would have loved to have come,' she lied.

'Ooh, a date? How exciting! Who with?'

'A man called Joe.'

'Local lad?'

'Well, sort of. He lives in Lutton. But he works at the church.'

'Oh, really? Casworth church? Is he the new gardener? Tall, good looking?'

Lorna grinned.

'Yes, that's him.'

'You lucky so and so! I'm glad you're dating again. Especially after the horrible time of it you had last year.'

'Thank-you. And yes, I'm much happier now. Joe is lovely.'

Verity winked at her and rubbed her arm.

'Good for you.'

'Right, I'd better be off. I've got bridal bouquets to make.'

'Oh yawn... are they a dreadful chore?'

'Not really but some people don't have a lot of imagination when it comes to their wedding flowers. The two bouquets I'm arranging today are practically identical.'

'But I bet they'll still be beautiful.'

Lorna nodded, climbed into Cherry and started her engine.

'And remember if you are at a loose end on Saturday after your date... you could both come over for a swim?' Verity

141

called after her.

Lorna waved back and slowly drove back down the stupidly long driveway, through the huge iron gates and turned left onto Bluebell Hill.

'We will!' she shouted in reply, waving her arm out of the window and looking at Verity through the rear-view mirror.

'Not,' she added, under her breath.

The drive back down into the village was a joy. The horse chestnut trees were at the height of their summery perfection – their large, flat, spanking-new leaves unfurled, creating a canopy of vivid lime green that looked oddly surreal. Lorna felt as though she was driving through a watercolour from a bygone era, when horses pulled carts and the harvest was cut by scythe and gathered by hand. These were the moments she held onto. The ones she safely stored deep in her memory for darker times – for when winter tightened it's grip and everything around her was dead and grey and lifeless – for times when she needed to lift her spirits. On those occasions, all she had to do was close her eyes and reach into the depths of her memory and pluck them out one by one, reliving and remembering, admiring them for all their worth. And when she had finished, she put them back again, alongside all the other memories she had safely stored, like autumn apples wrapped in newspaper, for another day.

She thought about Joe and felt a shiver of excitement shudder down her spine. She couldn't wait to see him again. He was starting to infiltrate every second of every minute of every hour. In fact, she couldn't think of anything but Joe.

It took all of her efforts to put together the twin bridal bouquets. But by the end of the day they were finished and lying in water-misted cellophane tents in the cold store. They were, as Verity predicted, absolutely beautiful and she felt extremely pleased with herself. She imagined Verity in her Blue Ginger dress, slashed to the thigh, playing the hostess with the mostest, telling anyone who would listen all about the flowers from Hawaii that she can't quite remember the name of and her addiction to spray tans and painter and decorators. She had met some characters over the years, but none were more colourful than Mrs. French.

After such a busy day, she was glad to be having dinner at her parents and not having to try to concoct something for herself. She dropped by her flat to pick up a remedy she'd brewed up for her bedridden father and a hanging basket she'd made for them to hang outside their front door.

As she pulled into their drive, she noticed the absence of cars, which meant her brothers were both out. They still lived with their parents – which always puzzled and slightly irritated Lorna. She let herself in through the unlocked door and called out to her parents, just to make sure they knew it was her entering their property and not some masked intruder.

Her father appeared from the sitting room, in his dressing gown and slippers, looking pale and weary.

'Oh Dad... you look awful!' she cried, hugging him tightly.

'Thanks.'

'Sorry but you do! Get back in there. Where's mum?'

Her father shuffled back through the sitting room door and plonked himself down on the sofa. He reached inside his dressing gown pocket and pulled out a handful of tissues.

'She's in the office. She needed to get some display ads

booked in. She'll be through in a minute.'

'And where are the boys?'

Phillip dabbed at his red, peeling nose and sighed.

'Nick is on a night shift and Ryan's just left to pick Polly up. He's taking her to see a play or something. You've just missed him.'

Lorna raised her eyebrows and looked at her dad.

'Shame... I've almost forgotten what he looks like. I was hoping to refresh my memory,' she said sarcastically.

'Now, now... he's a busy lad. And Polly keeps him on his toes.'

Lorna reached into her bag.

'I'm sure she does. Here...'

She thrust a bottle into his hand and he peered at it, his eyes squinting to read the handwritten label.

'Tincture for Dad,' he read aloud. 'Another one of your potions? What's in this one?'

'Honey, ginger, lemon, eucalyptus, a dash of brandy, a drop of something secret... Take a shot of it every four hours. You'll feel better this time tomorrow.'

'I'll feel inebriated this time tomorrow, you mean?'

Lorna smiled.

'Yes and that. It's good stuff though dad. It works.'

He set the bottle down on the coffee table and nodded.

'I'm sure it works. All your potions do. You're very good at doing what you do. You know that.'

He reached over and patted her hand.

'Ah, hello darling. Sorry, I was just putting the finishing touches to this months issue. We've had all sorts of problems with last minute ad changes. Bloody advertisers. They never get any better, they only get worse.'

Jilly breezed into the sitting room and stooped to peck Lorna on the cheek.

'Hi, mum. I was just telling dad he needs to take this every four hours. Will you remind him?'

'If it makes him better I'll remind him every bloody half hour. He's been getting under my feet this week. Heaven help me when he retires. I might have to pack him off to the cottage in Holt permanently and visit him at weekends. He's driven me mad with his coughing and spluttering and wheezing. And he keeps getting hot and stripping off... and then he's freezing cold and shivering as though he's got hypothermia and needs six layers of duvets on him just to warm himself up. I jolly well hope your medicine does work. Because nothing else has! He must have been through three boxes of Lem...'

'For gods sake, mum! He's got flu! Poor dad! Give him a break!'

Lorna leaned over and put an arm around her dad's shoulders. Jilly looked at the pair of them on the sofa, shook her head, tutted loudly and flounced off in the direction of the kitchen.

'All I'm saying is he's over-reacting,' she called from the hallway. 'Like all men do!'

Lorna looked at her dad.

'I don't know how you've put up with her all of these years, dad.'

Phillip made a face and reached for the bottle. He opened it and took a hearty swig.

'Me neither,' he said, swallowing the sweet, spicy and

potentially addictive liquid. He wiped his mouth on the back of his hand.

'Bugger, that's good.'

The table in the kitchen was already laid for dinner. Jilly tied an apron around her waist and put her oven gloves on. Lorna had an overwhelming urge to burst out laughing. She very rarely saw her mother in the kitchen these days, let alone cooking. Phillip was a wonderful cook, completely self-taught, and if it wasn't him rustling up the evening meal, it was a take-away, or better still, dinner in one of the numerous restaurants in town.

Jilly opened the oven door and slid out a tray of pork chops strewn with sage leaves and chunks of roast potatoes, onions and carrots dotted between them. It smelled fantastic.

'Mum! You've surpassed yourself!' said Lorna, astonished at her mother's sudden resurgence to the art of cookery.

Jilly gestured to a book lying open on the worktop.

'Jamie Oliver. He's marvellous. And a very good teacher although it says here serve with a salad, which seems odd. I'm not very fond of hot and cold together, but if Jamie says that's what it's supposed to go with, then that's what it's supposed to go with.'

Phillip glanced at Lorna and raised his eyebrows and Lorna gave him a wry smile in return.

'Oriel introduced me to Jamie Oliver. She had all his books, you know. Her favourite was that Italian one. I was thinking about her this morning as I was flicking through it... it must be a year ago, I'd have thought? Early May time, wasn't it?'

Lorna glanced at her father, his head down, studying his napkin intensely, and then back to her mother.

146

'Yes. It must be.'

'Hmmm. Such a shame. Malbec or Riesling?'

As they ate, they chatted about the magazine and the florists and how hard Nick was working at the hospital. Mundane chit-chat which interspersed the courses. After the Jamie Oliver extravaganza came a shop-bought Eve's Pudding. And after that, a platter of cheeses and an oval wicker basket full of different crackers appeared. This was so much more appealing than a bowl of pasta with a dollop of pesto.

'Thanks, mum. This is great!'

'My pleasure. You need fattening up. Eat up!' Jilly retorted, her tongue loosening with every mouthful of wine she took.

'Do I? I'm the same weight I've always been?'

'Too thin. You don't eat properly when you live alone and only have yourself to cook for. It's a well-known fact. I've seen it on This Morning. I bet you live off ready-meals and toast. Your bones will thin and become brittle and when you get to my age, you'll be riddled with osteoporosis.'

'I won't! And I don't! I eat pretty well… considering…'

'Considering you're on your own?'

Lorna had been enjoying a pleasant evening with her parents up until this point. Now, she felt increasingly irritated and wish she'd stayed at home with her pasta and pesto.

'I'm not on my own actually,' she snapped, knowing full well she'd get the reaction she hoped for.

Her mother dropped her knife onto her Stilton and Cheddar wedges and popped a grape into her gaping mouth.

'You're not?'

'No. I'm not. I've met someone.'

'Who?'

'A local man.'

'A local man? From Casworth? Is he a millionaire?'

Trust her to have that thought first and foremost in her mind. Money. It always came down to money.

'No. He's not.'

Jilly shot her a look dripping with disappointment and disdain. She hunched her shoulders and pulled an unflattering face.

'So, what is he then?'

Here we go, thought Lorna. She braced herself for a tirade of verbal abuse, an endless speech about how one needed to find one's equal in life. Anybody of a lower class simply would not suffice in the world of Mrs. Jilly Mills.

'He's a gardener.'

Phillip was quick off the mark, leaping to her defense before her mother could even draw breath.

'Good profession. People always need their gardens doing, trees cutting, hedges trimming...'

'Shut up, Phillip! A GARDENER? Good heavens, Lorna,' she sighed deeply and made an awful groaning sound. 'I've heard it all now! You can't go out with a GARDENER! Where does he GARDEN?'

She drew breath rapidly before Lorna could even begin to answer her and started talking again.

'Or do you mean he is a landscape gardener, you know, with his own business...?' she added hopefully, an air of desperation creeping into her voice.

'No. He's not. He's a gardener for the church.'

'The church! A glorified GRAVEDIGGER? Heaven help

us!' she said throwing her hands up into the air. 'Wait until Nick and Ryan hear about this. You'll be the laughing stock of the family! We didn't send you to a private school to end up marrying a GRAVEDIGGER! Did we, Phillip? Phillip...?'

'Marry...? Mum, we've only just met!'

'We sent her to a private school so she could get a good education and a good job,' interjected Phillip, dabbing at his nose with a fresh batch of tissues. 'And a good education and a good job is what she got.'

He looked at his rapidly reddening wife with disgust.

'Lorna is her own person. She's not a puppet for you or I to control. How dare you dictate who she can and cannot see. She's twenty-eight years old. She is a wise woman, not some silly little teenager. She chooses her own destiny and if that means she dates a gardener, rather than a... what, what would you prefer... a bank manager or a bloody solicitor... then she has my full support.'

He reached over and took Lorna's hand.

'And my blessing.'

It wasn't very often Jilly felt the full wrath of her husband. But today she did. She stood up and quietly began stacking dirty plates and bowls.

'Very well,' she huffed, flinging her tea towel around like a demented bull-fighter. 'Have it your way. But it'll all end in tears. You mark my words.'

TWELVE

LORNA WOKE TO A rose pink sky brindled with lilac and a dawn chorus so deafening, it could have stirred the dead from their eternal sleep.

There was a heavy feeling in her chest that felt like a large, flat stone crushing her heart. She knew her mother was the cause of this oppression and she hated her for it. Jilly could never be happy for her. Even during the party Lorna held for the launch of the florists, Jilly found fault. The champagne wasn't cold enough. She didn't like the design of the shop front logo. And the showroom wasn't anywhere near big enough to create a successful business. Of course, Lorna had proven her wrong. But an apology never followed. Not even when Lorna was commissioned to do the wedding flowers for Lord and Lady Barrington's eldest daughter – a wedding that was featured in Hello! magazine and one which saw Lorna's name in print for the very first time. A photo credit in Hello! was a huge achievement and proved she was no longer Tobias's sidekick.

Lorna sat on the edge of the bed and thought of the all the times she had defended Jilly. Supported her through sad times and bad times. Times when she had stood by her as only a daughter would. Even to the point of stepping in and saving Jilly's marriage to her father. Something Jilly wasn't even aware of. She often wondered why she'd bothered. Why she'd used so much energy up on her mother over the years, why she'd risked so much for her. But Lorna knew the reason why. It was because Jilly was her mother. And even though she didn't much like her, she still loved her.

She sighed a deep, sorrowful sigh, and heaved herself off the bed and headed towards the bathroom. The first of the two bridal bouquets had to be delivered at nine and the second at nine thirty, so she needed to get a move on.

She was back in the village by mid-morning with two very satisfied, if a little giddy, customers. She loved seeing brides on the morning of their wedding. It made her heart sing and chased away any bad mood that may have been lingering.

The spectacular dawn had blossomed into yet another idyllic summers day. Cotton wool clouds floated across the cobalt sky and as Lorna parked her car next to the bakery, a Red Kite circled high above her, riding the thermals, hunting breakfast.

The door of the bakery, as usual, was wide open. Lorna pushed her sunglasses up on to the top of her head as she strolled from bright, glaring sunshine into the darker, cooler interior of the shop. There was a huddle of women at the counter, all clutching brown paper bags containing loaves of fresh bread and sugary doughnuts and they were gabbling away ten to the dozen.

'She doesn't even look like a witch.'

'I always knew there was something decidedly iffy about her.'

'I'm not going to set foot in her shop again, I can tell you.'

'Peggy said she contacts the dead via a ouija board set up in her front room.'

Lorna stood in the doorway and observed the women

for a few moments and then very slowly and purposefully, strode up to the counter, surveying with over-exaggerated interest the array of baked delicacies on display. The women fell silent and an uncomfortable hush descended on the shop. The huddle looked at her with fear in their eyes and moved aside, creating a pathway to the front of the shop like a parting of the waves – uneasy murmering enveloping her like the hum of swarming bees.

'Good morning, ladies,' she said cheerfully. 'Morning, Sue.'

Sue was the only one to verbally acknowledge her.

'Morning. What can I get you?' she replied matter-of-factly.

Lorna stooped to take a closer look at the goods on offer.

'I'll have two almond croissants, please. A large, white farmhouse loaf. And one of your lovely lemon tarts please.'

She took her sunglasses off her head and ran her long, slim fingers through her coppery mane of hair. Her green eyes coruscated wildly as she scrutinised the terrified faces that stared back at her.

'I am meeting my two best friends for dinner tonight. And it's my turn to take a dessert.' She turned to face Sue once more.

'I was toying with the idea of taking a bats blood soufflé or possibly even a snake venom sorbet with me,' she said airily 'but I think a lemon tart would be so much more pleasant on the palate, don't you? Even for a gaggle of nasty, old witches like us...'

There were collective sharp intakes of breath and the women scuttled out of the shop like a plague of cockroaches fleeing for the safety of darkness.

152

Sue nodded furiously – her face flushed pink, beads of sweat forming on her forehead. Without speaking, she placed two almond croissants into a paper bag, wrapped a large, white farmhouse loaf in paper and carefully lifted a lemon tart from the chiller cabinet into a shallow, white cardboard box and closed the lid.

'Will that be all?' she croaked.

'Yes, thank you Sue. How much do I owe you?'

Sue's hand trembled as she punched the number pad on the till.

'Er, that's £7.80 please.' She paused. 'The tart is £4.00,' she added, almost apologetically.

Lorna handed her a ten pound note.

'Sue...? Do these women really think all these things of me? And my friends?' she asked, her voice softening.

Sue looked embarrassed and opened her mouth to speak but nothing came out. She shrugged her shoulders and her lips quivered as she smiled a shaky, awkward smile.

'Well... you know what this village is like. Full of women with nothing else better to do than tittle-tattle about others.'

Lorna frowned and imagined them sitting around their coffee tables, cooking up a multitude of rumours between them.

'I'm surprised at you though, Sue. I didn't think you were like them. I thought maybe you had more sense than to believe idle gossip.'

Sue avoided eye contact and started busying herself by sorting through till receipts on the countertop.

'I did say I didn't believe a word of it. But you know what they are like... they are all god fearing people and... well...

witchcraft and the likes… we don't get many folk into things like that around here.'

She handed Lorna her change and she slipped the coins into her purse and clicked it shut. She picked up her bag of shopping and turned to walk towards the door.

'You'd be surprised what kind of folk you do get around here, Sue. You really would.'

LORNA LET HERSELF IN to Evelyn's garden by the side gate. Evelyn wasn't as green-fingered as Rose. Her garden comprised of a rectangular, raised decking area and several tons of gravel with lots of plants in terracotta pots dotted here and there. Considering her devotion to all things feline, it wasn't a particularly cat-friendly garden. No trees or bushes for her feline friends to climb up or hide under. Lorna was most definitely a dog person. She didn't get the concept of cats at all. Which didn't sit at all well with the stereotypical witch.

'Yoo hoo!' she called, as she crunched over the noisy stones to the back door.

'We're in the kitchen, love,' yelled Rose.

Evelyn's house was a haphazard Victorian terrace with sash windows and a Minton tiled floor in the hall. It was situated on the outskirts of a quintessential English village, equidistant between Lorna and Rose's homes. She'd renovated it herself over the years, exposing floorboards, stripping original pine doors and buffing up the ornate, cast iron fireplaces, of which there were four. Every room was stuffed to the ceilings – literally – with objects she'd collected over the period of a lifetime. It was like living in a museum dedicated to all things goth.

Evelyn was a hoarder – nothing was ever thrown away because everything had a purpose. Even if that purpose might not be glaringly obvious at that particular moment in time. She had hundreds of cushions scattered literally everywhere, and in every shade, shape and pattern imaginable. There were numerous lamps, candles and incense burners adorning any and every flat surface. Photos in frames, pictures on walls, books on shelves and stacked up in wonky piles. And ornaments – so bloody many ornaments. There were cats – not only six, furry, hissy, scratchy real ones – but cats made of metal, wood, china and fabric. Her rooms were dark and cavernous, with sofas draped in deep purple crushed velvet and windows swathed in acres of black lace. It was an arachnophobe's worst nightmare. And Lorna wasn't a spider person either.

The smells eminating from the kitchen meant only one thing. Evelyn was cooking her infamous Thai Green Curry. A dish that lingered for many days, in all sense and purposes.

'Hello you two!' she said, kissing both Evelyn and Rose on the cheek. 'Something smells good,' she lied.

She put the bottle of wine in the fridge along with the lemon tart. It was far too hot to keep either out on the worktop.

'Thai Green Curry. You might have known! I know you both love it,' replied Evelyn, stirring with one hand and wafting her face with the other. 'It's so hot – and we'll be even hotter after eating this. Why didn't I just do a salad?'

'We don't do salad,' Lorna and Rose chorused in unison.

Evelyn laughed. 'Ah yes… but we do do wine!'

155

She poured Lorna a large glass of rosé and handed it to her.

'Shall we sit outside?'

Lorna visualised the living room crawling with cats and spiders and shuddered.

'Yes. Outside. We must make the most of sitting in the garden drinking and eating. We don't have the opportunity very often.'

'True. Come on then.'

The trio sat at the green plastic patio set Evelyn had positioned on the decking, a large, cream parasol shading them from the setting sun.

'Good day?' asked Evelyn, looking from one woman to the other.

'Not really. I had two clients booked in this afternoon, one for a micro-dermabrasion facial and the other for an eye lift – both big earners for me – and both cancelled this morning. Can you bloody believe it? And then I made stuffed mushrooms for tonight and left them on the kitchen table. I've had a terrible day.'

'I've told you a hundred times, Rose. You must take a deposit for bookings over a certain amount of money. Then the client is less likely to cancel as they'll be throwing money down the drain. And if they do cancel, at least you've not lost everything,' muttered Evelyn, popping an olive into her mouth.

'Evelyn's right. I always take a deposit for big jobs.'

'But I haven't got sophisticated machines like you have – I just take cash or cheque – no cards. How do I take a ruddy deposit at the end of a phone?'

'Oh, I don't know.' Evelyn slugged back her wine like it was pink lemonade. 'Anyway, how are you and Fred Astaire?'

'He's not old! Well, to you he is, but not to me. And he's very well, thank you.'

'How did the back, sack and crack go?' laughed Lorna.

Rose grimaced.

'Not good. I did his back all right. He coped with that. But I only managed one strip down below and he almost passed out. Drew blood, it did. He said he never wanted me to mention waxing ever again. It could have finished us really,' Rose took a sip of her drink. 'What was I thinking?'

Evelyn and Lorna roared with laughter.

'Have you heard from the man you ran away from, Evelyn?'

'Rupert?'

'His name is RUPERT?' shrieked Rose.

Evelyn nodded and giggled.

'Awful, isn't it? And as a matter of fact I have. He won't leave me alone! He's been texting me, emailing me, inviting me for dinner. I've only just found out he's one of the Barrington's sons.'

'From Lutton? Lord and Lady Barrington?'

'Yep. I had no idea he was landed gentry, until yesterday. I got chatting to Sally in the shop. He goes in there to buy his paper. He's invited me to his parents annual Summer Ball.'

'And...?'

'Well, I said yes. Only to be nosey, really. It's next weekend. Didn't you do his sister's wedding flowers, Lorna?'

'Yes and I know exactly who he is! Evelyn, he's gorgeous! I met him before the wedding and on the day itself. He was such a gentleman. Oh my god, I can't believe you!'

'What?' said Evelyn, sneering.

'What do you mean 'what'? You've got one of the country's most eligible bachelors chasing you, he's absolutely minted and he is going to be a real-life Lord one day! You're crazy! I'd be waltzing him down the aisle within the year, if I were you!'

'Oh Evelyn! You silly girl! How old is he? I thought you said he was a PE teacher?'

'He's 31, and he is a PE teacher. He works for a sports tuition company. Well, that's a lie... he doesn't just work for them. He owns it.'

'Aren't you attracted to him at all?'

Evelyn rolled her eyes to the heavens and groaned loudly.

'I guess I am... physically. He is gorgeous, Lorna, you're right. And he's very sweet. He's just a bit... well, boring.'

'All men are boring, Evelyn! For heaven's sake! Just say yes to the Ball, buy yourself a beautiful dress, and dazzle everyone.'

Evelyn thought about it for a second.

'Shall I dye my hair back to pink?'

Rose and Lorna looked at each other and tutted disapprovingly.

'I think the Barrington's are quite conservative, Evelyn. If I were you I'd stick to blonde.'

'Bollocks to them! They either accept me as I am or get stuffed!'

Lorna smiled. She wished she was like Evelyn. She really couldn't care less what anyone thought of her.

'Oh... and Rupert said I could invite some friends. So I said I'd invite you two. And Twinkle Toes and Joe. It's a couples thing.'

Rose rubbed her hands together with glee.

'Ooh, Evelyn! Gosh – I am so excited! Really? Does this mean I have to wear a ball gown?'

'I suppose so. Have you got one?'

'No, but I can buy one!'

The three women discussed Ball outfits and fantasized about Evelyn one day marrying into aristocracy and becoming Lady Barrington until they were almost delirious with excitement. It was all too much for one evening and with the wine flowing like tap water, and their heads becoming increasingly light, they decided they must eat.

Over the ridiculously hot Thai Green Curry and sticky, Jasmine rice, the conversation turned to Lorna and Joe. She told them all about their first proper date by the river. She told them how quiet and genteel Joe was, how he didn't own a mobile phone or a car, how he uncorked a bottle of homemade Elderflower wine and poured it into chipped, china mugs. That he was alone caring for his sister after losing both parents. How he was a simple man, who pulled weeds and dead-headed roses for a living. And how fantastic he was at kissing.

'He sounds a bit weird to me,' sniffed Evelyn.

'Have you told your parents about him yet?' asked Rose.

'Why is he weird? And yes, I briefly mentioned him yesterday when I went round for dinner.'

'Bet that went down well with your mother…' said Evelyn sarcastically.

Lorna bit her bottom lip and gazed down at her hands.

'No it didn't, unsurprisingly. She was really quite nasty about him'.

She looked across at Evelyn and their eyes locked together. 'You didn't answer my question,' she said flatly.

Evelyn shrugged her shoulders and was silent for a while.

'I dunno. I just think it's a bit weird he hasn't got a phone. I mean everyone's got a phone nowadays. Even slum dwellers in Mumbai have bloody phones! And who on earth takes a woman on a first date down to a rat-infested river and makes her drink shitty home brew out of a mug?'

Rose laughed but Lorna didn't. She swallowed hard and willed the tears that were pricking the back of her eyes to stay hidden in their reservoirs. She didn't want to cry in front of her friends. First her mother, now her best friend. She was starting to feel a little downtrodden to say the least.

'The river is beautiful. And his gesture was very romantic,' Lorna said softly. 'Not everyone has money, Evelyn. Money can't buy you happiness.'

Rose patted her shoulder and frowned at Evelyn.

'It sounds like a lovely first date, my love. When are you seeing him again?' cooed Rose.

Lorna sniffed and smiled weakly, her eyes shiny from withheld tears.

'Tomorrow. He's coming to mine after work.'

'Are you cooking for him?' asked Evelyn, conscious of the fact she had upset her friend and bitterly regretting speaking so churlishly.

'Yes. But I'm not sure what, yet.'

Evelyn poured the remainder of the wine into their three glasses and stood to fetch the lemon tart from the kitchen. Rose excused herself and said she needed to use the toilet. Inside the kitchen and well out of earshot from Lorna, Rose sidled up to Evelyn and hissed in her ear.

'Don't be so hard on her, Evelyn. She's been through a lot lately, bless her. She deserves some happiness after everything that shit Dan did to her.'

'I'm just worried about her, that's all. You and I both know full well what Oriel did and the whole rigmarole of that sodding charm being dug up... It's making me feel very uneasy. It's all so soon, and something isn't right. I don't know what it is but...'

'She must do the spell again. She has to. I'll mention it to her when we go back outside.'

Evelyn retrieved the tart and a jug of cream from the fridge and carried them into the garden.

'Sweetheart... I was just thinking. The next waxing moon is only a few days away. How about you cast a new love spell, to reverse the one that was broken?' said Rose, her voice light and cheerful.

Lorna watched as Evelyn placed the dessert down onto the table and started to slice it into quarters.

'Like I said before – make a new one, a fresh charm, but use clary sage this time, not lavender. And bury it deep. Much deeper than you did before,' Rose continued.

Evelyn nodded in agreement with Rose and handed Lorna a plate. She picked up the old-fashioned white and blue jug and poured cream generously over the tart.

'I'm not going to do it again. There's no point.'

Rose looked at Evelyn with alarm, her eyes fearful and wide.

'But you must! To let it remain a spoiled spell is no different to having cast a curse. Lorna, please...'

'No. Why would I want to do the reversal love spell when I have found love? My initial spell, the charm I made, was to bring my soulmate to me. And he's come. I know he has.'

'But the consequences, Lorna... a ruined spell, as Rose rightly says, is as good as a hex. You must do a reversal! You'd be mad not to... absolutely bloody crazy!'

Evelyn sat down forlornly, a look of despair on her face. She twiddled her pentacle ring round and round on her middle finger, mentally willing Lorna to change her mind.

'Then I must be crazy,' said Lorna, spooning dessert into her mouth and sighing with pleasure. It was delicious.

Rose and Evelyn exchanged defeated glances. Lorna was very willful when she wanted to be. Stubborn and obstinate. Which is why she was such a good businesswoman.

Nothing more was said about the charm. They finished their meal and drank coffee in high spirits and chatted until late. Lorna told them about Verity and the workman and her encounter with the god-fearing women in the bakery. When it was time to go, they said their usual farewell.

Kneeling down, facing one other in a circle on the floor, each woman reached out her left hand to grasp the right wrist of the friend beside her. They lowered their heads and closed their eyes.

'Live each day as if it were your last, for one day you will be right.' said Rose softly.

'Love yourself first and foremost. For when you truly love yourself, loving those around you will come as easy as breathing. And we all must breathe.' whispered Lorna.

'Learn your life's lessons – each as it comes – for that is the reason we are here.' Evelyn said, giving Lorna a sideways glance, followed by a wink.

'Enjoy your life, because if you do not, someone else will enjoy it for you and your time on Earth will have been wasted,' chanted all three women in unison.

THIRTEEN

WHEN ORIEL FIRST mentioned witchcraft to the three friends, they were all blind drunk. The suggestion that they could become witches – the imagery, the intrigue, the mystery – thrilled them more than they ever thought possible. It sounded exciting. Taboo. A secret they could keep forever, a secret only party to themselves.

When their hangovers wore off, and far away from Oriel, they discussed her proposition endlessly, until curiosity finally got the better of them. They read the little books on witchcraft that Oriel had posted to them afterwards and researched the religion of Wicca at the local library. They discovered its meaning and its roots in paganism and it interested them.

'I'm basically a witch already,' muttered Rose, as she leafed thought a book entitled 'Wicca: The Complete Craft'. 'I grew up in the Welsh valleys after all. I was surrounded by bloody witches my entire life! Although I didn't really know what they were back then, of course… I just thought they were a bunch of old hags!' she retorted, her accent rising and falling like a Celtic folk song. 'Everyone always calls me an old hippy, anyway. And that's basically what being a witch is all about. They're just daft old hippies.'

'I like the idea of being powerful. Using energy, a force, to create something good. It must be a brilliant feeling to want something and ask for it and then get it,' said Evelyn.

'I'm not sure it's as simple as that, Evelyn. I'm sure if I became a witch and asked for Johnny Depp to show up on my doorstep, he wouldn't actually appear. I just find it all very romantic. I love the thought of taking forces from nature, and using them to enrich your life. Do you think our lives will change very much?' asked Lorna wistfully.

She was the youngest of the three and the most naïve.

'I suppose it will do, yes. It will give us a purpose. It will form a kind of bond between us. Something that is our own. That belongs to us and only us. Our own little world,' Rose replied confidently.

'I love that,' said Evelyn. 'Our own little world. Nobody will know that we are witches except us. Are we going to practice only good magic or are we allowed to cast bad spells as well?'

'Evelyn!' shrieked Lorna. 'Cast bad spells? On who?'

'Oh I dunno. People piss you off from time to time, don't they? Some worse than others. I just wondered if, say, you got really annoyed with somebody, it be acceptable to put a bad spell on them?'

Lorna and Rose laughed.

'It's called a curse, for a start, you daft sod. And I guess you could put a curse on someone but if it worked, you'd have to live with the consequences for the rest of your life...'

'I'm not talking about wishing the grim reaper on anyone! Just – you know – a little mishap, maybe.'

'You are evil, Evelyn! That can be your new Wicca name. Evil Evelyn.'

Evelyn laughed like a drain.

'Oh, I like that! It has a certain ring to it. Like Evil Edna from Chorlton and the Wheelies! What could Rose be called?'

Rose raised her eyebrows and smirked.

'As I am going to be a quiet, kind and highly discreet witch, I think my name should be Reticent Rose.'

'Ha! Very good! What about you Lorna? You're lots of things beginning with L,' laughed Evelyn.

'We all know she's obsessed with the moon – how about Luna Lorna? Or does that make her sound like she's a bit mad? How about Lily-white? Now that suits her down to the ground!' chuckled Rose.

'Ooh, I like that. Lily-white Lorna. It has an air of purity about it. And lilies are my favourite flower.'

'Evil Evelyn. Reticent Rose. And Lily-white Lorna,' sighed Evelyn. 'Jesus – we sound like a load of frigging pirates!'

A COUPLE OF WEEKS after Oriel's supper party, at the end of their weekly meditation class, the three friends waited until all the other members had changed and gone home and told Oriel they would be honoured to be part of her coven.

Oriel was delighted and said they must set to work straight away. This entailed a self-dedication ceremony, which she would perform personally at her home. They were asked to do two things before the ritual took place. The first was to bring along an offering, which they would present to the gods. A gift of wine or food, it was entirely up to them. The second was to make sure they were scrupulously clean before entering the house. This was the ritual of purification. They were to bathe and wash their hair, scrub their nails and remove all make up, perfume and nail polish.

The women had no idea what a self-dedication ritual entailed. Rose was convinced they would have to be stark naked apart from long, white robes. Evelyn was sure she'd read that these sorts of ceremonies involved having sex on an altar with a tall, gangly wizard with straggly hair and a long grey beard. And Lorna just kept very quiet on the matter. She didn't even want to know how she would be dedicated into the world of Wicca and she was quite happy to remain blissfully unaware until the actual event was taking place.

In reality, the ceremony was a very understated affair. The only real shock was to discover that Roger, Oriel's husband, was aware of the proceedings. None of the women had the slightest inkling that Roger knew his wife was a witch. They assumed he was quietly oblivious to Oriel's little secret but she explained that although he had known about her involvement in witchcraft right from the beginning of their relationship, he was not part of the Wicca movement nor did he want to be. He was quite happy to let her get on with it, as long as it didn't involve him or encroach on their marriage in any way.

Rose likened it to being married to a man that was heavily into football. You allowed him to watch Match of the Day and go down the pub afterwards to discuss it with their mates. On one condition. He never talks about football in the house or expects you to be drawn into any manner of football-orientated conversation. EVER. Oriel agreed it was just like that.

On the day of the ceremony, the three women turned up at Oriel's house, much the same way as they always did, together and by taxi.

Roger welcomed them at the door and ushered them through into the conservatory where Oriel was sitting, dressed from head to toe in pale lemon. She stood to greet them, embracing them one by one, and asked them to take a seat. Roger disappeared briefly only to return moments later with a tray of tea and biscuits. The three women looked at each other, puzzled. The afternoon had more of a tea party feel about it than a Wicca self-dedication ceremony.

Oriel poured the tea and Roger offered around a plate of delicate shortbreads and wafer-thin lemon cookies. They indulged in idle chit-chat – talking about the weather, Lorna's floristry course at college, Evelyn's tedious job in the hospital kitchen and Rose's newly qualified status as a beauty therapist. When all the tea was drunk and the biscuits devoured, Oriel did a funny little hand gesture, which was obviously a signal for Roger to leave them alone. He did so very obediently, taking with him the tea tray and the dirty cups and saucers. Not long after, they heard the front door open and close, which indicated he had left the house altogether. Evelyn breathed a sigh of relief. She thought he might be the tall, gangly wizard – minus the straggly hair and long grey beard – that was about to gang bang all three of them.

Oriel appraised the women slowly, her ebony eyes shining like onyx, narrowing to slits at times, as only cat's eyes do.

'Well, we all know why we are here. And what we are about to do. I don't think we ought to wait a second longer. Do you?'

The women shook their heads.

Oriel stood and with a swish of jet black hair, turned and walked through the sitting room.

'Follow me,' she called, beckoning with her perfectly

manicured hand. 'And bring your offerings with you.'

They walked through the house and up the grand staircase, along a wide landing, to a room right at the end of the corridor. Oriel told them to wait outside. She took their offerings from them and entered the room, closing the door behind her briefly before reappearing seconds later, holding three coat hangers. From each hanger hung a long, white robe. Rose desperately wanted to squeal 'I told you so' but bit her lip and refrained from saying any such thing.

'I want you to wear these garments for the ceremony. I'll show you where to get changed.'

She walked back down the landing and opened a door halfway down on the left. It was a huge, light, airy bedroom overlooking the water meadows to the front of the house.

'It's totally private here. We're not overlooked at all. Through that door is a dressing room and through that one is a bathroom. So take your pick.'

'Do we have to be naked?' asked Rose.

Oriel threw back her head and roared with laughter.

'Of course not! Goodness me! This isn't Macbeth or some god-awful B movie! Rose, please… keep your undies on! Oh and when you're ready, just knock on the door, just to let me know.'

Oriel disappeared and closed the bedroom door quietly behind her.

The friends looked at each other and made mock horror faces before dissolving into a fit of giggles. They were very aware Oriel was the other side of the door and tried desperately hard to stop. This was a very serious occasion. Not one to be entered into lightly. They were about to become witches, for heavens sake!

They each took a robe and changed into it, leaving their bras and knickers firmly in place. They congregated by the bedroom door, huddling together like lambs to the slaughter. They looked each other up and down anxiously.

'I'm nervous,' said Lorna.

'Me too,' agreed Evelyn.

'Don't be so bloody daft. It's only a bit of fun!' hissed Rose, reaching out and knocking on the door.

Oriel opened it and led them back along the corridor to the room at the end. She had changed her clothing too. Gone was the lemon ensemble, replaced by a gown the colour of ripened damsons, tied at the waist with a silvery braided cord. She was barefoot and around her neck hung a silver pentacle. Her hair was loose and for a woman in the autumn of her life, she looked pretty spectacular.

Inside, the room was sparse. The pine floorboards had been stripped and stained, the walls painted pure white and the long, sash window was draped in swathes of sheer, white voile. Gently flickering candles resting in black, iron holders were dotted all around the floor and at the far end of the room, opposite the window, garlands of meadow flowers adorned a low, wide table covered in crisp, white linen that became immediately obvious as the altar.

Evelyn looked at it and gulped. In her atheist mind, altars were quite sinister objects. Used for sacrificing animals and people, conjuring up images of blood and death and rape. She shuddered and steadied her breathing. A tall, white candle stood at the centre of the altar and Oriel had placed their offerings to the gods either side of it.

In each corner of the room there was a symbol painted in white on the floor. The women recognised them instantly as the astrological elements for Air, Water, Fire and Earth. In the centre of the room a perfect circle had been painted onto the floorboards, also in white, which measured roughly six feet in diameter.

Oriel walked to the circle and sat at the very top of it, with her back to the altar. She asked the other to sit around it, Evelyn opposite her, Rose to her right and Lorna to her left. Then she asked everyone to form a closed circle by holding one another's wrists. She bowed her head briefly and whispered words that only she could hear and then raised her head, looked at the women and smiled reassuringly.

'We are here today to celebrate and rejoice together, to begin a whole new chapter in – not only your lives – but also in mine. New beginnings. The ceremony I am about to perform is called a rite of self dedication – a celebration of the rite of passage as you declare yourselves a follower of the path of Wicca.'

She slowly shook her head from side to side and her face suddenly hardened.

'This is not, I stress, an initiation ceremony. That special and very private ceremony can only take place once you have studied Wicca for at least a whole year. Only then, when you are truly at one with the practice, can you be initiated fully.'

She smiled a secretive, almost unnerving smile. 'And what a year it is going to be!'

Oriel broke the circle of hands, got to her feet and walked behind the altar. She summoned each woman to the front of the table in turn, where she handed them the offerings they

171

had brought to the ceremony. They placed them gently in the middle of the circle – Rose setting down wine, Evelyn bread and Lorna fruit – and once Oriel had returned to the group, they again linked wrists, encircling their offerings.

Oriel bowed her head and the others followed suit. It was deathly quiet. A gentle breeze stirred the gossamer voile through the open window and the smell of meadow flowers filled the air.

'I, Oriel Agnes Trewhellor-Fitzpatrick, High Priestess and direct descendant of Madgy Figgy of St. Levan, stand before you on this day, to lead you onto the path to Wicca, where you will begin your journey to spiritual enlightenment, freedom, fulfillment and eternal love. You will be joined in a marriage, a lifetime bond, between your soul and the gods and goddesses that surround you. This is a new beginning, a life-long study and dedication to Wicca. Once a witch, you will remain a witch until your heart beats no more. Let us begin.'

Oriel broke the circle once more and walked to the altar. She moved the candle to the end of the table and next to it, placed a small, earthenware bowl.

'Rose, please step up to the altar.'

Rose's face was ashen, her eyes wide. Her stomach felt as though it was full of wasps, stinging her repeatedly, generating pain and fear. She wasn't entirely sure she wanted to do this after all. This wasn't a bit of fun. This was a very earnest, sinister affair. And she was frightened.

She faced Oriel over the altar and stepped up onto it, before lowering herself onto the covered surface and lying flat on her back. Oriel dipped her forefinger in the oil. Rose could smell it. It reminded her of her herb garden at home. Oriel made a pentagram sign with the oil on Rose's forehead.

'Repeat after me. May my mind be blessed so that I can accept the wisdom of the gods.'

Rose repeated the chant in a whisper.

Oriel then softly anointed both of Rose's eyelids.

'May my eyes be blessed so that I see my way clearly on this path.'

Again Rose echoed Oriel's words.

Oriel went on to anoint Rose's nose to breathe, lips to speak, heart to love, hands to heal, abdomen to create life and feet to walk side by side with the gods. Each anointment involved the pentagram symbol, and Oriel gently blessed each part of Rose's body, until Rose had dedicated herself to Wicca.

When the ritual was complete, she opened her eyes. It was bright in the stark, white room and she blinked several times to adjust to the light. She sat up and breathed deeply, her lungs grateful to be swelled with fresh air once more.

Oriel then placed a necklace around Rose's neck, a simple silver chain, from which hung a delicate, silver, filigree pentacle.

'Wear this at all times. It will protect you from harm, give you strength and keep your spirit guarded.'

She then handed her a small, leather-bound book. She opened the front cover, and inside, in Oriel's distinctive lavender calligraphy, was a passage of words.

'Rose, please say these words aloud to complete your dedication ceremony.'

Rose glanced down and took another deep breath. She

felt different. The wasps had gone, replaced now by delicate, fluttering butterflies. And her heart was light and her mind clear.

'On this day, I pledge my dedication to the God and Goddess. I will walk with them beside me, and ask them to guide me on this journey. I pledge to honour them, and ask that they allow me to grow closer to them. As I will, so it shall be.'

Oriel smiled, the corners of her eyes crinkling, and her charcoal eyes sparkled like smouldering coals in a winters fire.

Rose walked back to her place in the circle, clutching her book to her chest, and glanced at Evelyn and Lorna. They no longer looked anxious. Relief flooded their faces and Lorna had tears in her eyes, overcome by the sheer simplicity and emotion of the occasion. In turn, they too were anointed with the scented, salty oil and all three descended into the world of Wicca with an intense feeling of belonging and acceptance.

THE FOLLOWING YEAR, as Oriel predicted, was a wonderful adventure. A year full of surprises, wonder, mystery and knowledge. They learned their craft well and with extreme dedication. Oriel was an outstanding teacher and together the four women practiced witchcraft on a regular basis, meeting once a week without fail. By the end of the year, and with a deep contentment instilled within their very being – they were officially initiated into the movement and became fully-fledged, practicing witches.

Oriel was a constant presence in their lives, existing solely under the guise of meditator and good friend. She was like a strong, wise, grand-motherly figure to them all. She became friends with their nearest and dearest, and along with Roger, effortlessly and successfully immersed herself into her new, extended family, becoming loved and respected by all.

The three women's lives changed for the better almost instantly. And with alarming velocity. Rose's business took off and for the first time in her life, she was earning her keep, paying her way and was firmly in the black. She even managed to buy a home of her own and quite often, especially after several glasses of wine, mentally raiseded two fingers at the ex-husband who maintained she would be nothing without him.

Evelyn found peace with herself after a troublesome upbringing and a difficult childhood. The asthma that had plagued her throughout her life – at times hospitalising her for days – all but disappeared overnight. For the first time ever she felt well. Healthy. Alive. And she could breathe freely without the help of inhalers and steroids.

And Lorna found success in her working life. She was good at her job, loved by everyone and grew more talented by the year. She launched her own shop at the age of twenty-four, something she was immensely proud of, bought a home and her beloved Cherry.

All three women had everything they could possibly wish for in their happy, healthy, contented lives. Everything apart from the one thing that all women desire the most… the hardest thing to find and the hardest thing to hang onto. Love. Some search their entire lives for it and never find it. Men rolled in and rolled out of their lives like a persistent sea mist over the ten years that were to follow, but neither Rose, Evelyn or Lorna found that special someone. They were spurred on by the notion that good things come to those that wait. And everybody has a soulmate out there somewhere. It was just a small matter of finding them.

FOURTEEN

LORNA LEAFED THROUGH her diary and crossed off orders and deliveries with silvery, diagonal lines drawn in pencil. She had one more bouquet to deliver but as the order stated it was for a Sunday birthday, she had arranged with the customer to drop it off after she'd closed the shop that evening. She also needed to go to the bank but that would have to wait until Monday morning. Most of her transactions were by credit card and paid directly into her business account but for some reason, this week had seen an increase in customers paying in cash and she had quite a large amount of money sitting in her till drawer.

She sometimes wished she had somebody to help her. A Saturday girl maybe, to run the shop while she delivered orders and carried out essential errands. But employees didn't come cheap and she couldn't justify paying a wage to anyone but herself at the moment. She was doing well. She'd built up a very good business over the last four years, but she wasn't quite at the stage where she could afford to employ somebody to do her dirty work while she kicked back every now and then.

Rose always lended a hand in the shop during the immediate run up to Valentine's Day and Mothering Sunday. February and March were quiet for Rose in her line of work. She often sold vouchers as gifts for loved ones, but they were rarely redeemed until spring had sprung. And then she was rushed off her feet. Helping Lorna in her hour of need was a pleasure. Rose enjoyed the change of scenery – working from her spare bedroom was sometimes isolating and Rose loved pottering around the shop, chatting to customers and sniffing everything in sight. Lorna was more than a little grateful to her, especially as Rose was happy to be rewarded for her kindness with dinner and a bottle of wine.

Lorna closed the diary and gazed around the shop. She was trying very hard not to think about the evening that lay ahead of her. If Joe had counted properly and remembered that today was Saturday, he would be on her doorstep at seven o'clock prompt. She swallowed hard and a tight ball of nauseating nervousness began to form in the pit of her stomach. She wanted him to stay the night. From the very first moment she'd set eyes on him, as he strolled around the bend at the bottom of the hill and she'd almost killed him, she'd wanted him to stay the night. Every time she allowed herself to think about running her fingertips down his naked back, no mater how fleetingly the thought, her heart palpitated and she felt dizzy.

'This won't do,' she said aloud to herself. 'You need to keep busy.'

She began rearranging the shop. It was a long overdue job and today, a baking hot Saturday in May, was the perfect time to do it. Outside, the streets were deserted. Casworth was only an hours drive from the coast and if half the village hadn't flocked there today, they'd be holed up in their vast back gardens, stoking up the barbecue, lying flat-out and oiled-up on matching teak sun-loungers and splashing about in swimming pools and hot tubs. Lucky sods, thought

Lorna with a sigh. The pitfalls of self-employment in retail – weekend working and having to open up come rain or shine, whether you liked it or not.

By the end of the day, the shop had been totally transformed. Entire areas had been shifted around and it looked great. Lorna even changed the window display, which had needed doing for weeks – draping pretty, patchwork floral bunting around the edges of the frame and filling old watering cans with flowers to create an ambiance of days gone by.

She'd had a few customers too, buying an assortment of odds and ends from pot plants to plant pots and single bunches of flowers to trays of assorted garden herbs. She received several telephone orders for bouquets for the following week and best of all, a request to supply the flowers for the summer ball at the Barrington's the following weekend. She didn't tell the anonymous caller who placed the order that she would be attending the ball herself as a guest, she was just very grateful to have been commissioned to do the job. She knew it was a big deal for one person to do – the Barrington's requested two podium displays for the entrance to the marquee, along with posies for every table inside, of which there were twenty. She would have to place an order for the flowers on Monday morning and spend all day Thursday and Friday assembling everything. She needed to deliver the flowers on Saturday morning, probably in two runs, and be as fresh as a daisy at seven o'clock that evening for the start of the ball. All after a full days work. It was a tall order but the Barrington's were paying her a lot of money for the honour, just as they had for their daughter's wedding flowers. She would make sure she got the job done – and done well, at that – even if it meant working through the night.

With Cherry parked and locked up for the night, Lorna let herself into the flat, slinging her handbag over one of the coat hooks in the hall. She sank down, exhausted, onto the cool leather of the oversized sofa that dominated her living room. She glanced up at the clock on the mantelpiece. She had approximately one hour, to not only rustle up the makings of an edible dinner, but shower, wash and dry her hair, dress and make herself look as ravishing as she possibly could. For one as naturally beautiful as Lorna, this meant applying mascara, lip gloss and perfume and would take her all of two minutes. But as Lorna was oblivious to her beauty, she fretted that she would run out of time and open the door at seven o'clock looking a complete and utter state.

Fifty minutes later, she looked in the mirror. Her hair was loose and hanging in silky tendrils over her shoulders and down her back. Her pale skin, as soft as butter, was scented with fragrant white musk. The fluid, navy blue, polka dot fabric of her halter-neck dress skimmed over her breasts and hips and accentuated her tiny waist. She was lucky enough not to have to wear a bra and she'd put her best cream silk knickers on. Just in case. She slipped a thin silver bangle onto her right wrist – it co-ordinated perfectly with the delicate, silver pentacle that hung from her neck. She pushed her feet into leather, beaded sandals and fastened the tiny buckles at each ankle. She was ready.

She dashed around the flat, one final time, checking that cushions were plumped and everything was in its rightful place. She'd remembered to change the sheets, pillowcases and duvet cover that morning so the bed was clean and inviting and the whole room smelled enticingly of freshly-washed linen.

She cautiously tiptoed to the kitchen window and peered through the slats of the blind. The pavement below was empty. Her heart was racing. It was almost seven o'clock. She walked to the hob and stirred the gently bubblng pan of chilli. She filled another pan with water and set it down on the back burner for later. She was just about to open the fridge door to retrieve the garlic ciabatta she'd bought to accompany the meal when the doorbell rang. She almost jumped out of her skin. She walked into the hall and pressed the intercom button on the wall and talked into the microphone.

'Hello?'

'Oh… Hello. Is that you, Lorna?'

A smile crept across Lorna's face.

'Yes! Of course it is! Is that you, Joe?' she asked playfully.

'Yes. It is.' Joe studied the row of numbers and buttons on the panel outside the main door.

'How do I get in?'

Lorna laughed.

'I'll come and get you.'

She flew down the staircase two steps at a time and opened the front door wide. Joe didn't say a word. He just cocked his head to one side and smiled, and with that one simple gesture alone, took Lorna's breath away. She held out her hand and he took it, stepping inside the hallway and wrapping his arms around her, kissing the top of her head. Lorna closed her eyes and laid her face on his chest, her hands caressing his back through his crisp, white cotton shirt.

'I've missed you.' Joe whispered.

'I've missed you too,' replied Lorna.

She tightened the grip on his hand and led him upstairs to her flat.

Once inside, she locked the door and slipped the chain guard on. She looked through the peephole, just to make sure nosey, old Peggy wasn't craning her neck up the stairwell to see who she'd just taken upstairs. She wouldn't put it past her to creep up the stairs after them and crouch down, listening, her ear pressed up against the door.

There was nobody there.

'Come through into the living room, Joe, and I'll get you a drink.'

Joe's eyes wandered around the flat as he took everything in. He unlaced his boots and placed them on the doormat.

'You have such a beautiful home.'

He walked over to the fireplace and pondered over her collection of framed photographs of friends and family, which had been arranged neatly on the mantelpiece either side of a huge vase of flowers.

'Who are all these people?' he asked curiously.

Lorna walked up behind him, gazing at the outline of his broad shoulders through his shirt, his tanned, athletic body just waiting to be explored. She loved the way his hair was cut, the sexy shape of the nape of his neck, the way he stood. Good grief, she was losing the plot.

'These two are my brothers, and these are my parents. This one is of my grandmother – my other grandparents have all died. This one is Rose, this is Evelyn – my best friends. And then there's this one of us altogether! Er... this is me on my graduation day and these are all my cousins – on my dad's side,' she said, pointing at each photo in turn.

'His brother lives in Australia and has six children. They all came over to stay with us a couple of years ago. It was great fun. But crazy!'

'Australia? The other side of the world! Everyone looks so happy... and you look so beautiful.'

He turned and gazed into her eyes and very gently stroked her cheek with his index finger.

'But you look even more beautiful standing here in front of me.'

A flush of pink crept over his cheeks. Lorna instinctively stood on her tiptoes and tilted her chin upwards. Their lips met for just a moment.

Take your time, she told herself. You have all night.

'Thank you. That is... very kind of you.'

She took a deep breath and looked around her, feeling slightly flustered. 'Now, what would you like to drink?' she asked, her voice faltering slightly.

'I don't mind. Anything.'

'Well, would you like wine or beer? Or something stronger? I have whisky, vodka, gin...'

'Beer. Beer is fine.'

He followed her into the kitchen and watched her quietly as she levered the top off the beer bottle and handed it to him. Then she uncorked a bottle of decent white wine and poured herself a glass.

'Cheers.'

'To your good health,' he replied.

'Come on, let's sit down. Dinner is almost ready, and I don't know about you, but I am starving.'

'It smells wonderful. What have you made?'

'Chilli con carne. With proper steak too, none of your minced beef rubbish! I followed a recipe and everything! Are you impressed?'

'I have no idea what that is but I love steak so I am sure I will love it.'

'You don't know what chilli is?' asked Lorna incredulously.

'No. What is it?' replied Joe, shaking his head and taking a swig of ice cold beer.

'It's Mexican! Beef, tomatoes, kidneys beans, chilli. You eat it with rice. It's quite spicy.'

She looked at him, her left eyebrow arching, a mischievous smile playing on her lips.

'Are you messing around with me...?'

Joe looked surprised.

'No!' he insisted. 'I've never heard of it before! Mexican food?' he laughed. 'I've only ever eaten English food!'

God, he was strange. It was as though he'd led some bizarre, sheltered life, stuck within the confines of the local area, never straying much further than into town or, at most, a day trip to the coast. She'd never met anyone quite like him before. He intrigued her. And he seemed totally unaware of his enigmatic demeanour. Which is why she was totally smitten by him.

'I hope I don't poison you then! If you've never eaten spicy food before, it might not agree with you! And by the way, your beer is Mexican too!'

Joe grinned.

'Is it? I've got a cast iron stomach. I'll be fine.'

They talked about the last few days as they slowly sipped

their drinks. Lorna told Joe about her father's flu and how she'd made him a remedy to make him better. She didn't divulge how she had become such an expert in potion making nor did she mention any of the hostility towards her concerning the womenfolk of the village. Lorna never told Dan that she was a member of a coven when they were together. It was part of her life that had nothing to do with him. And the same would go for her relationship – should it blossom into one – with Joe. He need never know that she was a witch. He seemed so unassuming – almost cloistered in his life – that the very thought of him finding out what she was, other than being a simple florist, could frighten him off altogether. And she didn't want to let him go. She knew she'd found what she'd been searching twenty-eight long years for. As the seconds ticked by, she fell deeper and deeper in love with him. She just hoped he felt the same way about her.

Again, Joe talked about little other than life in Lutton, his work in the churchyard and his friendship with Victor. Lorna was surprised to hear that Victor was a man in his eighties but Joe was obviously very fond of him and enjoyed spending time with him, probably because he was the father figure that Joe no longer had in his life. He touched briefly on the subject of Alice, but only after Lorna asked him how she was. He told her that Alice was confined to bed and was now receiving daily visits from a lady, who Lorna assumed was a nurse. Lorna wondered why on earth she wasn't in hospital, or a hospice, being cared for around the clock. But it wasn't any of her business so she didn't question him further.

They moved back into the kitchen together and he stood observing her again as she cooked. All she had to do was steam the rice, bake the ciabatta and throw together a simple coleslaw salad, but he was mesmerised. He watched her like a hawk, his eyes never straying any further than her hands as she prepared the food, and her face as she talked.

They ate at the little round table in the corner of the living room with candles flickering and soft music playing. They drank red wine, laughing and chattering, as though they had known each other for a thousand years. The atmosphere was relaxed, effortless and natural. They both knew it was right because it felt right.

So right, that after the dishes had been loaded into the dishwasher and the table cleared, they found themselves back on the sofa – the only luminescence from the dying candlelight and the room scented with the intoxicatingly, exotic perfume of burning patchouli oil. The sound of evening birdsong drifted in through the open window and the soothing, haunting strains of Einaudi heightened the intensity of the moment.

Joe set his glass down on the side table next to the sofa and turned to face Lorna.

'Will you dance with me?'

His face was serious, the tone of voice sincere, his gesture entirely charming.

Lorna swallowed her mouthful of wine with a gulp.

'Dance with you?' she spluttered.

'Yes… dance with me.'

He slowly got to his feet and held out his hand. Lorna took it and stood up, kicking off her sandals as she did so.

'I don't know how to dance, Joe… I've never danced with anyone before!'

'Then I'll teach you.'

His left hand slid around her waist and his right hand intertwined with her left. She placed her right hand on his shoulder and their eyes engaged. He drew her towards him and the butterflies in her stomach began to dance along with her. As they moved, in an unhurried, rhythmic motion, she followed his lead and was surprised at how well she could dance. He held her firmly, pulling her close, her face resting on his shoulder and his jaw nestled against her sweet-smelling hair. She breathed in his scent again. It was evocative, stirring something deep inside her. She longed to feel him against her, skin to skin. His hand caressed the small of her back through the gossamer sheerness of her dress. As they moved in time with the music, she tilted her chin to look at him. For the second time that night, he took her breath away.

Their eyes locked, their breathing quickened and their lips met. As they kissed passionately and more urgently, their body language became more frenetic.

Joe pulled her to him assertively, one hand stroking her hair, the other placed securely on the small of her back. She could feel his body through his clothes. Her head was swimming, a deep aching pulsated through her body until she was at breaking point. She took the lead and ran her fingers up his body to his collarbone. The top button of his shirt was already undone, so she unfastened the second, and then the third. Joe pulled away from kissing her, his breathing was fast and low. He watched her intently as she unbuttoned his shirt, exposing his upper body. She gasped as she touched his skin. She ran her hands up either side of his rib cage, lingering briefly as her fingertips grazed the livid, puckered scar that disfigured his chest. She continued up to his broad, strong shoulders and removed the shirt from his body in one swift move and let it fall to the floor.

Lorna held out her hand and Joe took it. She led him through the hallway and into her bedroom. He looked around the room nervously. Lorna sensed his apprehension and gently stroked his face, kissing him again tenderly.

'Don't look so worried,' she whispered. 'I don't bite.'

Joe's eyes widened, his breathing now even deeper and slower than before. He looked forlornly at the floor and then the bed and then at Lorna.

'It's just… I… I'm…' he stammered, finding it hard to find the right words without sounding like a complete idiot.

'Lorna, I've never done this before,' he said awkwardly, his expression one of shame and humiliation.

He looked like a child standing before her, innocent, pure and totally untouched. She had no feelings of shock or surprise at his revelation. Intuition had already told her that this may be the case. All she felt was an inclination to strip him and push him backwards onto the bed.

He stepped forward and gathered her into his arms again. Lorna could feel his heart beating hard against his chest wall as he buried his face into her hair, his lips against her ear lobe, his soft breath warm against her cheek.

'But I want to.'

She traced her middle finger down the arch of his spine and she felt him tremble.

'Undress me,' she breathed.

He didn't need any further persuasion. In seconds he'd

undone the halterneck tie around her neck and unzipped the back of her dress, allowing it to glide effortlessly to her feet. He undid the buckle of his belt with some urgency, then the buttons of his trousers, pushing them down his legs, stepping out of them and kicking them to one side.

They both stood opposite each other, naked apart from their underwear. Joe's eyes roamed all over Lorna's breathtaking body and she tingled from head to toe as she looked at him standing before her, the most prepossessing man she'd ever seen. And here she was – about to make love to him.

He scooped her up in his arms as though she was a feather and lay her down gently on the bed.

'Lorna, you are so incredibly beautiful...' he murmered, his eyes wandering lustily all over her body.

He kissed her mouth, her ears, her neck, working his way down to her breasts. He stopped for just a moment, his emerald eyes gleaming, and glanced up at Lorna as if asking for permission to go further. Lorna nodded without hesitation and his tongue traced around each nipple, his hands caressing every inch of her body as he licked and sucked her to a state of blissful oblivion. His lips trailed further and further, brushing over her navel, and across her tummy. Again he stopped momentarily, as if relishing every single second, before touching the sheer silk of her knickers, working his thumb around and around the wet, delicate fabric, until Lorna could bear no more.

'Joe... please... now...' she pleaded.

Joe removed his underwear – and hers – in a heartbeat and moved on top of her, his mouth exploring hers, their tongues entwined like ivy. His pushed one arm under her back and the other scooped under her bottom, raising her leg slightly. Lorna wrapped her arms around him, breathing in his smell, the highly sexual feeling of naked skin on naked skin, her hands holding him tightly. She'd never felt so turned on in her life.

And then he was inside her. That first push, the acute awareness that there was no going back, the intense sensation as two bodies become one took her breath away – for the third time in the space of three hours.

She cried out as the full force of his body entered hers. Her back arched and she closed her eyes as she breathed out a long, lingering sigh. Her fingertips ran up his back to his neck and then the back of his head. Her fingers raked through his hair as she pulled him to her and kissed him wildly.

She pulled away and ran her tongue up the side of his neck and bit his earlobe, tugging at it lightly with her teeth. She bit harder and felt him suddenly lurch inside her. He groaned with pleasure as he continued to move in and out of her rhythmically, forcefully, but with a lustful desire that made her feel like the only woman alive. The way he touched her, kissed her, bit her, licked her, teased her. She couldn't believe this was his first time. He knew exactly what he was doing. He was either lying or he was able, gifted and talented rolled into one.

'Joe, lie on your back.'

He rolled over, doing as she said, beads of perspiration on his forehead and his chest. He closed his eyes and gulped huge lungfuls of air. She swung her right leg over his body and positioned herself on top of him. She shifted her hips and guided him inside her again. She lowered herself onto him, crying out as he thrust upwards, taking her by surprise, feeling him so deep inside her, it almost hurt. But the pain was a rousing pain – exhilarating, explosive – she felt as though a million tiny electrical impulses were coursing through her body. She felt on fire.

Joe grabbed her buttocks and squeezed them hard, pummeling her flesh with his powerful hands. Lorna's fingers pulled at her nipples as she gyrated her hips. Joe went into meltdown. He gazed up at her, enraptured, and his breathing became rapid, his thrusting harder and faster.

'Lorna... he rasped. 'I'm...'

Lorna reached forward and clasped both his hands in hers, shifting her weight forward, relying on his strength to hold her. She threw her head back, her beautiful hair cascading down the curve of her spine.

'So am I...'

Joe wrapped his arms around her and she rested her head on his chest. She stroked his smooth, damp skin and he kissed the top of her head. The room was quiet and still and outside night had fallen. Somewhere in the garden, amongst the trees, a lone, predatory owl was on its twilight quest for food, it's haunting cry echoing through the darkness.

In the half-light, Lorna studied the profile of Joe's face. She watched as he blinked, his eyelashes long and thick, framing the pools of sea green she so badly wanted to gaze into for a lifetime. She could hear his breathing and watched the rise and fall of his chest as it mirrored hers, their heartbeats calm and thudding methodically in time with one another. They kissed again. This time it was tender and loving – a kiss that cemented their mutual attraction for one another, a kiss that confirmed what just happened, should have happened.

'That was… like nothing I've ever experienced before,' he whispered, breaking the silence.

Lorna felt a rush of blood to her head as it dawned on her that she had just taken Joe's virginity. It seemed incredible that he, at the age of twenty-four, and looking the way he did, had never had a sexual partner before. So many questions filled Lorna's head, stacking up one by one, each one more pressing than the last. She wanted to know more. She wanted to know how he knew what to do. And how old he actually was. And how he'd got such a horrendous wound to his chest. But now wasn't the time. She had plenty of opportunity to ask him all the questions she wanted answers to later.

'You were amazing… You made me feel amazing. I… I can't believe I was your first…' she whispered.

She knew it was wrong to doubt his claim that he'd never had sex before but she couldn't help herself.

'Why can't you?' he said, tightening his embrace and rubbing his nose on her temple.

'I don't know. I suppose it's quite rare these days to get to your mid-twenties and still be a virgin. And, Joe…' she shifted up onto her elbow and looked into those mystical eyes of green. 'You are the most beautiful man I've ever seen. You could have anyone.'

Joe looked embarrassed and blushed deep crimson.

'I'm not… and I haven't.' He lowered his eyes and started to play with the pentacle resting upon her décolleté.

'I've just never met the right girl before.'

'Have you ever had a girlfriend?'

'Yes, of course I have. I've taken girls out, on dates and things, but I've never had a serious relationship before. And I was brought up to wait until I met the right girl… you know, before going further with anyone.'

Lorna's heart somersaulted. That must mean she was the right girl. He'd chosen her, above all the other girls! And there must have been a pretty long orderly queue lining up for him. She wanted to sing from the rooftops.

'I'm glad you waited. I'm glad that girl was me.'

Joe kissed her and as he did so, his fingers trailed gently across her pale, naked breasts, across her abdomen, circling her navel and lower. Much lower. Lorna gasped with pleasure as he started making love to her again.

'Now I've got you, I'm not going to let you go. Ever.'

FIFTEEN

WHEN LORNA WOKE the next morning, Joe was gone. There was no trace of him in the flat. Not that he'd turned up with much – just the clothes he stood up in. There was no note explaining his departure either.

Lorna wandered from room to room, checking that he wasn't in the loo or making a cup of tea. But no. He'd definitely gone. The door key lay on the doormat, as though he'd just got up, dressed and left, locking the door behind him and pushing it through the letterbox.

She walked back to her bed, sinking down onto the soft, springy mattress, and looked at the pillow, where just hours before, Joe lay peacefully asleep. She ran her fingertips across the white cotton pillowcase and then drew her knees to her chest and hugged them tightly, her eyes rapidly filling with tears of dismay.

She'd met bastards before. Only a handful, but they were still there nonetheless – part of her distant past, faces now blurred, names forgotten, but their shadows still lurked in her memory along with a dirty, shameful feeling that never really went away. The worst part of a one night stand was the humiliating realisation that someone you'd genuinely liked, had used you just to get their leg over.

But she never believed for a single minute that Joe would spend all night shagging her – no, it was more than that – making love to her, and then upping and leaving without so much as a kiss goodbye.

She made a cup of tea and took it back to her bedroom. She felt despondent. With each sip of scalding, sweet tea she felt as though a lead balloon was sinking down painfully slowly from her throat to the depths of her stomach. She reached for her phone and glanced down at the screen. There were three unread texts from Rose, Lorna and her dad.

Rose's text was typical Rose. All it said simply was enjoy yourself. Evelyn's message was Evelyn through and through.

< Don't do anything I wouldn't... lol... and don't forget to wear a jonny. Him. Not you J X >

The text from her Dad, however, warmed her heart.

< Hello darling. Tried calling but your phone was off. I'm sure you're ok and having a lovely evening. Just to let you know your potion did the trick and I feel fighting fit once again. You are a good girl. And very clever! Your mother is out tonight with the ladies so I'm going to watch the Lottery and an Audience with Simon Cowell. Even though I can't stand the bloody man. Anyway, hope you are well and see you soon. Love you lots. Dad xx' >

It always made her smile when he signed his texts with the word Dad. Just in case she didn't know who he was. She replied, telling him she was glad he was feeling better and that she would pop round soon. She didn't mention Joe. Some things were too private to be shared with parents.

Her texts to Rose and Evelyn were of a very different tone and after she'd tapped the long, rambling message into her phone, she read it back to herself and promptly burst into tears. She pressed send and within minutes Evelyn's name flashed up on her mobile.

'Hello?'

'Hello babe. So he did a runner, did he…?'

Lorna sighed.

'I'm not sure I'd call it a runner, Evelyn. I woke up and he'd gone. We had such a lovely time last night as well. He's like nobody I've ever met before. We ate dinner, we danced…'

'Danced? What to?'

'What do you mean, 'what to'?'

'What to? Do you mean a slow dance or what?'

'Yes, you idiot. We're hardly going to start doing the Night Fever routine in the middle of the living room are we?'

Evelyn laughed.

'Blimey. A slow dance. That's a bit Mills and Boon, isn't it?'

'Evelyn, you are the most unromantic person I know. I didn't expect you to get the whole slow dance thing.'

'Carry on… what happened after that.'

'We went to bed. And we did it. And I was his first.'

'AY? His first WHAT? His first partner?'

'Yes.'

'Fucking hell! You bagged yourself a virgin?'

'Evelyn! You sound like a bloke.'

'Was he crap?'

'No! Of course not…' she said, suddenly overcome with shyness. 'He was the best I've ever had.'

Evelyn tutted.

'Hmmn… obviously lying then.'

'I don't think he was lying, actually… he was so nervous before we got down to it. He said he was brought up to respect women and he'd waited for the right girl to come along before doing it. And I believe him.'

'So you're the first girl he's ever met that he's done it with? How old is he? 15?'

'No! Shut up! I don't know exactly how old he is... about 24, 25?'

'How can you not know how old he is? Haven't you asked him? He could be a teenager for all you know but just looks older!'

'Course he's not! You can just... tell...'

'I dunno, Lorna. It all sounds very odd to me.' She fell silent for a moment. 'Anyway... you woke up, after this amazing night of passion, and he was gone...'

'Yes. He'd locked the door and pushed the key through the letterbox. I found it on the mat. He didn't leave a note or anything.'

'Have you checked? He hasn't got a phone either has he, so you can't call or text him. Jesus, Lorna – you do pick 'em.'

Lorna ignored her.

'Anyway, are you about today? I've got to pick up a job lot of cat food and half a ton of litter tray stuff from that big new pet place in town. I'll drop by afterwards if you're in.'

'Yeah, I'm here. I need to clean the flat and get my washing done.'

'Ok. See you later. Probably about two ish.'

'Alright. See you then.'

LORNA DRESSED, ate breakfast and set about cleaning the flat. She threw the windows wide open, welcoming in the sweet smell of fresh morning air and the comforting peal of church bells. Their ringing evoked memories of Joe and the night before. She imagined him up at the church, hoe in hand, getting on with his work. There must be a valid reason why he'd left this morning without waking her. Maybe a gut instinct told him to get back to Alice. Maybe he felt guilty for leaving her in the first place, seeing as she was so ill. She was sure there was a logical explanation, although when that explanation would come to light was another matter.

She had no idea where he lived, how to get in touch with him or anything. She would have to sit and wait for him to make contact first. Which would be difficult. She had no doubts he wouldn't get in touch but the waiting would be unbearable. She was desperate to see him again. The emotions he stirred in her were too strong to enable her to switch off and casually get on with life until he reappeared. She loved him. It was as simple as that.

She swept, scrubbed, polished and bleached the flat until it looked and smelled like it did the day she moved in. She even washed down the walls and the skirting boards and feather-dusted away all the cobwebs that floated like wisps of candyfloss in hidden corners of every room. She emptied the bins, removed the fading flowers from the vase in the living room and replaced all the candles that had burned down to puddles the night before.

As she ran the hoover around the bed – the same bed in which she'd lay with Joe just hours before, swathed in linen she couldn't bear to change – she didn't notice the handwritten note lying on the floor on the side of the bed where he'd slept. The stream of air from the cleaner's motor blew the note even further underneath the bed so it was totally out of sight. A torn scrap of paper on which Joe's slanted, old-fashioned handwriting told her the sun was rising and he needed to go back home to make sure his sister was alright. The note in which he told her he would be back for her in two days time. And how beautiful she was and how he'd cherish that night forever. The note in which he told her he loved her.

Lorna unplugged the hoover, wheeled it out of the room, and closed the bedroom door behind her.

The buzzer sounded in the hall. Lorna released the lock on the downstairs door and Evelyn made her way up to the flat. She unslipped the chain from the lock and opened the door and waited for her friend to appear.

Evelyn looked fantastic. Not many women could wear black skinny jeans slung from the waist, a torn white vest, black flip flops, an armful of tattoos and what looked like a tangle of chains around her neck and look totally stunning. She'd carried out her word and dyed her peroxide blonde hair baby pink again.

Lorna wondered, in the nicest possible way, what Rupert saw in her. Evelyn was so far removed from the type of woman he normally socialised with but perhaps that was the attraction. Her dry and intensely wicked sense of humour, combined with the fact she looked like she should be the front woman of a notorious punk band, obviously stirred something in his loins. Her nonchalant trick of playing hard to get only added fuel to the fire and he was desperate to claim her as his own.

Evelyn grinned, her wide mouth revealing the sexy gap between her two front teeth. She draped her arms around Lorna and hugged her.

'Have you heard anything?'

Lorna closed the door and they walked through to the living room where Lorna had already placed two mugs of tea on the coffee table.

'No. Not a dickie bird. But apart from turning up on my doorstep, I'm not going to, am I? He's not got a phone…'

'Still can't get over that,' Evelyn butted in.

'… and no landline. Well, not that I know of. I don't even know where he bloody lives.'

'I thought you said he lived in Lutton?'

'Yeah, he does. But even though Lutton is miniscule, I don't know exactly where his house is.'

'I bet Rupert does.'

'Do you think so?'

'No, of course not… I mean, his parents are only Lord and Lady of the Manor! They practically own all of Lutton, and half of Casworth as well. Of course he'll know him! I'll ask him when I see him tonight. What's Joe's surname?'

'I don't know.'

Evelyn pretended to scream and pull her hair out.

'Lorna! You are fucking useless! You've slept with this man and you know fuck all about him!'

'Stop swearing. It's not very lady-like.'

'No and neither am I.'

'You might be one day,' she muttered.

She sighed and took a sip of tea.

'There can't be that many Joe's in their mid-twenties with a sister called Alice in Lutton, for god's sake. We'll find him. Don't you worry. I'm on the case.'

Lorna nodded woefully and drank her tea. She suddenly put her mug down and looked at Evelyn .

'Oh! I knew I had something else to tell you! Somebody called from Lutton Hall last week and booked me to do the flowers for the Summer Ball!'

Evelyn raised her eyebrows.

'How funny! Did you politely decline and explain that you're frightfully sorry, but you are a guest at the ball and not a domestic?'

Lorna smiled.

'Of course not! I bit their hand off. They're paying me nearly a thousand pounds! Mind you, it's going to almost kill me to get the job done for next Friday – on top of everything else I've got to do next week.'

'Have you asked Joe to be your plus one?'

'No, not yet. For some reason, the Ball clean slipped my mind last night...'

'I bet it did. You dirty cow. Did you use a condom?'

'I think you mean did we use condoms, don't you? Emphasis on the plural?' she replied with a cheeky grin.

Evelyn mocked a look of utter shock.

'You did it more than once? At your age? I thought only teenagers could manage that!'

Lorna continued sipping her tea.

'I'm saying nothing... and no. We didn't use anything. I had this perverse notion that if we used a condom we wouldn't really be having sex? Like it would be a barrier between us? Is that very stupid?'

'Extremely stupid. What if he...'

'I'm sure I'll be fine. I've only just finished my period. So I'm pretty sure I can't get pregnant this week. And seeing as he was a virgin... he's hardly going to be riddled with

201

syphilis, is he?'

Evelyn sighed.

'You are a law unto yourself… and a complete fucking nutcase.'

The buzzer in the hall suddenly sounded, startling the two women. They stared at each other motionless.

'Are you expecting anyone?'

Lorna shook her head and looked puzzled.

'No… nobody. Unless it's Joe…'

'Oh god, please let it be Joe! I want to see if he's a good looking as you say he is!'

Lorna leapt up from the sofa and practically ran to the hall.

'Hello?'

'Absolutely ridiculous, these buzzy things. I bet she can't even hear me, even if I shout into the damn thing. Why she couldn't have bought a proper house, I will never know. I hate flats. It must be a nightmare to carry all your shop…'

'I can actually hear you mother!' yelled Lorna down the tannoy. 'I'll let you in.'

She looked over her shoulder at Evelyn in the living room and grimaced.

'I hope she was talking to my father out there and not standing on the street, prattling away to herself.'

Evelyn made a face. She didn't much care for Jilly. She found her very snobbish and opinionated and much preferred, as Lorna did, her father Phillip.

Lorna opened the front door to thankfully see both parents standing on the doorstep.

'I wasn't expecting to see you today!' she said cheerfully –

glad at least to see her father looking so well.

Jilly air-kissed both her cheeks and dumped a carrier bag into her arms.

'What's this?'

'Just a few bits and bobs. Some veg from Ted next door's allotment and an apple pie your dad made.'

She prodded her stomach with a bony forefinger.

'You need fattening up.'

Lorna's eyes glided from her mothers to her fathers and over to Evelyn's.

'You sound like the witch from Hansel and Gretel. I'll put the kettle on, go through to the living room – Evelyn's here.'

Jilly's neck jerked like a demented hen.

'Oh! Oh! What a lovely surprise!'

She scuttled into the living room and stooped to air kiss Evelyn.

'Hello dear. Ooh, your hair is rather 'out there'! I thought you worked in a school?'

'I do. But I'm a cook not a teacher. And I have to wear a hat at work,' replied Evelyn matter-of-factly.

Jilly sniffed and sat down on the sofa.

'Hello my love. You look well,' said Phillip, as Evelyn stood to hug him.

'So do you, Phillip. Lorna tells me you've been really poorly.'

'Oh, just a touch of flu. Nothing a bit of rest and a few brandy's couldn't fix.'

'I'm just relieved he's not moping about under my feet all day long anymore,' moaned Jilly.

Evelyn embraced him. She wished she had a dad. She didn't

even know who her dad was. All she had was a name in black ink on her birth certificate. Phillip was such a wonderful dad as well. Always there for his daughter, no matter what. She was jealous of their relationship. She'd never had a father figure in her life at all. Her mother married a man she met at work when Evelyn was six years old. But he turned out to be a gambler and a drinker and bled her dry. She kicked him out a year later and vowed to never get involved with another man again. And she didn't. She found comfort in a friend down the road called Liz and they moved in together. It was a huge scandal at the time – the talk of the village. And Evelyn suffered very badly because of it. She was bullied throughout primary school and couldn't wait to leave. Secondary school was much better. It was a large comprehensive in town and she became anonymous. Nobody knew her and that's the way she liked it. It was only after she'd left school, and won a place at a prestigious catering college, that she really came into her own. She formed friendships with people like her – loners, social misfits and the misunderstood – and she had the time of her life. As she matured, she came to understand and be glad that her dire childhood was responsible for the adult she was today – it had shaped her into a strong, assertive, colourful and above all, free-spirited woman. And she wouldn't want to be anything else. She even forgave her mother for becoming an overnight lesbian. She and Liz had given her everything she'd ever needed – a warm, secure, loving home – and for that she was eternally grateful.

'I love your hair,' Phillip added with a wink.

Lorna came into the living room with a tray of tea and cake. She topped up her and Evelyn's mugs and poured her parents a fresh cup each.

'Did I tell you Evelyn is going out with Rupert Barrington, mum?' Lorna asked mischievously.

Evelyn knew exactly what she was doing.

Jilly recoiled from the tea tray as though she'd been bitten by a viper.

'As in one of the Barrington boys? From Lutton Hall?'

'Yes! Isn't it wonderful? We're all going to a ball together at the Hall next weekend, as Rupert's guests.'

'Who is 'we?" spluttered her mother, desperately trying to chew carrot cake and talk demurely at the same time.

'Rose and her new man. Me and Joe…'

'Oh. Right. So, you're still seeing the gardener then?'

Lorna noticed her dad giving Jilly the look he always gave her when she was about to kick off.

'Yes, mum. Joe. That's his name.'

'Hmm. Are you going to attend a Ball at the Barrington's with pink hair, Evelyn?'

'Yes. Rupert loves it. And I'm going to wear a strapless, backless ballgown that shows off all my tattoos. Especially my pentacle one.'

Phillip grinned from ear to ear and Jilly shifted uncomfortably in her seat.

'What is it with these pentacles? Lorna has one around her neck, you have one on your arm, Oriel wore them all the time… are they in fashion or something?'

'Something like that, yes,' nodded Evelyn, taking a huge bite of cake and glancing sideways at Lorna.

Lorna dug her nails into the palms of her hand to prevent herself from laughing. Jilly had no idea what a pentacle was, let alone what it stood for and who wore them. Phillip, of course, knew exactly what they were. Just as he knew the two young ladies sitting before him were witches. He also knew Rose was a witch and that Oriel was one too. When she was alive.

Lorna glanced at her father and caught his eye. For a split second the smile faded from his lips, his eyes clouded and his brow furrowed. But then he winked at her and he was dad again.

'Ah, I miss all the parties Oriel and Roger used to hold. We had some fabulous times with them, didn't we Phillip? That beautiful house of theirs, the garden, the pool… goodness! And what terrific hosts they were. Always the very best food, the very best wine. Do you remember the time they had that gigantic firework display at the end of their summer barbecue? Professional display fireworks they were. Huge, great things. It must have cost them an absolute fortune.'

She shoveled more cake into her mouth.

'Yes. They were good times. I'm glad Lorna introduced us to them.'

'Do you still hear from Roger?' asked Evelyn.

'Occasionally,' replied Phillip. 'You know he retired after the funeral, don't you?'

Evelyn nodded.

'Well, he rented the house out and bought a boat and the last postcard we had from him, ooh, round about Easter time, he was sailing around the Med.'

'Lovely… what a life!'

'It's been a year now, you know,' Jilly chipped in.

'Yes. We were only talking about it the other day, weren't

we Lorna? This last year has flown by.'

'Do you visit her grave much?'

'Not really, no. I always think graves are... well... odd places.'

'How do you mean?' asked Jilly, jabbing at cake crumbs with her finger and licking them off.

'Well, I kind of think once you're dead, you're dead. Ok, you have to be buried – or cremated – so you have to be stuck somewhere. But it's not you down there in the ground. Or in the urn. It's an empty vessel than no longer contains your soul. You don't exist anymore. Why visit a grave when all that is there is a patch of grass and a bit of stone with writing on it. Seems pointless. I'd rather remember the person they once were.'

'That's a very strange way of looking at things, Evelyn!' gasped Jilly. 'Your loved one's remains are there! Surely that is reason enough to visit a grave?'

'I don't agree with you at all. Nobody is there! I hate churches as well. Religion brainwashes people. It only ever causes evil...'

'Goodness gracious...'

'Any more tea, anyone? Cake? There's loads left...'

Lorna interrupted the conversation swiftly and put a halt it before it developed into a full-scale war. Phillip calmed the situation further by diverting the topic of discussion to the warm weather they'd been having recently and how he and Jilly were planning a trip to the little holiday cottage they'd bought last year to make the most of the sunshine.

Evelyn made her excuses and left shortly after. She hugged Lorna at the door and whispered in her ear.

'Sorry babe… nearly lost it there. God, she's a pain in the arse.'

'Yep. And she's my mother. Lucky me.'

'Let me know if you hear anything from Joe. And I'll see you in the week sometime.'

'Ok. I will do. Thanks for coming round. I'll ring Rose later.'

Lorna's parents chatted a little more and then announced they needed to make a move so they could get the Sunday dinner on. Or rather Phillip had to make a move so he could get the Sunday dinner on. Jilly would lie in the bath for an hour, with a glass of wine, an anti-ageing firming mask plastered all over her face and Radio Two on. She said all four things kept her young. At times, she would even sing along to the music. Which in itself was worse than listening to a drowning cat.

LORNA WAS RELIEVED to have her flat back to herself. She cleared away the tea things and after an early shower and a jacket potato in front of the tv, she took herself off to bed. She lay on the side Joe had slept on and hugged his pillow to her chest, burying her face into the pillowcase and breathing in the scent of him that still lingered on the soft, white cotton. Delicious, intoxicating and uniquely him.

She wondered where he was right now. Surely he must be at home. It was Sunday evening. She doubted he was sat in the pub or out with friends. He'd be at home, looking after Alice. She wondered if he was thinking about her too. She checked again underneath the pillows and in between the sheet and the duvet, looking for a note – anything that could reassure her he'd not deserted her. But there was nothing.

She drifted into an uneasy sleep full of strange, muddled dreams featuring Oriel, sailing boats and carrot cake. And all the time, as she tossed and turned, through to the small hours when she finally fell into a deep slumber, Joe's note lay just inches away from her, resting on the floor directly beneath her head. Unread and gathering dust, his words of ardor calling out to her like the sough of lost souls on a bleak, restless wind.

SIXTEEN

AFTER SUCH A restless night, Lorna slept right through the jangling alarm clock and finally woke at nearly nine o'clock, which for her, was extremely late indeed. She had orders to place with the wholesaler and she really wanted to go to the Monday morning WI meeting. She knew most of the village's womenfolk would be there and something niggling away inside her wanted to gauge the reaction her attendance would cause.

Some of the women now blatantly ignored her in the street, scuttling to the opposite side of the road whenever they saw her walking towards them. Others maintained eye contact and said a polite, if a little brusque, hello as she passed by. And a handful of women – those who possessed the most open of minds – treated her as they always had, with good-mannered decency.

The meeting started at eleven o'clock so she needed to get a move on if she was going to get there in time. She flipped open her laptop and set about logging into her Flowers Direct account. Once she was in, she browsed and clicked her way through the entire weeks' plant and flower order, including the huge allocation of roses, lilies and greenery for the summer ball commission. The order was one of the biggest she'd ever placed and the final costing made her eyes water. She paid for the flowers by credit card – the arrow on the screen hovering reluctantly over the confirmation button for several minutes until she finally bit the bullet and clicked, sending the order and all her money flying off through cyber space to the Flowers Direct HQ in Guernsey. If the Barrington's cancelled now, she'd be in big trouble. Why, oh, why didn't she take a deposit from them? She mentally cursed herself and closed the laptop.

The village hall was adjacent to the church and a tree-lined, graveled lane ran off the High Street uphill to both buildings – the village hall on the left, the church with it's old, stone wall and towering cedar trees, to the right. Cars weren't granted access to this ancient and protected part of the village so Lorna travelled to the meeting on her faithful bicycle. Church Walk was a steep climb so she hopped off her bike half way and pushed it to the top of the lane, propping it up against the wall and leaving it unlocked, as usual. Nothing of any significance ever happened in Casworth, least of all petty crime.

Lorna inhaled the summery air. It always smelled so wonderful in this part of the village, with its' abundance of trees and blossoms and foliage. It smelled almost as good as her shop. She walked to the wooden gate that led through into the churchyard and pushed it open, surveying the jumble of graves and tombstones, looking for Joe. But there was nobody to be seen. Everything was still and quiet with the exception of an occasional, gregarious rook cawing in one of the treetops high above.

She turned and walked back across the lane and into the courtyard surrounding the village hall. It was a lovely, peaceful place. The villagers took great care of their communal spaces and the courtyard was full of lots of little pots containing herbs and plants and flowers, along with a couple of wrought iron benches painted white and a beautiful stone sundial, bought by the parish to commemorate the year 2000.

Lorna stepped inside the entrance hall and stuck her head around the kitchen door. A couple of ladies were inside filling a large urn with water and slicing up and buttering what looked like malt loaf. She walked through to the main double doors that led into the hall and peered through the glass panel to have a look inside. It was practically full, which was unusual. All at once and without warning, she wished she'd never come. Her presence at the meeting would only incite trouble and she had an overwhelming urge to turn around and leave the building as quickly as she could. She'd said her piece at the bakery the week before. That should have been the last of the matter. Coming here was a stupid idea. But before she could turn and run, one of the doors swung open and Barbara Claypole, a good-natured, friendly lady whose husband had recently passed away, burst through, almost sending Lorna flying.

'Oh, goodness me, dear! I'm so sorry! I didn't even see you standing there! Blind as a bat...'

Lorna rubbed her shoulder and smiled feebly at Barbara.

'It's all right. Serves me right for loitering behind swing doors.'

'Are you sure you're ok?' she asked, looking deeply concerned she might have hurt Lorna's arm.

Lorna nodded.

'Are you coming in, dear? We've a guest speaker about to start and I don't want you to miss it.'

'Oh? Who is it?'

'It's that Geraldine lady. The one from Gretton, you know, the one who came second in The Great British Bake Off last year? She's doing a talk on what it's like to be on the telly and how to bake the perfect loaf.'

'Sounds interesting,' replied Lorna, grateful that the meeting wasn't just the regular sit-around-and-have-a-cup-of-tea-and-a-natter-type affair. And the speaker wasn't talking about their collection of thimbles from 1725 to 1958.

'Mary Berry would have been much better but she's far too famous for the likes of us! Go on in and help yourself to tea and biscuits. Mrs Pollard has baked a batch of Cornish Fairings.'

Lorna sidled into the hall hoping to go unnoticed, but she immediately sensed a lull in conversation as she skirted around the side of the room and found herself a seat on the back row. She glanced around the hall fleetingly and then lifted her bag onto her knee and pretended to rifle through it, searching for some imaginary object. She'd already spotted Sue and Peggy and the women she'd layed into from the bakery. She suddenly felt very self-conscious and the back of her neck started to feel hot and prickly.

She put her bag down on the floor and shuffled over awkwardly to the tressle table positioned against the back wall of the hall. She made a cup of tea and helped herself to two of Mrs Pollard's biscuits. They were still warm and smelled delicious. Just as she was about to sit down, she felt a tap of her shoulder. Her heart leapt. Expecting to be engulfed in a cloud of putrid fag and coffee breath, she spun round, spilling half of her tea down her pretty floral dress, only to see Verity French beaming at her.

'Oh, it's you!' she gasped, breathing a huge sigh of relief.

'Who did you think it was going to be?' laughed Verity. 'You daft sod!'

Verity followed Lorna back to her chair on the back row and sat down next to her. She reeked of perfume, albeit the very expensive variety, and Lorna could hardly taste her tea for the intense aroma of musk, orange and neroli that overwhelmed her senses.

'Are they still being bitches to you?' Verity murmured into Lorna's ear, nodding her head towards nobody in particular.

Lorna shot her a sideways glance.

'It depends who you mean but, yes, kind of. It's sort of fifty, fifty. Some ignore me – at worse politely avoid me. And some are ok.'

'Stupid cows. Just ignore them. They'll soon find something or someone else to gossip about. It's usually me to be honest, so I'm glad you've given me a bit of respite,' she joked.

'Thanks,' Lorna replied, smiling weakly.

With that, Margaret Redhead, the chairwoman of Casworth WI, stood and introduced Geraldine Wheeler and the surprisingly entertaining and informative presentation began. It came to a close an hour and a half later with Geraldine having demonstrated several types of bread. The members tasted them all and Geraldine received a hearty round of applause for her efforts. During the tea break half way through the talk, a number of women made polite conversation with Lorna, some even going as far as laughing and joking with her, but she was acutely aware of the caustic huddle of hags towards the fringes of the group who were quite obviously talking about her. Every now and then one of them would look at her over their shoulder or she would catch sight of a shocked expression or a sneer on one of their faces. Verity stuck by her side the entire time and was a very welcome ally.

Afterwards, she gathered up her things and said goodbye to Verity. She had just about made it all the way to her bike, when she heard footsteps behind her on the gravel, followed by a familiar voice.

'Not so fast, sunshine.'

It was Peggy. Lorna watched as she flicked the top back on the packet of Silk Cut she was holding and placed a cigarette between her lips. She lit it and took a long, heavy drag, breathing nicotine deep into her lungs and exhaling between her yellowing, tar-stained teeth.

'What the hell do you think you're doing here?'

Lorna recoiled as a toxic cloud of cigarette smoke swirled around her head.

'Lovely...'

'What?' spat Peggy.

'I don't smoke.'

Peggy looked bewildered.

'Didn't you hear me? What are you doing here?' she repeated.

'I did hear you, Peggy. Sorry, I didn't realise I'd been banned from the WI. Nobody told me.'

'You haven't been banned... you've just got a nerve showing up here, waltzing in like butter wouldn't melt, laughing and joking as if you'd done nothing wrong!'

'I haven't done anything wrong!' snapped Lorna.

'You think? You're a witch! You're evil! You go against

215

everything that's good in this village!'

She took another long draw on her cigarette.

Lorna shook her head and suppressed a scornful laugh.

'Everything that's good in this village?' she echoed. 'And what exactly is good in this village, Peggy? People like you? Narrow-minded, insular, prejudiced people who have nothing better to do with their time than spread false accusations about other people? I've seen you all gossiping together like a load of old fishwives. You're pathetic.'

The adrenalin in her body made her heart race and her limbs begin to shake uncontrollably. Peggy's eyebrows shot up theatrically and her mouth opened wide as she gasped.

'How dare you speak to me like that!' she yelled. 'I'm a respected member of this community, old enough to be your grandmother. You nasty little cow. You're not wanted here anymore. Not you, your friends, or your shop! We don't want people like you in this village, meddling with the forces of nature, dabbling in black magic!' she screeched.

A small group of women had gathered near the village hall door. Lorna looked up at them and watched in disbelief as they all started to slowly shake their heads in silence. She didn't have to stand there and be intimidated by a pack of god-fearing, old women. She turned, and without saying a single word, walked out of the courtyard, closing the iron gate behind her gently. Inside her blood was boiling but her exterior conveyed an unperturbed calmness that infuriated Peggy all the more. Once out of sight, she leaned up against the wall and breathed deeply, gradually feeling her heartbeat return to a steadier rhythm and the beads of perspiration that drenched her skin dissipated and cooled her hot, clammy body.

'I need to find Joe,' she muttered to herself, leaving her bike leaning up against the wall and walking over the lane towards the church.

The graveyard was cool and shaded by trees that had stood for hundreds of years. The flagstone path beneath her feet was pale and smooth from centuries of footfall. She watched as two creamy butterflies flittered and fluttered a dance of courtship on the gentle breeze. All around her roses were in full bloom, their petals pristine and delicately scented, tinted every shade of summer, from peach to cream, lilac to yellow. She could sense Joe everywhere. She could see his handiwork in all directions – carefully trimmed hedges, manicured lawns, clipped bushes and straight, neat edging. There wasn't a single scrap of litter or solitary weed to be seen; the entire churchyard looked immaculate.

She ambled around the grounds alone, listening for the sounds of digging or mowing or another human being at the very least, but all was quiet. A sleepy kind of hush descended upon the graveyard and aside from intermittent bursts of birdsong, the only sounds were that of her own feet as she walked and the swish of cotton against her calves.

When she'd searched for Joe for at least twenty minutes, and without success, she reluctantly decided to make her way back to her bike and cycle home. She had jobs to be getting along with and they wouldn't get done if she spent all day hanging around graves.

Just as she stepped onto the gravel path that ran around the perimeter of the church, she caught sight of something out of the corner of her eye. She turned her head sharply to see a man sitting on a bench, his back to her, his shoulders hunched over. It had to be Joe. She couldn't quite see properly so she edged closer to get a better look. He was sitting in the shade but as she grew closer, she could see the man was old. She could tell by the way he was sitting. His back and shoulders were boney, his neck as scrawny as a chicken destined for the pot. It definitely wasn't Joe. Her heart sank and she started to tiptoe away from the man but he turned, almost intuitively, and saw her.

'Mornin'!' he called out.

Lorna smiled cheerfully and raised her hand to acknowledge him.

'Morning! Lovely day!'

'And long may it continue.'

'I hope so.'

'Not had a summer like this since I don't know when. Not this hot, like, since Easter and well into May. Unheard of.'

'No, I don't suppose we have. Last summer was awful.'

'It were a wash out. Nothin' went right. Growin', harvestin', frosts killin' everythin' off early and the rain finished off whatever did manage to grow.'

Lorna nodded in agreement, not quite knowing what to say. She walked closer to the bench out of politeness and to get a better view of him. He looked so old. She wondered if he was here, sitting quietly on the bench mourning somebody but then she noticed he had a shovel by his feet.

'Live round here, do ya?'

His accent was broad Fenland. The same accent Joe had, but Joe's was much softer, and at times hardly even detectable.

'Yes... yes... at the far end of the village. I run the florists.'

The old man looked at her with surprise.

'Do ya really? You don't look old enough to be runnin' a florists?'

Lorna smiled.

'Well, I am twenty eight... I'm quite the grown up now!' she quipped, smiling broadly.

The old man grinned a gappy, toothless grin.

'Girls these days look younger and younger. All that muck you slap on your faces. 'Spose it does do summat after all.'

Lorna took that as a compliment. She concluded women nearing their thirties in his day must have looked well past their sell by date.

'What about you? Do you live here?'

'Jeeees! I've lived here all my life! Man and boy. Worked in this graveyard since I were a nipper. Me father too, and me grandfather.'

He stood up slowly – Lorna could almost hear his bones creaking – and wiped his hand on his trousers, before thrusting it out towards her.

'Victor Freshwater.'

Lorna could hardly believe it. So this was Victor Freshwater! She smiled at him, her face the picture of surprise.

'Victor! I've heard so much about you! My name is Lorna. I am Joe's... a friend of Joe's.'

She placed her hand in his and he gave a firm, strong handshake in return. Not so creaky after all, she thought.

Victor eyed her warily.

'Friend of Joe's, hey?'

'Yes. We're... very good friends. I was just looking for him actually… hoping to catch him before I headed off home.'

'Ah. He's not about today. But he'll be around tomorrow though.'

'Will he?'

'Why do you ask?'

Lorna started to feel uncomfortable.

'No reason… I just haven't see him or heard from him for a couple of days. That's all.'

'You'll know Alice is very ill…'

Lorna didn't know if he was telling her or asking her but she wanted to find out more. She had to keep the conversation going, even if Victor scared her slightly.

'Oh yes, I know. Poor Alice. Joe's desperately worried about her. It's her heart…' she added nonchalantly.

'She's in a bad way, poor gell. I've known her since she were this high,' he said, gesturing to the level of his knee with his hand.

'Lovely family. Tragic the way the mother and father went one after the other like that. And now this. The last time I saw Joe he told me the next grave I would be diggin' would be for his Alice…'

Lorna was taken aback. She had no idea Alice was so ill. She'd assumed she was on some never-ending hospital waiting list, like thousands of others, patiently killing time until it was her turn to be poked and prodded and hopefully healed. Poor Joe must be at his wits end. She felt guilty for not having been a little more sympathetic when he'd talked of her illness.

'I'd like to pop by with some flowers. Do you know their exact address? I know they live in Lutton…' she quickly

220

added.

Victor eyed her suspiciously and shook his head. She had a feeling he knew exactly where Joe lived but for some reason wasn't willing to divulge any further.

'All I know is the old house is on Lover's Lane somewhere.'

He chewed thoughtfully on a long stalk of grass he'd wrenched from the ground and hummed a tune to himself.

Lover's Lane. How romantic, thought Lorna.

'Thanks. I'll find it.'

Victor nodded and continued chewing, gazing into the distance, lost in thought.

Lorna picked up her bag and slung it over her shoulder.

'Bye then. And thank you again.'

Victor didn't say a word. He just raised his hand and bowed his head.

She practically skipped back to her bike, immensely pleased with herself for finding out so much information about Joe. She'd spoken to his friend – a person who knew him and his family well. She'd found out, unfortunately, just how sick Alice was and now she knew exactly where he lived. Lover's Lane. It sounded idyllic. A rose-tinted vision of herself barefoot and pregnant popped into her head, picking apples and baking bread and waiting at the white, painted garden gate for Joe to come strolling home down Lover's Lane after a hard days work.

She dumped her bag in the basket on the front of the bike and started to pedal back to her flat. As she turned onto Main Street she could see Peggy and her clutch of cronies standing near the pub in a circle, arms folded, shaking heads, mouths opening and closing ten to the dozen. Lorna knew exactly what they were talking about. Peggy was clearly re-telling the account of the spat she'd just had with her in the courtyard. No doubt she was exaggerating it beyond all recognition and painting herself as the poor, defenseless victim.

As she rode by them, she put her hand in the air and waved.

'Morning!' she called cheerily, an enormous and extremely false smile on her face. She could almost hear their collective gasps as she cycled off down Main Street towards her flat.

But she didn't stop at the little gate leading to the alleyway down the side of the shop where she kept her bike. Instead she pedalled on, down to the bend in the road where the village signpost stood, across the junction, over to the lane that led to Lutton.

The hedgerows had sprung to life with the recent spell of hot weather. Flowery hawthorn tangled harmoniously with elder, blackberry and sweet briar and the air was warm and fragrant. Nettles, buttercups, cow parsley and meadowsweet grew in abundance alongside the verges and the joyful sound of birdsong reverberated all around her, making the ride to Lutton one filled with delightful anticipation.

She crossed the little stone bridge into the village and looked around her. There was no pub, no shop, no school. There was nothing to really go there for apart from if you so happened to live there. The houses were a mixture of old and new but all of them highly desirable. She didn't know the village at all. She'd only ever been there once or twice, on route to an idyllic, little picnicking spot down by the river.

She had no idea where Lover's Lane was but it sounded like the sort of place that had been named a long time ago so she figured it must be somewhere close to the oldest part of the village – that being the church.

She found it very easily. The lane to Lutton led to the hamlet, looped all the way around the houses and back out to Casworth again. There was one way in and one way out. She found the heart of the village – a collection of crooked, stone, thatched cottages – and here she found the church. It was small and unimpressive compared to it's majestic neighbour in Casworth but it was still beautiful. It had a simple hedge encircling it, a small bell tower, intricate medieval carvings all around its chancel arch and a mere scattering of archaic, crumbling gravestones.

Lorna dismounted her bike and looked at the building over the hedge. Lover's Lane must be close by. She spotted a small lane that ran alongside the churchyard. The house on the corner – a sturdy, stone cottage with a bright red post box inserted into the wall and ivy covering the entire front façade – indicated that this was the right place. Just underneath a first floor bedroom window, a white painted sign edged in black bearing the words Lover's Lane had been bolted to the wall.

The hairs on her arms stood to attention as goosebumps swept across her skin like an avalanche racing down a mountainside. Her heart beat a little faster as she looked down the lane, knowing Joe lived somewhere along its shady trail. She couldn't see any houses at all, just a dense arch of foliage either side of the road that merged in the middle creating a dark, leafy tunnel. Half way down, it seemed to veer off to the right. She didn't even like to guess where the lane led or how long it was. She seemed to remember cycling down there to go blackberry picking once when she first moved to Casworth. But she wasn't entirely sure it was the right lane. Her memory was sketchy at the best of times.

Instinct told her not to go any further. For the second time that day, she suddenly regretted her actions. She felt like a stalker. What if Joe suddenly appeared and asked her what she was doing here, lurking around the bottom of his road like a total weirdo? She looked around her sheepishly. For all she knew he could live in the house on the corner with the post box and the sign and was watching her right now from behind the half-drawn curtains. And what exactly was she going to say to him if she did see him? Hi there, you didn't leave a note or say goodbye the other night, so I just thought I'd cycle nearly two miles in the blistering heat to ask why? He would think she was mad and that would be the end of Joe.

She jumped onto her bike and began pedaling as fast as she could out of the village and back down the lane towards Casworth. She flew over the bridge, past the picture postcard cottages and out of Lutton, back along the overgrown lane and its shielding hedgerows. She breathed a sigh of relief and slowed down a little when she was within sight of the village. If he materialised in front of her now at least she could pretend she'd been for a bike ride, or some fresh air, a little exercise maybe. But he didn't.

Within minutes she was back home – hot, sweaty and in need of hydration. She cooled down in the cold store and drank a pint of water too quickly, giving herself hiccups. As frustrating as it was, she had no choice but to sit and wait for Joe to come to her. And he would. She knew he would. She could feel it in her bones.

SEVENTEEN

King James Bible. Exodus 22:18.
"Thou shalt not suffer a witch to live."

THE PIECE OF PAPER was stuck to the door of the florists with selloptape. It was a plain, white, rectangle sheet of paper and the biblical quotation was written in a strange watery, brown substance.

Lorna stood and stared at the message. She read it over and over again. She was starting to feel out of her depth. She reached up to tear it down, her hand shaking like a leaf. She glanced around her, looking up and down the road, but there was nobody around. She unlocked the door and went inside, slamming it shut behind her and locking it again quickly. She went to the window and peered out into the empty street, looking for signs of life. She had the feeling she was being watched but couldn't see a solitary soul.

She walked behind the counter and sat down, placing the note flat out on the table top in front of her. She gazed at it, her eyes becoming more and more hazy as they filled with tears. What made her saddest most was the fact that although ninety nine percent of the village now believed she was a witch – which in fairness was precisely what she was – they knew nothing about what she practiced and how peaceful and harmonious her craft was. She wasn't a bad person. She wasn't evil. Wicca was a way of life for her –

just as Christianity is to a church-goer – and she felt a better person for being part of it. But nobody else knew that about her. Or Rose. Or Evelyn. The villagers saw witchcraft as a terrible thing, profoundly immoral, dancing with the devil. In reality, all the three friends ever did was good. Together they cast love spells and incantations to cure sick friends and family. They concocted lotions and potions to heal and to enhance and they made charms to summon the sunshine and call upon the rain.

And now somebody was out to get her because of her beliefs. Maybe the note was the work of more than just one person. She had an inkling it was from Peggy but it could have been from anybody.

Her heavy tears landed on the counter top with a splash. She brushed them away with her hand and picked the note up again. It smelled peculiar. There was a strange odour emitting from the paper. She brought it closer to her face and sniffed at it tentatively.

'Jesus! It's shit!' she yelled.

She scrunched the note into a ball and hurled it over the counter onto the floor. She ran into the cold store where the tiny cloakroom was situated and promptly vomited into the toilet bowl. She was trembling all over and her eyes streamed with the onset of such violent retching. She pulled the chain and sat down forlornly on the toilet seat. She wiped her eyes and blew her nose, tossing the bundle of soggy tissues into the waste paper bin.

How could anybody do something so revolting? Her head reeled as she tried to think of what to do next. Should she report it to the police? Or would they just laugh at her and tell her to ignore it? It's not every day a woman gets a note written in shit pinned to her front door. She washed and dried her hands and walked back into the shop and picked up her mobile.

'Hi it's me.'

'Hello sweetness. How are you? Have you heard anything from lover boy?'

Lorna immediately dissolved into a flurry of tears.

'Goodness, whatever is wrong? Lorna? Lorna?'

Lorna heaved and sobbed for a few seconds, unable to speak lucidly. Eventually she regained her composure enough to tell Rose what had just happened. After an initial outburst of expletives, Rose regained her composure and returned once again to her usual cool, calm and collected self.

'Right. Now you listen to me,' she said sternly. 'You get that letter and you place it in an envelope and on the envelope you write today's date and the time you found it on the door.'

Lorna sniffed and reached for another handful of tissues.

'Why?'

'You're safeguarding yourself. You must keep it as evidence. Just incase you need it.'

'Ok. And then what?' she replied, stifling a sob.

'And then we will put a stop to all of this ridiculous nonsense. Once and for all! Tomorrow. Evelyn and myself will be round at eight. Don't worry about a thing, my lovely. This negativity is draining all of your positive energy and is making you ill. Forget about what happened this morning. Push it to the furthest reaches of your mind. Go freshen yourself up, go to that shop door and throw it open wide. Show the world you're afraid of nothing. And nobody.

Because you're not. You're Lorna. You are above all of this and you are far more powerful than they ever will be.'

Lorna started to cry again.

'I love you Rose.'

'As I love you. Now go and do as I said. And we'll see you tomorrow.'

LORNA LOOKED at her reflection in the mirror above the sink and swept powder and blusher over her face and slicked sheer coral lipstick onto her lips. She looked as bright as a button. She combed her hair and dabbed fragrant white musk oil onto her pulse points. Then, like an obedient child, she did as she was told.

She picked up the note, unfolded it and carefully slid it into an A4 brown envelope and wrote the date and time on the front in biro.

Then she strode confidently to the front of the shop and raised the electronic shutter in the window and opened the front door as wide as she could. She spritzed the inside of the shop with vanilla and set about moving pots of flowers and plants from the cold store out onto the little display area in front of the shop. She was still aware of eyes watching her every move but she showed no outward signs of being as deeply perturbed as she was. Quite the opposite. As the village sprung to life, she smiled and waved at passers by and folk popping to the shops for bread, milk or their daily newspaper. Villagers walked their dogs, children cycled to school, mums stopped to chat in the street. It was a picture of idyllic, everyday rural life, one that she hoped she was still very much part of.

JUST BEFORE LUNCHTIME, a Flowers Direct delivery lorry drew up alongside the shop. Lorna rummaged around underneath the counter to find her clipboard with this weeks order attached to it. She watched the driver jump out of his cab and stroll round the front of the vehicle and into her shop. She was expecting Peter. But this, most definitely, was not Peter.

'Oh! Hello! I thought Peter was back this…'

The tall, handsome stranger reached up to his ear and slid out the pen that was firmly wedged behind it.

'Not yet, no,' he interjected. 'He's taken an extra week off to spend with his wife and baby. He'll be back next week. So until then, unfortunately, you've got me.'

He looked at Lorna and grinned. He looked like the sort of man who could give a girl a good time.

'I don't mind that at all.'

He was very good looking. Not in the same league as Joe but welcome eye candy nonetheless. He was the opposite of Joe. Loftily tall, slim, blue eyed, blonde haired. He looked like he would be more at home on a surf board rather than clutching a clip board.

'So… is the owner about to sign for this lot?' he asked, tapping the order form with his pen and looking around him inquisitively.

Lorna found his question highly comical. First Victor and now the flower delivery man.

'I am the owner,' she replied, her eyes twinkling with amusement.

'You don't look…'

'Old enough?' she laughed, finishing his sentence.

He shrugged and grinned broadly at her.

'No. You don't. Most florists I meet are old – hang on, no… let me re-phrase that – most florists I meet are more mature ladies. And you don't look a day over twenty-one.'

Lorna raised her eyebrows and looked down at her outstretched hands on the counter top, feeling overcome with shyness all of a sudden.

'I'm a few years older than that, but thank you very much.'

He leaned in closer and looked her squarely in the eye.

'My pleasure.'

She felt slightly uncomfortable and cleared her throat a little too loudly.

'Now… where do I sign?'

She'd signed hundreds of delivery forms over the years. She knew exactly where to sign.

'Just there please… sorry, I didn't catch your name?'

'It's Lorna. And yours?

'Matt. Matt Coulson.'

'Pleased to meet you Matt Coulson.'

She scribbled her signature on the last page of the form and handed him the clipboard. He took it from her and shoved his pen back behind his ear.

'I'll start unloading. There's a lot of stuff in here,' he said, nodding towards the lorry. 'I hope you've got room for it all?'

'Yeah, I've got tons of room out the back. I'll show you where it all goes.'

Fifteen minutes later the cold store was full to bursting point. The sight of so many flowers unnerved her slightly as she remembered the huge amount of work she had to do that week.

'Right. I'll be off then. Everything you ordered is there apart from the palms – they'll be delivered next Tuesday. Something to do with a delayed shipment from the Canaries. But you saw all that on the footnotes, didn't you?'

'Yes, I did thanks. I've initialed it to say that's fine. I only ordered two of them to see if they'd sell. I've never sold palms before. If they don't sell, I'll have them for my flat!'

'Ah, you can't be doing that! That's like a landlord drinking away his profits!'

Lorna grinned. She thought about Kevin at The Vine in the village.

'I'm not quite that bad!'

'Didn't think so. You look far too sensible. Anyway, I've got to get another three loads delivered today so I'd better make a move.'

He walked towards the door but hesitated as he reached it and turned to glance at her over his shoulder.

'I don't suppose you're free one night are you? For a drink?'

Lorna felt quite touched. He was a nice enough lad, although not for her. She was done with loveable rogues.

'I'm sorry… I've just started seeing somebody,' she replied softly.

He pulled a hapless face and sighed.

'Bugger! Just my luck!' he muttered. 'Well, he's a lucky bloke. I hope he knows that,' he added, with a wink. Lorna smiled and Matt climbed up into his cab, waving at her as he pulled off down Main Street.

She sat down on the stool behind the counter and popped a few raisins into her mouth and chewed. She was expecting

Verity to call by at some point today. Today was order day. She didn't know whether to mention the note to her or not. Verity knew everything that had gone on so far but she didn't know there was any truth behind the accusations. Lorna would never divulge such information to anyone, regardless of who they were. It was a closely guarded secret. She got a kind of buzz from the surreptitiousness of being a witch.

She decided that when she saw Verity, she would tell her about the note written in shit. Verity knew everyone after all. She could indulge in a spot of discreet investigation, which could, with any luck, reveal the culprit.

Just as she was lost in thought, her mouth full of raisins and her finger entwined around several strands of hair, she was aware of somebody walking into the shop. She briefly glanced over towards the door and simultaneously felt her heart leap through her ribcage.

'Hello, darling,' whispered Joe with a shy smile.

He walked straight across the shop floor, around the side of the counter and threw his arms around her. She was so astounded by his sudden appearance she could hardly breathe.

'What... I... hello... I...' she stammered, her brain not engaging enough to enable coherent speech.

'I've missed you,' said Joe, kissing her gently. 'I know it's only been two days but it's seemed like a lifetime to me.'

'I didn't think I'd see you again.'

Joe looked confused.

'Why ever not?'

'Well, you know, you just left, without telling me... I woke up and you'd gone.'

His eyes looked sad.

'But I left you a note…'

She looked up at him, her stomach doing treble back flips. He was breathtakingly beautiful.

'You did…?'

He nodded slowly and stroked her hair.

'I didn't see it.'

'I left it on my pillow. It said I had to get back to check Alice. And it said thank you for such a wonderful night. And I'd be back in two days time. And…'

She held him tightly and kissed his velvety lips. He smelled like a delicious blend of freshly cut hay and fragrant, seasoned timber.

'It doesn't matter…' she interrupted. 'You're here now. And having you here means the world to me.'

There was a playful glint in his green eyes that she'd never seen before. He almost looked like the loveable rogue she was trying to avoid.

'Come on… let's do something!'

'Like what?' she laughed.

'I don't know… anything!'

'I can't! I'm working!'

'Well, stop working!'

'I can't!'

'You can…'

She looked through those eyes of green and into the soul inside. It was calling her name, goading her to run free, to throw caution to the wind.

'You're right. I can…'

She pushed him gently to one side and marched across

the wooden floor of the florist, pressed the button next to the light switch and lowered the shutter. She pulled the buckets and baskets and tubs in from outside and into the cold store, as Joe leaned back against the wall and watched with amusement.

'There. From this second on, I am closed for the day.'

She flipped over the sign on the door, closed it firmly and locked it shut.

'Come on! What are you waiting for?'

Joe laughed.

'I didn't think you'd do that, I must say. But I'm very glad you did.'

They held hands as they walked down the lane to the water meadows – the sky above them the colour of sapphires and the gently swaying trees that lined their promenade as verdant as emeralds.

When they reached the river, they crossed over the footbridge and followed its silvery, snaking path until they reached a point where it widened slightly on one side, creating a natural bathing pool.

'This is where the Roman's used to bathe, you know,' Lorna exclaimed.

'Really? How do you know that?'

'Oh I read it somewhere. Probably in the parish news. It shelves gently and is almost oval in shape, look. Like nature's own swimming pool.'

'Fancy a swim?'

'I haven't got my swimming costume with me!'

'We can go in in our underwear.'

Lorna eyed Joe.

'I do believe you're trying to lead me astray, sir...'

He grinned and started pulling off his shirt. Then he kicked off his boots, followed by his trousers. Lorna looked at his impeccable body, marred only by the ugly scar on his chest, and something stirred within her. She tore off her clothes and stood facing him in her underwear.

'I'm taking everything off.'

Joe didn't need to be told twice.

'Me too.'

He tossed his underpants onto the pile of clothes at his feet and led a naked Lorna into the cool, clear water.

'It's freezing!' shrieked Lorna, as she stood ankle deep in river water.

Joe waded straight in up to his waist. He caught his breath as he submerged his shoulders and swam gingerly across to his slightly more reluctant swimming partner.

'It's wonderful when you get in...' he gasped. 'Honestly, it's really not that bad.'

'Sounds like it! You can hardly speak! Right... I'm going to count to three!'

'Ok. Ready? One. Two. Three.'

Lorna plunged under the water and emerged looking like a beautiful water nymph – her long, red hair trailing across her translucent skin like slippery tendrils of seaweed.

Joe disappeared under the surface and Lorna felt his hands slide up her legs, over her buttocks and up either side of her waist. He appeared in front of her and flicked his hair out of his eyes, pulling her close to him, the invigorating scent of moss and minerals and rain enveloping them. He kissed her deeply, his tongue exploring her mouth and his breathing getting faster by the second.

She felt instant arousal as her hard nipples brushed across his chest. She could feel him pressing hard into her tummy. He scooped her up into his arms and she wrapped her legs around his waist. She became instantly weightless and he slipped inside her effortlessly. And there, in the middle of the river, they made love.

It was only afterwards, as they lay underneath a towering oak tree, wrapped in each other's arms, that it occurred to Lorna that anyone could have been watching them. The thought hadn't even entered her mind. Many people frequented the river every day, not just the locals.

'Do you think we were seen?'

'In the water?'

'Yes.'

'I don't think so. Not that I was paying much attention.'

Lorna groaned.

'Why? Are you worried about it?'

'A little bit, yes,' she replied. She thought of the ensuing scandal that was already engulfing her in the village. She didn't want any more.

Joe hugged her tightly.

'Nobody saw us. We were under the water anyway. There was nothing to see,' he reassured her, kissing her forehead and nuzzling her hair with his nose.

'Joe?'

'Hmm?'

'How did you get that scar on your chest?'

Her hand travelled up to where his scar lay beneath his shirt. He placed his hand on top of hers.

'I got shot.'

Lorna raised her head from his shoulder and looked at him intensely, her eyebrows furrowed, her senses heightened.

'You got shot?' she asked, staggered by this unexpected revelation.

'Yes.'

'When? How?'

'When I was a soldier.'

'A soldier? You never told me you were a soldier...'

Joe's face crumpled as he mentally relived his ordeal.

'The wound turned bad and I was discharged from the army.'

'I... had no idea you were even in the army?'

Joe nodded slowly and stroked her hand.

Suddenly, there was an almighty commotion above their heads and two agitated magpies swooped down from the branches of the oak tree and landed on the ground in front of them. They watched as the two birds scratched around in the dust looking for food. Dappled sunlight fell upon their ebony feathers, refracting metallic hues of intense purple and green.

'One for sorrow,' said Lorna.

'Two for joy,' Joe continued.

They looked at each other, interlocking their fingers, and grinned, both feeling ludicrously joyful.

'I've never been so happy, Lorna.'

Her head swam and the now familiar tingly, lovesick sensation radiated through her abdomen once more.

'Me neither,' she breathed. 'You're all I ever wished for.'

Joe shifted onto his side, propping himself up onto his

elbow. He stroked her face and gazed into her eyes.

'I love you,' he whispered.

Lorna's vision began to blur as she fought back a sudden onset of tears. She really didn't want to cry in front of him but those were the words she'd been longing to hear since the day she set eyes on him. He loved her. She could hardly dare to believe it.

'I love you too.'

EIGHTEEN

ROGER AND ORIEL'S large, eighteenth century house had a vast cellar. It was a warren-like network of four separate chambers, connected by short corridors, and had been hewn out of the soft local limestone for which the area was famous. It had pale, creamy stone walls and an intricately carved vaulted ceiling. Roger used the cavernous vault for the rightful purpose for which it was intended – to house his highly valuable collection of wine, champagne and port.

There was no easy way down into the cellar. The heavy trap door – in what used to be the old scullery – opened upwards and outwards to reveal a steep flight of stone steps into what was fondly known as The Abyss. Half way down the steps, a switch on the wall enabled the wonders of modern technology to flood the cellar with light and power and a complicated looking digital display panel at the bottom of the steps allowed Roger to regulate humidity and temperature. This ensured his precious collection remained in optimum condition and the whole intricate set up, which had cost a small fortune to install, was his pride and joy.

As Roger descended the precarious staircase, carrying a recently purchased case of Chateau Haut-Brion, Pessac-Léognan 1970, he immediately noticed a mark on the cellar floor. He wouldn't normally have paid much attention to insignificant details like that, but this mark – it looked like a red wine stain – had feathered into the oatmeal jute rug that covered most of the first chamber's floor and had made quite a mess.

He set the case of wine down on the sideboard that was positioned against the stone wall to his right and turned to look more closely at the mark on the floor. He never opened wine in the cellar. Ever. There was a huge American fridge next to the sideboard that housed numerous bottles of beer, which admittedly he did frequently open and swig whilst perusing and logging his dusty stash. But beer was pale gold in colour and most definitely not deep blackish red.

He knelt on the cold, flagstone floor and scrutinized the stain. The centre of the puddle was still a little tacky so he prodded at it with his index finger, raised it to his nose and sniffed. It smelled vaguely familiar, kind of metallic, like the vitamin syrup he was forced to take as a child. He possessed a good nose being a connoisseur of wine, but this smell baffled him. So he licked it. It was blood. And it was putrid.

He recoiled, feeling suddenly intensely nauseous. An icy trickle ran down his spine, making the hairs stand up on his arms and his entire body shudder. He shivered. How the hell had blood got into his cellar? He looked at the mark on the rug, and the way the stain had crept into the fibres of the jute, tainting it forever with something that had once flowed through a living thing.

The only other person who went down into the cellar was Oriel. And that was only occasionally, usually to hoik a decent bottle of red for the girls to quaff whilst watching some godforsaken rom com. But he had just seen her. All of ten minutes ago. And she certainly wasn't wounded. Or in pain. Or bleeding. Quite to the contrary! She was dolled up to the nines to go out to dinner with her gang – the ladies she'd befriended at the very first meditation class she'd taught in the town eight years ago.

Roger knew Oriel practiced Wicca. He'd always known. She'd been very open about her beliefs when she first met him, and in a strange kind of way, he enjoyed the thought of being married to a witch. She wasn't anything like he imagined a witch would be. She was educated, funny, charming, beautiful, and the most marvellous wife and companion any man could want. They were a team. She told him everything, as he did to her. There were no secrets in their relationship. Or so he thought.

His mind raced as he tried to figure out how blood, fresh blood, had got into his cellar. He tentatively looked above him at the cellar ceiling, just in case something was dripping through it and landing on the floor below. But that was a ridiculous idea. The vaulted ceiling was made of solid stone and at least three feet thick. Nothing could penetrate through that. Not even an entire abattoirs worth of blood.

He shuffled backwards on his knees and let out a deep, troublesome sigh. Something was very wrong. If Oriel was the only other person who had access to the cellar, then the blood must have something to do with her. There was no other explanation.

He ran his fingers over the stain on the rug. He'd never be able to get that out. It was ruined. He flipped the corner of the jute over to get a better look at how deep the stain was but immediately wished he hadn't.

Underneath the corner of the rug he saw two painted black lines that merged into a sharp point with another curved

241

black line running around the outside. He edged the rug back a little further, and then some more, his heart beating louder and heavier with each passing second. The lines continued towards the centre of the room and the border line was by now a semi-circle. He stood up and walked over to the opposite side of the rug and gradually rolled it back, rolling the rug into a long tight coil. It was only then that the artwork was fully revealed in all its glory. Emblazoned across the cellar floor, at least eight feet in diameter, was a huge, black, inverted pentagram.

Roger felt the blood drain from his face and his hands begin to tingle. He recognised the symbol immediately.

When he first met Oriel and she told him what she was, he researched it thoroughly and discreetly without ever telling her. He knew everything there was to know about Wicca. But his wife was a white witch. She only did good! It was all very harmless and quite charming, really. But this... this turned everything on its head. His wife wasn't who she said she was. She was living a lie. And, more gut wrenchingly for him, she had lied to him for all these years.

This ominous, black, blood-stained inverted pentagram was not a symbol of a peaceful, harmonious and, above all, good and wholesome way of life. It meant something far more sinister – a symbol of the dark side of Wicca, of black magic and pure evil. It meant only one thing. With one point facing downwards and two pointing up, many called it the sign of the cloven hoof. To Roger it was known quite simply as the footprint of the devil... an insignia of wickedness from which his wife – his clever, loving, devoted wife – worshipped Satan himself.

THE SICKLY, almost choking cloud of perfume hit Lorna before the source came into view. She glanced up from her notebook to see Verity striding across the shop floor in her gym gear.

'Hello you... and where were you yesterday, might I add?' she asked, somewhat accusingly.

Lorna lay down her pen and closed her book.

'I was ill. I closed the shop at mid-day and went home to bed. It's the first time in four years I've had to shut shop,' she replied as quick as a flash, hoping the blissfully loved-up look on her face didn't expose her as the complete and utter liar she was.

'Oh,' huffed Verity. 'Nothing serious I hope?'

'No, just an upset tummy from Monday night's dinner. A-bung-in-the-oven thing that I obviously didn't heat through properly.'

She was good at this lying malarkey.

'Feeling better now?'

'Oh yes. I feel great. I just needed lots of water and a good nights sleep.'

'Hmm. You still look a bit peeky. Mind you these things take a good twenty-four hours to get out of your system. You'll be back to normal by tonight.'

Cheeky cow, thought Lorna. I'm not even bloody ill.

'Right. I need to place my order. I hope you can still do it, seeing as you're a day out now?'

Lorna groaned inwardly. Verity's huge weekly order on top of the flowers for the summer ball didn't bear thinking about.

'Yes. Of course I can manage. I was only closed for half a day plus I am well stocked this week. Unless you want Blue Ginger again. I haven't got any of that.'

'Loved the Blue Ginger! But no. Something more simple this week please. We haven't got much on this weekend, amazingly. Only a simple family supper party. So, could I order your wonderful sunflower displays? Three of them please. Like the ones I had earlier this year. Lots of yellow and orange and green?'

Lorna laughed. Verity never was one for highly descriptive ordering.

'Of course. It'll be a pleasure. I'm getting fed up of everybody ordering roses and lilies all the time. People are very unimaginative on the whole.'

'Ha! Not me!' she laughed.

'No, not you,' giggled Lorna. 'I'll just put the order through.'

She set about filling in a customer order form and working out the cost of the displays while Verity browsed around the shop.

'Such a shame you couldn't make the party at the weekend. I was looking forward to meeting your new man,' she remarked, picking up a bottle of orange blossom body lotion, unscrewing the cap and sniffing it.

'Oh, I'm sorry Verity. We ran out of time, what with cooking and eating dinner, clearing away and everything. By the time we sat down to relax properly it was getting late.'

'I saw him today actually. Your man.'

'Did you?'

'Yes. Up at the church. He's a good-looking fella. Can't think why I've not noticed him before to be honest!'

'He is good looking,' replied Lorna pensively. 'He's... well, he's just perfect in every way.'

'My thoughts entirely!' cackled Verity. 'You lucky girl.'

'One Yorkshire or two?'

'Two please. I still can't believe you've cooked a roast dinner,' scoffed Evelyn.

'You're becoming quite domesticated, Miss Mills, aren't you?'

'Thanks Rose,' replied Lorna dryly, pouring gravy over the three plates of roast lamb and new potatoes.

They sat with their dinners on their knees in front of the television and ate in silence as they watched the latest episode of Eastenders.

'I don't know why I watch this rubbish,' muttered Evelyn as the title sequence rolled. 'It gets worse.'

Lorna cleared away their dishes and returned to the living room with a bottle of red wine and three glasses.

'So, when are you seeing him next?' asked Evelyn.

'Tomorrow night. He said he'd be back in two days time. I'm not sure why he can't just use the names of the days of week like anybody else.'

Rose glanced at Evelyn.

'Maybe he... er, doesn't know them?' She hesitated. 'Or something?'

'Don't be so bloody stupid! He's not a retard!' said Lorna crossly.

'I know that! It's just you've mentioned a few things about him before that sound a bit... quirky. That's all.'

'He's just unusual. And he's everything I could ever want,' she replied wistfully. 'I've fallen for him. He told me he loved me yesterday.'

'No! Did you tell you loved him back?' Evelyn shrieked in astonishment.

'Yes. Because I do.'

Rose and Evelyn looked at each other in amazement.

'Wow! That was quick.'

'You know when it's right though, Rose, don't you?' smiled Evelyn. 'I mean, you and twinkle toes must have said the L word to each other by now?'

'Actually no… we haven't. I'm not sure I do love him to be honest. He's alright but he has lots of peculiar little ways that irritate the hell out of me!'

'Welcome to my world!' laughed Evelyn.

'You're getting on with Rupert, aren't you?' asked Lorna, surprised.

'Yes, yes, of course. I just meant life before Rupert. Everyone I ever met before him irritated the hell out of me.'

'I seem to remember Rupert irritated the hell out of you when you first went out with him! You did a runner from the pub on your first date, I seem to recall!' roared Rose, taking a mammoth glug of wine.

'Yeah, he did I suppose. He's grown on me now,' she grinned. 'So, missy. Will we have the honour of meeting Joe on Saturday night?'

'I've not asked him yet. But I will do tomorrow. I promise.'

'Good. Now… where is this letter?'

Lorna looked glum and sauntered off to her bedroom to get it.

She came back with the large brown envelope and handed it to Rose.

Rose slid it out cautiously and grasped it in both hands, gazing down at the words from the bible depicted in excrement. She raised it to her nose and inhaled.

'Hmm,' she groaned. 'Just as I thought. It's not human shit, Lorna. It's cow dung.'

'WHAT? Cow dung? How can you tell?'

'I grew up on a two thousand acre farm remember. It's cow shit. And traditionally, in the olden days, the way to ward off a witch was by writing a biblical passage in cow dung on a piece of linen or parchment and nailing it to the said witches door.'

'So, whoever did this has done their research,' said Evelyn, taking the note from Rose and reading it.

'Yes. And they have access to cows. Do you know anyone who lives on a farm?'

Lorna nodded her head.

'Quite a few. The whole village is surrounded by farms and farm land but most of them are arable. I can't think of any livestock farms around here, apart from a few farmers with the odd field of sheep.'

Rose shrugged.

'I think there's only one thing to do, ladies,' she whispered, rising to her feet.

'The silencing spell?' questioned Evelyn.

'Yes. Let's get it done now and put a stop to this once and for all.'

Rose went to her bag in the kitchen and returned with a candle, a piece of slate and a small box. The three women knelt on the floor and bowed their heads. Rose opened the box and scattered marigold petals across the floorboards.

Then she lit the candle and gestured to the others to link hands to form a closed circle. She bowed her head and began to speak.

'If you place the Bible in the wind and the rain, soon the paper on which the words are printed will disintegrate and the words will be gone. Our bible is the wind and the rain,' she chanted softly.

She broke the circle and reached behind her to retrieve the note. She tore it in half and then in half again and held the squares of paper over the flame, scorching the scurrilous words until they were charred and black and burned to ash.

Then the three women took off their pentacle necklaces and began to swing the chains in a circular rotation. Slowly, steadily and in perfect unison with each other, the pentacles glinted in the candlelight like miniature pendulums.

Rose spoke once more, this time with intense fervency.

'Idle godsipp, womenfolk of this parish, be now silent. Let your bitter tongue be broken. Idle godsipp, womenfolk of this parish, be now silent. Let no evil words be spoken.'

The pentacles continued to rotate as the three witches raised their heads and looked skyward. All was silent apart from the gentle shushing sound each woman made with her mouth – a hush that would be carried by the wind to the lips of the scandalmongers, rendering them mute and unable to speak ill of Lorna ever again.

NINETEEN

LORNA GLANCED WEARILY at her watch. She hoped it told a different time to that of the old clock on the wall. But both said seven thirty. Dusk was falling outside and Lorna had been working continuously for twelve hours. She was very much aware that Joe was supposed to be calling by this evening but as she had no way of contacting him, she had no way of letting him know she wasn't at home and was still trying to finish the flowers for the Barrington's ball.

She'd had a bizarre day. She thought it would be one of those days that dragged by, void of all customers, slow and frustrating – the perfect day to spend concentrating on a commission. But she thought wrong. Today was full of people popping in and out all day long. Browsing, sometimes buying, placing orders, expecting a free cup of tea and a spot of idle chit chat.

The most unexpected event of the day was the appearance of Peggy. Lorna was more than a little surprised when she shuffled into the shop, a smile on her face as wide as the Thames estuary, wreaking of cigarette smoke and Tweed by Lentheric. All she did was walk up to the till, place a bunch of dahlias on the counter top, tell Lorna what a beautiful shop she had and how lucky they were to have her in the village. She handed over a five pound note and told her to keep the change – all fifty pence of it – rubbed her arm affectionately, gave her a cheeky wink and shuffled out of the shop again.

Lorna stared after her for what seemed like hours, finding it hard to believe just how swiftly the silencing spell had taken to work its magic. But it had obviously worked. Because later that day Sue from the bakery came in as well and bought a hanging basket and a bag of magnolia pot pourri. Barbara also popped by, purely for a natter and to give Lorna a dozen eggs courtesy of her ever-increasing brood of hens.

In between all of this social frivolity, Lorna managed to make up half of the table decorations for the summer ball. She figured if she worked into the evening she could finish off the podium displays too, which would leave ten posies remaining to assemble tomorrow.

That was until Joe popped his head around the door and gave her the fright of her life, particularly as she thought she'd locked it.

'I thought I might find you here.'

'God, you made me jump! I wasn't expecting you!'

'I told you two days ago I'd be here tonight! And here I am. I'm just sorry I couldn't get here any earlier. I was trying to coax Alice into eating something. It was like pulling teeth.'

Lorna wiped her damp hands on her apron and walked round the counter. She wrapped her arms around him and hugged him tightly. He looked very tired, there were shadows beneath his eyes and he looked so sad. She'd never seen him looking like this before. He was usually glowing with health, all scrubbed and shiny and immaculate, like a movie star working the red carpet.

'I needed that,' he whispered into her hair. 'I've missed you.'

'I've missed you too.'

She pulled away from him and placed her hands in his and looked into his sorrowful eyes. The glinting amber flashes had all but disappeared from the deep emerald green and they looked as grey and troubled as a dark, stormy sea.

'I'm worried about you,' she sighed, squeezing his hands.

He smiled weakly and squeezed her hands back.

'Don't worry about me. It's just been a long day. And I know we're not far away from... the end...'

Lorna's face crumpled.

'Don't say that. You must try to remain positive, Joe...'

He shook his head and frowned.

'There's no point in being positive. Everyone has to die one day,' he said dolefully. 'And now it's Alice's turn.'

Lorna breathed in a deep lungful of air and closed her eyes and sighed. Joe's words were so final, so melancholy. He had truly given up any hope of Alice ever getting well – that was only too clear. But it puzzled her how he could leave her alone at home if she really was so desperately ill, especially as he was leaving Alice alone to indulge himself in a brand new relationship – to be with her. She felt terribly guilty. What if Alice died and Joe wasn't with her? The thought made Lorna shudder. She wondered if she would ever meet Alice. She doubted she would but she decided to ask Joe if she could help in any way. Caring for her must be a huge burden on one so young. If she could be of any support to him, or to Alice, she would be there for them.

'Look. I've finished for tonight. Let's go for a walk. It'll do us both good to get some fresh air, some exercise. Have you eaten anything today?'

'No... I... I don't feel very hungry.'

'Don't be silly. You must eat. Or so my mother is fond of telling me anyway. I've got some bits and bobs that need eating up in the fridge. Let me nip back home, throw a picnic together and we can walk down to the river and eat it. It's still light and very warm. What do you say?'

For the first time that evening Joe smiled. And it was a big, happy smile that melted Lorna's heart.

'That sounds perfect.'

Lorna locked up the shop and closed the shutters and together, she and Joe walked the thirty yards or so to her flat. The communal front door was already open as Nicola and Joshua, who lived in the flat below Lorna, were just leaving the building to walk up to the pub.

'Hi!' said Lorna cheerfully. 'I've not seen you for ages!'

Nicola smiled widely and patted her tummy.

'I've been held prisoner in my bathroom – the worst five weeks morning sickness ever!'

Lorna shrieked with excitement.

'Wow! That's amazing news! Congratulations!' she said, kissing them both on the cheek.

She glanced over at Joe and he smiled and nodded at the expectant couple shyly.

'When are you due?'

'November. Gives us something to look forward to as winter draws in. Christmas will be very different this year! And I apologise in advance for the all the noise this little one will make!'

'Won't it just! And don't be daft! The walls are so thick – I won't hear a thing! I'm so pleased for you.'

'Thank-you. And how are you? Everything ok? Shop

always seems busy?'

'Going great thanks. I'm rushed off my feet at the moment. I'm doing the flowers for the Barrington's summer ball – you know, the family from Lutton Hall?' she asked.

They nodded and she looked again at Joe.

'But the perk is we get to go to the ball – Joe, I've got to talk to you about that – as well as getting paid, so it's a job worth doing. Even if it means I sleep all day Sunday!' she said with a wink.

Nicola and Joshua glanced at each other and then at Lorna.

'That sounds great. Right, well… we'd better get going then. Josh still likes his beer even if I'm now restricted to lemonade! Good to see you!'

'You too. And good luck with everything.'

Lorna and Joe walked into the entrance lobby.

'You may as well stay here, Joe. I'll run up and grab a few things and be down in a minute. Oh and watch out for Peggy,' she added in a whisper. 'She came into the florist today and was actually nice to me!'

Joe pulled a face at Peggy's door, which sent Lorna into a fit of the giggles.

She raced upstairs and grabbed a hessian shopper and threw in all sorts of things – a half eaten quiche, a tub of potato salad, a pack of chicken drumsticks, a baguette, brie, grapes, a couple of very ripe peaches and a bottle of chilled white wine. She added a handful of napkins, two plastic wine glasses, two picnic plates, a sharp knife and forks. It was a feast fit for a king. And his queen. And she was ravenous.

Joe was waiting for her at the foot of the stairwell, gazing up at her as she positively flew down the steps two at a time.

'You are amazing.'

'Me?'

'Yes! You!'

'Why am I?'

He leaned forward and kissed her tenderly.

'Because I say so.'

They walked down the lane hand in hand – the hedgerows still wide awake with birdsong and bees and butterflies, the sky the colour of lilac in springtime. Every now and then a rabbit would hop out of the undergrowth, turn to look at them in astonishment and disappear again into the safety of the brambles.

'It's such a lovely evening. Isn't summer magical?'

Joe looked around him, immersing himself in the beauty of the surroundings and the warmness of the still night air.

'It is. It's my favourite time of year. I love spring, how everything spontaneously bursts into life. And autumn for its' changing colours, the harvest... oh, and the clear night skies. But I hate winter. The ground is so cold. So hard. And it seems to go on forever.'

They reached the river and headed for the grassy patch by the lock and sat down underneath an ancient, gnarled apple tree that had stood there for centuries, bearing fruit that the local's scrumped every September and made into crumbles and pies and sauces. Lorna shook out the old tablecloth she'd brought with her to sit on and laid it down on the grass. She unpacked the bag and placed all the food in the middle of the cloth.

'This looks wonderful Lorna,' said Joe, his eyes roving over the lavish picnic Lorna had so effortlessly thrown together.

'Well, it all needs eating up so I suggest we get started!'

She uncorked the wine and poured Joe a glass. They piled their plates high and drank the buttery, rich, ice-cold Chardonnay.

Their stomachs full and the picnic devoured, they lay back beneath the tree, Lorna's head resting in the crook of Joe's arm, and gazed up through the branches to the violet sky beyond.

'Hand me that knife.'

Lorna looked alarmed.

'What on earth for?'

'You'll see,' he laughed, scrambling to his feet.

He walked up to the trunk of the apple tree and began hacking away at the bark.

'What are you doing?'

'Making us permanent. Don't look!'

He continued to carve away at the tree trunk – his body shielding his handiwork from view, keeping Lorna guessing. When he finally moved to one side, she gasped with delight.

She trailed her fingertips across the rough, mossy bark of the age-old tree and around the edges of the heart shape that was now deeply engraved into the wood.

'J.H + L.M,' sighed Lorna. 'You carved our names into a tree.'

She turned and smiled at him.

'You did that for me! You are so romantic. That will be there forever.'

'That was my intention.' He reached for her hand and kissed it gallantly, like a prince to his princess. 'Come on, let's dance.'

Lorna cocked her head to one side and frowned.

'Here?' she giggled. 'The wine's gone to your head.'

Joe grinned.

'It has not! Come on! You're getting good at dancing and anyway... it's romantic. Me, you, the river, the sunset.'

'We haven't got any music!' she protested.

Joe looked mildly flummoxed then smiled inanely.

'I will sing!'

Lorna dissolved into peals of laughter.

'Now there's an offer I can't refuse! Sing? Nobody had ever danced with me before until I met you, let alone sing to me at the same time!'

'Well, there's a first time for everything,' he said softly, pulling her to her feet. 'As we both know.'

He slid a hand around her waist and clasped the other close to his chest. He kissed her lightly on the lips and rested his cheek on the side of her head.

'Don't sit under the apple tree with anyone else but me...' he sang.

Lorna tilted her chin to look at him, unexpectedly overcome with shyness. It was weird being sung to. And she had no idea what he was singing.

'Anyone else but me, anyone else but me, no no no! Don't sit under the apple tree with anyone else but me, till I come marching home.'

She held him tighter, breathing in his smell and loving him to the moon and back. She'd never heard the song before but it was so lovely how was singing about an apple tree, when here they were dancing barefoot beneath one.

They carried on dancing as Joe continued to sing softly

and in perfect key, like a seasoned pro.

'Don't go walking down Lover's Lane with anyone else but me, anyone else but me, anyone else but me, no no no! Don't go walking down Lover's Lane with anyone else but me, till I come marching home.'

'Oh my god! Did you make that song up on the spot?'

'No!' laughed Joe. 'It's an old song!'

'Is it?' she said, genuinely surprised. 'It's just that it talks about the apple tree. And Lover's Lane... and you live down Lover's Lane...?'

Joe looked puzzled. He hadn't remembered telling her exactly where he lived. But he guessed he must have done.

'I suppose it is,' he said pensively, running his fingers through his dark, shiny hair.

They danced as he sang and hummed the song she'd never heard before but could now never forget. He pulled her over to the picnic spot underneath the tree and they lay down. The warmth of the day was evaporating rapidly and he wrapped his arms tightly around her to keep her from feeling the slight chill that now spiked the evening air.

'I wish I could spend more time with you.'

The corners of Lorna's lips curled and she closed her eyes.

'I wish you could too.'

'It won't always be like this, you know.'

Lorna thought of Alice lying on the sofa in the house down Lover's Lane, her life slowly ebbing away. She had a vivid picture of her in her minds eye. She imagined she looked a lot like Joe but with long, chestnut hair, strong bone structure and almond shaped eyes the colour of pistachios.

'I know it won't, darling.' She kissed his soft, pillowy lips.

'Look Lorna – over there!' Joe suddenly hissed, sitting up.

Lorna craned her neck to look in the direction Joe was pointing. There, by the rivers edge, were four fat black and white magpies.

'One for sorrow, two for joy...'

'Three for a girl, four for a boy.'

Joe placed his hand under Lorna's chin and tilted her face up to his. His eyes penetrated hers for a second, the freckles in their eyes perfectly aligned.

'One day we'll get married and have a baby,' he said, his words barely audible, the faintest of whispers caressing her ear.

Lorna felt as though a bolt of lightning had struck her. She could barely speak.

'I knew that earlier today when we met your neighbours. I was envious of them, being married, becoming parents. Imagine bringing new life into the world, Lorna... Can we? Shall we?'

Lorna felt tears prick her eyes and she desperately tried to swallow hard to stop herself from crying but it was no use and the tears flowed like the river they lay beside.

'Oh, Joe...'

'You will be mine for always, won't you?' he whispered. 'Please don't ever leave me, Lorna.'

'I won't Joe... not ever.'

Joe's chest heaved as he stifled a sob.

'I'll never leave you, please always remember that, my love. My girl,' his voice faltering, his cheeks wet with hot, salty tears. 'Even through the darkest of days... remember I'll always come back.'

TWENTY

'AM I GLAD TO SEE YOU!' Lorna rushed to the shop door and gave Rose an almighty hug.

'Sorry I'm a bit late, lovey. I got stuck at that bloody level crossing for twenty minutes. So many trains at this time of the morning.'

'That's ok – I'm just thankful you're here. Fancy a cup of tea? I've just made a pot.'

'Love one. I got up early today, with good intentions and all of that. But I ended up watching breakfast telly and only managed a slice of toast in the car on the way here!'

'What are you like? That's the trouble when you're used to working from home. Everything fits in with you – you become complacent.'

'I suppose you do…'

'It's a good job I went to the bakery first thing and got us a pain au chocolat each.'

'Ooh, you are a bugger!' chuckled Rose. "I'm supposed to be on a diet.'

Lorna took Rose's bag from her and hung it up in the tiny lobby out the back where the cloakroom and even tinier kitchen was. She rustled up a quick breakfast for them both and brought the tray through to the shop. It wasn't quite opening time so they had a few minutes to enjoy the freshly baked and still gooey in the middle pastries.

'So, anything to report?' asked Rose, pouring steaming tea

into two mugs.

Lorna smiled smugly.

'I saw him last night. It was the most romantic night of my life,' she cooed, brushing flakes of wafer thin pastry from her mouth.

'Did he propose?' joked Rose.

'More or less.'

Rose's jaw fell open, exposing a highly unattractive mouthful of chewed-up, mushy, pain au chocolat.

'Are you having me on?' she spluttered.

'No. We went for a walk down to the river and had a picnic. Then we danced and he sang this really old song to me – something about don't go sitting under an apple tree...'

'Oh yes! I know that one! My mam used to sing it to me when I was little,' Rose interrupted.

'And then he carved a heart into the tree trunk and put our intitals inside it!'

'Blimey! Go on... then what?'

'Well, then we had a kiss and a cuddle on the tablecloth...'

'On the what?'

'I didn't have a picnic rug to hand... stop butting in Rose, shut up a minute...' she said crossly.

'Sorry, love, carry on.'

'Then he pointed over to four magpies that were scratting around near the river. I said one for sorrow, two for joy... because we'd seen magpies before and we'd said the rhyme before...'

'And he said three for a girl, four for a boy...'

'How do you know?'

'A wild guess, my love. And?'

'And that's when he said we'd get married and have a baby one day. That it wouldn't always be like this – I'm assuming he meant with him having to care for Alice – and then he got upset and promised he'd never leave me.'

Lorna stopped and swallowed hard, her face fell and she looked troubled.

'Even through the darkest of days.'

Rose grimaced and stuffed the last chunk of pain au chocolat into her mouth.

'That must mean when Alice dies. God, how awful,' she said, still chewing.

The women looked at each other and without exchanging words, knew exactly what the other was thinking.

'He's going to need a lot of support afterwards, you know. He's lost his parents and now he's losing his only remaining family member. The poor lamb. Is he dreadfully upset?'

Lorna frowned and shook her head.

'No. That's the strangest thing about it. He seems so matter of fact about her dying, really. Yes, he's sad, and when I first saw him last night, he looked terrible. But I think he must have come to terms with her illness and the fact that she's going to die.'

'I suppose you do when people have a terminal illness. When my mother died I was relieved, which sounds odd, but I was glad it was all over. Then the grief hit me about a month after the funeral. I'd prepare yourself for that to happen to Joe, my love.'

Lorna hummed in agreement and drank the rest of her tea in silent contemplation. She was dreading Alice dying, even though she didn't even know her. The only person she'd ever known to die was Oriel. Even her grandparents were still alive albeit on their last legs. She'd never had to support someone through a death before. It always seemed so far off, like it only happened to you when you got older yourself.

'It's just such a shame you had to meet him now, in a way.'

'Why?' asked Lorna, confused.

'Well, if you knew him better you'd also know Alice and it'd be easier for you. You'd be in control a little more. And if you'd met him after she'd died, that too would be easier because you wouldn't have known anything about what he went through. Being in the first throes of love with someone as they lose someone dear is very hard. On both of you.'

'I hadn't thought of it like that before,' admitted Lorna. 'I've been too wrapped up with him and how he makes me feel and how lucky I am to have found him to have given it much thought.'

'I don't suppose he planned it this way either, lovey. You can't predict when you'll fall in love with someone. It just happens.'

Lorna took the breakfast things into the kitchen and washed them up while Rose opened the shop. The shutters and the door was only open for all of five minutes when Jilly swept in, all big hair and high heels and sharp tailoring. She air kissed both Lorna and Rose and plonked her overly large and extremely cumbersome designer bag on the counter.

'I haven't got long and I know you're busy but I just wondered… actually, me and you father just wondered… when we'd be meeting your gardener.'

Lorna breathed out a long, weary sigh.

'George?'

'George?' echoed her mother, staring at her daughter and blinking rapidly.

'Yes. George is my gardener. Why do you want to meet him?' asked Lorna, knowing full well who her mother was really talking about.

'I thought he was called Joe?' she replied sharply.

'Oh! Well, why didn't you say so? You mean Joe? He's my boyfriend not my gardener.'

Jilly looked uncomfortable. She knew Lorna was winding her up.

'Yes. That one.'

Lorna smiled and glanced over at Rose, who was trying very hard to busy herself with a stack of cellophane.

'I was thinking maybe next weekend. I will throw a party, or perhaps a barbecue if the weather stays like this. Are both you and dad free?'

'Er, yes,' stammered Jilly. 'Of course! I will tell your father to expect an invite, then. Friday or Saturday?'

'Saturday. Let's say Saturday. I don't have to work the next day.'

'Lovely. Right. I'd better dash. I'm having my infills done,' she said, waving her nails in Lorna's face. 'Everything else alright?' she added, a blatant afterthought.

'Yes thanks, mum. Everything is great.'

'Good. See you soon then! Bye Rose!'

'Bye, Jilly.'

And with that Jilly flounced out of the door without so much as a backwards glance.

'Your bloody mother gets worse.'

THE REST OF THE DAY passed in a blur. While Lorna arranged the remaining ten posies for the Barrington's ball, Rose held fort in the shop. She served customers, made tea, and even ran Verity's order up to her in Lorna's Morris Minor. By mid-afternoon, Lorna was flagging and emerged shivering from the cold store for a sandwich and to warm herself up a little. All day in the cold had chilled her to the bone despite wearing several layers of clothing and a pair of fingerless gloves. If she got any colder she'd get frostbite and need digits removing.

'You're making me feel hot, Lorna. All those bloody clothes!'

'I'm freezing, even out here in the heatwave! Don't worry – I'll be back to a normal body temperature in about twenty-four hours with a bit of luck! Are you still getting ready at mine tomorrow night?

'Yes, if that's ok? And Graham will meet us there. He's looking forward to meeting you all. I can't wait! My dress is amazing! Bright red and really frill...'

'Oh my god!' shrieked Lorna, slamming her mug down so hard, hot, sugary tea sloshed over her paperwork.

'What?' exclaimed Rose, jumping out of her skin.

'I've not asked Joe to the ball!'

Rose clutched her chest with her hand and wafted her face with a stack of paperwork.

'Well, I mentioned it to him last night but I didn't actually give him any details!'

She started mopping up the spilled tea with a handful of tissues.

'I've got to find him. Tell him where and when. Can you

stay here and man the shop while I nip up to the church in the car?' She glanced at the clock. 'He should still be working.'

'You nearly gave me a heart attack, you daft bugger. Of course I can! Go on! You've not got much time left. He probably knocks off around now. When do these flowers have to be delivered?'

'Not until tomorrow morning, thank god, but I need to get them to Lutton first thing and then get back here to open up by ten. I've got a busy day ahead of me tomorrow and I was hoping to close a bit earlier so I could get ready without rushing.'

'Crikey, you do sail close to the wind, my girl. Get off then, and find Joe or you won't have chance to – seeing as you don't even know where he sodding lives.'

Lorna stuck her tongue out, grabbed her car keys and ran out to the van. She did a haphazard three-point-turn in the road and accelerated to well over the speed limit towards the church.

As she approached the heavily wooded area in the centre of the village, she noticed there were a lot more cars than usual parked on the side of the road, even lining the lane up to the village hall, which was normally reserved for pedestrians only. This could only mean one of two things – either a wedding or a funeral was taking place. And judging by the amount of people milling about wearing head-to-toe black, she figured it must be the latter.

She managed to squeeze Cherry into a parking space between two ginormous 4x4's and sidled up the lane into the churchyard, eager to remain as inconspicuous as possible. After all, she wasn't a mourner at the funeral and neither did she want to be seen as a morbid bystander, out for a gander at what was going on.

The funeral procession had only just arrived at the burial site and she could see the black-clad mourners gathering around the graveside over by the far wall of the churchyard. It was at that precise moment she spotted two figures underneath the trees, standing a fair distance away from the funeral party but watching the proceedings nonetheless. She instantly identified the two men as Joe and Victor.

She skirted hesitantly around the boundary wall until she was on the same side of the graveyard as they were. As she approached the two men, trying to make as little sound as possible, Joe was the first to turn and see her. His face, at first solemn and without expression, softened and broke into a smile as he recognised her. Victor eyed her suspiciously and tipped an imaginary hat towards her in an old-fashioned gesture of acknowledgment.

'What are you doing here?' whispered Joe, slipping his arm around her shoulders and brushing his lips across her cheek.

Lorna looked over at the funeral taking place just yards away and lowered her eyes, leaning into Joe's shoulder.

'I had to find you. It's about tomorrow night. I know I mentioned it yesterday but I didn't give you any details,' she replied, keeping her voice as low as possible.

'The ball, you mean?'

'Yes. I'm assuming you'll come with me,' she added shyly.

'But I haven't even asked you. So… will you? Will you be my partner?'

He squeezed her shoulders with his arm and kissed the

top of her head.

'Of course I will. It would be a pleasure. And an honour.'

Lorna felt a huge wave of relief wash over her. Now, at last, her best friends would finally meet him, they would adore him as much as she did and they'd no longer think she was dating the village idiot.

'Thank you. I'll meet you at the main gates in front of the hall at seven pm. Have you got a suit you can wear?'

Joe shifted uneasily next to her.

'No, not really, but we've got all my father's suits still. I could wear one of those?'

Lorna felt a pang of foreboding in the pit of her stomach. Dear god. His father's suits must be dreadfully dated. And as if that wasn't bad enough, his father was a much older man than Joe was, with probably very different tastes in fashion. She had visions of him turning up to the ball, with its over-the-top ostentation, looking like a drunk walking out of a bookies at kicking out time.

She cast her eyes over him and felt instantly ashamed of herself. She watched as he stared at the ground, kicking his foot back and forth in the dirt and fiddling with the corner of his shirt hem nervously.

'That will do just fine,' she whispered. 'You'll look very handsome.'

He looked at her from under his long lashes and a ghost of a smile spread across his beautiful face.

'Thank you,' he said, squeezing her hand tightly.

'I love you. See you tomorrow.'

And with a nod to Victor, who hadn't said a single word the entire time she was there, she edged her way around the graves, out through the gate opposite the village hall and drove back to the shop to finish off what she'd started two days before – a thousand pounds worth of floral displays. It was going to be a long night.

TWENTY-ONE

LUTTON HALL was teaming with people by the time Lorna delivered her third and final batch of floral arrangements. There were men in overalls who were erecting the biggest marquee she'd ever seen, electricians, caterers, musicians, pyrotechnics people, entertainers, people ordering other people about and various Barrington family members – who seemed to be either pitching in and seriously grafting or milling about doing nothing much in particular.

Lorna spotted Lady Barrington as she was unloading flowers from the back of the Morris Minor and waved to her. She rushed over at once and congratulated Lorna on her spectacular work. They were to be stored in one of the stone barns until the marquee was completely set up for the ball and the tables and chairs were in place, fully dressed for the occasion.

It was a beautiful summers day and already the grounds looked like a film set. The lawns were as lush and manicured as a bowling green, the Italian garden – with its polished marble statues – was pruned to within an inch of its life and the water meadows beyond were dotted with fallow deer and rare breed sheep. The setting was stunning, like gazing at a rare Masterpiece in an upmarket art gallery. Lorna felt a tingle of excitement building inside her. She'd never been to a proper country house ball before and this one promised to be the ball to end all balls. Evelyn had given her sneaky snippets of information about the event that probably should have remained a closely guarded secret. Lorna knew what they were eating, which musical acts had been booked, the vintage of champagne they would be drinking and how much the firework display was costing. Lorna tried to work out how much the Barrington's were forking out for such extravagance but she lost count somewhere between the fireworks and the champagne.

As she surveyed the estate around her, she still couldn't believe Evelyn was in a relationship with Rupert Barrington. It all seemed so surreal considering Evelyn's humble background, but it was all the more bizarre to think this ancient, rambling, opulent pile could one day become Evelyn's family home. Rupert was the eldest child of four and therefore the first in line to inherit both his fathers' title and his vast country estate. Lady Evelyn Delilah Barrington had a certain ring to it, even if it was slightly unconventional. Lorna couldn't wait to see her tonight. She couldn't wait for tonight full stop. It would be one of those magical nights one wishes could go on forever. She would show Joe off to everyone and anyone. They would dance, laugh, eat, drink and spend the entire evening being the perfect couple. Which, in Lorna's eyes, was exactly what they were. This was the start of their lives together. She knew sad times were ahead but she was strong, she would get Joe through them. She could weather any storm that was thrown at her, that much she did know. He was hers and she intended to keep him.

WHEN SHE ARRIVED back at the shop, Rose was standing outside holding a long, zipped-up suit carrier containing her red, frilly ball gown and an overnight bag, which was most probably stuffed with several pairs of shoes, enough make-up to stock an entire John Lewis beauty department and her vast jewellery collection.

Lorna cashed up the till and locked up the shop and the two women headed to the flat to begin the painstaking metamorphosis from chrysalis to butterfly.

Two hours later, the flat resembled the backstage area of a fashion show. There were shoes, tights, stockings, various types of underwear, hairdryers, curling tongs, hair straighteners, lipsticks, bronzing powders and god knows what else, littered all over the floors of both bedrooms and bathrooms. The air was heavy with an interesting and slightly nauseating blend of cheap hairspray, Chanel No 5, Soir de Lune and half a dozen Oriental Nights scented candles. It smelled like a brothel.

'Jesus, what a mess! I can't be bothered to tidy up now. I'll do it in the morning,' muttered Lorna, emerging from her bedroom.

'It's nearly all my stuff. Sorry. I can never seem to make my mind up about anything,' Rose replied.

The two women stood opposite each other, motionless, mouths gaping. For the first time, they saw each other in all their finery.

'Rose,' breathed Lorna. 'My god, you look incredible!'

Rose beamed from ear to ear.

'Oh Lorna… so do you. You look like you've stepped from another era. You look absolutely beautiful.'

Each woman surveyed the other scrupulously, getting each other to twirl round to show their dresses off to full effect.

Rose's dress was a scarlet red, semi-fitted gown in tafetta – strapless, with a boned bodice and delicate buttons up the back – and boasting an amazing, tulle skirt that frothed out in a multitude of layers from her hips. For once, her ample bosom was firmly under control and the corsetry of the dress gave her the hourglass silhouette of Marilyn Monroe. Her snow-white hair was elegantly fashioned into a chignon and held it place with an antique barrette studded with tiny pearls. Her nails and lips were painted the same shade of red as her dress and as she walked, you could just about see the ivory satin and pearl-encrusted strappy high heels she'd finally chosen to compliment her outfit. She looked fabulous.

Rose was right when she said Lorna looked as though she'd walked straight out of another decade – she was a vision of 1920s glamour and sophistication. Her dress was a fitted silk sheath overlaid with the palest baby pink chiffon. The neckline was low, exposing her flawless, alabaster décolleté, and the angel sleeves that cascaded over her arms shimmered like gossamer wings as she moved. The gown was fitted to just under the bust but the skirt floated gently to her feet like a cloud.

She'd set her hair in pin curls for an hour, which created a mane of tumbling waves as smooth as silk and as glossy as a newly-emerged horse chestnut. Her porcelain complexion, delicate and fragile like a china dolls, needed no more than a light dusting of iridescent powder and the faintest flush of pink on her cheek bones. Her lashes were extravagantly long, thick and dark, and her lips were stained the colour of peonies. She was a sight for sore eyes and she knew she looked her very best. Her stomach was in knots at the thought of seeing Joe. She was desperate to see him. And desperate for him to see her.

'I suppose we'd better make a move, love. It's just gone a quarter to. I've texted Graham to say we're on our way.'

'Ok. Let me grab my clutch bag and we'll get going.'

'Have you heard from Evelyn today?'

'No. Have you?'

'Only first thing to say she was buzzing with excitement and going to get her hair done.'

'I bet she will look stunning. I'm looking forward to seeing Rupert again too. I've not seen him since Arabella's wedding. He's a lovely man, a bit gingery but very handsome.'

'Is he? Oh, I don't do ginger! I started reading that Fifty Shades of Grey last week. I quite liked the sound of Christian until I read he had red hair. Put me right off. I couldn't visualise him in my head after that. I had to give the book to one of my clients. Mind you, she read it in three days flat and said she was off to buy the sequel.'

Lorna and Rose roared with laughter.

'I'm ginger! I shouldn't laugh really! I'm just not overly keen on ginger men.'

'You're not bloody ginger, you daft mare! You've got a lush colouring all of your very own. Like Jessica Rabbit.'

Lorna smiled. Rose did say some weird things.

THE LANE TO THE HALL was on the outskirts of the village, not far from where Joe lived. She kept an eye out for him as they drove the short distance to the gatehouse but he obviously hadn't arrived yet as he was nowhere to be seen.

273

Two uniformed men wearing white gloves and peaked hats were standing in front of the huge iron gates as they approached Lutton Hall. One had a clipboard and was asking for the names of guests and ticking them off before allowing them to drive in. The other saluted the cars and their occupants as they drove by, which looked a touch pretentious and made the two women giggle.

Lorna gave the man with the clipboard both her and Rose's names and mentioned that she would be walking back down to the gates in a few minutes to meet her guest. Rose asked the man if somebody called Graham Dersham had arrived, and after thumbing through several sheets of paper, he confirmed he had.

They were saluted as they drove through the gates and broke into fits of hysterics when they were safely past the men and into the grounds.

'Goodness me!' cried Rose. 'Anybody would think this was a sodding royal function! Why was that man saluting us?'

'I don't know,' giggled Lorna. 'But I felt a bit of a prat driving past him in my Morris Minor! Look at all these cars, Rose!'

She parked Cherry amongst a sea of Bentley's and Rolls Royce's and very fast, sleek sports cars. Poor old Cherry stuck out like a sore thumb but at least she was clean and shiny.

As they got out of the car, a tall, elegant-looking man started to walk towards them. He was dressed impeccably in a black dinner suit, a blue bow tie and expensive leather shoes and he had the look of a man who was very well-groomed and definitely used moisturiser.

'Hello sweetheart!' he called, beaming broadly at Rose.

'Graham! You look wonderful!'

'Me? I'm far more interested in you!' he exclaimed, looking at Rose with wonder. 'Wow! You look sensational!'

Rose blushed and they embraced.

'And you must be Lorna...?' he asked, turning to her and taking her hand. 'I've heard so much about you. Rose loves you to pieces.'

He lifted Lorna's hand and kissed it.

'You look beautiful.'

Lorna fleetingly remembered Joe kissing her hand and smiled.

'Thank you! You must be Graham. It's so lovely to meet you at last.'

Rose's eyes twinkled and she looked happier than she ever had done. If she ever dared say she didn't fancy Graham again, Lorna would wallop her one. He was every middle-aged woman's dream! And she obviously fancied him rotten! As he clearly did her. He kept turning to her and shaking his head in disbelief and Rose would giggle like a girl and coyly pretend to wave him away. They were like a pair of lovesick teenagers and Lorna thought it was absolutely wonderful.

'Right. I'd better go and get Joe. It's seven o'clock on the dot. He'll be waiting for me. Tell Evelyn I won't be long.'

Rose and Graham walked off in the direction of the marquee and Lorna walked down the sweeping gravel driveway towards the gatehouse. The powder blue evening sky was dotted with flamingo pink clouds and the air was scented with the heavenly aroma of sweet peas in full bloom. She inhaled deeply and felt an intense sense of contentment. Her heart rate was beginning to gather pace and her stomach had transformed into a cage of butterflies once again.

The two guards acknowledged her as she approached them and exchanged glances of admiration to one other as she glided effortlessly past, such was her perfect posture and poise and graceful beauty. Of course, Lorna was blissfully unaware that she had this effect on every man who set eyes on her. In her mind, she was very ordinary but to everyone else around her she was extraordinary – captivating, alluring and almost certainly out of bounds.

Her eyes focused to see in the rapidly descending twilight as she scanned the dusky lane in front of her. Joe wasn't where he said he would be, dressed in his father's suit, waiting for her to whisk him to the ball, like a gender reversed Cinderella. There was nobody there. Every now and then, an expensive car would draw up to the gates and be waved through. She waited for over half an hour. It grew darker and darker – the shadowy trees lining either side of the lane becoming more menacing by the minute. Rose and Evelyn would be wondering where she was. They would be finishing their canapés and champagne by now and about to take their seats for dinner.

Lorna was aware her breathing was becoming quicker and shallower, her heart was racing and she felt sick. Joe said he would be here. He promised. And then it hit her like a thunderbolt. What if he had already gone inside? She walked back through the gates only to see the two guards walking up the drive towards the hall, holding their peaked caps in their hands and whistling a merry tune. All of the guests must have arrived, which is why they were knocking off duty.

'Excuse me?' she called after them.

One of the men turned and peered at her through the gloom.

'Is everything alright, madam?'

'No… no it's not. I'm waiting for my guest to arrive. But it has just occurred to me he may already be inside. Did you check off any guests who arrived on foot this evening?'

The guard frowned momentarily before answering.

'Yes, I think we did madam. What's your guests name?'

He took out a pocket torch and flicked it on, shining it onto the guest list fastened to the clipboard.

'It's Joe.'

'Joe?'

'Yes. Joe.'

'And his surname, madam?'

'I… er… I don't know.' She replied, feeling extremely idiotic. How the hell did she not know Joe's surname? For god's sake, she was sleeping with the man!

The guard looked bemused.

'You don't know, madam?'

Lorna trawled frantically through her memory. He'd never even told her his fucking surname! Think, Lorna. Then she remembered the initials carved into the tree trunk.

'It begins with an H. I'm sorry that's so vague but… I don't know what else to say.'

The guard sighed and flipped through the guest list and then went back to the first sheet and double-checked it again.

'I'm sorry madam. There is no Joe H on here. What's your name?'

'It's Lorna. Lorna Mills.'

He scrolled through the list again.

'Yep. You're here. I ticked you off when you drove in. All it says next to your name is 'plus one'. Which I assume is your Mr H, madam?'

Lorna nodded wearily. Where the hell was he?

'Yes. That's him. I was supposed to be meeting him here, you see. Outside the gates. He lives in Lutton, only a few minutes walk away. I... I don't know where he is.'

The guard nodded sympathetically. What fool would stand her up, he thought to himself. Whoever he was, he must be a loaf short of a picnic.

'Thank you anyway,' she muttered and started to walk towards the marquee. She could see her beautiful flower arrangements standing proudly in the entrance and the warm glow, the excitable chatter and the haunting strains of chamber music from within raised her spirits a little although deep inside, she was absolutely petrified.

THE MARQUEE WAS alive with the sounds and smells of people enjoying themselves. The internal walls were strung with row upon row of tiny fairy lights, which danced and twinkled and made her feel as though she'd entered a fairy grotto. Each table was adorned with one of the floral arrangements she had made, a huge candelabra and enough bone china and solid silver to sink a ship. Waiters and waitresses wandered around with trays of champagne, Kir Royale and fresh orange juice and great silver platters laden with exquisite, little morsels to nibble on.

It didn't take her long to spot her friends. Rose's red dress was highly conspicuous, as was Evelyn's pink hair. She weaved her way through the throng towards them, stopping briefly to scoop up a flute of champagne and a smoked salmon blini.

'Lorna! Where have you been?' screeched Evelyn, looking over Lorna's shoulder curiously.

Lorna popped the blini into her mouth and chewed.

'Looking for Joe.'

Evelyn kissed her cheek.

'God, you look fucking amazing.'

'I don't,' said Lorna flatly. 'But you really do look amazing.'

Evelyn had carried out her double promise by wearing the strapless, backless, tattoo-exposing black dress and dyeing her pixie haircut baby pink. Lorna couldn't quite fathom out how her dress was staying upright, let alone on. It fitted her like a glove. The back was so low it grazed the base of her spine and showed off the trail of ivy that ran its length up to the nape of her neck beautifully. Her elfin face was flawless, her eyes huge pools of black and her lips a sheer, pale, glossy pink that mirrored the shade of her hair. The intricate pentacle tattoo on her right arm drew glances from everyone around her and with the two women standing next to each other, nobody quite knew who to look at first – Evelyn because she looked so unconventionally beautiful and Lorna because she was quite simply beautiful.

'You do, Lorna. What's wrong? Where is he?' she replied softly, sensing Lorna was upset.

'I've no idea. I waited until it was almost dark in that lane and he didn't show up. I'm sad and angry.'

She glanced at her watch.

'It's almost eight o'clock. He's nearly an hour late. I was looking forward to seeing him so much, to introducing him to you and Rose, to just being with him really…' she trailed

279

off, biting her bottom lip and trying not to cry.

Evelyn stroked her arm tenderly and reached out to another passing tray and grabbed two glasses of champagne.

'Here. Drink this.'

'I've already got one.'

'Then drink both. Even if Joe doesn't show, I'm determined you're going to have a good time tonight.'

Lorna downed the two glasses of bubbles one after the other and immediately felt better. It never ceased to amaze her how quickly the effects of alcohol could turn a negative situation into a positive one. By the time she'd drunk her third glass she was feeling quite cheerful.

Evelyn introduced her to Rupert, who she found utterly charming and who was also clearly besotted with his new, avant garde girlfriend. He couldn't take his eyes off her the whole time they were together and after the group had stood and chatted for a while, he excused himself and Evelyn, and whisked her off to introduce her to his friends and family. A prospective Ladyship didn't seem so out of the ordinary after all.

At eight-thirty precisely, the sound of a gong resonated around the marquee, indicating it was time for everyone to take their seats for dinner. It was only as Lorna took her seat next to Graham, she realised the chair to her left was intended for Joe. She stood again briefly and scanned the marquee, hoping that Joe was somewhere inside and trying to find her. But all the guests were seated and the only people walking around were the waiting staff.

Rose and Evelyn could see the look of despondency on Lorna's face. Their hearts went out to her. Here they were, all three of them, dressed like queens and sitting in beautiful surroundings, being waited on hand and foot and both Rose and Evelyn had their men beside them but all Lorna had was an empty chair. They tried to cheer her up by telling her how amazing her flowers were and constantly topping up her champagne glass but it was no good. Lorna was inconsolable.

She felt even more miserable when the immaculately uniformed waitress set down a plate of dressed crab with avocado and melon in Joe's place. Lorna explained that her guest was ill and wouldn't be attending. The waitress apologised profusely and said she would inform the maitre d' immediately, which caused Lorna to feel terribly guilty and insist that she shouldn't be the one apologising, it should be herself for causing such a fuss.

The table of eleven ate their delicious starters, followed by a divine main course of tournedos of beef with ox cheek and celeriac and wrapped up with vanilla panna cotta served with almond and poached rhubarb. It was a splendid meal and champagne flowed throughout the gastronomic revelry. Even Lorna had to admit it was the best meal she'd ever eaten and she got off her chair to tipsily tiptoe around to Evelyn to give her a hug and tell her how thankful she was for the invitation.

After coffee and petits fours, the tables were cleared and the entertainment began. A colourful group of wandering minstrels sang and played music on a variety of instruments, along with playing tricks on guests and performing magic and telling jokes. They were like latter day court jesters and everyone found them hilarious. A five-piece band struck up a bit later on and started to blast out familiar songs and before too long the dance floor was crammed to bursting point.

Lorna sat at her table while the other two couples went to dance. The champagne had numbed her from the inside out and she no longer felt angry at Joe. Instead she felt tremendously hard done by and really quite stupid. She'd spent a small fortune on looking her very best, all for Joe's benefit. She'd told her friends he'd be here tonight and they would meet him at last. His absence had caused food to be wasted. And she was having to spend the whole night by herself when everyone else had partners.

As she sat and stewed, she became more and more curious as to why Joe hadn't showed up. He lived in the village for gods sake. Even if something dreadful had happened, couldn't he at least have gotten a message to her or the men on the gates?

She stood up from her chair and wobbled slightly on her heels. With red mist descending faster than fog rolling in off the North Sea, she teetered unsteadily through the marquee and out into the fresh air. It was pitch black and the sky was sprinkled with a billion stars. She headed down the long, sweeping driveway, past the gatehouse and through the huge iron gates into the unlit lane. She glanced up at the sky and saw the moon hanging above her like a great, celestial glitterball. It illuminated the lane enough for her to make her way to the end and onto the main road which wound through Lutton. The alcohol coursing through her veins along with occasional spikes of adrenaline made her feel brave. She would find Joe, right now, and give him a bloody piece of her mind.

The staggered through the village, past houses and

cottages, over the tiny, stone bridge and up to the church. She stood in front of the house on the corner of Lover's Lane, the one with the letterbox set into the wall, and looked up at the windows. The house was in total darkness. She had no idea where Joe lived. It might be this house, it might not be. She wandered a little further down the lane. In the distance she saw more houses, some had lights on, others were black and still. Her heart was beating harder and harder as she sensed she was getting close. She could almost smell him. The frustration and emotion of the day rose within her like a dormant volcano on the verge of eruption. She felt dizzy and sick and her head was starting to spin as the cool night air began to sober her up. She kicked off her shoes and the coldness of the ground beneath her feet began to slowly creep up her legs.

Suddenly she called out to him. His name echoed through the night, a tormented wail saturated with sorrow and pain.

'Joe! Where are you?'

The village was still and silent. She took a deep gulp of air and called again.

'Joe! Please! Joe! Where are you?'

She stood in the middle of the road and reached both arms skywards. Tears streamed down her face as her eyes searching the heavens, looking for answers.

She began to sob uncontrollably and still she called to him. She called his name again and again as she stumbled barefoot up and down the lane. She called until her voice was broken and hoarse and every ounce of energy had been drained from her body. But he never came.

Car headlights flicked to full beam and Lorna stood in

their glare, shielding her eyes from the bright, white light, momentarily stunning her into stillness. The rear doors of the car opened and Rose and Evelyn leapt out and ran to her.

'What the hell…?'

Rose flung her arms around her. She was freezing cold.

'Oh Lorna…'

Lorna continued to sob all over Rose's bare shoulder and down the front of her beautiful, red dress.

'I can't find him,' she gasped. 'I've called and called but he's not here.'

'Let's get you home.'

Rupert turned the car around and drove to the end of Lover's Lane, stopping briefly by the church before turning right onto the main road and out of the village.

UPSTAIRS IN THE HOUSE on the corner – the one with the letterbox set into the wall – the shadowy figure of a young man observed the commotion in the street below from his bedroom window. He watched in silence as the beautiful woman in the baby pink dress paced the lane – weeping, wailing and calling his name over and over again.

He bowed his head and closed his eyes as the car carrying her disappeared around the corner and great, big teardrops spilled from beneath his lashes and rolled down his cheeks. With his body wracked with sobs and the acidic sting of remorse spiking through his soul, he slid down the wall into a heap on the bare, wooden floor and there he stayed until the sun began to rise once again, marking the start of another new day.

TWENTY-TWO

'SHE'S IN BED ASLEEP. I've never seen her that drunk before.'

Rose gently closed Lorna's bedroom door and tip-toed softly into the living room where Graham and Rupert sat, both looking tired and somewhat bemused by the evening's events. Evelyn rustled into the room in her black ball gown, carrying a tray of fresh coffee and set it down on the table.

'She's going to feel like crap tomorrow. Has she been sick?' she asked Rose, handing everyone a mug.

'No. It might be better for her if she was.'

They sipped the hot coffee in silence.

'Look at us all sat here in our glad rags! We look like we've just walked off a cruise ship!' joked Rose, trying to make light of the fact they'd had to abandon the ball to find Lorna and effectively cut short their night out.

'Rupert, if you want to go back, please do,' said Evelyn apologetically. 'I feel so terrible that you're missing out.'

'No! Don't worry about me. I'm just glad we found her and she's home safe and sound. It could have been a lot worse. The lane to the hall is so dark. You don't know who's lurking about, for one. She could have been hit by a car or anything.'

'I knew she'd gone looking for Joe the second she vanished into thin air like that. One minute she was chatting, laughing, jigging about to the band, the next she was gone,' replied Evelyn solemnly.

'I'm desperately worried about her. I wanted to meet

Joe tonight so I could suss him out, see if he really is this wonderful man she says he is. He seems like such an odd character to me, from what she's told me about him, anyway,' said Rose, shaking her head and cradling her mug the way they did in the hot chocolate advert.

'How do you mean?' asked Graham.

'Well...' she said, pausing dramatically. 'She said he lives with his dying sister, which could be true of course, but would a young man be looking after a young girl on her death bed? Surely she'd be in a hospital or something? And he doesn't go out or have any friends, he doesn't have a car...'

'Or a mobile,' interrupted Evelyn.

'Or any money. Look at that time they went for a picnic and he took chipped china cups to drink out of?'

'And he doesn't know the days of the week! He sounds illiterate. She mentioned he'd served in Afghanistan but was injured so he was discharged on medical grounds. Then, in the next breath, she's saying she is his first girlfriend and he's never had sex before! It doesn't add up.'

'A virgin soldier in the British Army? I don't believe it for a second!' scoffed Rose.

Rupert shrugged.

'And you say he lives in Lutton?'

'Yes! I was going to ask you last week but completely forgot about it. Surely you must know everyone in the village?'

Rupert frowned and cocked his head to one side.

'I know I don't live there anymore but I can safely say I know the occupants of every single house in that village, yes.'

'And...?'

'I've never even heard of a Joe. I can't even picture who he

286

might be? Whereabouts does he live in Lutton?'

'This is it... we... she... doesn't actually know,' sighed Rose.

'Oh. So she's never been to his house before?'

'No. He always comes here. He's never asked her to his place.'

'I suppose that's because of Alice, is it?' added Rose hopefully.

'I'll do some detective work. Mum will know who he is. We'll soon find out if this Joe exists or not.'

Rose and Evelyn turned to each other in alarm.

'Oh god. I hadn't even thought of that. What if she made him up?'

'She wouldn't do that, would she? I mean... she's not bloody crazy!'

Rupert looked at Graham and then at the two women and raised his eyebrows.

'Well, we'll soon find out, won't we?'

LORNA KNEW she'd drunk too much before she even opened her eyes. Her head felt heavy and there was a dull pain somewhere in the centre of her brain that became sharp and throbbing every time she moved so much as a centimeter. She knew she must lie as still as possible and she'd feel alright, but she desperately needed the loo and putting it off would just create more pain albeit in a different region or, at worse, result in a possible toileting accident. Neither of which she particularly relished the thought of. She heaved herself to a sitting position, looked at her disheveled reflection in the mirror opposite and groaned.

She downed several glasses of water in the bathroom and took herself back to bed, again lying as motionless as possible in a bid to will away the hangover. Her mind becoming active, she then began to worry that maybe she'd drunk too much water in the bathroom and her kidneys were about to fail, causing sudden and violent death. She'd read loads of stories in the newspapers about people who'd perished in similar circumstances but to be fair, most of them had taken various narcotics in nightclubs which had induced severe thirst, which in turn had caused their kidneys to fail. Lorna had only drunk several glasses of champagne – hardly hardcore substance abuse.

Her anxiety wasn't so troublesome as to keep her awake fretting for hours on end because she awoke, feeling bright and breezy, three hours later. She reached out for her mobile and checked the time. It was nearly noon. She hadn't slept for that long since she was a toddler.

There were several text messages awaiting her. One from Rose saying how worried she was. One from Evelyn letting her know that she and Rupert had gone back to the ball and continued partying so please, whatever she did, don't feel guilty about spoiling the evening. Another was from Tobias, who she hadn't heard from for ages, informing her he was cruising the Caribbean and would she like to join him for the final leg – a week in Florida? And the fourth message was from her mother, demanding – not asking – that her barbecue be held on the Friday night and definitely not the Saturday night, because she and Lorna's father had been invited to a Million Pound Drop charity event. And they couldn't decline the invitation because the mayor was also attending. And it would look bad if they didn't go.

Lorna read all of the texts but replied to none of them. Instead she padded barefoot into the kitchen, where she cooked herself a full English breakfast, and ate the lot, including three rounds of toast and two mugs of tea, in bed.

She was still mightily pissed off about Joe's absence the night before. She'd not only made a complete fool of herself in front of her friends and their respective partners – and most likely a host of other people as well – but she'd ruined their night and woken half of Lutton up with her incessant wailing at the same time. She needed to find Joe as soon as possible, even if that meant banging on every single door in Lutton until they were answered. And if that took a month of Sunday's, then so be it.

Today was her only real day off and after showering and dressing, she went to the shop, where the landline was cheaper to use than her mobile phone, and called Rose, Evelyn, Tobias and her mother in turn. Both Rose and Evelyn were relieved to hear she'd escaped a hangover from hell but even more relieved to hear that she was all right. Lorna told them she'd changed the barbecue date from Saturday to Friday to fit in with her parents. The only obstacle remaining was to make sure Joe was there. A second no-show would not only be humiliating but disastrous, particularly if her parents were involved. Her mother would positively gloat if he didn't turn up. It would be a total told-you-so moment with much whispering under her breath and Lorna wasn't going to give her mother the satisfaction of delighting in her own misfortune.

It was a joy to speak to Tobias after so long. Lorna hadn't

seen him since his annual Christmas party and a catch up was long overdue. He was semi-retired these days, his assistant doing the day to day running of his shops, with Tobias overseeing the business side of things and undertaking only the very best commissions. He was currently on a six-week cruise around the Caribbean with his partner Freddie, who was a good twenty years younger than him and as perfectly preened as a catwalk model. Visually they were an odd couple – Tobias, short, plump, all teeth, tan and too tight trousers and Freddie, tall, slim, blonde and gorgeous – but they loved each other dearly and were planning to get married and possibly even adopt a child together, such was their commitment to one another. It was all very Elton and David.

Tobias pleaded with Lorna to take a week off work and meet them in Miami but she couldn't. She wasn't fortunate enough to have a significant other to run the shop for her and a holiday was out of the question until she was. She also didn't want to leave Joe, even though the merest mention of his name made her blood boil at this present moment in time. She told Tobias all about him, conveniently omitting certain details from the conversation including the ball fiasco, but Tobias seemed genuinely pleased and very excited that she'd finally found someone who she loved and who loved her in return.

The call to her mother was brief. Lorna didn't really want to speak to her and a text message would have sufficed but she loved talking to her dad and always hoped he'd answer the phone instead of Jilly. Unfortunately, Phillip was out digging the garden when she finally got off the phone from

Tobias and dialed her childhood home. She had to talk to Jilly after all. She confirmed Friday was fine and she'd see them at 7pm. Jilly said they were looking forward to meeting Joe very much and her father couldn't wait to get some gardening tips off him. Lorna groaned as she replaced the receiver. She couldn't imagine anything worse than standing around, burger in one hand, beer in the other, discussing green fly deterrents and the composition of a good lawn feed. She was regretting this whole barbecue thing already.

She sighed and bent to pick her bag up off the floor when she heard a tapping at the window. She got off her stool and walked over to the shop door and peered through the glass. There, looking disheveled and repentant, was Joe. His face was pale, his eyes filled with sorrow. Lorna's heart melted into a gooey puddle and she flicked back the deadlock on the door and opened it wide.

'How did you know I was here?'

'I tried your flat. The shop was next on my list.'

'You'd better come in.'

Joe stepped into the shop, his head bowed, his shoulders hunched.

'I'm so sorry, Lorna…'

'Sorry? You stood me up! You made me look like a complete fucking idiot in front of my friends. It wouldn't surprise me if they think I'm lying about even knowing you!'

Joe's face crumpled and he glanced nervously up to meet her eyes and then looked down at the floor again. Lorna's voice was starting to get louder and higher as the anger she felt last night came flooding back.

'Where were you? Why didn't you come? I walked around

291

Lutton calling your name like a demented lunatic!'

'I...'

'And more importantly, why didn't you just let me know you couldn't make it? You only live around the fucking corner!'

'I didn't know how to let you know. I couldn't leave the house. Alice was so poorly, I thought she might pass away. I was frightened to leave her all by herself.'

'You are so weird, Joe! You haven't even got a fucking phone. Why haven't you? I don't know anyone else on the planet who hasn't got a phone.'

'I... I've never needed one before.'

Lorna huffed and laughed maliciously.

'Oh really? Don't you think living with a dying person might warrant you getting a phone? Isn't that a good enough reason? What are you going to do if you need an ambulance in the middle of the night? Send a carrier pigeon? Joe, you don't live in the real world. Honestly... I've never heard such a load of crap.'

Joe lifted his face and his eyes were misty with tears. He blinked and they fell onto his cheek.

Lorna wished somebody could have slapped her face right there and then. If Joe had done it, she'd have congratulated him. She couldn't believe she could be such a hard-hearted bitch at times. Before her stood the man she loved, a man whose only living relative was dying in front of his very eyes, and here she was effing and blinding at him, reducing him to tears. She could almost hear her mother chastising her, telling her she ought to be ashamed of herself and to apologise at once.

292

'I'm sorry, Lorna.'

Joe held out his hand and Lorna bypassed it, throwing her arms around him, pulling him close and breathing him in.

'I'm sorry, Joe. It's me that should be apologising. I just wanted to see you so badly. I wanted you to meet my friends. I wanted us to have a special evening together. I'm so, so sorry for shouting at you. You must think I am such a cow.'

He tightened his arms around her and shook his head.

'I don't think that at all. I'm just glad that you still love me.'

Lorna felt as though her heart had been ripped out of her chest and squeezed so tight that every drop of blood that once flowed around it lay in pools around her feet.

'I love you with all my heart.'

She kissed him and all the fury and frustration she felt earlier ebbed away. He was here now and she didn't want to let him go.

'And Alice...?' she whispered, holding her breath, not wanting to hear his reply.

Joe swallowed and momentarily closed his eyes.

'She's still hanging on. She's a fighter. She has a lady with her today and tonight. She's been sent in to care for her. I didn't know she was going to come. She just turned up this morning. I watched her bathe Alice and brush her hair and give her sips of tea. Poor Alice... she looks like a child...'

His voice faltered and he struggled to continue speaking.

'Is there anything I can do?' Lorna pleaded, feeling inadequate and utterly useless. There must be something she could do, surely. Even if it was just sit with Joe by Alice's bedside. Joe shook his head again.

'No. It's just a matter of time. But today I want to be with you. And tonight. Please. If it's all right by you, that is?'

Lorna couldn't love him any more if she tried. He may be weird, unusual, quirky even, but he was everything to her.

'Of course.'

They walked the short distance back to her flat and ate lunch together overlooking the garden. They lay on the sofa and watched old movies, played cards and talked and laughed. Joe sang to her again and waltzed her around the room until she was dizzy and when evening began to fall, they undressed each other slowly and sank into a deep, warm bath scented with lavender and rosemary and piled high with frothy, sparkly bubbles. In the candlelight, Joe lathered and washed Lorna's hair, rinsing the suds away with jugfuls of fragrant water. Next he poured shower cream into the palms of his hands and sensually massaged every inch of her wet, naked body, washing her gently and expertly as though he had done it a thousand times before.

As they lay entwined, somewhere in the furthest reaches of her mind hoped that their love for each other would culminate in something magical within her body. She wanted Joe's baby. She'd never wanted anything more in her life. And tonight was the night to conceive. The moon hanging above them in the inky sky was full, her body was fertile and the hawthorn tree was in full blossom. The merry month of May was almost over and the tarot cards she'd dealt just hours before predicted a Valentine's baby.

Evening slid into night and night faded into dawn and still Joe slept on by her side. As the sun rose, and the cock crowed, and the scent of pea flowers drifted in through the open bedroom window, Lorna stirred from her sleep. She opened her eyes tentatively but her fears were unfounded. She could feel his skin next to hers, his soft breath on her neck, his intoxicating smell enveloping her like a cloud of never ending sweet dreams. He was still with her.

TWENTY-THREE

A year ago...

AT FIRST, ORIEL was in a state of complete denial about her cancer. She sat in the oncologist's stark consultation room, with Roger at her side, and practically laughed in the doctors face as he told her, with compassion and a great deal of sensitivity, that she had stage three breast cancer which had spread to her lymph nodes, lungs and spine. There was no cure, palliative treatment only would be offered, and she was – in short – going to die.

She was in constant pain, there was no disputing that, but she still looked the picture of health. Her raven mane still shone, her ageless skin still glowed and her deep brown eyes still sparkled. Not only did she refuse to believe she was dying, she went into overdrive trying to prove the hospital had made some terrible mistake. They'd clearly mixed up her results with some other poor, unfortunate woman. How could she be dying? She had never had a day's illness in her life! She had held back the ravages of time for so many years with her vegetarian diet, rigorous exercise regime and her holistic approach to life. She drank only the finest red wine – she called it nature's medicine – and had never smoked, even as a hip, young thing in the seventies. And at the very foundation of all the good she bestowed upon herself to promote rude health and wellbeing, were the dark forces of evil that she used day in, day out, to ward off all things bad. She believed so strongly that her devotion to black magic would protect her and guard her for all eternity, that when she faced death head on, she could not, would not, accept her credence had failed her.

That was until she started to cough uncontrollably, her body doubled over in agony, pain so severe she thought her ribs might crack. She began spitting blood the colour of ruby port and struggled to catch her breath. Next she started losing weight. Oriel always was a slender, toned woman but her clothes began to hang off her body like limp rags despite never losing her appetite. Her face became gaunt and pale and it's ethereal beauty started to fade. And then she slept. Long, deep periods of sleep, waking for an hour or so at a time, sometimes enough to watch a movie from start to finish, before returning to the arms of Morpheus.

Roger cared for her meticulously at home and together they chose a hospice – one with a beautiful walled garden, a pond full of lily pads and an abundance of trees – where she would spend the final days of her life. Her friends rallied round her, keeping her cheerful, often turning up out of the blue with a bottle of wine or a homemade cake, snippets of gossip and tales to raise a smile. They talked about death and dying and how every one of them had to return to nature eventually. That was the cycle of life. They discussed the Summerland and the afterlife and eventually Oriel accepted her fate and faced her rapidly approaching death with dignity.

Roger never revealed the horror he'd found on the cellar floor that evening. To Oriel or the other three women. He kept it to himself, a dark secret hidden deep within, and he lived with it – at times with great difficulty – with a sense of ironic denial. He did what so many people do when faced with a situation that is beyond their ability to process, comprehend and accept – he buried his head in the sand and the world continued its perpetual rotation.

Oriel was only in Magnolia House for three days when she became gravely ill. Her skin became mottled and took on a slightly bluish tint, her breathing was irregular and shallow and she stopped eating and drinking. She was damp to the touch but felt as cold as ice. Roger knew it was the beginning of the end and he called Rose, Lorna and Evelyn.

That night the three friends visited Oriel as she lay in her bed overlooking the pond with the lily pads and the cedar trees. She drifted in and out of consciousness as they spoke to her, one after the other. Lorna was the last person to go into the room. Rose and Evelyn were equally distressed after saying their last goodbyes to a friend who had been part of their lives so intimately for the past nine years, and they took themselves off to the café downstairs for a much-needed coffee.

The room was dark and quiet and smelled faintly of antiseptic and freshly-washed linen. Lorna sat by the bed and reached out to touch Oriel's hand. Oriel jerked as though a current of electricity has passed through her fingertips and she slowly opened her eyes.

'Lorna… I'm so glad to see you,' she whispered.

Lorna smiled at her.

'Rose and Evelyn have just been to see you too. But you were asleep.'

'Have they? Was I? I'd have liked to have seen them.'

Her words came sporadically and were obviously laboured.

'They've gone to get a coffee. Can I get you anything? A sip of water?'

Oriel shook her head and blinked very slowly. Her breathing was strange, rasping, noisy – and at times it sounded as though she wasn't breathing at all.

'But I could… murder a gin and tonic,' she said, her lips dry and her smile weak.

'I've got something… for you. My bag.'

Lorna frowned and reached for the tan leather shoulder bag that sat on the chair next to hers.

'In here?'

'Yes. Inside. Pocket.'

Lorna unzipped the pocket and fished around inside. Her fingers closed around something cold and smooth. It was Oriel's pentacle.

'I want… you to have it. Wear it Lorna. For me.'

Lorna opened her hand and looked down at the bespoke, silver pentacle that Oriel had worn around her neck for forty years. She closed her fist around it and squeezed it tight, the corners of the pentacle digging into the palm of her hand, hurting her.

'I want nothing of yours, Oriel,' she snapped.

She got up from her chair and walked over to the window, opening it as wide as possible and threw the pentacle into the pond below.

Oriel struggled to turn to see what Lorna was doing but she knew she'd discarded the most precious possession she had ever owned.

Lorna walked round to the side of the bed again, leaned

forward and softly whispered into Oriel's ear.

Oriel tried to scream but the only sound she could make was a strangulated croak. She reached for the panic button by her side, fumbling to locate it, her breathing becoming rapid and shallow and distressed. Her hand shook violently as she tried numerous times to press the button, without success, her strength diminishing by the second.

Lorna burst through the bedroom door into the corridor outside where Roger sat reading a magazine.

'Something is wrong, Roger. She just started shaking and gasping.'

'Oh god,' cried Roger and ran into the room. 'Go and find the others.'

Lorna did as she was told and headed off in the direction of the coffee shop.

Oriel lay in her bed, trembling all over, her face contorted with rage.

'Oriel? My love? What is it?'

'I... Oriel Agnes Trewhellor-Fitzpatrick, High... Priestess and... direct descendant of Madgy Figgy of St. Levan...' she gasped, 'curse Lorna... Mills... and hereby order that she will never... find...'

She began to cough. Roger stared at his wife in disbelief. She was revealing her true self to him right there, on her death bed.

'...the thing she wants the... most... true love. Let this curse be done and final and without... severance for... eternity.'

Roger leaned over her and pressed the alarm. Two nurses came scuttling into the room immediately and within

300

seconds, Oriel was sedated and in a deep sleep.

She never woke from that sleep. Just before midnight, her chest rose and fell but failed to rise once more. Her heart beat it's final beat and her body became eerily still. The women had long since returned to their homes but Roger was by her side and stayed with her until her body turned colder than he ever thought possible.

THE FUNERAL, a week later, was a sociable affair. Oriel wanted a traditional funeral but stressed there was to be no religious connotation whatsoever. Roger organised a simple but elegant ceremony in the local crematorium followed by a wake in a country house hotel. It was more like a wedding reception than a funeral, with a string quartet and canapés and tray upon tray of champagne. Around two hundred people attended, including Jilly and Phillip and the cream of Stamford society. Everybody wore black of course – Oriel was adamant there would be none of this everyone-should-wear-an-item-of-pink nonsense that was becoming de rigeur at modern day funerals. She wanted black and black is what she got. It was almost like watching a fashion show with ladies in towering heels and striking hats and immaculately cut Italian suits.

Roger was the perfect host, as always. He looked tired, and sad, but the occasion itself was far from sombre. It was a celebration of Oriel's life and although the guests mingled and chatted about her, sharing stories and reminiscing about good times now past, there were no tears shed. Oriel had been very good at being a friend to everyone but she'd been even better at concealing her inner self from everyone. Nobody ever really knew the real Oriel. All of her relationships were at surface level and that is just the way she wanted them.

Towards the end of the day, when people were gradually filtering home, Roger glanced fleetingly around the beautiful glass conservatory, trying to locate Rose and Evelyn. He needed to speak to them urgently and they had to be alone. He found them outside, sitting on the patio drinking wine and thankfully, Lorna was nowhere in sight.

'I'm glad I've found you both. Where is Lorna?'

'She mentioned going to have a look at some floral arrangements in the dining hall. She spotted them earlier and said they were stunning. I think she was a bit peeved they were so good, to be honest! She wants to find out who did them!' laughed Evelyn.

'Good. I need to speak to you both. I'll keep it brief, incase she suddenly materialises.'

'Is everything all right, Roger?' asked Rose, sensing a foreboding tone to his voice.

'No. Not really.'

He scratched his head and sighed deeply.

'I don't know where to start.' He took a deep breath. 'Oriel wasn't who you think she was. She wasn't a white witch. It was all a smokescreen. She was into the occult. I discovered an inverted pentagram on the cellar floor. And blood. And all sorts of other things afterwards. She was evil. Truly evil.'

The two women stared at each other, mouths open in sheer disbelief, their hearts beating like the clappers.

'What...?' stammered Rose, wondering if Roger had lost the plot.

'Let me continue. On the night she died, when you two

went down to the café, Lorna went into her room and reappeared minutes later saying Oriel was acting oddly. I went inside and Oriel cursed Lorna. Right there in front of me. She said she'd never find true love. She came out with all sorts of stuff, long names I'd never heard of before. It was like looking at a different person…'

'But why would she do that?'

'Why would she curse her?'

'I've no idea,' he said, shaking his head. 'But I wanted you to know. A curse is a curse. And from what I've found out about Oriel these last couple of years… I think she might have been pretty good at them.'

'What do you mean?'

'I spent a long time researching the occult after I found the pentagram. And I gained access into her personal email. And her phone. She used black magic to gain everything in her life, including me I suppose.'

'And us?'

Roger nodded.

'She had strings of affairs, used men… and women, for money, for power, for eternal youth. I realise now why she was so unaccepting of her illness and death. I think she truly believed she was immortal.'

Rose and Lorna were astounded. They had never seen any evidence of Oriel dabbling in anything other than white witchcraft. They wouldn't have suspected her of being involved with the occult in a million years. It was a lot to take in. Oriel wasn't who or what she said she was.

'Is there anything you can do?' asked Roger in despair. 'To help Lorna?'

They looked at each other and nodded.

'We'll try.'

RAIN POUNDED the rooftop of the Maltings, waking Lorna from her sleep. She peered at the alarm clock. It was eight-thirty a.m. Thunder rumbled overhead and the rain fell even harder. She slipped out of bed and peered through a slat in the blind. The garden was drenched and so was the washing she'd pegged out on the line the night before. She watched as a solitary magpie hopped about under the cherry tree by the shed, trying unsuccessfully to dodge the rain and keep himself dry.

'One for sorrow,' she said to nobody in particular, a force of habit that had stayed with her since childhood.

The spell of hot weather had finally broken. She could feel the freshness in the air through the open window, so she reached her hand between the wooden slats and pulled it shut.

Typical. The weather would have to change just as she was planning an outdoor party in four days time! She could always hold it in her flat instead, if the worst came to the worst, but somehow that option didn't seem quite as appealing.

She debated whether she should go to the weekly coffee morning in the village hall or not but as she had so much to do due to her lost weekend, she decided against it. She cleaned the flat from top to bottom and fetched the soggy washing in from the equally soggy garden, spinning it again in the washing machine before draping it over the rails of the drying rack in the kitchen. Next on her list was a trip to the florists to wash the floor and give the shop a good tidy. She hadn't had chance to clean it since shutting up early to go to the ball on Saturday and she knew it must be a tip. She took her laptop with her and placed her weekly order to the wholesalers and set about scrubbing the shop. By lunchtime, everything was in order and she felt very pleased with herself. She was determined to do something nice for the rest of the day, seeing as it was supposed to be her day off, so she text Rose to see if she was free. Amazingly, she didn't have any clients booked in until later that evening so Lorna jumped into Cherry and drove over.

The two-mile journey was atrocious. There was no sign of the rain letting up anytime soon – it pelted down relentlessly, resulting in little rivers of water flowing down either side of the road and culminating in huge, great puddles in every hollow. In some parts, the road was almost impassable. Cherry wasn't the most reliable of cars in wet weather so Lorna heaved a sigh of relief when she could see the rooftop of Rose's cottage in the distance.

Rose had a pot of tea mashing on the side and was cutting a fruit cake into slices as Lorna let herself in through the back and into the kitchen. She was soaked.

'This is a nice surprise! How are you? Apart from wet! Good weekend?' she laughed, handing her a tea towel.

Lorna raised her eyebrows, pushing the wet hair off her face.

'It was in the end, thank you.'

'Have you heard from Joe?'

'I spent all day yesterday and last night with him!'

'You never! I hope you gave him what for!'

Lorna looked sheepish.

'I did actually. But he was so sweet, so apologetic and… well, he had a valid reason for not showing up. Alice took a turn for the worst and he couldn't leave her. Apparently, they have a nurse going in to help now. She was there all day yesterday and last night. I suppose she must be from Macmillan?'

'Yes. She must be. Doesn't bode well, does it?'

Lorna bit her bottom lip and shook her head.

'We had the loveliest day though, Rose. I've never been so happy. He held me in his arms all night. He woke me at six this morning and said he had to go, which I understood, of course. I went back to sleep for a couple of hours but the bloody rain woke me up. So much for a lie in! I hope he didn't get drenched walking home. I should have driven him really but it was such a beautiful day first thing…'

'It was, I know. I woke up early and put a wash on. The sun was blazing, not a cloud in the sky. And then it went as black as the ace of spades and the thunder started. Scared me to death. Mind you, we need the rain, lovey. My garden was suffering and I must have spent a small fortune using the bloody hosepipe all this month.'

She picked up the tea tray and carried it into the small sitting room.

'So, will Joe be at your do on Friday?'

'Yes. I asked him and he said he'd be there come rain or shine, which seems quite apt now considering the weather. I suppose the only reason he won't be there is if Alice…' she trailed off.

'Dies. Yes. That's quite understandable. The poor girl.'

Lorna and Rose drank tea and ate cake all afternoon. When Lorna finally upped and left, Rose went straight upstairs where the signal was better and dialed Evelyn's mobile.

'It's me. Lorna's just been round. I'm getting really worried about her. She said he was with her all day yesterday and last night. And she said he's coming to the barbecue on Friday but I can almost guarantee he won't be there.'

'I can guarantee a hundred percent he won't be there. He doesn't exist, Rose. Rupert called me earlier. There's no Joe in Lutton. There's not even a young man of the age and description she gave us living in sodding Lutton. All of the residents seem to be either school age, over forty or pensioners. I think she's having some sort of nervous breakdown.'

'Oh dear god, no...' groaned Rose. 'Or of course...'

'The charm she made, the spell she cast, the botched one, has turned into a curse.'

'You read my mind. They were my thoughts exactly. We did the reversal spell but she didn't finish it off by casting the love spell again, did she? She'd already met Joe by then. Or so she says.'

'You told her there'd be serious repercussions if she'd didn't bury the charm again.'

'I know I did. And she wouldn't listen, would she?'

'Well, let's see what happens on Friday night. That's all we can do, Rose. We can't say anything to her just yet, in case he is real. And we've got very vivid imaginations.'

'Well he doesn't live in Lutton. And that's a fact. We'll just sit and wait. But I think I know the ending to this story already, don't you?'

'I think so, yes.'

TWENTY-FOUR

'HELLO, PETE!'

Lorna rushed round from her side of the counter towards the door as she spotted a familiar face entering the shop, clipboard in hand.

'Hello, Lorna! You look well!'

'And so do you! Fatherhood is obviously suiting you! Crikey! You look like a different man!'

Pete blushed and beamed from ear to ear. He did look like a different man!

'So… tell me then! What have you got?' asked Lorna excitedly.

'A beautiful baby.'

'I know that!' she laughed. 'But what is it? A boy or a girl?'

'A boy. And he's the spit of his mother. Here…'

Pete rummaged around in his overall top pocket and pulled out a Polaroid of his wife holding the most angelic, tiny baby Lorna had ever seen. He handed her the photo and Lorna gazed at it, suddenly feeling quite emotional and misty-eyed.

'Oh, Pete… he is adorable.'

She knew what this meant to Pete. A bachelor for so long but now a happily married, father-of-one.

'You must be the proudest man alive. And what a gorgeous lady you're wife is. Wow! If I looked like that shortly after giving birth I'd be a very happy woman indeed!'

Pete took the photo back from Lorna and looked at it with love in his eyes.

'Ah – she was incredible. Seventeen hours in labour, no pain relief. She's a remarkable woman. All I did was stand by her side and hold her hand. And she gave me this! A son. I never thought I'd be a dad, you know.'

He shook his head, Lorna unsure which he emotion he was feeling the most – disbelief or total wonder.

'You make the most of every second. You've been given a gift to treasure. I bet he's spoilt rotten. What did you call him?' she asked.

'He is at that! Never seen so many clothes and toys and teddy bears. We called him Kye.'

'Well… here's a present from me to Kye. It's not much but I'm sure you will make use of it.'

She reached down under the counter and handed Pete a cream gift bag tied with a big satin bow and a picture of a stork on the front carrying a baby in a blanket.

Pete put his hand inside and pulled out a gift wrapped meticulously in layers of pastel-coloured tissue paper. He tore it off, revealing a stunning silver filigree photo frame.

'Lorna! Thank you! I don't know what to say! It's beautiful!'

'You don't have to say anything! But I do. Congratulations! Come here!'

She threw her arms around his big, clumsy frame and planted a kiss on his cheek.

'You're an angel. Thank you.'

He carefully wrapped the frame up in the tissue paper and slipped it back into the bag. Then he handed Lorna the clipboard and took the pen from behind his ear.

'Now. Where were we?' he said, tapping the first page of the order form. 'Make sure it's all there, love.'

She ran through the order quickly, making sure it was correct, and signed the top copy.

'Yep, it's all there thanks, Pete.' she said, handing him the clipboard.

'Right you are, I'll go and unload.'

Lorna smiled and folded her arms. Some things never changed.

'I'll help you'.

LORNA WAS UNPACKING sheets of delicately-patterned flower wrapping paper when Verity strolled in looking every inch the Casworth housewife – mid-blue fitted jeans, pale pink and cream striped Joules rugby top – with the collars standing up, naturally – navy blue padded gilet and leather pumps the colour of sand. It was a uniform all the ladies in the village from their mid-thirties onwards adhered to. They sported similar hairstyles too. Highlighted bobs of varying lengths, all of which had been chemically straightened. Their uniform varied very little from season to season. In summer, sleeves got shorter and jeans morphed into cropped chinos, in winter the gilet and pumps were replaced with quilted, belted jackets and Dubarry boots. It was a practical yet stylish uniform and all the womenfolk wore it well.

'Ooh, hasn't it turned chilly?' she moaned as she approached the counter, a newspaper in one hand and her purse and a packet of cigarettes in the other.

'I've just seen your man next door!' she added with a cheeky wink.

Lorna's back straightened and she stopped counting packs of wrapping paper.

'My man?' she asked, not really knowing why she felt so surprised that Joe was in the shop next door.

'Yes! He's got his gardening gear on. He's buying a paper and a can of Coke I think. God, I sound like a stalker!' she laughed.

'Er… do you mind if I just pop next door? I need to have a word with him and he might not come by the shop today. He knows Tuesday is a busy day for me.'

'No, of course not! I'll stand behind the counter and read my paper. Go on, off you go!'

There was a queue at the till in the village store. It was a small shop that sold just about everything but in minute quantities – a vague attempt to cater for every eventuality Casworth might throw at it. Tins of beans sat alongside toilet rolls and cans of dog food and boxes of sellotape were stacked next to a top shelf boasting an impressive range of porno magazines.

Lorna scanned the line of people standing at the counter. There was a grey-haired old lady buying milk and digestive biscuits. A young mum with a toddler who kept repeating the words chocolate and stars over and over again. A middle-aged man in oily overalls. And at the end of the queue, a very handsome gardener in dark green work trousers, a paler green polo shirt and heavy, muddy boots. But he wasn't Joe.

The queue of customers gaped at Lorna as she stood in the doorway staring at them. She glanced around the rest of the shop but there was nobody else there. How odd, she thought. Clare, the shop owner, gave Lorna a look of total bemusement and carried on serving the old lady with the biscuits who now also wanted an ounce of Old Virginia.

'You must have been mistaken, Verity. That wasn't Joe,' she said breezily as she got back inside the florists.

'What, next door? The dishy man in green?'

'Yes. He's not Joe. I've no idea who he is. I've never seen him before.'

'That's who I thought you meant… you know, when you said you were seeing the new church groundsman. I thought you meant him!'

Lorna was confused.

'Does he work at the church then?'

'Yes. He's been there for… ooh… about two months or so? He's got all the local ladies hot under the collar, I can tell you. That's why I assumed he was your man!'

Lorna shook her head and started fiddling nervously with her hair.

'He's got a landscaping business, so I hear. Does a bit of tree surgery, or whatever they call it. Oh, and maintains the church grounds along with lots of other properties. Got himself a little goldmine going, I shouldn't wonder.'

Yeah, I bet he has, thought Lorna. He sounds like the type of gardener my mother wants me to marry.

'I don't think he digs graves though. That's probably what your Joe does then, does he?' she continued.

Lorna didn't really know what to think. At this moment in time she'd quite like Verity to stop waffling and shut the fuck up. If the handsome man in green was the church gardener, then who the hell was Joe? She'd seen him working in the grounds! Pruning, trimming, weeding. She couldn't make any sense of it at all.

'I… I don't know, Verity. Maybe he is the gravedigger, although I think an old man does it.'

'A couple of men do it actually but I haven't got a clue who they are. It's a good job I didn't say anything to the man in the shop just now! He'd have thought I was bonkers!'

Lorna smiled weakly.

'Right, well, thanks for looking after the shop for me. I expect I'll catch up with Joe a bit later on today. Now… what do you fancy ordering for Friday?' she asked, trying to make light of the inner turmoil she felt.

'I've been looking round actually and I love those irises. Can you do something with them? Something quite dramatic! Use your imagination. I'm giving you a blank canvas here, Lorna. You're so clever, I'll love whatever you do.'

Praise indeed. She wished all her customers were like Verity.

'Thank-you. You are sweet. And you're my best customer. Just don't tell anyone I said that.'

As soon as Verity left the shop, Lorna dialed Rose. Evelyn would be at school cooking toad-in-the-hole for a hundred children so she wouldn't be able to stand around and chat. Luckily Rose picked up on the second ring. If she was with a client the call would switch to the answer machine.

'Rose's Beauty Room! How may I help?' Rose sang, her Welsh accent sounding so much stronger on the telephone.

'It's me. I thought I'd give you a quick ring.'

'Is everything alright?'

'No, not really. It's all a bit strange. Verity has just been in to place her weekly order and she'd been to the shop next door before she came to me. She told me Joe was in there. I asked her to hold the fort...'

'...like you did me.'

'Yes. Like I did you. And I went to see him. But he wasn't there. There was a tall, handsome man queuing, wearing gardening gear, but it wasn't Joe.'

'She just made a mistake, that's all, love.'

'No. That's the thing. She hadn't made a mistake. She'd seen the church gardener before – apparently he's new – put two and two together when I told her we were seeing each other, and thought that he was my boyfriend.'

There was silence on the end of the line.

'Are you there?'

'Yes. But you've totally lost me.'

Lorna tutted with irritation.

'Right. I'll start again. Joe told me he was the church's gardener. I've seen him with my own eyes in the churchyard. Gardening.'

'Yes, I get that bit.'

'But the man in the paper shop is the new church gardener. And I've never seen him before in my life. But Verity has.'

'Oh I see. And she thought he was Joe, did she?'

'Yes!'

'But he's not, is he? Obviously.'

'No! He's not!'

'I get you... So, who is he?'

'Oh Rose! He's the church's gardener. Which means...'

'Who is Joe?'

It was Lorna's turn to be silent. She thought for a second.

She didn't have the answer.

'I've no idea.'

The bell over the door jangled and Lorna hastily ended the conversation. She'd have to ring Rose back later. Bloody hell, she was hard work at times.

'Good... afternoon!' called Lady Barrington, hesitating momentarily as she peered at the clock above the counter.

'Good afternoon! How are you?'

'Very well, thank-you. I've popped in for a couple of reasons actually. The first to say a huge thank-you on behalf of my husband and myself for the wonderful flowers you arranged for the Ball. They were spectacular and we received so many compliments on them.'

Lorna flushed a delicate shade of pink.

'Thank-you! I was very pleased with them. It was a big job but I was more than happy with the result. Thank-you for asking me to do them!'

'Well, you did such a good job with the wedding flowers, you were the only woman for the job! I'm just sorry we didn't get to speak to you much on the night. We were rushed off our feet! I don't think we got round to half of our guests. Not properly anyway. You know what these occasions are like.'

Lorna didn't but she nodded anyway.

'It was a lovely evening. Everything was just delightful.'

It wasn't a lie. Everything had been delightful up until the point she'd drunkenly stumbled out of the marquee and spent the entire evening wandering the streets wailing like a banshee.

'Super!'

She took off her Burberry raincoat and stood her umbrella

up against the wall to drain onto the doormat. She was immaculately dressed in a pale beige cashmere sweater, calf-length tan Capri pants and expensive, chestnut leather ankle boots. She may be a pensioner but she had serious style.

'That's better. I can't believe how the weather has changed. Mind you, we needed the rain.'

Lorna wished she had a pound for every time a customer, friend or family member said that to her over the years. Working in a shop meant you had to talk to all and sundry about all sorts of things but the main topic of conversation was always the weather.

'Now, I'm here on other business too. An old housemaid of ours has just passed away. She'd been ill for some time, very brave towards the end. I've been tending to her personally these last few days but we found her this morning, bless her soul. She'd died in her sleep.'

'Oh goodness. That's so sad.'

'It is. She doesn't have a penny to her name so we are paying for the funeral and any other expenses it may incur, so I'd like to order a floral tribute for her coffin if I may.'

'Do you have anything specific in mind?'

Lady Barrington took a moments thought and shrugged her shoulders.

'I'm not sure, Lorna. I know she adored roses? Or is that a trifle dull?'

'No. Not at all. Roses are very popular for wreaths as they keep their form well and smell wonderful for days. Any particular colour scheme?'

'Pretty, summery colours would be lovely, don't you think?'

'Pinks, yellows, oranges with some cream or maybe

white?'

'Perfect! The prettier, the better. Just like her. Oh, she was a beautiful girl in her day... Could you write on the card that they are from everybody at Lutton Hall Estate please? And Lorna, don't worry about cost. Just send us the bill.'

'Of course. Leave it with me. Could I just have the name of the deceased and address of the chapel of rest please?'

'Certainly. Her name is... was, sorry... Miss Adelaide Hardy. And she is... hang on... mind like a sieve...'

She rooted around in her handbag and pulled out a leather pocket diary and flicked through the pages until she found what she was looking for.

'She's at the Stamford Chapel of Rest. The one on Broad Street. Not the other one on the outskirts of town. Oh... and the funeral is this Friday. Hence the rush. We were so lucky to get a slot with Casworth church. I think the vicar pulled a few strings for us, between you and me. Funerals can take up to two weeks to arrange nowadays, you know?'

Lorna was an expert in how long it took for funerals to be arranged. Just as she was an expert in how predictable a bridal bouquet could be.

'Friday is fine. It'll be a much quieter week than last week, to say the least!'

'Bless your heart. Thank-you Lorna and it's lovely to see you again.'

'You too.'

Lady Barrington picked up her coat and umbrella and disappeared from view. Lorna looked at the rain running in rivers down the window pane and watched as a lone magpie swooped down and started to bathe in a puddle just outside

317

the door.

'One for sorrow,' she said miserably under her breath, reaching for the phone to call Rose and finish off the conversation she'd started half an hour earlier.

TWENTY-FIVE

THURSDAY CAME AND WENT – shrouded in a grey, misty, veil of rain that didn't lift all day. The temperature had plummeted, causing Lorna to dig out last winters tights and cardigans for added layers of warmth. She hadn't seen or heard from Joe for three days, despite him telling her that he would come to see her every day now that Alice was being cared for. She kept finding herself slipping off her stool and wandering to the front of the shop, almost in a daze, and squinting through the drizzle, trying to catch a glimpse of Joe making his way to or from work. But she didn't see him, not even once.

She painstakingly arranged fifty roses for Lady Barrington's housemaid after lunch – an explosion of colour wired into a stunning teardrop design, finished off perfectly with trailing fronds of deep green ivy. It was beautiful and it helped cheer up the soggy afternoon. She used slightly more blooms than she normally would for a standard funeral wreath but she'd been told money wasn't an issue and to do a good job regardless of cost. She chose a fitting gift card from a selection she kept in a drawer – plain white with a candle on the front – and she penned the heartfelt message Lady Barrington had dictated to her on Tuesday in her hallmark, swirly, pale blue handwriting. Then she drove the flowers to the chapel of rest and handed them over to a large, surly-looking gentleman in reception, hoping to god his wasn't the first face every grief-stricken customer saw as they walked through the front door of the funeral parlour.

During the night – as torrential rain hammered down onto the roof tiles, keeping her awake – Lorna tossed and turned for hours, unable to switch off long enough for sleep to take over her troubled mind. She kept going over and over everything that had happened to her over the past few weeks, almost as though she was watching a silent movie in her head on repeat. Her thoughts were like laundry in a washing machine. No sooner had they tumbled into a gentle rhythm, becoming quiet and soothed, than they launched into a spin cycle that whirled them around and around angrily. She needed answers to questions, the main one being who exactly was Joe. If he wasn't the church gardener, then who was he, and more importantly, why had he lied to her? She was madly in love with this man. She loved every single thing about him. If she could make a charm to summon up the most perfect man alive, Joe would appear before her very eyes. She thought about the charm she'd made and buried only for it to be unearthed again. Rose and Evelyn were wrong. It had worked. She really did believe her wish had been granted. She wanted to spend the rest of her life with him, to bear his children and grow old and grey with him. These teething problems needed to be ironed out and fast. A relationship built on mistrust wasn't going to last five minutes, she knew that only too well. She decided if she hadn't heard from him by Friday evening, she'd go to Lutton and find him herself. She always swore blind she would never chase a man, not after Dan. But Joe was different. He wasn't like any man she'd met before. It couldn't be that difficult to find him –

Lutton was practically one road and a cluster of houses – and she kicked herself for not having found out where he lived right from the start. She should have been more assertive. Like Evelyn. She should have asked to meet Alice. To insist she helped look after her. To be more involved in Joe's life. But everything had happened so quickly. She'd barely had time to catch her breath. They had endured a whirlwind romance, the stuff of movies, and she'd been well and truly swept off her feet.

Suddenly she remembered the barbecue she'd arranged for Friday night. The weatherman predicted more rain, she'd seen it on the news that morning. At this rate she'd be able to swim to bloody Lutton. But something much more than the weather was troubling her, leaving her unsettled and feeling on edge. She didn't want a barbecue – whether Joe turned up or not. She'd organised it under duress by her maddening mother. Her week had been horrendous enough as it was let alone making it ten times worse. She wasted no time in picking up her phone and sending a group text message to everyone she'd invited cancelling it – citing the weather and the fact she felt a bit fluey as excuses. The first pretext was true, the latter of course was completely fabricated. She never caught colds.

FRIDAY WAS AS WET and miserable as Thursday, and Wednesday, and the rest of the week put together. The ongoing inclemency was obviously taking a toll on the villagers who passed by her window, judging by their sullen faces and hooded eyes. The online grocery order she'd placed on Monday was delivered first thing that morning and she'd been faced with more packs of burgers and sausages than she knew what to do with. She didn't realise she'd ordered so much food. There were bags of salad, tubs of coleslaw, trays of dips, baps and finger rolls and enough beer and wine to keep Kevin from The Vine pissed for an entire week.

She crammed as much as she could into the freezer, the rest went into the fridge, and she wished she'd invited Evelyn and Rose over for supper after all. Together they could eat her out of house and home and would polish off a truckload of salad and a few hot dogs in no time. She also desperately needed cheering up. And if Joe showed his face, as he promised he would, it would be a win-win situation. They could eat, drink and be merry all together! She made a mental note to call the girls later when she had more time on her hands.

CONSIDERING IT WAS such a dismal day, the florist's was busy. She took more money during the morning than she had done all week. Maybe people were buying flowers to lift their spirits in what was now officially the coldest, wettest week in May since records began. She closed the shop briefly at lunchtime to deliver Verity's regular order. As Cherry rumbled up the sweeping driveway, Lorna noticed yet another white van parked in front of the house, this time with a logo emblazoned across the side bearing the owners name, business and telephone number. Apparently Verity's visitor was a certain Michael Pepper and he was an electrician. Lorna wondered which electrical implement in Verity's ultra-modern and fully-functioning home could possibly need repairing. The dishwasher? The vast American-style fridge-freezer? Or was it more likely to be the

322

hairdryer? One of these days Verity was going to get caught red-handed. Unless, of course, she'd already been caught red-handed. There was no telling with Verity. She was hardly discreet. Her dentist husband could quite easily call by the house at anytime, particularly as he owned the practice and the clinic was located only two miles away. Lorna smiled as she pictured Verity straddling some young, fit handyman on her circular water-bed as Johann made his way unexpectedly up the drive.

Verity appeared at the colossal, Ancient Greek-inspired front door wearing a leopard print bikini, a matching sarong and a smile. Absolutely fine if it was this time last week, thought Lorna. But it was a goosebumpy twelve degrees at most. Hardly bikini weather. Michael was most definitely there to fix the hot tub. Or at the very least, to pretend to.

'Come in, lovely!' she called. 'Have you got time for a glass of champagne?'

Lorna glanced down at her watch.

'Not really, Verity. I've got to get back to the shop and open up. I've had a great day today and I want to keep the momentum going!'

'Are you sure? I'm celebrating having my Jacuzzi fixed. It was out of action for nearly a week, you know. Disaster! And you know how I love my bubbles. In both senses of the word. I was going to suggest a dip!'

'Not today, but thank-you. Some other time, perhaps?'

'You're welcome any time, you know that. Just pop up. And bring that man of yours along! I'm gagging to meet him!'

'Yeah. Me too,' Lorna replied, sarcastically.

Irony was wasted on Verity. Her head was full of mid-day

champagne and a possible session in the hot tub with Mr Pepper.

Lorna drove back down the sodden hill into the village, splashing through puddles and watching Cherry's decrepit windscreen wipers trying to cope with the driving rain. As she passed the church, she noticed the flag on the steeple was at half-mast and the lane to the village hall had bright orange traffic cones positioned across its entrance. Either a wedding or a funeral was about to take place. Then she remembered. It was the housemaid from Lutton Hall's funeral. If she got back in time, she would be able to watch the cortege drive past the shop. She hoped the Barrington family were pleased with the display she'd arranged. She wondered if she'd gone a little over the top with it, using too many flowers, too many colours, too many varieties of rose. It wasn't a typical funeral wreath, granted, but Lady Barrington had requested pretty and pretty is what Miss Hardy had got. It was just a shame she'd never get to see it.

Lorna opened the shutters and flipped the closed sign to open just as a sleek, glossy hearse came into view around the bend by the village sign. Lorna opened the door and stood in the doorway out of the rain. She'd read somewhere that rain falling on the day of a funeral implied the deceased had passed away before their time. She glanced up at the blackened sky above her, heavy with storm clouds and laden with a million celestial teardrops. In the distance, she could hear the church bells tolling – each one meticulously-timed, forbidding, sombre chimes announcing Adelaide's imminent arrival.

Lorna watched as the hearse carrying the coffin, draped

in roses and ivy, drove slowly past. A second black, shiny limousine followed close behind carrying the chief mourners. As the car drew level with the shop, Lorna recognised Lord and Lady Barrington and several other family members sitting in the passenger seats. It was a solemn moment, watching the dead make their last journey. She bowed her head as a mark of respect as the procession passed in front of her and she stood in the doorway until the cars disappeared from view and the bell tolled no more.

Miss Adelaide Hardy had reached her final resting place.

LORNA CLOSED THE DOOR to her flat and kicked off her shoes. She was exhausted. This week had been mentally exhausting and for the first time in her career, she didn't much feel like opening the shop in the morning. She wanted to stay in bed and sleep for a month. The week had started out so well but was now ending so badly. Her stomach was beginning to churn at every opportunity – a sickening nervousness tying it in a multitude of knots. Every now and then, her heart would flutter, filling her with alarm and an overriding fear that she was about to have a heart attack. She knew deep down that the cause of her anxiety was Joe and the thing she needed to do most was to calm down but that was easier said than done. She was never usually one to worry. But then she met Joe. Now every little niggle seemed to escalate into a full-blown crisis. She felt an intense sensation of ominous foreboding, a sixth sense that something was very, very wrong. She was almost bracing herself for her world to shatter into a billion pieces.

She went into the kitchen and pulled a bottle of Rioja from

the wine rack. She opened it and poured herself a large glass and took a swig from it, swiftly followed by another. She mooched from room to room, her eyes filling with tears as she sat on the side of the bed where Joe had slept and stroked his pillow as if it were a fluffy kitten. She drained her glass and poured herself a second. She'd completely forgotten to call Rose and Evelyn with all the activity in the shop and she cursed herself. She wished they were here more than ever.

She missed Joe so much. She longed to see him, even if it was only for five minutes, just to reassure herself that he was alright. It was almost five days since she last held him in her arms, gazed into his eyes of green. Five days since she'd kissed him with a love she'd only ever known for him. She wondered if something had happened to Alice. But surely Joe would find a way of letting her know if his sister had died. She'd not heard of anyone called Alice dying in Lutton. Only poor Adelaide. And it was such a tiny village... the odds of two people from a sleepy, handful of houses dying in the same week were so remote...

Somewhere in the murky depths of her subconscious, a light bulb flickered on. She had to sit down. If she continued standing, her legs would most likely buckle and give way and she'd fall to the floor. She reached for the laptop by the side of the bed and flipped the top up, shouting at it like a naughty child for being so slow to boot up. Her hands shook as she typed the words 'Name Meanings – Adelaide' into the search engine and pressed the return key. Pages and pages of Christian name websites flashed up before her eyes. She had no desire to waste any time looking at them all so she clicked on the site at the top of the screen and drummed her fingers on the keyboard impatiently as it loaded painfully slowly.

'Adelaide. Of French origin derived from the Germanic name Adalheidis,' she read aloud. 'Hmm… sounds a bit like Edelweis…'

Her eyes scanned further down the text and she read on.

'Diminutives of the name include Ada, Alison, Alicia… Alice.'

She gasped and her hands began to tremble so much she could hardly shut down the computer.

'Oh god. She's dead,' she whispered. 'I've got to find him. You stupid, stupid idiot!' she screamed at her reflection in the mirror opposite her bed.

The flowers she made were for Alice! She'd stood in her shop doorway that very morning and watched Alice's coffin pass her by. Bowed her head. Listened to the bells tolling for her. Jesus! Joe must have been in the limo with the Barrington's… She was furious with herself for not making the connection before. She must be stupid! Poor, poor Joe! He'd gone through all of this week totally alone. She should have been there by his side.

She wracked her brain to recall snippets of conversation from Tuesday when Lady Barrington came into the florists to place the order. Adelaide was pretty, she remembered that much. She was a housemaid at the Hall. She was penniless. Did she mention anything about her having any family? She couldn't remember. She swigged back the remainder of the wine and ran into the hallway, scooping up her bag, car keys and pushing her feet back into the pumps she'd kicked off just a few minutes before.

She was very aware she'd drunk half a bottle of red

wine on an empty stomach as she drove cautiously towards Lutton. It was a quiet, country lane but even so. The last thing she needed right now was to get stopped by the police, breathalised and banned from driving for a year. It would destroy her livelihood in one fell swoop.

As she crawled into Lutton, she drove to the centre of the village and parked next to the church. She was still shaking but had calmed down considerably, probably due to the red wine that was now infiltrating her bloodstream.

She locked the car and began walking towards the first huddle of cottages, the ancient, thatched ones that stood higgledy-piggledy along Lover's Lane. As she approached the house on the corner, the one with the postbox set into the wall, she saw a small van parked on the verge next to the gate that led through to the cottage's garden. The rear door was open and from somewhere inside the vehicle she could hear the curious chirruping of birds. Lorna stood next to the wall and peered into the van and then over the wall into the wild, tangled garden. There was a solitary faded, yellow duster on the washing line and the grass was over a foot high.

A scruffy man in filthy, torn dungarees suddenly emerged from the garden carrying what appeared to be dozens of tiny finches in old-fashioned, metal birdcages. He looked startled as he glanced up nonchalantly only to see Lorna standing just inches away from him.

'Can I help?' he asked suspiciously, taking a step backwards.

'Er… I'm not sure. I'm looking for somebody.. I know they live… lived… around here somewhere, but I don't know where exactly…'

'Oh, well, I'm not from the village but I know a bit about

the people who live here. I've worked on the estate for forty-odd years. I'm collecting these birds. The owner's just died.'

'The owner?'

'An old lady. Worked all her life at the Hall. Buried her this morning, they did,' he sniffed, shoving the cages roughly into the back of the van without any regard for the poor creatures inside them. He slammed the doors shut.

'An old lady? Oh, no. No. I'm looking for a much younger woman. I don't think this is the right house, but thank-you anyway.'

'Adelaide Hardy, her name was. Lived here all her life. An' a sorry ol' life, it was an'all.'

Lorna frowned and gulped.

'I think you must be mistaken. The Adelaide I am looking for is in her late teens, early twenties at most. They call her…'

'Alice. Yes, that's her. Alice for short. Only the hoity toity brigade called her Adelaide. But we all knew her as Alice. Beautiful girl, in her day. Whatever gave you the idea she was a young gell?' he jeered, grinning and displaying a mouthful of blackened teeth.

Lorna's heart started to bang so loudly she thought it might smash through her rib cage. Alice was old? How did that figure?

'I… I don't know. I'm confused. This Alice…you say she had a sorry life…?'

'She did, the poor old sod. All her family died when she was a gell. Eighteen she was, when the ol' boy died. The only family she ever had was the estate workers. She never married or owt. Stayed here, she did. Her mam and dad used to run the old Post Office before the war.'

329

Lorna felt close to collapse. Before the war? Just how old was Alice? She'd lost her entire family when she was a girl? And what did he mean 'when the ol' boy died'?

The sound of her own heartbeat resonated throughout her head as hot, sticky blood surged through her veins. She felt faint. Nothing made sense anymore. She struggled to think coherently.

'Old Lord and Lady Barrington looked after her well – as did the present ones, mind. Paid for her funeral an' everything.'

The tatty man in dirty dungarees was still prattling away to himself as she turned and ran to the car. Her legs felt as though they were made of spaghetti and she was so dizzy she thought she was going to throw up. These stories didn't add up. She had to get to the church in Casworth, to see for herself exactly who Alice was.

As she reversed and slammed the car into gear, accelerating hard, there was a loud thud and a flurry of black and white feathers swirled in front of the windscreen. The dead magpie lay on the bonnet of the car for a second before it slid off, landing with a splash in a muddy puddle. Lorna slammed her foot down onto the break and skidded to a halt. She'd never killed anything in her life. She burst into tears of exasperation and sat gripping the steering wheel tightly for a few moments, trying to comprehend what was happening, before pulling herself together enough to drive at high speed towards Casworth.

THE SKY HAD DARKENED to a menacing shade of battleship grey and the wind blew in from the east, driving the rain sideways, striking Lorna's face and arms like a thousand lashes of a whip. Her legs felt heavy as she ran uphill towards the church, her feet becoming slippery in her shoes, her peripheral vision blurring into an almost tunnel-like world of slow motion. She burst through the entrance into the graveyard, steadying her gait briefly as she tried to navigate her way through the rain to the area of ground reserved for modern day burials. She crunched along the gravel pathway, the stones wet and shiny beneath her feet, down the side of the church, in the direction of the rose garden and beyond. She ran past the elderly mulberry tree with the circular bench and the quiet, shady corner where the little ones slept.

She stopped for a second and peered further along the path. In the distance she could see a mound of earth covered in flowers. She stood for a moment, soaked to the skin and surveyed the grave. Slowly, she walked towards it, her heart beating faster with every step. She knelt down at the foot of the recent burial, panting, trying to catch her breath, and read one of the message cards attached to a wreath in the shape of a car.

'Darling John. We will miss you always. Forever in our thoughts. Pam and family.'

This wasn't Alice's grave.

She scanned the plots again but none of them seemed any more recent than John's. There were others, of course, huge piles of earth, too new for headstones, but their flowers had wilted and discoloured and decayed. She wandered around looking for the flowers she'd arranged – the teardrop of summer roses and trailing ivy – but it was nowhere to be seen.

She continued walking around the graveyard aimlessly, the relentless rain stinging her skin, a sense of confusion and bewilderment engulfing her mind. She'd gone mad. She'd heard about people losing their minds over the most trivial of things. This must be how it felt. Panic started to rise from the pit of her stomach and she had an overwhelming desire to run and run and keep on running.

Alice must be here somewhere, for gods sake! She had to be! She'd seen the funeral cortege pass by that morning. Lady Barrington said they'd pulled strings with the vicar to get a burial slot at Casworth church on Friday. It usually took two weeks! She hadn't imagined all that. If she had, she needed sectioning. And quickly.

She began to dart between the graves once again, the wet grass brushing against her ankles, her lungs beginning to hurt, and made her way down the edge of the churchyard towards the cedar trees. It was darker there, the trees were so old and majestic, their evergreen branches blocking out much of the light from above.

She stopped running and held onto the back of the bench that overlooked the trees. Her eyes wandered from one gravestone to another as she read the names aloud.

'Clarence George Fitzjohn. Katherine Lillian Happisford. Victor Edwin Freshwater.'

She read the name again. And then again. An icy shiver trickled down her spine and the hairs on her arms stood on end. She read aloud the inscription on the stone.

'Victor Edwin Freshwater. A loyal soul who tended this parish for a lifetime. Born April 16, 1867. Died August 3, 1956. Aged 89 Years.'

She could barely breathe.

'But I've spoken to him... I've seen him with my own...' she whispered.

Just then, out of the corner of her eye, she saw colour. She held onto the bench for support and looked beyond Victor's stone, over to the graves that lay beneath the shelter of the cedar trees. She could see flowers – fresh, vivid, beautiful flowers – lying unperturbed amongst a sea of darkness.

With her breathing slow and low and her eyes wide and frightened, she edged cautiously over to the wreath, instantly recognising it as the one she'd made with her very own hands. It was placed on top of a mound of new, black, peaty earth. There were no other flowers to be seen. She crouched down on the wet ground and read her own distinctive handwriting, neat and feminine and in the palest, baby blue ink.

Her gaze shifted hesitantly to the gravestones next to Alice's plot. They were tall and grey and almost identical, apart from the inscriptions engraved upon them. The headstone on the left bore the name Elizabeth Mary Hardy, and the stone to the right belonged to her husband, Edward John Hardy. Alice had been laid to rest alongside her parents. She reluctantly allowed her eyes to deviate further – to the stone standing next to Elizabeth's. A white slab of marble, a good deal shorter than the other two – polished and gleaming and as pristine now as the day it was erected.

Lorna trailed her fingertips across the expertly engraved script, her mouth dry and eyes scarcely believing what they were reading.

'Lance Corporal Joseph Edward Hardy. Who died of wounds received in Normandy, 1942 aged 23 years. January

25th, 1920 – February 11th, 1943. Brave To The Very End.'

An intense, searing pain deep within her chest cavity tore through her body as her heart ripped in two. She fell to her knees and gripped the sides of the cold, white marble, unable to breathe, choking on nothing but fresh evening air. The whole world was spinning violently around her and she couldn't focus properly. An almighty clap of thunder reverberated high above her and the heavens opened once again. Her shoulders dropped forward and her mouth opened wide but she made no sound. Her fingernails clawed furiously at the wet, mossy, blanket that had covered Joe for over seventy years. There was a high-pitched ringing in her ears and she began to see small patches of black, tiny at first, but growing bigger and bigger by the second until all was black and she could see no more.

TWENTY-SIX

ROSE TRIED CALLING Lorna at eight pm. The phone rang and rang and then switched to voicemail. Perturbed, she dialed again. And again. Then she sent a text message. Followed by three more. At just before ten pm she called Evelyn, who, unbeknown to Rose, had also been trying to contact Lorna, albeit rather less persistently. They decided to drive over to the flat immediately. For all they knew, Lorna was having a good time with Joe and deliberately not answering their calls and messages. But both women had a gut feeling that all was not well.

They arrived at the Maltings at almost exactly the same time, parking their cars on the side of the road in front of the communal front door. Rose pressed Lorna's buzzer and waited. There was no answer. She pressed it again. She took a step backwards off the pavement and into the road and craned her neck to look up at Lorna's windows. The flat appeared to be in darkness.

'Let's go round the back – we can see if the bedroom or living room lights are on,' whispered Evelyn.

'Good idea. Although even if they are on, we can't gain access, can we? What if she's lying there dead inside?'

'For fucks sake, Rose! You do talk a load of bloody rubbish. She's not lying there dead inside!'

Rose muttered something under her breath and the two women made their way around the corner and down the little track that led to the garage block and the back gate into the shared garden. They unlatched the door and crept inside.

'I feel like a burglar,' hissed Rose.

They stood under a maple tree and surveyed the rear of the Maltings. The flat where Peggy lived was ablaze with light, as was the flat directly underneath Lorna's. The other was in total darkness and Lorna's was too, apart from a tiny glimmer of light coming from the living room.

'That'll be from her sticks…' said Rose.

'Sticks?'

'Yes. Those sticks in the corner with the little lights on them. She's always got them on.'

'Oh. Yeah. Well… it doesn't look like she's home. Maybe she's just gone out. Her car's not here either,' she replied, peering over towards the garage block.

'It doesn't feel right though, does it? I feel very unsettled. Shall we try to get inside the building just to check?'

'Rose, I think you've seen too many horror films. Let's just go home. If she came back now and caught us lurking around her flat she'd think we'd well and truly lost our marbles.'

'Well, I'm going to check, whether you like it or not,' she said, marching off into the darkness.

Evelyn heaved a huge sigh of frustration and scuttled off after her. When she finally caught up with her, Rose was already pressing number 2 on the buzzer keypad. It was getting late and Evelyn was starting to regret even being there. Now they were about to wake up the residents of the building and Lorna would be furious with them when she found out.

'Yes…?' croaked a husky female voice.

'I'm so sorry to bother you at this hour but we are friends of Lorna Mills from flat number three. I wonder if you could possibly let us in please? She's not answering her buzzer.'

There was a muffled sound at the other end of the line as the woman relayed the conversation word for word to someone else in the flat.

'Hang on...'

There was a click followed by footsteps and the front door creaked open slowly. Peggy stood in the hall in her dressing gown and slippers.

'Oh. It's you two. I recognise you both. I was just saying to my husband that if I didn't recognise you I wouldn't let you in. But I do. So... you'd better come in.'

Rose and Evelyn stepped inside and thanked Peggy. They started to make their way up the staircase but Peggy wasn't letting it lie there.

'Are you sure she's not gone out? Have you checked the garages?'

'Yes. Her car's not there but... well, we just want to make sure everything is ok.'

'Oh, well, I'm sure she's alright. Just out gadding I expect, young gal and that. Mind you, next door saw her last week and said she was talking to herself.'

Rose and Evelyn looked at each other in alarm.

'Talking to herself?'

'Mmm. They said it was most peculiar. As if she had someone next to her, like. She kept looking at them and gesturing to them. But there was nobody there. Always did think she was an odd...'

She stopped short of finishing her sentence and looked at

337

the two women blankly.

'Anyway, thanks for letting us in, again... er... Peggy. You'd better get back inside. It's a bit chilly out here,' said Evelyn.

Peggy huddled her dressing gown around her tightly and shivered.

'It is a bit. Sodding weather. Doesn't know what it's doing.'

The two women got to the top of the stairs and waited until Peggy was safely inside her flat.

'Fucking woman. Imagine living in the same building as her.'

'At least she let us in. She could have told us to piss off.'

Rose knocked on the bottle green front door and waited patiently. Then she fished out her mobile phone and scrolled through a list of names until she got to Lorna's and pressed the call button.

'It's ringing,' she told Evelyn unnecessarily.

Evelyn had her face up against the door trying to look through the spy hole.

'Not sure what you're trying to achieve there, Evelyn. They were invented so you could look out and see who was at your front door. Not so peeping toms could look in and spy on you in your underwear.'

'Shut up, Rose. I can hear something.'

Rose pulled a face and mumbled something to herself in Welsh. Evelyn was always telling her off.

'I can hear her mobile ringing.'

'What...?'

'Ssh...' Evelyn pressed her ear up against the door. 'I can hear it. It's that stupid ring tone of hers – the one from that comedy she likes.'

'Are you sure it's not the telly?'

Evelyn looked at Rose with pure disdain.

'Are you being serious? The telly isn't even on. We'd have been able to see it through the window. It's her phone, I'm telling you.'

'But why would she go out without her phone?'

'That's what I'm worried about.'

'What shall we do? She wouldn't go anywhere without it. She even takes it to bed.'

'Her car's not here so she must have gone out somewhere.'

'But she never, ever drives without having her phone on her. Look how many times she's told us off for not having our phones with us when we travel anywhere. It doesn't add up.'

'What do we do then? We've no way of contacting her. We can't go to the police. What the hell would we say? 'Excuse me, officer, but our friend's gone out without her mobile phone. Please can you send out a search and rescue team.' They'd lock us up.'

'We'll have to sit and wait.'

Evelyn glanced at her watch.

'It's nearly ten-thirty. I'll tell you what... you drive to Lutton and see if you can see her car. I don't know where Joe lives but if she's with him, you're bound to see it somewhere. It hardly blends into the background. And I'll stay here and sit outside until you come back, in case she shows up.'

Rose nodded and zapped her car with the remote unlocking device.

'Good idea. I'll go straight away.'

She drove the mile to Lutton and checked every road and

driveway in the village while Evelyn sat in darkness and scrutinised every car that drove by and every person that passed. Neither woman had any luck.

It was nearly eleven-thirty by the time Rose drove back into Casworth. She parked her car behind Evelyn's and Evelyn got out of her car and into Rose's. She needed warming up.

'Well?'

'Nothing. I literally drove into every nook and cranny of that damn village and she's nowhere to be seen. I take it you had no joy either?'

'No. Or I'd be inside there with a glass of wine and not half frozen to death in my car,' she said, pointing a finger at Lorna's flat.

'I guess we just sit and wait. If it gets to some silly hour and she's not back then we know something is wrong. She'd never stay out all night without having some means of communication on her.'

Evelyn agreed and they prepared themselves for a long night.

THE CHURCH WARDEN was doing his final check of the grounds before locking the gate and turning in for the night. There was a time when there was no need to lock the gate. But times had changed and only four months ago an extremely valuable stone effigy was stolen from the church porch. Graves had also been vandalised in recent years and a blatant attempt to steal precious lead from the roof was foiled thanks to vigilant passers by, who ended up throwing rocks and stones at the thieves to scare them off.

It was still raining heavily and the warden was dressed for

the occasion in a heavy waxed jacket, waterproof trousers and wellies. He doubted anyone in their right mind would be out on a night like this, let alone out stealing or up to no good, so he stuck to the perimeter of the grounds, shining his torch casually here and there as he made his way around the inky graveyard.

As he crunched along the gravel path that ran underneath the grand cedar trees, he noticed something unfamiliar to him. He knew the perimeter pathway like the back of his hand and the area beneath the colossal evergreens was the darkest, stillest, most eerie part of the burial ground. But in the pitch-black of night he could just make out something light-coloured lying on the ground to the left of the path, only a few feet away from him. He flicked his torch onto full beam and shone it onto the object. He squinted through the rain, the light from the torch illuminating the raindrops so they resembled a multitude of sparkling crystals flying through the air. He edged closer to get a better look and that's when he saw feet, legs, bare arms and long, long, red hair. His heart leapt in his chest and he briefly saw stars. A hundred and one thoughts and scenarios raced through his mind and he began to shake. He braced himself for what might happen next. He'd never seen a dead body before, let alone discovered one.

He crouched by the woman and shone the torch up and down the length of her body. She was lying face down on top of a grave. Her clothes clung to her and her fingernails were embedded in the lichen and moss beneath her. He quickly flashed the light up to the tombstone at her head and read the name upon it. Joseph Edward Hardy. Then he positioned the torch on the wet grass beside the grave and with trembling fingers, pushed tendrils of hair from her face. He leaned in towards her and reached for her wrist. Her skin was as cold as ice. She was sure to be dead. He felt for her pulse and at the same time lowered his head towards her mouth. Simultaneously he felt her breath on his cheek and her heartbeat coursing blood through her veins. She was alive.

Relief washed over him and he took a deep breath to steady his jangling nerves. He was too scared to move her in case she was injured so he took off his waxed jacket and lay it gently over her frozen body. Next he rifled through his pockets until he found his mobile phone. He very rarely carried it around with him at night but this night, intuition told him to take it with him. He dialed 999, calmly explained to the operator that he had just discovered a young lady face down in a graveyard and gave her his precise location. Then he waited patiently for the ambulance to arrive.

THE FIRST EVELYN and Rose knew that something was wrong, was when Rose's mobile rang and woke the pair of them up. They had fallen asleep in the car waiting for Lorna to materialise and the piercing shrill of the ring tone made them jump out of their skins. Rose fumbled in the darkness trying to answer her phone, her heart racing, and after several attempts, finally managed to connect to the caller. She gained full use of all her senses when she heard Phillip's voice on the other end of the line. He was composed and his usual softly-spoken self as he explained gently that Lorna had been found by the church warden in Casworth churchyard at around midnight. Lorna was fine – there was no sign of any injury or assault – but she was bordering on being hypothermic and her blood pressure was quite low as a result. She was in the city hospital and being very well cared for. She'd been sedated and was now sleeping. She would be assessed in the morning and they would take it from there. And that was it.

Rose stared at Evelyn, her mouth agape and unable to speak.

'Rose, what's happened?'

Rose shook her head and continued gawping.

'Rose!'

'She... she was found in the graveyard. She's got hypothermia. She's been sedated,' she eventually managed to say, her voice barely audible above the whirr of the fan heater in the car.

Evelyn peered at the clock on the dash. It was two o'clock in the morning.

'Sedated? Why? Why was she in the graveyard? Has she been hurt?'

Rose shook her head and her eyes started to fill with tears.

'No... nobody has done anything to her. The church warden found her at midnight. I've no idea why she was there, Evelyn. Or why she's been sedated. Poor Lorna.'

Rose burst into tears and her friend slipped an arm around her shoulders and gave her a comforting squeeze.

'Rose... are you thinking what I'm thinking?' asked Evelyn after a few moments contemplation.

Rose raised her chin to look anxiously at Evelyn, her eyes bloodshot and her cheeks shiny and wet with tears.

'That she's had some sort of breakdown...?' she asked croakily.

Evelyn didn't respond with words. She only need nod her reply. The two women sat in silence, holding one another's hand, watching little rivers of water run down the windscreen and listening to the hypnotic pitter-patter of rainfall on the roof above them.

TWENTY-SEVEN

AFTER BEING THOROUGHLY checked over and given a clean bill of health, Lorna was discharged from hospital the following lunchtime. Jilly and Phillip were adamant she would not be returning to her flat and would be much better off recovering at their home instead. Lorna, still woolly-headed from the sedation, agreed to go home with them without so much as an ounce of resistance.

Once back in her childhood bedroom, she showered and changed into a pair of her brothers pyjamas and sat on the edge of her bed, as still as the night, looking out onto the lush and verdant garden that her parents lavished so much time and money on. A weeks worth of rain had replenished it, rejuvenated it – the yellowing grass was now emerald green and the borders were a riot of radiant colour. She gazed at the sky. The bleak, grey clouds of the past week had all but disappeared, replaced by fluffy white balls of cotton wool drifting across a never-ending vastness of ultramarine.

'I didn't think I'd see the sun again,' she whispered to her reflection in the window.

An overwhelming ache rose from the depths of her soul and her eyes were suddenly brimming over with tears. They spilled down her cheeks and dripped like a leaking tap off her chin onto the white and blue ticking of her brother's pyjama trousers.

'Oh Joe, where are you?' she breathed.

She got up off the bed and walked to the window and placed her hands upon the glass.

'You said you'd never leave me…'

She stood for what felt like hours staring out at nothing in particular, silent tears streaming down her face, a river that refused to run dry. She felt a hand on her shoulder, and turned sharply, only to see her father standing behind her. She hadn't even heard him open the door and come into the room. She glanced down and saw he'd placed a tray at the end of her bed.

He gently wrapped his arms around her and held her until her sobbing receded and she was still again.

'I've bought you up some tea. I thought you must be hungry. But it might be a bit cold now. Shall I do you some more?'

Lorna reached for the box of tissues on her dressing table and blew her nose loudly. She looked at her reflection in the gilt-edged three-way mirror she'd had since childhood and saw a red, puffy face gazing back at her.

'God, I look awful.'

Phillip smoothed her hair back and placed a finger under her chin and tilted her face up to his.

'You look beautiful. You always do. Now come one, eat something.'

Lorna eyed the plate of scrambled eggs on toast and felt her stomach growl ferociously. She'd not eaten for an entire twenty-four hours and she was ravenous.

'I'll try it.'

Ten minutes later, she'd eaten everything on her plate and drunk her mug of warm, sweet tea.

'Are you up for visitors, love?'

'It depends who they are…'

'Rose and Evelyn want to come over. They've been desperately worried about you. They sat outside your flat for most of last night. I called Rose after you were found and discovered they were both asleep in her car outside the Maltings.'

Lorna began to cry again. What had she ever done to deserve such friends like them.

'Yes… of course,' she sniffed. 'I want to… need to… see them. They don't know that Joe is dead yet.'

Phillip nodded slowly and took her hand.

'You've had a terrible shock. It would do you the power of good to see them. I'll tell them to come over when they are ready.'

Lorna went into her little bathroom and washed her face and hands and combed her hair, before tying it back in a loose ponytail.

It didn't take Rose and Evelyn long to drive over to the Mills' house. Rose cancelled all her appointments for the day and Evelyn had stayed the night at her cottage. They'd hardly slept, waiting for a phone call from either of Lorna's parents to let them know how she was and when she'd be going home. Jilly didn't tell them very much when she finally did call, only that Lorna was deeply traumatised and extremely tearful. She said she'd explain everything to them when she saw them.

It was Phillip who answered the front door. Jilly's car wasn't on the driveway, which both women thought was a bit odd but Phillip was quick to explain her absence.

'Jilly's just popped over to Lorna's flat – to pick up some clothes, toiletries, bits and bobs.'

'We wondered where she was...' said Evelyn, stepping into the hall with its beautiful, terracotta tiled floor.

Both she and Rose embraced Phillip. They had known him for ten years and were both very fond of him. Rose in particular had a soft spot for him, often wishing she'd met him before Jilly had. He was dream husband material and in Rose's world, dream husbands were as rare as hen's teeth.

'Oh Phillip... how is she? What the hell has happened?'

He ushered them through into the lounge and closed the glass double doors.

'I'll make it snappy. She's up in her room, I'm not sure if she's awake or asleep.'

The two women sat down on the sofa and looked at him expectantly.

'Well?' urged Rose.

Phillip leaned forward, his hands clasped together between his knees, and took a deep breath.

'She was found by the warden at Casworth church, seemingly unconscious and wet through. We don't know how long she'd been there. Anyway, he called the ambulance and they took her in and then we got a phone call.'

'How did they know who she was?'

'She'd parked her car in the lane alongside the graveyard and had her car keys in her hand when she was found. The warden knew the car belonged to her – it's pretty distinctive – and he gave the hospital her name and address. I suppose from there, they traced us. I've no idea how they do these things but we were contacted within the hour. Amazing really. We just got out of bed, got dressed and drove to the hospital.'

'But what happened Phillip? Why was she there?' asked Rose, her face crumpled and her brow lined with worry.

'By the time we got there she was on a ward and had warmed up a little. She'd already had blood taken and things like her oxygen levels tested, blood pressure, an ECG, all that. And medically she was ok. But she was rambling, mumbling, frightened. She kept saying Joe was dead and he'd been dead for seventy years. At one point she got really hysterical and that's when they sedated her. I must say it was all very distressing – for her and for us. We still don't really know what she meant... saying Joe has been dead a long time. She keeps crying and since she's been home, she's not said a word.'

Rose and Evelyn sat in dumbfounded silence, trying to process everything they had just been told.

'Can we go up?' asked Evelyn eventually.

Phillip nodded and opened the lounge door.

'You know where to go.'

They found Lorna in her room. It was bright and sunny and quiet and she was lying on her side on the. bed with her back towards them. Evelyn sat down next to her and Rose edged around the bed and knelt by her side. Her doe eyes opened slowly and they were filled with fear.

'I'm glad you're here,' she murmured.

Rose stroked her hair and reached for her hand.

'We've been worried sick...'

'I know. Dad said. I'm so sorry.'

Her voice was soft and low, her eyes red from crying and

her eyelids puffy and swollen.

Evelyn smoothed her hair.

'Don't be silly... you'd have been worried about either one of us if the tables were turned.'

The three friends sat in silence for a few moments until Lorna got up and began to talk.

She told them how she'd gone home from work and realised the funeral cortege she'd seen that morning was Alice's. She told them how she'd got into her car and driven to Lutton to try to find Joe and got talking to a man who was loading cages of birds into the back of his van. She soon discovered the birds belonged to Alice and the man told her Alice had worked in the Hall as a housemaid all of her life and had lost her family as a young woman. She'd never married, had died on Monday and was buried that morning. But he said Alice was an old lady. Rose and Evelyn looked at each other and an icy shiver ran down their spines. Both were starting to piece the puzzle together mentally and had an inkling of what was about to come.

Lorna continued, stopping every now and then to dab at her eyes or blow her nose. She told them how she drove like a woman possessed to the church and ran frantically around the graveyard trying to find Alice's grave. She told them about Victor Freshwater and her shock at seeing his name engraved upon a gravestone. Then she told them she found Alice's grave, all new and fresh with the wreath she'd made placed on top of the dark, wet earth.

Rose and Evelyn sat on the bed gripping Lorna's hands as she began to cry.

'That's when I saw him... his gravestone was... is... next

to his mother's. He died in the war. Of injuries received in France...' she sobbed. 'The scar. On his chest. Where he got shot...'

Rose looked at Evelyn, her eyes filled with horror. Neither woman could muster up the strength to speak. Lorna's words left them bewildered, speechless and filled with terror.

'But he was real...'

Evelyn draped an arm around Lorna's shoulder and pulled her towards her.

'I'm sure it felt that way, sweetheart.'

Lorna lifted her head from Evelyn's shoulder and glared at her.

'What do you mean? You think I imagined him? That I made all this up?'

'Well...no... but the mind is capable of so much more than we...'

Lorna shoved Evelyn away with a ferocity that she had never seen before.

'How dare you!' she hissed. 'You of all people. You with the most open of minds, capable of casting spells that do bad as well as good, you... who has seen and experienced things most others haven't.'

Evelyn was lost for words. Everything Lorna was saying was true.

'Lorna... darling... I don't think Evelyn meant to upset you,' interrupted Rose, her voice calm and soothing.

'And what do you think Rose? The same as Evelyn, I suppose? That I somehow conjured Joe up like a magician or that he lived in my imagination?'

'No, sweetheart, no... it's just...'

Lorna raised her arms in the air and laughed sarcastically. 'Oh here we go... It's just what, Rose?'

Rose's cheeks flushed pink and she swallowed nervously.

'It's just that we never met Joe. Nobody did. Nobody saw him. Then you said Verity told you the new church gardener was somebody else – and not Joe. And last night Peggy mentioned your neighbours had chatted to you recently and you were... you were... talking and gesturing to somebody next to you who wasn't... actually... there.'

Her voice trailed off to a whisper as she looked down at Lorna's hands resting in hers.

'Oh my god... what have you done to your hands?' she cried, gently splaying Lorna's fingers and staring at the broken, bloody nails, ripped from the end of each finger tip.

Lorna's eyes filled with tears again as she held her hands out in front of her and gazed at them.

'I was trying to reach him,' she breathed, her voice hoarse and muted. 'In the ground.'

She looked into Rose's eyes, like a little girl lost.

'Rose, have I gone mad...?'

Rose and Evelyn threw their arms around their heartbroken, fractured, shattered friend and tried their utmost to reassure her and console her and soothe her the best they could. They stayed with her until she drifted off to sleep and then they crept quietly out of her room and down the stairs, where they sat drinking tea until the sun set and the moon rose, relaying the entire sorry tale to Jilly and Phillip, urging them to get Lorna assessed by a psychiatrist as soon as possible.

TWENTY-EIGHT

EVELYN'S PHONE BUZZED, waking her from a bizarre dream in which she was in the middle of a battlefield in Normandy digging graves for fallen soldiers. She felt a wave of relief flood over her as she opened her eyes and realised she was in her own dark, velvety cocoon of a bedroom and not up to her knees in mud surrounded by the walking wounded. She reached for her phone, expecting the incoming text to be from Rose but saw it was from Rupert.

Last night they'd enjoyed dinner together in the same pub they'd ventured to for their first, disastrous date. This time round things were very different. She'd disliked Rupert in the beginning, thinking him dreary, posh and far too dull to ever consider becoming romantically involved with. But he was persistent, attractively so, and over time, she'd grown to love him. Not merely as a friend but as a partner. She really did love him. He was witty, funny, affectionate, and treated her like a lady.

Over dinner, she told him about Lorna and the ordeal she had endured. She thought he might be judgemental and form strong opinions about her personality or her state of mind but he was quite the opposite. Evelyn was relieved to discover he was as broad-minded as she was as he started to talk about the possibility of other factors that could explain Lorna's encounter with a man who had been dead since the 1940's. He also agreed it would be a good idea to get her

353

assessed by a psychiatrist and he gave Evelyn the name of a good friend of his who worked as such at a nearby private hospital. She promised she would pass the information on to Jilly and Phillip straight away. They discussed Lorna until it was kicking out time and Evelyn, exhausted both physically and mentally, went home and straight to bed.

She pressed the envelope icon button and read Rupert's text.

< Hello, my darling. I hope you had a good nights sleep and feel much better today. I hope you don't mind but I've spoken to mum about Lorna. She would very much like to talk to you. I know we were planning a quiet night in tonight, but would you come over to the Hall for dinner? >

Evelyn was baffled as to why Lady Barrington wanted to talk to her but seeing as there was a connection between Lorna and Lutton Hall by way of Alice, she accepted the dinner invitation without hesitation. She was intrigued.

EVELYN SWEPT through the gates of Lutton Hall in her black Mini Cooper. As she drove along the private road to the beautiful, stone manor house, she surveyed the majestic surroundings that had been an integral part of her boyfriend's noble family for generations. The grounds that unfolded before her, for as far as the eye could see, had entertained lords and ladies and kings and queens over the centuries, and she felt extremely lucky to be part of such a family, no matter how long or brief the privilege.

Rupert met her in front of the house, with its wide flight

of smooth stone steps leading down to a perfectly circular, gravelled forecourt bordered by pristine box hedging. He watched as she pulled up to the house and parked, then crunched across the shingle, looking every inch the country gentleman, and opened the car door for her. He kissed her cheek and gallantly took her by the hand, leading her up the steps and into the house.

Inside, the formidable air of grandeur quickly faded to one of a very ordinary family home. The large, formal drawing room was furnished with vast sofas upholstered in linen and leather and draped with luxurious, tactile throws of chenille and pashmina. An immense television dominated one side of the room and a towering fireplace filled with great hunks of wood the other. Despite the magnificence of the room, it felt homely and lived in and before long, Lord and Lady Barrington had joined them and they were sat listening to classical music, drinking aperitifs and chatting about the weather, the success of the summer Ball and their upcoming holiday to Mustique.

At seven o'clock sharp, a uniformed gentleman appeared at the doorway and announced dinner was about to be served. They picked up their drinks and walked through a network of stone hallways, subtly lit and furnished with vases of flowers on elegant side tables and outsized, ancestral oil paintings.

The dining room was stunning. In the centre of the room stood an enormous oval table, swathed in linen and groaning with plates, glasses and cutlery. Evelyn wasn't expecting a full-on state banquet – a bowl of chilli in front of the telly and a few glasses of red would have sufficed.

'Wow... you really shouldn't have gone to so much trouble

Lady Barrington,' Evelyn exclaimed.

'Evelyn, dear... no titles please. Call me Arabella,' she announced with a wry smile. 'Ok?'

Evelyn grinned and nodded. They took their seats, the four of them, and the uniformed gentleman – who Evelyn soon discovered was called Robert and was the house butler – served them carrot and coriander soup in dainty, little, white china tureens with freshly baked bread rolls. Conversation didn't turn to Lorna until they'd ploughed their way through chicken chasseur with new potatoes and spring vegetables, summer pudding and cream and were half way through coffee and petits fours. Evelyn bit her tongue several times during the meal, desperate to ask Arabella what information she had to pass on that was so amazing, it had to be accompanied by a four course dinner served by a butler.

'Your friend Lorna...' she began tantalizingly.

Evelyn's heart skipped a beat and she hastily swallowed a mouthful of chocolate truffle.

'Yes...?'

'How is she?'

'Not good. I spoke to her parents today, before I came here. She's been in bed for most of the day although she is eating.'

'Hmmm. Rupert told me what happened. He said Lorna was in a relationship with a man called Joe? And Joe's sister was Adelaide? You'll know her as Alice... Is that correct?'

'Yes it is. I believe she was a housemaid here at the Hall?'

Lady Barrington took a genteel sip of rich, black coffee and dabbed at the corners of her mouth with a linen napkin.

'She was, yes. She began service here when I was a young girl. I remember her first day vividly. I must have only been around four years old. I was a lonely child, having no brothers or sisters for company. I had plenty of people around me, of course, a nanny to care for me, and many of the servants had children who I played with, but Adelaide was different.'

'In what way?'

'She was only around sixteen years of age when she came here. And very, very beautiful. She looked to me like a fairy... tiny, perfectly proportioned, dainty with fine features. Her father ran the post office in the village and her brother was a farm worker. Until, of course, the start of the Second World War, and all of our lives changed literally overnight.'

She gazed down at her coffee cup and swirled it around like brandy.

'Adelaide – Alice – became my friend. She worked in the house, making beds, sweeping carpets, polishing wood and silver. But she would always make time to play with me every single day. She would sing to me. And read me stories. I adored her.'

She drained her coffee cup and poured herself another, this time adding cream and two spoonfuls of sugar.

'Her mother died shortly after giving birth to her and her father raised both Alice and her brother single-handedly. And he did a sterling job. But, as you may already know, he died very suddenly when she was eighteen years old. It was his heart, we think. She took it very badly and the whole, frightful ordeal was made all the more traumatising for her when Joe was called up to fight in the war. He joined the army at the beginning of 1940 and managed to survive for three years. Unfortunately, by then, he was a Lance Corporal and he was posted to the battlefields of Normandy. He

357

received dreadful wounds to his shoulder and chest and was sent home to recuperate. By then Alice was twenty-one and the Post Office had been taken over by a lady in the village, although the house still belonged to the Hardy family and Alice continued to live there alone. Alice cared for Joe on his return whilst continuing to work at the Hall. But sadly Joe's wounds never healed and he died from septicemia a few months later.'

Evelyn sat nursing her wine glass and looked across sadly at Rupert and Lord Barrington. The room was silent with the exception of the hypnotic tick from the grandfather clock in the corner.

'How dreadfully sad… the poor girl.'

'I remember my parents accompanying Alice to both her father's and her brother's funerals. And from that day on, after Joe was buried, they looked after her as though she was their own daughter. They always remembered her birthday and she spent every Easter Sunday with us, and Christmas Day too. And she came to church with us on Sundays and dined with us afterwards. She was never a housemaid on those occasions, but a valued and treasured member of our family. We all loved her dearly.'

'Did she ever marry or have children?'

'Never. She devoted her whole life to us, the Barringtons, and to her beloved birds. She kept zebra finches and budgerigars and canaries and absolutely doted on them. It was as if we, and they, were her family and by way of thanks to us, for looking after her and giving her some sort of family life, she repaid us with a lifetime of unbroken service. She finally retired at the age of seventy but continued to be part of estate life until she fell ill.'

Lady Barrington began to weep and Rupert leapt from his chair to find her a handkerchief, while his father put a comforting arm around her and kissed the top of her head.

'I'm so sorry, Evelyn. It's just still very raw, with her passing so recently and so forth...'

Evelyn took a gulp of wine and wondered where all this was leading. What did this have to do with Lorna? No sooner had she thought the thought, Lady Barrington composed herself enough to continue the conversation.

'Which brings me to your dear friend Lorna. In the final days of Alice's life, I personally took care of her. I practically moved into her home and tended to her every need. When I broached the subject of moving her to the Hall to be looked after in greater comfort, she vehemently declined my offer and was adamant she would die in her own home. She said she felt close to her mother, father and brother there. She also refused to go to the doctor or have any medical intervention. She was extraordinarily stubborn when she wanted to be!'

Everyone laughed and the mood, for a brief moment, was lifted.

'As I sat by her side, and she drifted in and out of consciousness, she spoke of Joe and how he was in the house with her. She described him to me on several occasions, detailed accounts about what he was wearing, the cut of his hair, how handsome and youthful he looked. She talked endlessly of him, sometimes scaring me to death by saying he was in the room with us and that she could see him standing behind me or next to me. And at times, you know, I really did sense something there with us in the room. I never saw him but I felt his presence. I smelled him, you know… as odd as that may sound – a beautiful, clean smell – of cut grass and hay, summer sunshine and ozone. It used to drift in and out of the room but I knew it was him. But what really, really convinces me that your friend Lorna is telling the truth is this…'

Evelyn, Rupert and Lord Barrington sat staring at her, mouths open, perfectly still and almost unable to breathe.

'Alice told me Joe had met someone. That he had fallen in love… for the very first time. A girl with skin the colour of alabaster and hair as red as the setting sun and she sold flowers to make people smile. And that made Alice happy. Oh, it made her so, so happy, Evelyn. A week ago today, I sat with her and I witnessed her talking to Joe. I will never forget it for as long as I live. I couldn't see him, of course, but I knew he was there and that she was dying. He had come to take her. Her eyes sparkled and she looked so beautiful as she spoke to him. She reached out her thin, pale arm as if she was taking hold of his hand and she told him she was ready.'

She held the crumpled handkerchief to her face and wept like a child.

'At the time…' she sobbed, 'I assumed Alice was hallucinating, having visions and experiences caused by the dying process. Now everything has fallen into place. But what really swung it for me…'

Her bloodshot, puffy eyes stared intently from one person to the next, all of who were shaking their heads in response to her question, nobody even daring to guess what she was going to say next.

'…the one thing that has turned all of my previous

convictions regarding death and the afterlife completely on their head? Last Sunday morning, the day before she died, as I got Alice washed and changed into a clean night gown for what was to be the final time, she lay on the sofa, covered with her green blanket, and told me she'd heard dreadful crying during the night – relentless, heartbroken weeping coming from the street outside the house. She called out to Joe and eventually he came. But he was a broken man. His body wracked with sobs, he explained to Alice that the woman outside was his love. And she was calling to him but... for reasons we can only assume... he couldn't go to her.'

She drummed her fingertips on the table and shook her head sorrowfully.

'Rupert told me that on the night of the Ball, Lorna disappeared – only to be discovered wandering the streets of Lutton calling Joe's name. Is that true, Evelyn?'

Evelyn felt a chilling shiver run down her spine, commanding every single hair on her body to stand to attention.

'Yes... we went looking for her. Me, Rose, Graham and Rupert. Rupert drove, didn't you?' She glanced at Rupert and he nodded dutifully. 'We found her on the corner of Lover's Lane. She was in a terrible state. Cold, barefoot, mascara all over her face... she was inconsolable because Joe had let her down.'

Lady Barrington poured herself a large glass of brandy. This unexpected outpouring of grief had drained her emotionally and she needed something to fortify her nerves.

'As incredible and totally absurd as this may sound, the girl Joe was talking about, the girl he fell in love with... was

Lorna. There's no two ways about it. Lorna is telling the truth.'

LATER THAT NIGHT, after undressing and bathing, Evelyn sat on the edge of her bed in her dressing gown, with a towel wrapped around her head, and picked up the phone.

'Rose, it's me. I hope you're sitting down... I've got something to tell you...'

TWENTY-NINE

DR MATTHEW O'LEARY strode purposefully into the hallway of the Mills' house and was ushered straight into the living room. He didn't look like a psychiatrist. He was very young for a start – tall, fair, broad-shouldered. He had a confident air about him, verging on cocky. Jilly went into automatic flirt mode, flattering him with comments about how she wished her doctor looked like him and how flattering the cut of his suit was. Dr O'Leary smiled and took her flattery in his stride. He was obviously a seasoned pro at fending off middle-aged housewives.

Lorna welcomed the idea of being mentally assessed. Even in her confused state of mind, she understood the fact she had endured a month long relationship with a dead man was more than a little unusual and although she felt she was quite sane, there was an element of self-doubt gnawing away at her like a persistent rodent.

She sidled shyly into the living room after hearing the front door close and muffled voices downstairs. Dr O'Leary stood to shake her hand and all at once she felt extremely self-conscious, almost as if she was in trouble and was about to be told off. She felt like a young child again, being watched by her parents and this very tall man, this unfamiliar male doctor.

'Don't look so worried, Lorna. I'm not going to bite,' Dr. O'Leary joked, a feeble attempt to lighten the mood.

Lorna smiled weakly and sank down onto the sofa.

'Can I get you any tea? Coffee?' asked Jilly, batting her eyelashes at the poor man.

'Er, yes, thank you. That would be very nice. Tea please.'

'I'll be right back – I'll leave you two in peace for a while,' she said with a wink and a wiggle.

Lorna looked at the doctor and rolled her eyes. He grinned at her, not having to say a single word in response.

He unclipped the sturdy, leather briefcase that was placed on his knees and took out an A4 notebook and a series of forms along with a fancy-looking, tortoiseshell fountain pen.

'Do you mind if I take down a few particulars about you, Lorna? Name, date of birth, occupation, etcetera?'

'No... no... that's fine.'

He asked question upon question and jotted Lorna's answers down in meticulously neat handwriting. Jilly appeared with tea and a plate of assorted biscuits on a tray and set it down on the glass-topped coffee table in front of them. She disappeared again, thankfully minus any suggestion of coquettishness.

'Right, that's all of the paperwork done,' he said, filing the papers away and pouring both Lorna and himself a cup of tea. 'Let's move onto the reason why I am here...' He smiled kindly at her.

'...you. Now, tell me – in your own words, at your own pace – about everything you have experienced over the past month or so?'

Lorna took a deep breath and began to talk, embarrassed at first – it felt strange discussing personal details about yourself with a total stranger – but she gained confidence and fluency as the words started to flow more freely. Dr. O'Leary allowed her to talk, cry, sit in silence and sob, with out any interjection at all. He made notes when necessary but for most of the time he listened considerately and watched her like a hawk, paying close attention to her facial expressions, her body language, the tone of her voice, the constantly changing reflections in her eyes.

When Lorna finally stopped talking and sank back into the squashy sofa, absolutely worn out, he reached out and placed a hand on her forearm.

'Thank you, Lorna. I could tell that was very difficult for you at times. Now, if you don't mind, I have one last piece of paperwork to complete. It's a psychiatry analysis and although at times you may think the questions I am asking you border on the ridiculous, surprisingly, they do make sense to me!'

Lorna found herself feeling suddenly overcome with nausea. This must be the point where he decides if I'm mad or not, she thought.

'Fire away…' she said, her voice faltering slightly.

The doctor asked all sorts of bizarre questions in quick succession, the purpose being so Lorna didn't have time to dwell on any of them. There were no right or wrong answers but the overall assessment results would give Dr O'Leary a very detailed picture of Lorna's state of mind.

'And we're finished,' he said, closing his notebook and reaching out for his teacup.

'What now?' asked Lorna, relieved her ordeal was over but wondering if the men in white suits were waiting just around the corner to cart her away in a straight jacket.

'I will send you, or your parents, a report on my findings but from what you've told me, from my observations and my initial findings, you are, I'm glad to inform you… totally sane.'

Lorna rested her head onto the back of the sofa and closed her eyes.

'So I've not gone mad… you're not going to section me or anything?'

'No, far from it. I can't explain why you experienced what you went through. I don't have the answers to that. But in time I think all will become clear to you. In the meantime, get plenty of rest, drink and eat well, lots of fresh air and exercise and maybe book an appointment to see your GP. He will be able to prescribe a mild anti-depressant to see you through the next few weeks. But only if you need it, of course.'

Jilly waved Dr. O'Leary off like a lovelorn teenager saying goodbye to her first ever boyfriend and sighed as she shut the front door.

'Mum, you are pathetic,' muttered Lorna, as she stomped up the stairs to her bedroom.

For once, Jilly bit her tongue and gracefully accepted she probably was more than a little humiliating at times.

Lorna picked up her phone and tapped out a text message to Rose and Evelyn.

< I've had a doctor here all morning. Apparently I'm completely normal. >

Evelyn was the first to text back.

< I know you are. Lorna, we have to talk. >

LORNA WOKE THE NEXT morning and decided she wanted

to go back home. Her faculties were reassured that she wasn't barking mad but she was still struggling with the memory of Joe and the notion she would never see him again. She desperately wanted answers, the most pressing question being why did he come to her.

As she lay in bed, sunlight streaming through the filmy curtains at the window, she cast her mind back to the day she first encountered him. Baking hot, a cloudless sky, careering down the hill on her bike, pretending she was a young girl again. And there he was. Without warning, standing in the middle of the road. She pictured his face and the squeal of her brakes as she fought hard to control the bike and avoid slamming into him at the same time. He came to her, not the other way round. She hadn't imagined him, or conjured him up in a dream. He was part and parcel of real, every day life. And she'd touched him, spoken to him, kissed him, eaten with him, had sex with him. She'd stroked his hair, smelled his skin, brushed her fingertips across the ugly, livid, puckered scar that disfigured his chest. She knew intimate details about him, about his family, his life, the war, his favourite smell. And he'd left his mark on the world as well as her heart. He wasn't just a name engraved into gleaming, white marble. His initials and hers were tattooed into the trunk of a tree. His scent impregnated onto her pillowcases. His lip imprint still visible on the beer bottle he'd drunk from. Oh, he was real all right. He was more than real. He was her everything. And he said he'd come back for her, no matter what. And every single bone in her body ached for him to come back for her.

She plodded down the stairs, heavy with bags, and

dropped them in the hallway. Phillip wandered through from the kitchen and eyed the bags.

'Going somewhere?'

'Home. I've got to dad. I'm very grateful to you and mum for looking after me but I need to go home. Back to normality. Work. Friends. Life. I'm not ill. Just heart broken.'

Phillip nodded reluctantly and gathered her into his arms.

'I know. I know. I didn't expect you'd stay long. Are you sure you'll be alright by yourself?'

'I won't be by myself,' she answered cheerfully. 'I've got the girls coming over this afternoon and they are quite determined they are staying with me for a couple of days.'

Phillip grinned.

'Oh, good. You're lucky to have those two, you know. Not many people have friends like them in their lives. I certainly don't. Neither has your mother. Speaking of your mother, where is she?'

'In the pantry rustling up a food parcel for me, no doubt.'

Phillip shook his head in a gesture of disbelief.

'I know she's rather maddening at times, Lorna. But she means well.'

Lorna leaned forward and kissed her father on his cheek. He'd used the same aftershave for as long as she could remember and it was a comforting reminder of their closeness and just how much she loved him.

'I know she does.'

'Right, Lorna. This will keep you going for a while,' trilled Jilly, shuffling down the hall with a huge cardboard box full of groceries in her arms. 'Plenty of tins, pasta, rice, biscuits, tuna, bread, butter, tea, sugar, a nice bottle of squash – not that ghastly artificial stuff that's never had so much as a whiff of a real orange near it – and one of your father's fruit cakes. And make sure you keep eating. You need...'

'Fattening up. Yes. I know.'

NO SOONER HAD Phillip pulled away from the Maltings, Rose and Evelyn arrived. They too were laden down with groceries, but of a very different kind. They made Lorna sit in the living room with a cup of tea and the tv on while they unpacked pizzas, potato wedges, crisps, chocolate, boxes of wine in all three colours and enough fresh cream doughnuts to give them all a coronary.

Rose pottered through with Lorna's little lacquered drinks tray, on which three humongous glasses of white wine wobbled precariously.

'Where the hell did you get those glasses from?' giggled Lorna.

'Ha! I knew they'd make you smile! I spotted them on the market stall yesterday and they called to me! Begged me to buy them! I thought they would come in useful,' she replied, handing Lorna a glass almost overflowing with wine. 'And they have!'

Evelyn joined them with a wooden bowl full of crisps and three smaller dishes filled with creamy dips.

'A light aperitif... before we go the whole hog and commit refined carbohydrate and alcohol suicide.'

Lorna smiled faintly. This time yesterday she never thought she'd smile again but being here, surrounded by her own personal belongings, her memories, with her two best friends and a goblet of wine, life didn't seem so bad. Even if it was only until the inevitable hangover wore off the following morning.

'What did you want to talk to me about, Evelyn?' she asked, taking a mouthful of wine and swallowing it, feeling a delightful, icy chill trickle down her oesophagus. It felt good.

Evelyn knew the question was coming but she didn't expect it would come so soon. She cleared her throat and picked up a handful of salty crisps and began to nibble at one. She looked into Lorna's eyes and fleetingly saw a frightened little girl looking back at her. She was the baby of the group and both she and Rose had always felt protective over her. She seemed so young and fragile sat before her in her oversized, floral patterned pjyamas, her hair scooped back off her face, her green eyes wide and doll-like.

'I saw Lady Barrington on Sunday evening. Rupert invited me for dinner. He finally got to speak to her about Joe and Alice and that is when she dropped a bombshell. Rupert had no idea Alice was in fact Adelaide – he knew Alice all of her life but always by her full name.'

Lorna stared into her wine glass and her eyes misted over at the mention of Joe's name.

'What was the bombshell?' she said softly.

Evelyn retold the entire conversation she'd had with Lady Barrington that night almost word for word. As she spoke, Lorna's bottom lip trembled and her eyes occasionally filled with tears, but she didn't crumble. She listened intently, never averting her gaze, concentrating on every single word that Evelyn said.

'So you see… that's why she is convinced your story is completely true.'

'Alice told her she heard me crying and Joe was upset because he knew it was me?'

'Yes. She even described you Lorna. She described your skin, your hair, she even knew you sold flowers for a living... how could she know all of that if Joe hadn't told her first? Alice was bed-ridden. House-bound. Dying.'

Lorna nodded and Rose broke down in floods of tears, unable to speak.

'I saw him the next day. It was our last day together. And we had the most wonderful day. It was magical... We cooked together, watched old movies right here,' she said, patting the sofa she sat on. 'And we danced and kissed and went to bed. And he stayed with me all night. I kept waking up and looking at his beautiful face in the moonlight as he slept. I stroked his cheek and his eyelashes and kissed his lips. He woke early and said he had to go to check on Alice. He said she had a carer... who I now know must have been Lady Barrington... The sun was shining and the sky was blue and I watched him walk away. I went back to bed but when I woke again a little later, it was dark and gloomy and raining. It rained every day for a week.' Her voice got quieter and quieter as she spoke until her words were barely audible. 'I never saw him again.'

Hot, salty tears spilled down her cheeks and Rose and Evelyn cried along with her.

'I just need to know why... why he came into my life... and why he has gone again,' she sobbed.

Now it was Rose's turn to speak. She glanced anxiously at Evelyn and Evelyn nodded at her encouragingly.

'We think we know why.'

Lorna's brow furrowed and she appeared perplexed,

wondering what on earth Rose was talking about.

'Why? Go on, Rose... please tell me...'

'We should have told you this a long time ago but... we were trying to protect you...'

'Tell me!'

Again, Evelyn urged Rose to continue and topped up everyone's glass, knowing what was coming.

'Oriel cursed you.'

Lorna recoiled and spilled some of her wine down her pyjamas.

'Cursed me?'

'Yes. She cursed you. As she lay dying.'

'H... how do you know?'

'Roger told us after the funeral.'

'Roger knew?'

'Of course he knew... he witnessed her doing it. She wasn't what she appeared to be, Lorna. She was evil. She practiced black magic and used it to enrich her life. Everything she ever got was the result of her involvement with the occult. She used Wicca and white witchcraft as a smoke screen to conceal her true identity. She used everybody, including us, to get what she wanted in life – friends, money, power, men...'

'How do you know all this?'

'Roger discovered an inverted pentagram on the cellar floor – purely by accident of course. He went down there one day to store some vintage wine he'd just bought and he noticed a wet mark on the rug. He thought it was wine but soon discovered it was blood. He tried to clean it off and ended up rolling back the rug – which is when he saw the pentagram.'

Lorna stared at Rose, unable to process these shocking revelations in her already overloaded brain.

'He did his homework and read anything and everything he could on the subject of the occult. But he never, ever said anything to Oriel about his discovery. He kept it to himself, lived with it, and she died thinking she'd taken her secret to the grave with her.'

'For reasons we will never know, she chose to curse you as she lay dying,' added Evelyn.

Lorna shifted uncomfortably in her seat.

'What was the curse?' she asked shakily.

'A curse to prevent you from ever finding what you desired most in life – a soulmate, your one true love. She wanted you to die alone and unloved. Why? We just don't know. We've thought about it and talked about it over and over again...'

'Roger told us what Oriel said, the words of her curse. He said he was horrified to watch her revealing her true self to him as she lay dying. Evelyn and I knew we had to try to make it right. There was only one thing we could do. And that was a curse reversal spell.'

'That night, after the funeral, we went to Rose's house and gathered oils, plants, herbs, candles and we sat and made an effigy of Oriel and of you. At midnight we performed the spell and we sat and waited for months, hoping upon hope that together, our magic was strong enough to compete and to overcome the curse Oriel put on you,' said Evelyn.

'We knew only time would tell if it had worked or not. But then you made that bloody charm to invoke your soul mate. We knew something could quite possibly go wrong...' said

Rose quietly.

'Why didn't you warn me?' cried Lorna.

'How could we? You and Oriel got along so well. She gave you her precious pentacle, for gods sake. How could we turn around and tell you that she'd cursed you? Damned you for all eternity?'

Lorna sat in silence, staring at the floorboards, lost in thought.

'The charm was unearthed by your stupid gardener and you never did a love reversal spell to counteract the harm that may cause... We tried to tell you, we urged you to do make the charm again, didn't we Rose? But you were having none of it. Joe had appeared in your life by then... It was too late. You'd fallen in love,' Evelyn cocked her head to one side and placed her hand on Lorna's hand.

'You summoned Joe to you, my love,' Rose whispered soothingly. 'And he came. The charm worked. He was... he still is... your soul mate... but our magic just wasn't powerful enough to make him real, of flesh and bone... of this world. Instead he was of another time, another place... a force of nature that once walked this earth and breathed air but who no longer does. It was never meant to be this way, my darling... but it is what it is. And there is no going back.'

'Our spell changed the outcome of Oriel's curse – she yearned for you to go through your life alone and unloved – but her magic was too strong. Instead, you found love but on a higher stratum,' Evelyn conjectured. 'I'm just so sorry we failed you...'

Lorna put her head in her hands and breathed deeply. Her mind was in turmoil. It was all her fault. This whole desperate situation was entirely her fault. And her friends, the two people she loved and valued most, were totally oblivious to what she had done to cause it. Instead they had gone all out guns blazing, to try to change the path of destiny for her. And they had succeeded to a degree. Now here they were, caring for her, pacifying her, supporting her, listening, talking, analysing – when all along Lorna had kept a terrible, sinister secret from them. Her actions and nobody else's had caused untold destruction and the time had come to reveal her wrongdoing.

THIRTY

Two years ago...

LORNA SWUNG THE CAR into the drive and parked behind the brand new, gleaming white Range Rover that was taking up most of it. She knew instantly it was Oriel's monstrosity. The number plate announced to the world it belonged to her. ORI 3L. A showy, tinted-windowed, gas guzzler.

'What's she doing here?' Lorna muttered to herself, turning off the engine and jerking up the temperamental handbrake. One of these days it would come off in her hand.

Lorna loved Oriel. She was like the glamorous, sophisticated, fountain-of-all-knowledge aunt she never had. She could talk to Oriel about anything whereas conversations of any importance with Jilly always ended up, somehow, revolving around her mother. So she didn't bother anymore. Rose was her surrogate mother, Oriel her surrogate aunt and Evelyn her surrogate sister. And that's the way she liked it.

Oriel had grown very close to all three women and their families and flitted between the three quite comfortably. But she relished being with the Mills family the most because neither she, Rose or Evelyn had been blessed with children and Lorna's brothers were an endless source of amusement as they grew from spotty youths into charming and witty young men. Jilly enjoyed Oriel's company and the two women also grew close, often shopping together, indulging in the odd spa day here and there and trips to the cinema or theatre. Phillip found Oriel a little intimidating but he and Roger shared a passion for sailing and motorsport and became good friends too. It was all very amicable.

Lorna knew Jilly was out. On Monday mornings she went to a small, exclusive tennis club in town and received private tuition followed by a game with whoever was willing to take her on. She was an enthusiastic player but her hobby was a relatively new one and in reality, she was useless at it. In her head she was Martina Navratilova – never one to admit she was anything less than accomplished at anything she turned her hand to.

Lorna usually spent Monday's catching up with housework, accounts, placing orders and the obligatory coffee morning at the village hall. But today she fancied driving over to Stamford to spend the morning with her dad. He probably had work to do on the magazine but she was quite happy to sit in the office with him, make him tea and pitch in with ideas for forthcoming articles or photo shoots.

She placed the key to her parent's house in the lock and turned it. The house smelled of furniture polish and fresh coffee and she wandered down the hallway into the kitchen to pour herself a cup. Two coffee cups were on the worktop next to the sink, one of them possessing a deep, scarlet red, lip imprint around its rim.

Oriel must be in the office with dad, she thought, and walked through the conservatory and out through the open patio doors, across the lawn and down the path to the pretty log cabin nestled at the bottom of the garden. The door was open and the computer switched on but nobody was inside.

Puzzled, she turned round and walked back into the house. She peered through the glass doors into the lounge and stuck her head around the door into the dining room, but all was quiet.

She stood in the hall, hands on hips, the gentle ticking of the clock the only sound to be heard. How odd.

Then there came a noise from upstairs. A faint noise but a definite one. She walked to the bottom of the stairs and craned her neck to look up the curved staircase to the landing above. She stood on the bottom step and then edged her way a little further, trying not to make a sound.

Why was her father and Oriel upstairs? There were only bedrooms up there.

Her heart started to bang loudly in her chest as adrenalin flowed through her veins. She stopped half way up the stairs and listened again. There were definite noises coming from the bedroom furthest away. She crept up the rest of the stairs like a cat burglar, barely making so much as a creak as she went. She hardly dare breathe. She stood on the landing and began to tiptoe along the corridor towards her parent's bedroom. She could hear soft moaning – a man – and there… a female voice, muffled but unmistakable in it's tone and cut-glass refinement. It belonged to Oriel. Laughter. A shriek of excitement. A groan of pleasure.

Were they having sex? Surely not! Her father and Oriel? Her head spun and she felt sick. She froze in horror. She should leave – turn round right now, walk downstairs and back through the front door, out to her car and drive away. Forget all about it. Bury her head in the sand. Or should she confront them? Throw the bedroom door open wide and ask

378

them what the hell did they think they were doing!

And then, without warning, her father was standing in front of her, naked, sweaty, his hair all over the place. Over his shoulder, on the bed he'd shared with her mother for thirty something years, lay her friend – Oriel – her bare breasts exposed, a sheet covering the lower half of her body, her raven hair tousled and falling around her shoulders seductively.

Lorna stared at her father, his eyes fixed on hers, as scared as a rabbit in the headlights, his body frozen in terror. Lorna shifted her gaze to the bed. Oriel blinked and with a hint of a smirk, deliberately pulled the sheet from her waist as slowly as she possibly could, sliding the white cotton up her body until her nipples were covered.

Lorna felt a rage well up inside her until it overflowed and she flew down the landing, arms flailing, claws at the ready. Phillip tried to stand between her and the door but she pushed him with such force, he careered backwards and landed with a sickening thud against the corner of the wardrobe.

Oriel began to scream hysterically. Lorna was on the bed in seconds, her left fist gripping Oriel by the throat, her right pulling her hair out by the handful. She let out a battle cry as she rained blows down onto Oriel's head.

'You fucking bitch! He's my father!' she screamed, her face the colour of calves liver, her eyes almost popping out of her head, her hair as wild as a stormy sea.

'Phillip... she's... strangling...' Oriel gasped, trying frantically to kick her legs, her hands grasping Lorna's wrists in a desperate attempt to prise her off.

'Lorna! Please! Stop! You'll kill her!' he shouted, his voice fraught, his face filled with fear.

Lorna wanted to kill her. She hadn't wanted anything more in her whole life. This woman, a trusted friend, a woman she cared for and loved like a member of the family, had betrayed her. And betrayed her mother. Oriel and Jilly were friends! And here she was, fucking her friend's husband and father as though it was a perfectly acceptable thing to do – lying there, looking like the cat that got the cream. There was no explanation, no remorse, no apology. Only a smugness that made Lorna feel sick to the core.

Lorna sank back onto her heels and shoved Oriel one last time back onto the headboard.

'You make me sick,' she spat, wiping her mouth with the back of her hand.

She looked at Oriel. Long black hairs lay strewn around her where they'd been torn from her head. Her eye was bruised, her nose bloody and her lip split.

'Get out!' Lorna screamed.

Oriel whimpered and slid off the side of the bed, into the shower room and closed the door. Lorna heard her gasp in shock and begin to weep as she caught sight of her reflection in the mirror. She appeared minutes later, dressed and holding a wad of damp tissue to her face. She practically ran from the house only to scuttle back into the hallway moments later, sobbing.

'Please can you move your car, Lorna. I can't get out.'

Lorna smiled smugly to herself and hurled the keys at her over the top of the banister. They narrowly missed her, landing with a clattering crash at her feet. Minutes later she was gone.

Lorna sat in the kitchen and waited for her father to appear. He had some explaining to do. He sidled into the room anxiously, fully clothed, his hair neat and tidy once again. She watched him as he eyed her nervously and slid onto a stool at the breakfast bar alongside her. His put his head in his hands and rested his elbows on the worktop.

'I don't know what to say... ' he breathed. 'What do you say when you've been caught with your trousers down.' He paused. 'By your daughter.'

He avoided her gaze by intensely studying the patterns in the formica.

'But Oriel, dad? I didn't think you even liked her that much.'

Phillip scratched his thumbnail back and forth on an imaginary speck of dirt.

'I didn't. I don't, really. She's always scared me a bit. A bit like your mother does,' he glanced up fleetingly. 'But she bewitched me. I didn't have any say in the matter. She set out to get me and she succeeded. I knew it was wrong. I knew if your mother ever found out, that would be the end of it. And I would lose you, her, the boys, everything I've worked so hard for all my life,' he groaned.

'So what made you take the risk?'

Phillip shifted uncomfortably on the stool and returned to studying the worktop.

'She lavished attention on me. She made me feel like a man again. I've spent so long being a husband and a dad, I'd forgotten what it feels like to...' he cleared his throat. '...to be a lover.'

Lorna closed her eyes and sighed. As angry as she was

with her father for betraying her mother, she could see where he was coming from. Life with a domineering, demanding woman such as Jilly can't have been easy.

'Your mother hasn't so much as kissed me for... ooh...' he looked up at the ceiling 'fifteen years or so? Oriel makes me feel alive. She does something to me that your mother never has.'

Lorna felt a wave of sympathy wash over her and she reached out and gently took his hand in hers.

'I had no idea,' she whispered.

'I'm not unhappy though,' he said, his face brightening. 'Far from it. I can't imagine a life any different from this one. And I wouldn't want any other life. I love my life and you children and I do love Jilly... in my own way.'

'Oh dad...' said Lorna, shaking her head sadly. 'And what about her? Do you love her?'

'Oriel? I don't think so. Are you going to tell your mother?'

'No... I'd never do that. It would break her heart. She does love you, you know. I can see it in her eyes, even if she is rubbish at showing it.'

'I'm so sorry Lorna... you must hate me.'

He gripped her hand and his eyes misted over with tears. She'd never seen her dad cry before.

'I could never hate you.'

'Thank you.'

'So what happens now?'

'I've no idea. I suppose I need time... time to work out what's best for me and your mother. Things have to change between us, even though that may be impossible after all this time. Oriel is like a drug... I tell myself no but then I keep going back for more. It's like she has put a spell on me... If I never see Oriel again, if I end it today, here and now, never must mean never. She needs to disappear from my life forever.'

Lorna slid off her stool and walked over to the kettle. She stood in a daze as it boiled, clouds of steam rising around her.

'Be careful what you wish for...' she whispered to herself, as she poured the scalding hot water into the teapot, idly watching the tea leaves inside swirl round and around like autumn leaves on a windy day.

LORNA STEPPED FROM THE WARM, scented bath water onto stripped wooden floorboards, wrapped herself in an over-sized cream towel and looked down at the puddle collecting around her feet. She must remember to buy a bath mat. And a wok – necessary household objects she desperately needed but always forgot to buy. So for now, the floor – and a frying pan – would have to do.

She smoothed white musk lotion onto her body and massaged it in gently, inhaling the familiar scent that had cocooned her since she was a teenager then slipped her white cotton nightdress over her head and let it fall to her ankles. She looked at her reflection in the full-length mirror that stood by her wardrobe then padded across the hall into her tiny sitting room. There she gathered together a white candle, a china plate, a tiny bottle of clary sage oil, a Victorian well filled with black ink and five nettle leaves. Next, went into the kitchen to retrieve the box of matches she kept under the kitchen sink, along with parchment paper and a pen, and took all of the items back to her bedroom.

She looked out of the window and up to the sky. The moon

above her, suspended in an inky infinity of stars, was getting larger by the day, moving from new moon to full moon. Tonight the moon was a waxing moon, which meant tonight was the perfect night for casting spells.

She moved into the centre of her room and walked slowly round in a perfect circle, sank to the floor and carefully lit the candle. She ripped the nettle leaves into tiny shreds and placed them on the china plate. Next she unscrewed the lid off the bottle of clary sage oil, tipping it forward slightly so that three drops spilled out and landed silently on the leaves. Then she tore a small strip of parchment from the sheet and in black ink wrote, in a hand as steady as a rock, the name Oriel Agnes Trewhellor-Fitzpatrick.

She tilted the burning candle so that the molten wax dripped onto the oil and leaves. She waited patiently until the whole candle had melted. Next she squeezed the pipette into the well and filled the glass phial with pitch black ink. She dripped the ink drop by drop onto the molten wax until the clear liquid became as dark as her intentions. She rolled the strip of paper bearing Oriel's name into a tight coil, no bigger than her little fingernail and held it as she spoke aloud.

'Body and soul that at present is pure, be blackened with cancers for which there is no cure.'

Her delicate fingers mixed and moulded the wax, ink, leaves and oil together into a small effigy of a woman and into the warm wax body of the figure, she pushed the coil of parchment, until it was totally concealed. When the effigy was cold and hard, she tiptoed barefoot into the dewy garden, and amongst a sea of daffodils and tulips, she buried it deep beneath the evergreen branches of a holly tree.

A HUSH DESCENDED on the sitting room. Candlelight danced and flickered and a gentle breeze wafted in through the open slats of the blind.

'You cursed her first...' Evelyn breathed.

Lorna held her gaze and nodded her reply.

'I wanted her gone.'

'I always like to think I am a perceptive kind of person, but I can honestly say I had no idea any animosity existed between the two of you...' cried Rose incredulously. 'Even after doing what she did to you, and you did what you did to her in retaliation... you remained friends? I mean... she didn't disappear, tail between her legs, never to be seen again? We still did things together, the four of us?'

'Mmm,' Lorna hummed. 'She never mentioned it from that day on – the day I found her and dad together. She lay low for a couple of weeks until the bruising and swelling went down and then continued life as normal.'

'How did she explain the state of her face to Roger?'

'I really haven't got a clue. I expect she told him she did it falling off a horse or something.'

'And your dad? Did their affair continue?'

'I'm pretty sure it ended there and then. But I can't be certain. I think, looking back, he did have feelings for her. When she announced she was dying...'

'I remember it vivdly. We were all at her house, weren't we? Watching the Olympics opening ceremony...'

'...I looked over at dad and I could see the hurt in his eyes. It caused him great pain.'

'But what if they were meant to be together, Lorna?'

'She never intended to keep him. I knew that from the sickening smirk she gave me when I found them in bed together. She used him. Just like she used all of us. When you told me she was a black witch, any guilt or regret I may have harboured inside of me melted away. She was evil to the core. She bewitched my father – my loving, adorable father – and she betrayed me and my mother. She betrayed our friendship. She betrayed Roger and she betrayed you. She betrayed all of us. The bonds of friendship do not bend so that rules can be broken. I'm glad I did what I did.'

Rose picked up her wine glass and took a generous mouthful.

'Even if that means you've jeopardised your own future happiness in the process?'

'If you hadn't told Oriel what you'd done as she lay dying, she would never have known and she would never have put this curse on you that can't be broken…' Evelyn said sadly.

'I needed to tell her, Evelyn. For my own peace of mind. Just to let her know she hadn't gotten away with it. She thought she had! She sailed through that last year of her life, with all of her friends rallying around her, Roger waiting on her hand and foot, everybody none the wiser. But I couldn't sit back and watch her behave so appallingly. So I told her. She died knowing my magic was as strong, if not stronger, than hers and that is what killed her. She knew she had ultimately failed. She knew that white overshadowed black in the end.'

The pieces of the jigsaw slowly but surely slotted together, forming a picture so detailed and intricate, so vivid and incredible that it was hard to believe it was real and if it were told as a story – written down in the pages of a book – most would say it was extraordinary.

LORNA SAT ON THE EDGE of the bed and gazed at her short, stubby fingernails, still bruised and stained with blood. She gently slipped off her rings and placed them next to her and reached for the jar of hand cream on the bedside table beside her pillow. As she massaged the cream into her hands, one of her rings slid to the floor and disappeared from view. She got off the bed and crouched on all fours, peering under the metal bed frame, trying to locate it in the semi-darkness. She could see it just out of arms reach so she shifted herself lower to the floor and stretched out to retrieve it. She felt her fingers brush against the cool metal of the ring and then touch something else lying next to it. It felt like paper. She pressed her fingers down onto the object and dragged it, along with the ring, out from the darkness. She slipped the ring back on her finger and sat back on the bed. She held the paper out in front of her and blew away the thin layer of dust from its surface – a torn scrap of paper on which Joe's slanted, old-fashioned handwriting was etched in ink.

To my dearest Lorna,

The sun is rising as I watch you sleep by my side. You are the most beautiful creature to ever grace my life and meeting you has been a gift I thought I would never receive. I need to go home now to see Alice but I will be back in two days time. Tonight has been the most wonderful night of my life. I'll never leave you because quite simply, I love you with all of my heart.

Yours truly,

Joe

He had left her a note after all, just as he said he had, and he really had been there with her. He wasn't a dream, a figment of her imagination, he was real, and in that instance, missed him more than she knew was humanly possible. She clutched the note to her breast, words of love permanently preserved for all time, her body aching with grief and paralysed with sobs and wept until the sun began to slowly rise in the sky once more.

THIRTY-ONE

LORNA WOKE SUDDENLY with a jolt, her heart thudding in her chest as though she'd had a terrible shock in her sleep. Her head was fuzzy from the hangover she predicted she'd have and she felt dehydrated and a little woozy still. All at once, like a flash of lightning, she remembered the events of the night before. Rose and Evelyn were here with her in the flat, the shocking confession she'd confided in them and Joe's note...

She sat bolt upright in bed and wondered if she'd dreamed everything. But as the tantalising aroma of sizzling bacon and fresh coffee wafted through into her bedroom and she spotted the beautifully hand-written note lying on top of her duvet, where it had lain all night, she knew this was no dream.

She picked up the piece of paper and read it again, her already swollen and reddened eyes filling with tears, then got out of bed and padded barefoot into the hallway to find her friends.

She didn't have to go very far. They were stood in the kitchen assembling a monster of a cooked breakfast. There were pots and pans on every ring of the hob, bottles of ketchup, jars of mustard, plates of bread and butter. Her stomach growled with hunger.

'Oh hello love! We were just about to wake you. How are you feeling?' said Rose, turning towards the door, pinny on, spatula in one hand, mug of tea in the other.

'Sad. Hungover. Starving. In that order.'

Rose pulled a face at her, all down-turned mouth and doleful eyes.

'You'll feel much better when you get this little lot inside you!'

'Rose has cooked enough breakfast to feed an army of truckers. You'll be eating sausages all bloody week.'

Lorna held out the hand that was clenching Joe's note and watched as Evelyn, with Rose looking over her shoulder, read it.

'Where did you find this?'

'Under my bed. Last night. I dropped a ring and it rolled underneath the bed frame. I fished the note out along with the ring.'

'But why was it under there?'

'I don't know. That morning when I woke up, and Joe had gone, and I was really upset and phoned you because I thought maybe he was just after a leg over…?'

'Yeah…?'

'Well, when I finally did see him again, he said he'd left me a note before he left. But I thought he was lying, trying to make things better, smooth things over… because I never found it.'

Her eyes filled with tears and they trickled in a steady stream down her cheeks.

'He wasn't lying. He did leave me a note. I suppose I must have got out of bed that morning and sent it flying. I feel terrible for doubting him.'

Evelyn put a comforting arm around her.

'You weren't to know it'd fallen under the bed, you silly sod. But how wonderful to have found it eventually, hey? You can treasure it forever, a reminder of him, a precious memory.'

'But I don't want a precious memory! I want him! I want him to come back to me,' she sobbed.

Rose and Evelyn looked at each other, neither knowing how to respond, what to say to her to make things better. They had no doubt Joe had been real, but what now? He was a jumble of bones and decaying scraps of fabric and leather and metal, lying six feet under in Casworth graveyard.

'Come on. Let's eat.'

They sat around the small, circular table Lorna kept in her living room and tucked into bacon, eggs, sausages, tomato, mushrooms and baked beans. It was delicious and just what the doctor ordered.

'I'm going to get dressed and go for a walk,' Lorna announced as they were washing up.

'Not to the church, love? Rose asked anxiously. 'I'm not sure you're up for that just yet...'

'No. No. I want to take you somewhere. I want to show you something.'

'Ok,' said Evelyn hesitantly, glancing at Rose who was nervously trying to avoid her gaze.

'What do you want to show us?'

'You'll see. Come on, let's get dressed. It's a beautiful day out there. And the fresh air will do me good.'

An hour later and the three women were strolling down the lane that led to the water meadows, the mill and the river. It was indeed a beautiful day. The sun shone down from a cloudless sky, creating shimmering heat haze mirages on the road in front of them. All the trees were now in full leaf and above them, the soft whisper of the stirring boughs sounded like gentle waves breaking onto a deserted beach.

Lorna talked of nothing else but Joe during the entire walk down to the river. By the time they reached the small, disused railway crossing next to the overgrown, tumbledown station, Rose and Evelyn felt as through they knew him personally. Lorna led them through the meadow and over the tiny bridge, along the towpath and to a clearing next to the river, overlooking the breathtaking seventeenth-century mill house.

'Tell me I didn't imagine it...'

Rose frowned. 'Imagine what?'

Lorna pointed to an ancient, gnarled apple tree, under which a soft, green carpet of moss lay.

'Joe carved our initials into a heart on that tree trunk.'

She hesitated, then swallowed.

'Will you go and see if it's there? Please?'

She watched as Rose and Evelyn walked over to the tree and knelt on the green velvet beneath its leafy branches. Their hands caressed the rough bark of the tree as they surveyed the trunk. And then they saw it – an intricate carving in the shape of a heart, with the initials JH and LM tucked inside. Rose turned to Lorna and smiled.

'It's here.'

She closed her eyes, tilted her head back and beamed with pure joy. She rushed over to the tree and looked at the carving, tracing her index finger around the heart and over the precisely chiseled letters.

'I need to go to him,' she said excitedly, her eyes wide, her cheeks flushed a delicate shade of rose pink. She looked alive. She felt alive. Every nerve ending in her body tingled with anticipation.

'But where is he?' asked Evelyn, confused.

'I don't know yet but tonight I'm going to bring him back.' She looked at them, her eyes darting wildly from one woman to the other. Her sudden enthusiasm instilled a deep fear within them.

'I'm not so sure, Lorna…' said Evelyn shakily.

Rose shook her head and apprehensively raked her fingers through her long white hair.

'We can't go around messing with stuff like this, Lorna. Evelyn's right. If Joe comes back to you it will be on his own terms. When he is ready.'

'The charm I made brought him to me and the curse took him away again. If I make the charm again, he will come back,' she insisted. 'He said he would never leave me. And I believe him.'

The three women stood and stared at each other in silence.

'Please! I beg you! Together, our magic will be at it's strongest. Please say you'll help me. I can't live without him!' she cried.

I can't live with out him. The words reverberated around them like a sonic boom, piercing Rose and Evelyn's souls like shards of glass following an almighty explosion. Both were dreading the utterance of those very words but both knew they were coming. It was inevitable. Lorna was in love. And she wanted her man back. But what if they couldn't get him back? What if he never, ever came back? The repercussions

393

didn't bear thinking about. They knew they had no other choice but to try to help her. This was Lorna in her hour of need. She needed their support and skill as witches to awaken Joe from the dead one final time. It would be a hard task to execute but all they could do was try. And they owed it to their dearest friend to try as hard as they possibly could.

'Ok. Ok!' cried Rose. 'We'll cast a new spell tonight. But we can do it only once. And it has to be exactly the same spell as you did before only I have to bury it for you. Your hand cannot touch the charm once it's made.'

'Thank you,' she breathed. 'Thank you from the bottom of my heart.'

THAT EVENING, after a riotous afternoon watching Bridget Jones Diary, eating pretzels and drinking rosé, Lorna announced she was going to have an early bath in preparation for the charm they were about to make and the spell they were about to cast.

She poured white musk bubble bath under the running hot tap and watched as mounds of foam turned the water into a cloud. She slipped into the bubbles and inhaled the same scent she'd enveloped herself in for as long as she could remember.

She lay back and thought of Joe. She wondered if he was thinking about her too, wherever he was. She felt a shiver of anticipation as she imagined setting eyes on him again. The picture of him in her mind was so vivid. She closed her eyes and imagined him walking towards her, a ghost of a smile playing on his lips, his hair slicked back, his fern green eyes glinting with specks of gold. She longed to run her hands up his back to his neck, to smell him again, to kiss those butter soft lips, to hold him in her arms one last time… even if it was ultimately to say her final goodbye.   .

She chose a knee-length, cotton halter-necked dress, pale lilac with violet flowers and dainty white butterflies, and slipped it on. Next, she combed her long, auburn hair and embellished it with a silver and jade dragonfly slide. She glossed her lashes with black and her lips with apricot and added silver hoops to her ears. Her pentacle hung around her neck and rested on her breastbone like some mysterious, spangled star.

'You look lovely!' exclaimed Rose, as Lorna appeared all scrubbed and shiny and new in the living room.

'Thanks. I felt like I needed a bit of a makeover. I just wish my nails didn't look so hideous.'

'They'll grow back – or you can always go and get yourself some lovely, shiny, plastic ones like Verity's!'

'Er… no… I think I'll wait until they grow back,' she grinned.

'Right, ladies… Are we ready?' asked Evelyn, her voice tinged with an ominous sense of foreboding.

'Yes. I think so,' said Lorna quietly.

'Have we got everything we need?'

Lorna gestured to the coffee table where a woven basket held all the items they required to concoct a charm. Rose picked it up and, without even saying a word to one another, started to weave their magic. The walked round in a perfect circle and sank to the floor. Rose laid out a pink candle, a china plate, a tiny bottle of geranium oil and two, pristine white rose petals. When everything was just so, she glanced up at Lorna and bowed her head, signaling to her that she must now make the charm.

With her left hand, she carefully lit the candle and pushed it into the centre of the circle. Next, she placed the petals onto the plate and unscrewed the lid off the bottle of geranium oil, tipping it forward slightly so that three drops spilled out and landed silently on the petals.

She spoke softly and slowly, her voice as innocent as a child's, every so often faltering and stalling with emotion.

'Love's truth burns bright, return my soulmate to me this night.'

She tilted the burning candle so that the molten wax dripped onto the petals. Her delicate fingers molded the wax, petals and oil together into a coin-shaped disc and when it was cold and hard, she handed it, still only using her left hand, to Rose.

Rose wrapped the charm in a white cotton handkerchief and clutched it tightly to her chest.

'I will bury this under the rose bush you used in your original spell. You may watch me from the window but you must not set one foot on the soil for at least 30 days after it's burial for fear of hindering it's enchantment.

'I won't,' whispered Lorna.

Rose got up from her place in the circle and walked out of the living room, down the hallway and through the front door. She trod cautiously down each step, across the black and white chequerboard tiles to the back door of the building, stopping briefly to pick up a trowel from the tool box, and made her way out across the garden. She was acutely aware of the two pairs of eyes following her every move as she picked her way across the lawn to the rose bush directly opposite Lorna's living room window. She knelt down with her back towards the Maltings and placed the charm, still wrapped in cotton, by her side. She dug a hole about twelve inches deep then tossed the trowel to one side. Next she picked up the handkerchief and unfolded it carefully. She took out the charm and in the blink of an eye, slipped it inside the pocket of her skirt, worn specifically for the purpose of concealing a secret. Then she held her hand out and dropped nothing but fresh air into the foot-deep hole, dramatically discarding the cloth in view of the spectators behind her and began to fill it with earth until the ground appeared as smooth and untouched as it had ten minutes before. She stood and turned towards the building, picking up the trowel to her right and the empty handkerchief to her left.

There was no way on this earth she was going to stand by and watch Joe materialise once more. He'd done enough damage already in her view and caused nothing but untold suffering and unsurpassed chaos. This was one soulmate Lorna could do without a repeat visit from.

She strode confidently to the back door, knowing full well she was still being watched, and dropped the trowel back into its wooden trug. Out of view, she skipped jubilantly across the tiles and up the stairs, back into the flat where Lorna and Evelyn were waiting expectantly for her in the hall.

'It's all done,' she said as convincingly as she could, handing Lorna the hankie. 'Excuse me for a moment – I desperately need to use the loo.'

She went into the bathroom and locked the door. Once inside, she pulled a yard or so of toilet tissue off the roll and delved into her pocket, fishing out the charm. She placed it in the centre of the paper and scrunched it into a ball. She flushed the toilet and dropped the wad into the swirling water and watched as it spiraled round and round and then disappeared from view.

She stood at the sink and washed the earth from her hands. She looked at her ageing reflection in the mirror and breathed in a deep lungful of air and exhaled slowly. Her hands shook as she toweled them dry, adrenalin flowing fast and furiously through her veins. An overriding, and somewhat bewildering, sensation of relief, joy and regret flooded through her as she realised what she'd just done. She'd tampered with fate, changed the path of destiny. But it was too late now. The secret was hers to keep and Lorna need never know.

AS THE SUN slid towards the horizon and the early evening star studded the violet sky like a solitary diamond, Lorna became increasingly restless. She pushed her dinner plate away from her, having toyed with her food for almost half an hour but barely eating a thing. She started to get up from her seat, wandering to the window, looking out across the darkening garden and then returning to her chair. It was as if she was waiting for something to happen.

'Sit down Lorna, for god's sake,' snapped Rose. 'You're making me feel jittery.'

'Me too,' quipped Evelyn.

'I'm sorry – I'm just feeling a bit odd. On edge. I can't sit still.'

'Have another drink. That'll make you sit still if you have

enough of it.'

'No. I don't want any more. You'll turn me into an alcoholic at this rate.'

'Well you can't keep getting up and down. What do you want to do?'

Lorna stood at the window, watching the shadows lengthen and a new smattering of stars appearing with each blink of the eye.

'I want to go to his grave.'

'It'll be getting dark soon.'

'It's June! It won't be properly dark for ages! For goodness sake… I'll be alright. I'll take a torch with me.'

'I'm not so sure, Lorna…'

'Rose. I am twenty-eight years old. Not six. I am quite capable of visiting a grave and putting some flowers on it. And tomorrow I am opening the shop.'

Rose baulked at the idea.

'Are you ready for that? Opening the shop I mean… you've hardly touched your food tonight. I'm not convinced you've recovered fully. It's only been four days since you were in hospital…'

'Rose… I know you're worried about me but you worry about everything. You even fret when one of your cat's cough up a hairball. Honestly, I will be fine. I'll take my phone. Along with the torch.'

Evelyn sat in silence, her eyes firmly fixed on the television, her lips pursed.

'Go on then. But if you're not back in an hour, I'm coming to get you.'

Lorna was out of the flat in seconds, out on to the street

below and along to her shop. She unlocked the door and grabbed the nearest bunch of flowers to hand, locked up again and retrieved her bike from the passageway that ran down the side of the florist. She placed the flowers in the wicker basket on the front of the bike and switched it's little headlamp on.

She cycled through the twilit village, past the stone cottages, the busy pub filled with the sound of laughter and mouthwatering aroma of griddled steak and fermenting hops. Further still, through the tunnel of mingling branches and onwards towards the church.

She jumped off her bike and wheeled it up the lane until she reached the side gate that led into the churchyard. She propped it up against the wall and took the flowers out of the basket. She unlatched the gate and stepped into the churchyard, allowing the gate to swing back to its rightful position with a clatter.

She made her way slowly up the gravel path to the front of the church. The porch lantern was on, bathing the ancient wooden door and surrounding rose garden in a glorious, golden glow.

The air was heavy with the captivating scent of linseed flowers, carried on the breeze from miles around, hanging like a fragrant cloud above the village. Lorna inhaled deeply and sighed. This was her most favourite time of year and the arrival of the scented breeze announced that summer was here at last.

In the stillness of the evening, standing alone in the churchyard with nobody else around and remembering the events of the week before, she began to feel a tight ball of apprehension form in the pit of her stomach. She clutched the flowers to her chest and edged slowly around the perimeter path of the graveyard. The last time she was here it was sodden and sinister and eerie. This time it felt different. It was calm, peaceful, welcoming almost. She walked past the elderly mulberry tree with the circular bench and the quiet, shady corner where the little ones slept, down further, to where the cedar trees stood guard over countless resting souls.

As she approached the area where Joe lay, heavily shaded and tranquil, she saw the figure of a man sitting on the bench overlooking the graves. As she inched closer, her heart rate began to increase rapidly, the sound of pumping blood booming in her ears like a big bass drum. She could see the man was wearing a white shirt and the outline of his head, his ears, neck and shoulders looked all too familiar. And then suddenly, as if he knew she was there, he stood and turned. Lorna dropped the flowers she was carrying on the floor and all around her, time stood still.

They stood opposite each other, neither saying a word, staring at one another for what seemed like an eternity – their identical green eyes flecked with amber perfectly aligned, the rise and fall of their chests mirroring each others as they breathed in time.

'You came back,' whispered Lorna.

'I never went away.'

'But…?'

Joe raised a finger to his lips in a gesture of silence.

Lorna was confused. If he never went away, where had he been all this time? She'd just made a charm to bring him back to her. She'd watched Rose bury it before her very eyes.

Joe walked around the side of the bench, treading with a degree of trepidation, not knowing how Lorna would to respond to his sudden appearance. He stood in front of her, within touching distance. Lorna closed her eyes, raised her right hand in front of her and with her thumb and index finger, firmly pinched the skin on her left forearm. It hurt. She opened her eyes. He was still there, a look of bemusement dancing across his face.

'Just to make sure you really are here.'

'I am.'

He was even more beautiful than she remembered. She reached out her hands and they curled around his, their fingers entwining. His skin was smooth and warm. Lorna gazed at his face and her eyes brimmed with tears. He pulled her to him and they were one again. His hand brushed up her back, to her neck, his fingers becoming entangled in her hair. His lips trailed along her jawbone, up to her ear, then back to her mouth. She felt as though she was drowning in delirium as they kissed. He smelled exactly the same and he felt exactly the same. She ran her hands over his upper body, her fingers lightly brushing over the wound that had killed him, sensing his strong arms through the thin fabric of his shirt, the muscular form of his broad shoulders, his lean, curved back and the soft, sweetly-scented neck she loved to nuzzle into.

'I don't understand, Joe...' she whispered.

He took her hand and led her to the memorial bench where they sat down alongside one another. He slipped his arm around her shoulders and drew her to his side.

'It's the way it's always been done, my Lorna. You come back to guide your loved ones through to the next life, the next stage of their journey. We have many lives. This is just the beginning. I came back for Alice but as I waited for her life to end, something extraordinary happened to me. Something I can't explain... even to this day.'

'Did the charm bring you to me?'

Joe looked puzzled and turned to face her.

'The charm? I don't know anything about a charm...?'

'Then what...?'

'That day, on the hill behind the church, when you were on your bike, and you almost collided with me... well... you could see me!' He laughed incredulously. 'You saw me in the road and you swerved and I fell backwards. And then you spoke to me! Nobody else could see me, Lorna! Only you. You were never meant to see me. But you did. And you can...' He leaned over and gently kissed the tip of her nose. 'And there was this feeling I got, a feeling that we were meant to be. I've never felt anything so intense before. I've never been in love before.'

'I could see you. I can see you!' she looked at him in wonderment, placing her hands on his cheeks. 'But I could see Victor too...'

'I know. When I realised you could communicate with Victor as well...' he blew out his cheeks and raised his eyebrows. 'That truly amazed me. Your mind is open, Lorna... willing to see and believe what others refuse to. Even when it is staring them in the face.'

'But you are dead, Joe! I've lain on your grave! I've seen your name engraved upon a headstone. This is just crazy! Do you have any idea how that felt? To find your final resting place, to read your name? To see that you died seventy years ago...' she cried. 'I thought I'd gone mad.'

Joe smiled weakly.

'You're not mad. Just incredibly special.' He leaned forward and kissed her tenderly. 'And I love you very much.'

She stroked the side of his face, looked deeply into his eyes and her stomach lurched. She couldn't be angry with him. This was all her doing. She should never have made a charm, or cursed Oriel, or even got involved in Wicca in the first place.

'I love you too... but how can this work?' she asked sadly. 'We can never be together.'

He embraced her tightly and kissed her hair.

'We can. If you'll come with me.'

Her stomach churned and the bitter taste of bile rose in her throat. She swallowed and tried to breathe normally. She looked at him in total disbelief.

'Come with you?'

Joe nodded. 'Come with me.'

'Where to?'

'To the place we all go to after we die.'

Lorna's head spun. She couldn't comprehend what Joe was asking of her. She closed her eyes and tried to steady her breathing. This couldn't be happening. It was a dream. Surely. It must be a dream. Any second now she would wake up, in her flat, sunlight streaming through the slats in the blinds and she would roll over and Dan would be lying beside her – the past two years or so just a dream. A disturbing, realistic, sick dream.

She opened her eyes. She was still in the graveyard. Surrounded by evening bird song, the earthy scent of moss and fern, with Joe sitting by her side, gazing into her eyes and clutching her hands. This was no dream.

'You... you're asking me to give up my life? To die for you?'

'Please, Lorna. Come with me...' he pleaded.

She stood, shaking like a leaf, her head swimming, her vision fading. She felt vulnerable and suddenly very afraid, standing alone in this darkening garden of ghosts. An avalanche of thoughts, memories and emotions rained down on her psyche, causing her to become disorientated and unsteady on her feet. She clutched the back of the bench with both hands to stop herself from falling. What Joe was asking of her was over and above the call of duty. It was shocking, unexpected, totally unthinkable. She looked at him, her body aching with love for him, knowing that time was running out and soon he would be nothing but a memory.

'Joe... I can't.'

'PLEASE Lorna...'

He reached across the bench and grasped her wrist.

'No Joe!'

Her face crumpled and she burst into tears.

'Joe... my darling, darling Joe... I love you with all my heart. You have shown me a love I never knew could exist between two people,' she sobbed, 'But I can't go with you. I can't give up my life on this earth to follow you into the unknown... I love my life, Joe! My family. My friends. My job.'

Utterly bereft, he leapt up from the bench, rivers of tears running down his face.

'Please don't leave me, Lorna. I've waited a lifetime for you.'

'Oh, Joe... please don't do this to me.'

She rushed to him, kissed his butter-soft lips, gazed into his viridescent eyes, ran her fingers up the sides of his face and cradled his head in her hands. She desperately wanted this moment to last forever. She let out a sorrowful cry and in the silence that followed, you could almost hear her heart breaking in two.

'I love you. I'll always love you. Until my dying day. But that day is a long, long way away. I will die when I am old and grey. I will live a long and happy life. I will be a mummy and a granny and I will treasure each and every moment of my life. And when my day comes, and I take my last breath and my heart ceases to beat, I will close my eyes and see you there waiting for me,' she wept.

Joe's body heaved with sobs as he gathered her hands in front of him and raised them to his lips, kissing each and every fingertip.

'I'll be there.'

'Do you promise?' she sobbed.

'I promise.'

Their lips met one last time. Lorna could taste the saltiness of Joe's warm tears mingling with hers. The love she felt for him would stay with her a lifetime.

'Now you must let me go.'

He released the grip on her hands and they fell to her side. They stood opposite each other, the agony of separation almost too painful to bear. She took a brave step backwards, followed by another, the distance between them widening.

'Thank you for everything... the love you showed me, the flower you gave me, the heart on the tree. For singing to me, for teaching me to dance, for the love letter I will treasure for always...'

'You found it?'

Lorna nodded and took another step back.

'I'll never forget you,' she whispered into the darkness, only the silhouette of the man she loved now visible.

She stepped onto the path, and without a backwards glance, turned and walked away. She heard nothing more, no calling after her, no footfall behind her, only silence. It took every single ounce of inner strength to continue walking away from him, her pace increasing with every footstep, not daring to look back. She got to the gate and unlatched it, only then allowing herself to look over towards the majestic cedar trees, which stood tall, and proud, shading the souls of those who slept beneath their aromatic, evergreen branches. Joe had gone.

She got onto her bike and rode down the gently sloping lane to the main road, stopping only to unclip the chain around her neck and dropping it, pentacle and all, through the iron grid of the drain cover at her feet.

THE FLOWERS DIRECT delivery van drew up alongside the shop at 10am prompt. Lorna rifled around underneath the counter for her clipboard with this weeks order attached to it. She watched as the driver jumped out of the cabin and strolled around the front of the vehicle and through the florist's door.

'Oh... hello!' she said cheerfully.

The tall, handsome driver reached up to his ear and slid out the pen that was firmly wedged behind it.

'Hello, stranger! Bet you was expecting Peter!'

'I was, yes… is he ok?'

'He's on holiday. Taken the wife and nipper off to Spain. Good time of year to get away, with the kids back at school and all that.'

Lorna looked outside at the changing scenery. The vibrancy of summer was fading fast, verdant green leaves replaced with shades of gold and red and orange. She loved autumn.

'How are you, anyway?' she smiled.

'I'm good, thanks. And you're looking as beautiful as ever,' he said cheekily, handing her the delivery form to scan through and check. She took it from him and blushed like a schoolgirl.

She read through the order, cross-checking it against her own copy, without really reading it at all and scribbled her signature on the last page of the form and handed him the clipboard. He took it from her and shoved his pen back behind his ear.

'I'll start unloading then. There's a lot of stuff in there,' he said, nodding towards the lorry. 'Hope you've got room!'

Fifteen minutes later the cold store was full to bursting point. The sight of so many flowers unnerved her slightly as she remembered the huge amount of work she had to do that week, namely for Evelyn and Rupert's engagement party.

'Right. I'll be off then. Everything you ordered is there apart from the Blue Ginger – something to do with an air and sea strike in Hawaii. But you saw all that on the footnotes, didn't you?'

'Yes, I saw it thanks,' she lied.

'Right, I've got to get another five loads delivered by the end of today so I'd better make a move.'

He walked towards the door but hesitated as he reached it.

'I don't suppose you're single again are you?'

Lorna flushed pink again and smiled.

'I am as it happens, Matt.'

'You remembered my name!'

'A girl never forgets a name,' she replied playfully.

'You've made my day! So, can I take you for that drink?'

'Next Friday night?'

'That's great! I'll pick you up from here shall I? Say, seven ish?'

'Seven ish is perfect.'

He ran a hand through his mop of blonde curls and gave her a cheeky wink before jumping into the cab and driving away with a toot of the horn.

Lorna waited until he was out of view and clapped her hands like an excited schoolgirl. The grin on her face was a mile wide as she reached for her mobile phone. She scrolled down and clicked on Rose's number, followed by Evelyn's.

< Guess who's got a date next Friday night!!! > she tapped, before gleefully pressing send.

She sat back and waited for the inevitable replies from her two best friends. It took them all of thirty seconds.

THE CHARMING
WICCA PHILOSOPHY OF LIFE

LIVE…
Live each day as if it were your last, for one day you will be right.

LOVE…
Love yourself first and foremost for when you truly love yourself, loving those around you will come as easy as breathing… and we all must breathe.

LEARN…
Learn your life's lessons – each as it comes – for that is the reason we are here.

ENJOY…
Enjoy your life because if you don't, most likely someone else will enjoy it for you, and your time here will have been wasted.

Printed in Great Britain
by Amazon

78998498R00234